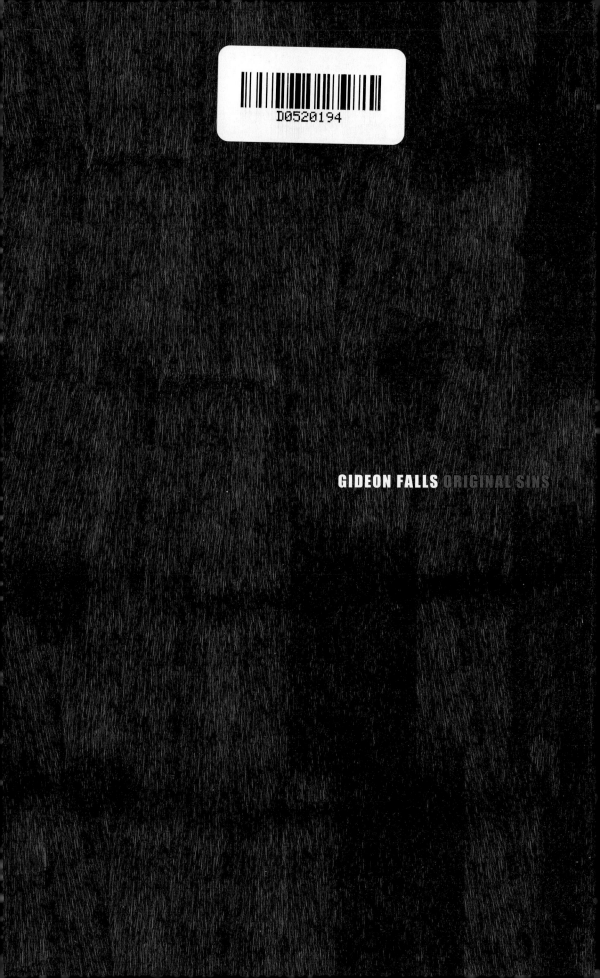

GIDEON FALLS ORIGINAL SINS

LAYOUT & PRODUCTION BY RYAN BREWER

IMAGE COMICS, INC. • **Robert Kirkman**: Chief Operating Officer • **Erik Larsen**: Chief Financial Officer • **Todd McFarlane**: President • **Marc Silvestri**: Chief Executive Officer • **Jim Valentino**: Vice President • **Eric Stephenson**: Publisher / Chief Creative Officer • **Corey Hart**: Director of Sales • **Jeff Boison**: Director of Publishing Planning & Book Trade Sales • **Chris Ross**: Director of Digital Sales • **Jeff Stang**: Director of Specialty Sales • **Kat Salazar**: Director of PR & Marketing • **Drew Gill**: Art Director • **Heather Doornink**: Production Director • **Nicole Lapalme**: Controller • **IMAGECOMICS.COM**

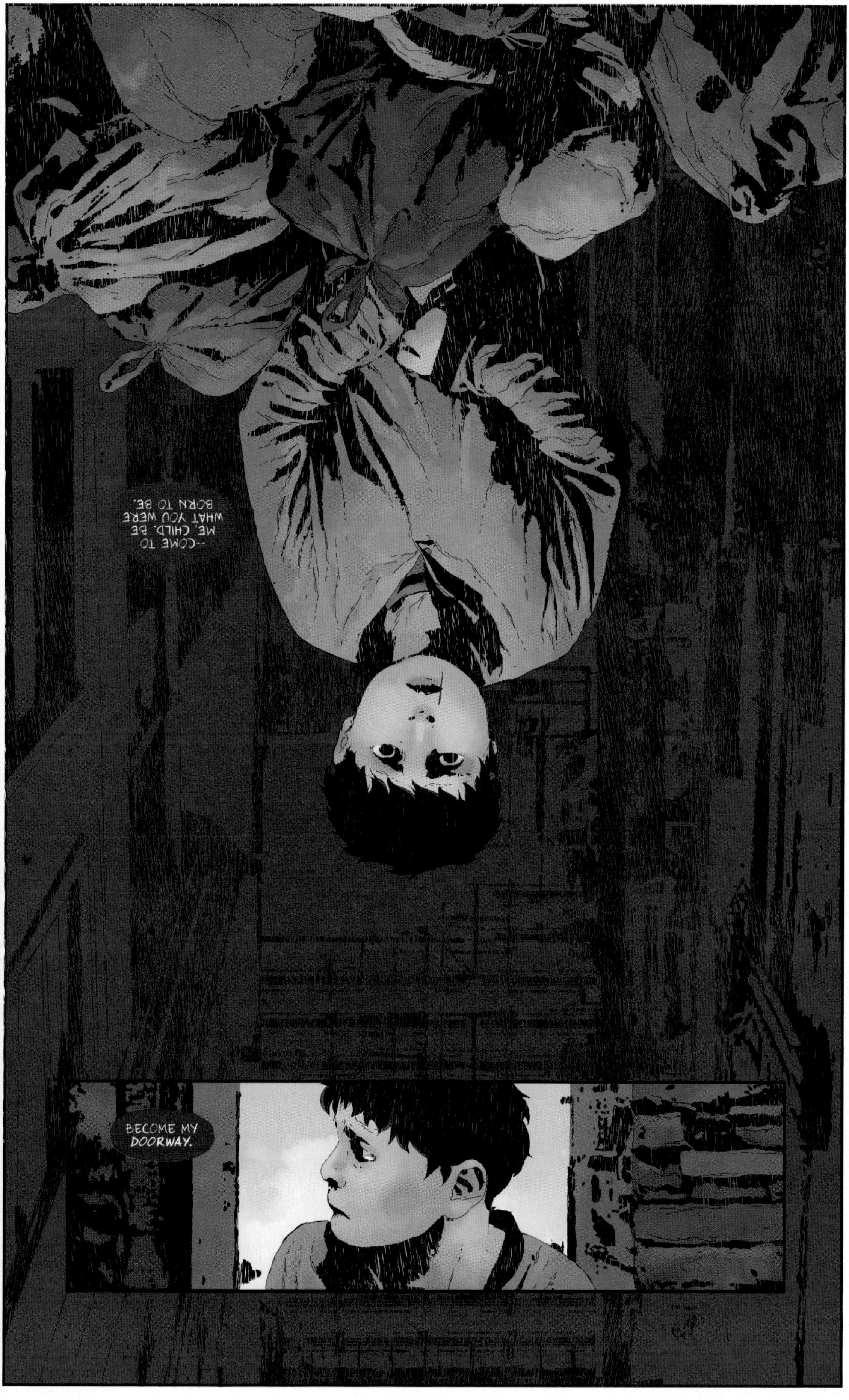
--COME TO ME, CHILD. BE WHAT YOU WERE BORN TO BE.
BECOME MY *DOORWAY.*

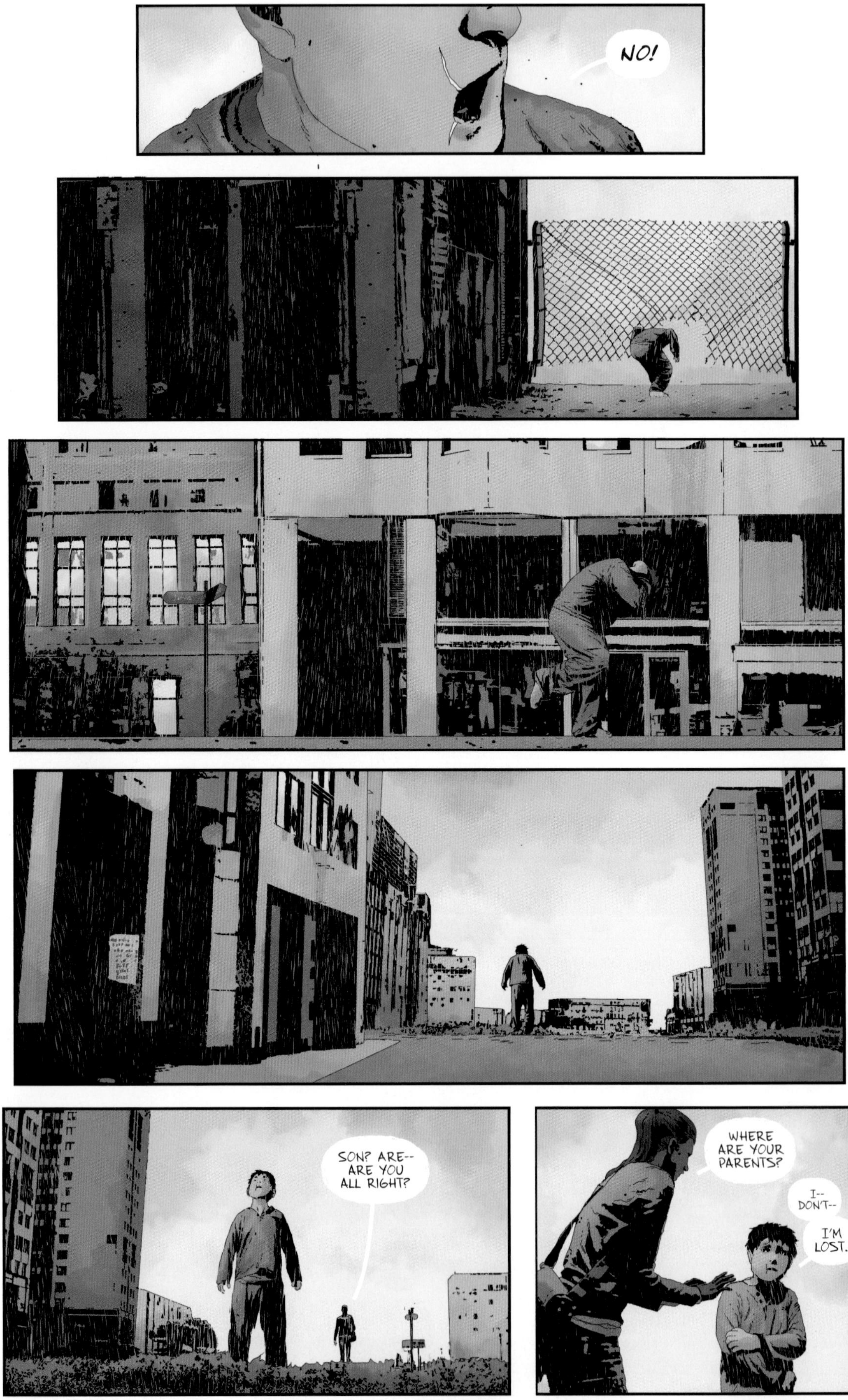
NO!
SON? ARE--
ARE YOU
ALL RIGHT?
WHERE
ARE YOUR
PARENTS?
I--
DON'T--
I'M
LOST.

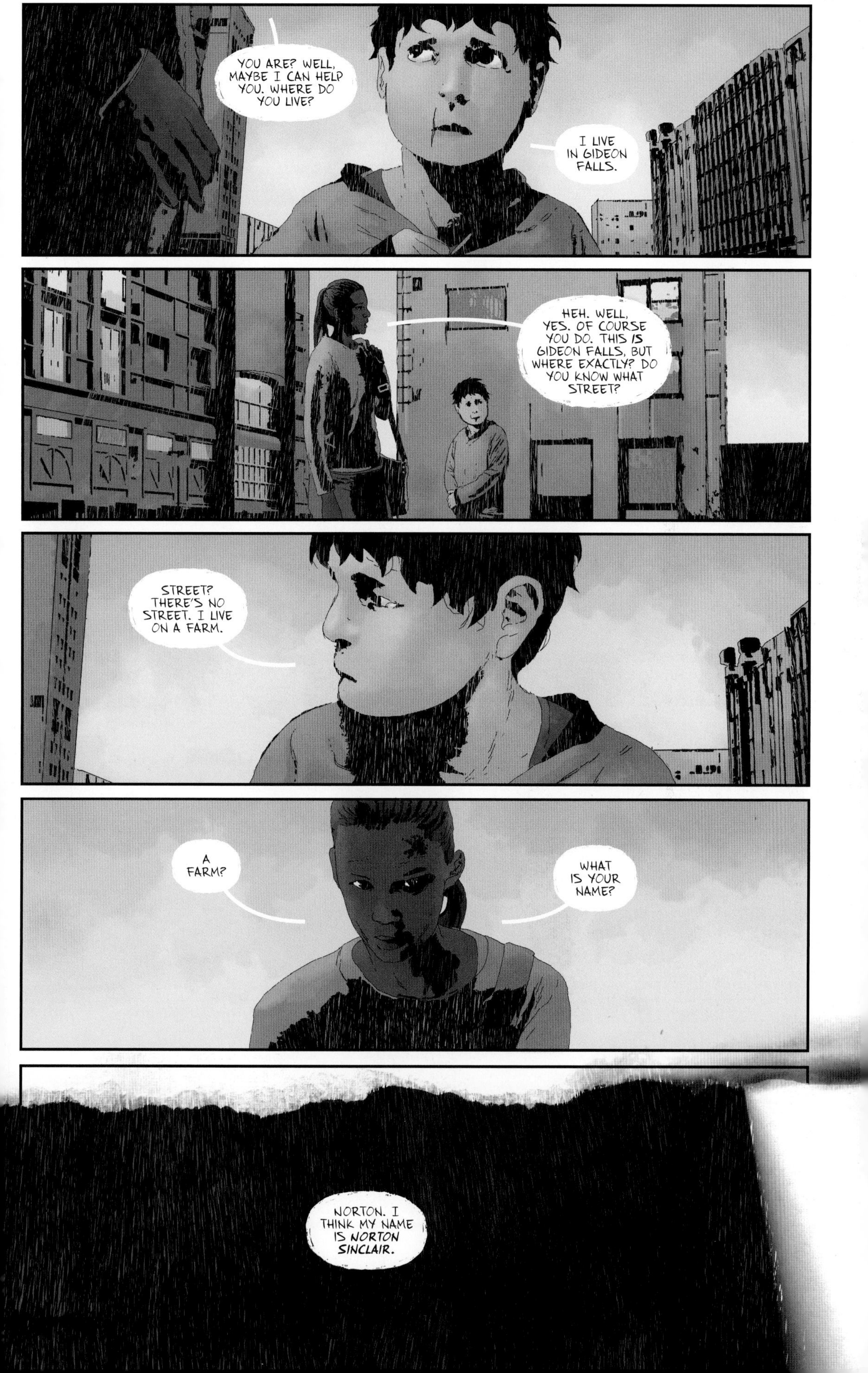
YOU ARE? WELL, MAYBE I CAN HELP YOU. WHERE DO YOU LIVE?
I LIVE IN GIDEON FALLS.
HEH. WELL, YES. OF COURSE YOU DO. THIS IS GIDEON FALLS, BUT WHERE EXACTLY? DO YOU KNOW WHAT STREET?
STREET? THERE'S NO STREET. I LIVE ON A FARM.
A FARM?
WHAT IS YOUR NAME?
NORTON. I THINK MY NAME IS NORTON SINCLAIR.

JEFF LEMIRE

ANDREA SORRENTINO

DAVE STEWART

STEVE WANDS

WILL DENNIS

GIDEON
FALLS

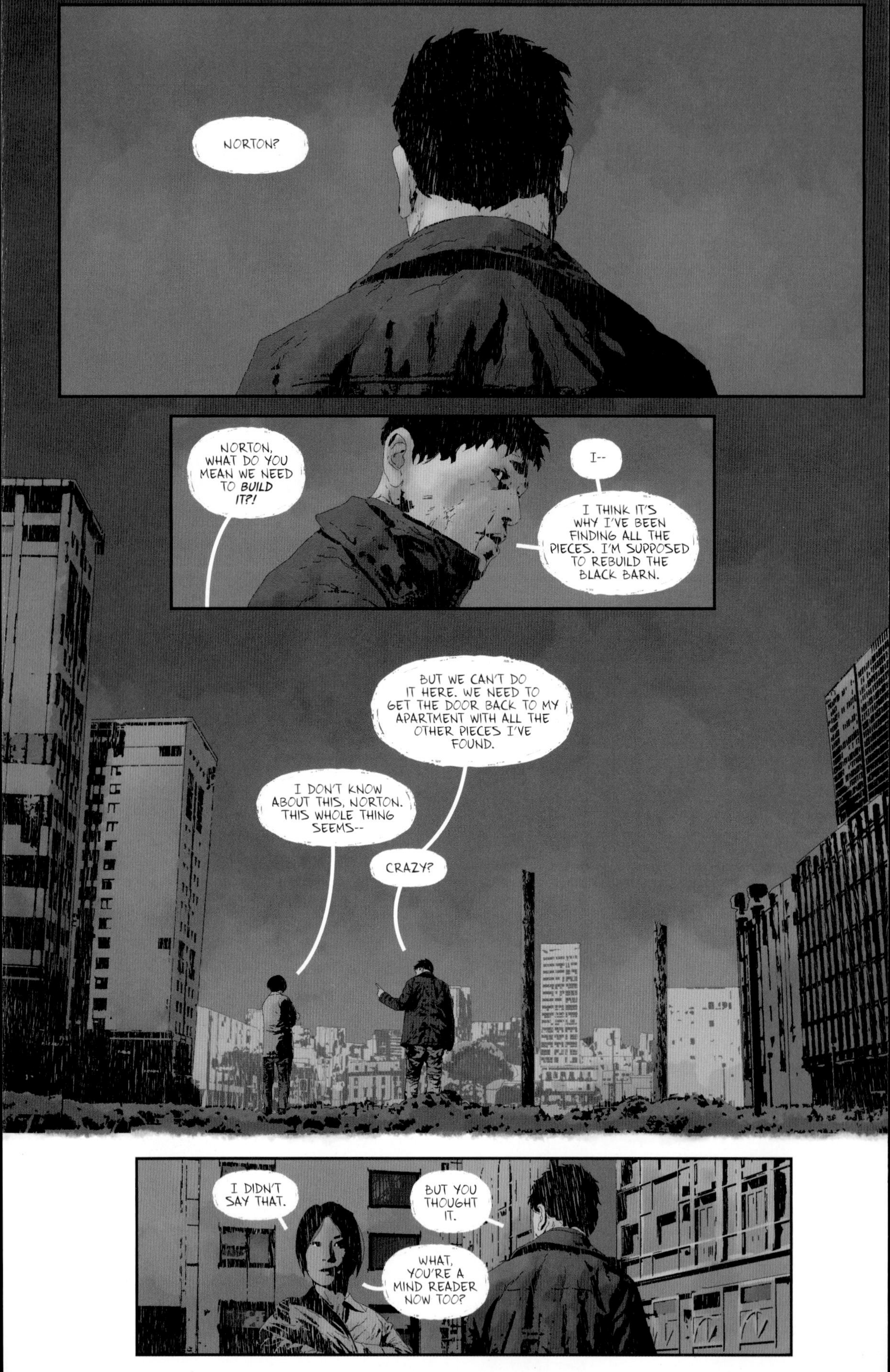
NORTON?
NORTON, WHAT DO YOU MEAN WE NEED TO **BUILD IT?!**
I--
I THINK IT'S WHY I'VE BEEN FINDING ALL THE PIECES. I'M SUPPOSED TO REBUILD THE BLACK BARN.
BUT WE CAN'T DO IT HERE. WE NEED TO GET THE DOOR BACK TO MY APARTMENT WITH ALL THE OTHER PIECES I'VE FOUND.
I DON'T KNOW ABOUT THIS, NORTON. THIS WHOLE THING SEEMS--
CRAZY?
I DIDN'T SAY THAT.
BUT YOU THOUGHT IT.
WHAT, YOU'RE A MIND READER NOW TOO?

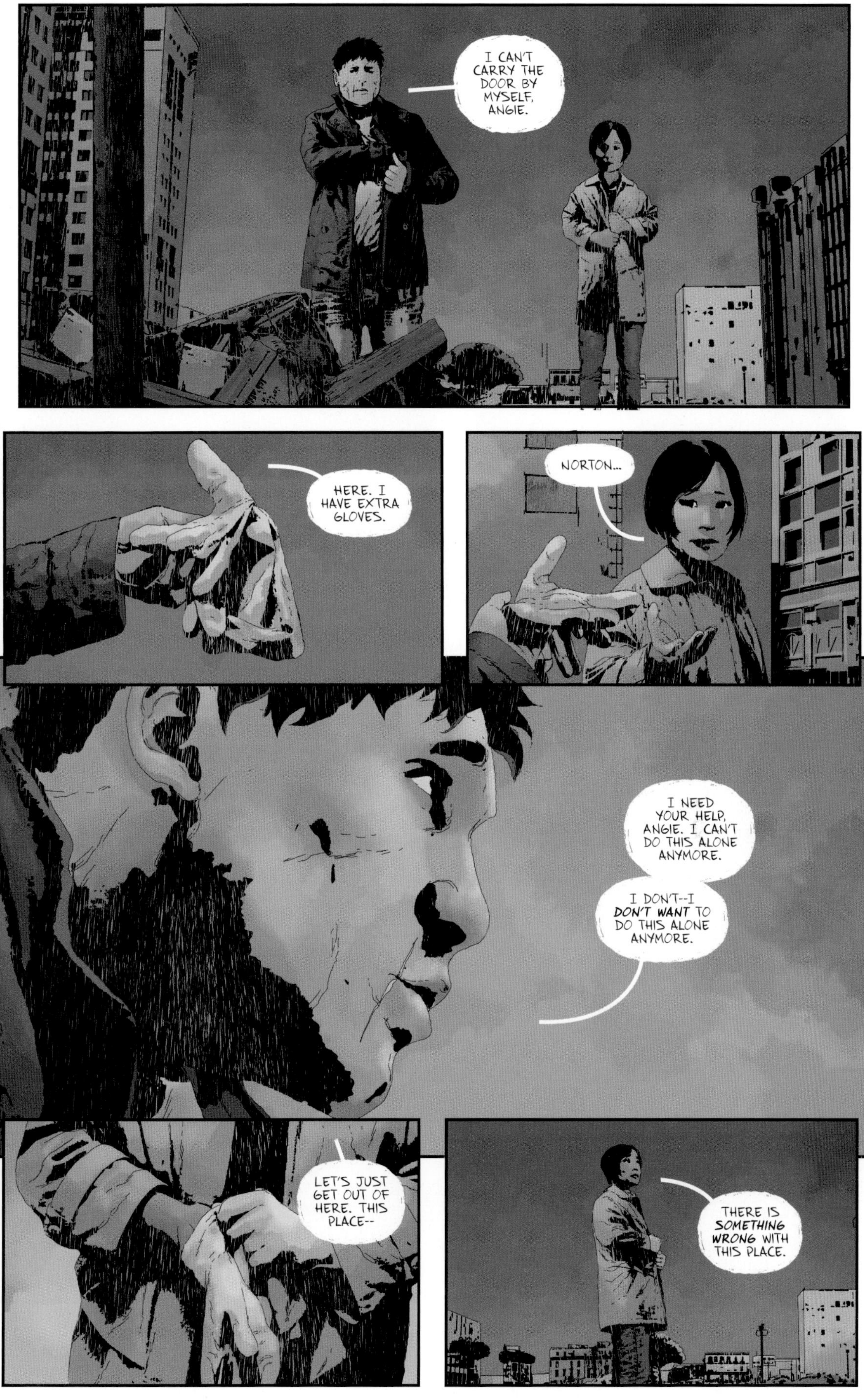
I CAN'T CARRY THE DOOR BY MYSELF, ANGIE.
HERE. I HAVE EXTRA GLOVES.
NORTON...
I NEED YOUR HELP, ANGIE. I CAN'T DO THIS ALONE ANYMORE.
I DON'T--I **DON'T WANT** TO DO THIS ALONE ANYMORE.
LET'S JUST GET OUT OF HERE. THIS PLACE--
THERE IS **SOMETHING WRONG** WITH THIS PLACE.

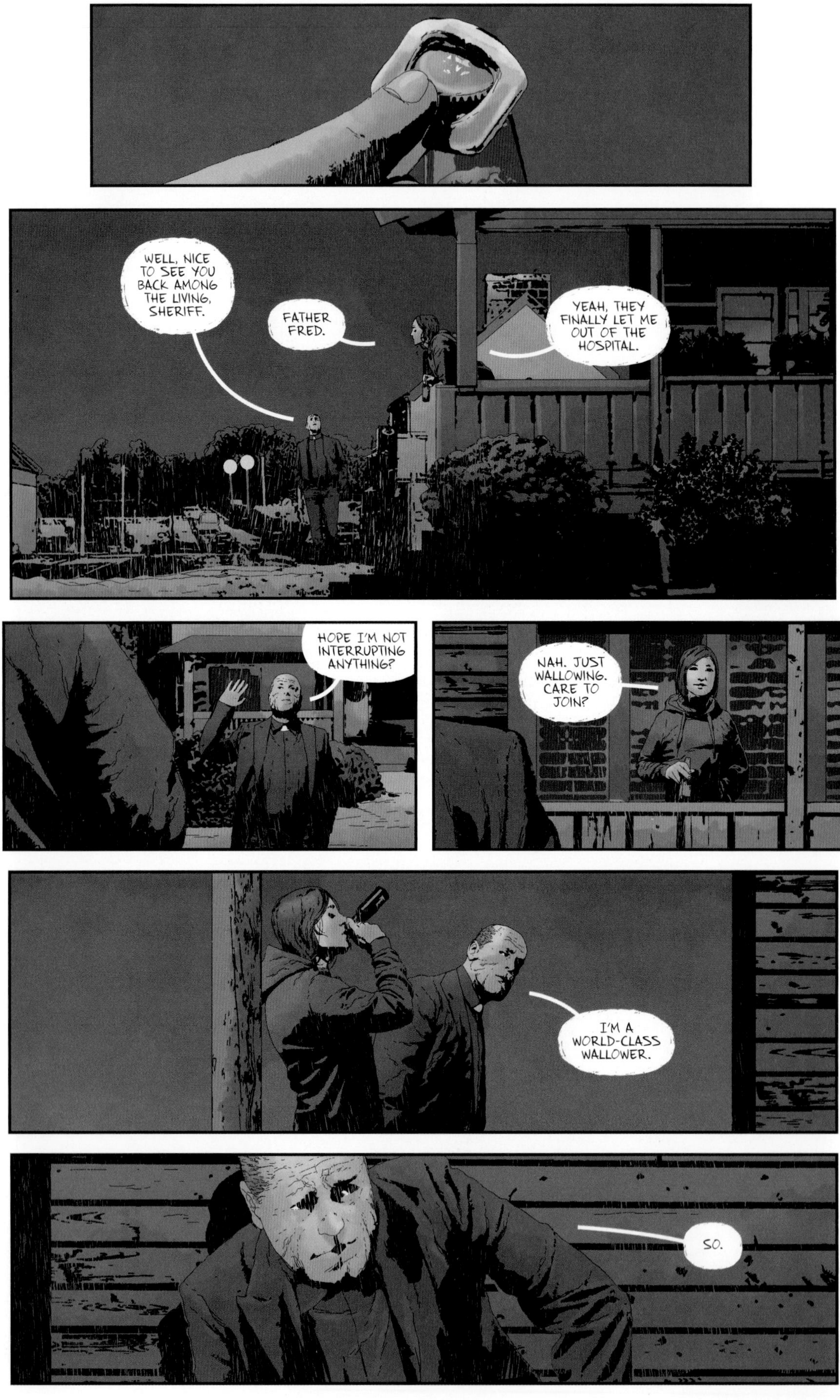
WELL, NICE TO SEE YOU BACK AMONG THE LIVING, SHERIFF.
FATHER FRED.
YEAH, THEY FINALLY LET ME OUT OF THE HOSPITAL.
HOPE I'M NOT INTERRUPTING ANYTHING?
NAH. JUST WALLOWING. CARE TO JOIN?
I'M A WORLD-CLASS WALLOWER.
SO.

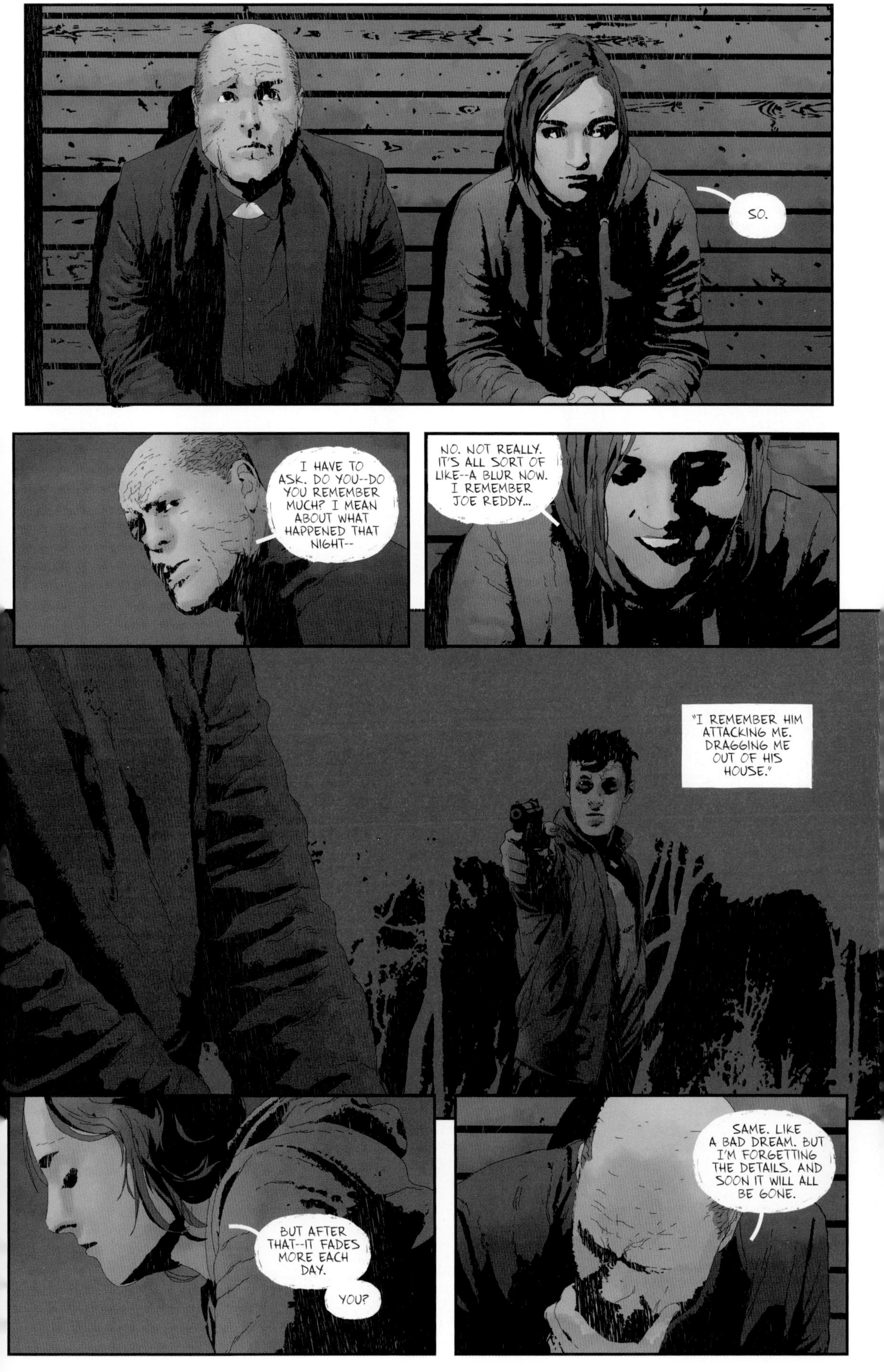
SO.
I HAVE TO ASK. DO YOU--DO YOU REMEMBER MUCH? I MEAN ABOUT WHAT HAPPENED THAT NIGHT--
NO. NOT REALLY. IT'S ALL SORT OF LIKE--A BLUR NOW. I REMEMBER JOE REDDY...
"I REMEMBER HIM ATTACKING ME. DRAGGING ME OUT OF HIS HOUSE."
BUT AFTER THAT--IT FADES MORE EACH DAY.
YOU?
SAME. LIKE A BAD DREAM. BUT I'M FORGETTING THE DETAILS. AND SOON IT WILL ALL BE GONE.

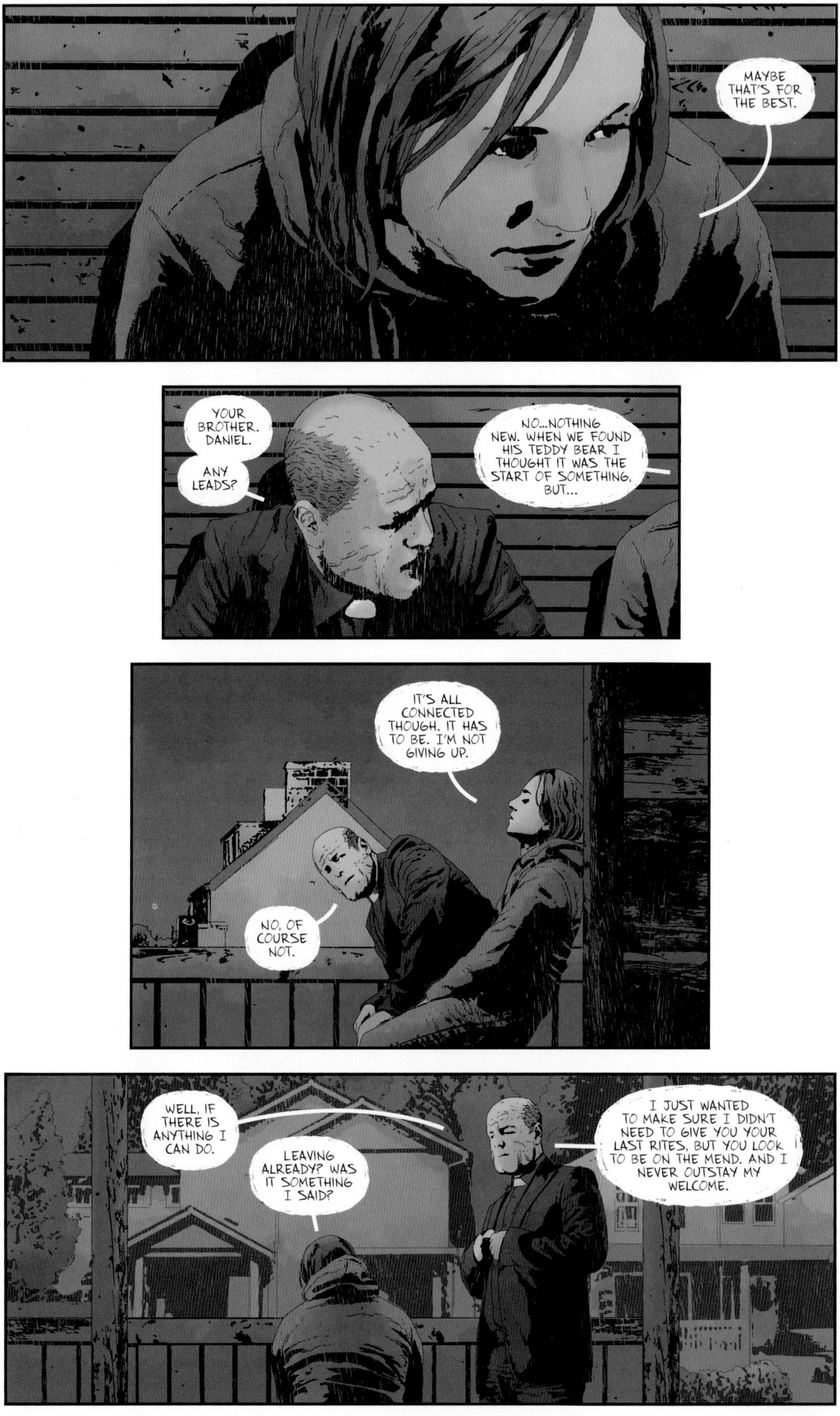
MAYBE THAT'S FOR THE BEST.
YOUR BROTHER. DANIEL.
ANY LEADS?
NO...NOTHING NEW. WHEN WE FOUND HIS TEDDY BEAR I THOUGHT IT WAS THE START OF SOMETHING, BUT...
IT'S ALL CONNECTED THOUGH. IT HAS TO BE. I'M NOT GIVING UP.
NO, OF COURSE NOT.
I JUST WANTED TO MAKE SURE I DIDN'T NEED TO GIVE YOU YOUR LAST RITES, BUT YOU LOOK TO BE ON THE MEND. AND I NEVER OUTSTAY MY WELCOME.
LEAVING ALREADY? WAS IT SOMETHING I SAID?
WELL, IF THERE IS ANYTHING I CAN DO.

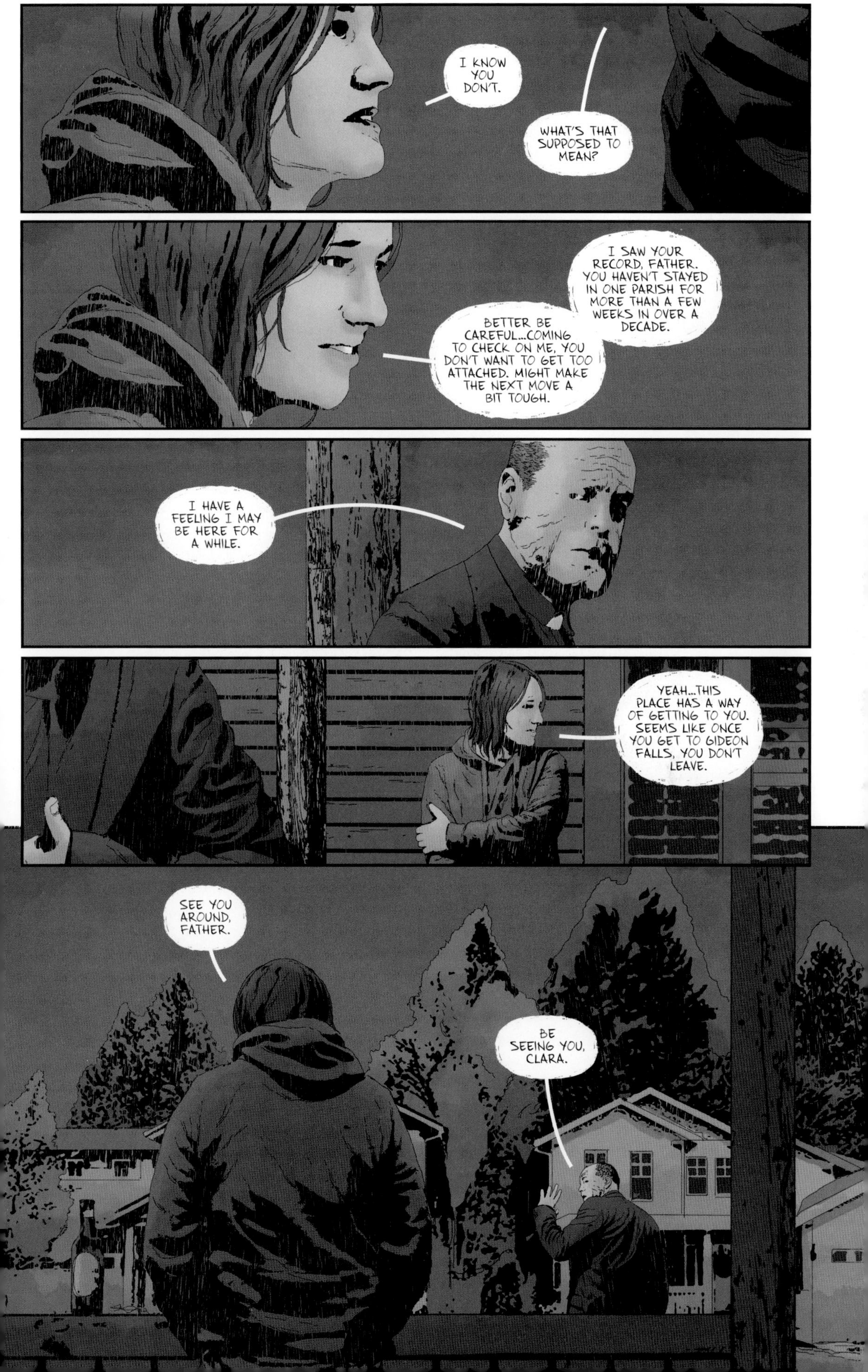
I KNOW YOU DON'T.
WHAT'S THAT SUPPOSED TO MEAN?
I SAW YOUR RECORD, FATHER. YOU HAVEN'T STAYED IN ONE PARISH FOR MORE THAN A FEW WEEKS IN OVER A DECADE.
BETTER BE CAREFUL...COMING TO CHECK ON ME, YOU DON'T WANT TO GET TOO ATTACHED. MIGHT MAKE THE NEXT MOVE A BIT TOUGH.
I HAVE A FEELING I MAY BE HERE FOR A WHILE.
YEAH...THIS PLACE HAS A WAY OF GETTING TO YOU. SEEMS LIKE ONCE YOU GET TO GIDEON FALLS, YOU DON'T LEAVE.
SEE YOU AROUND, FATHER.
BE SEEING YOU, CLARA.

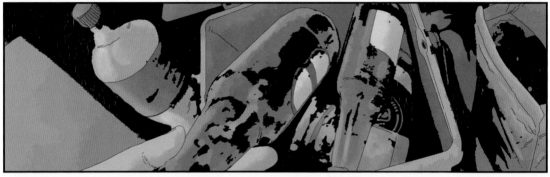

"WHAT A BABY!"

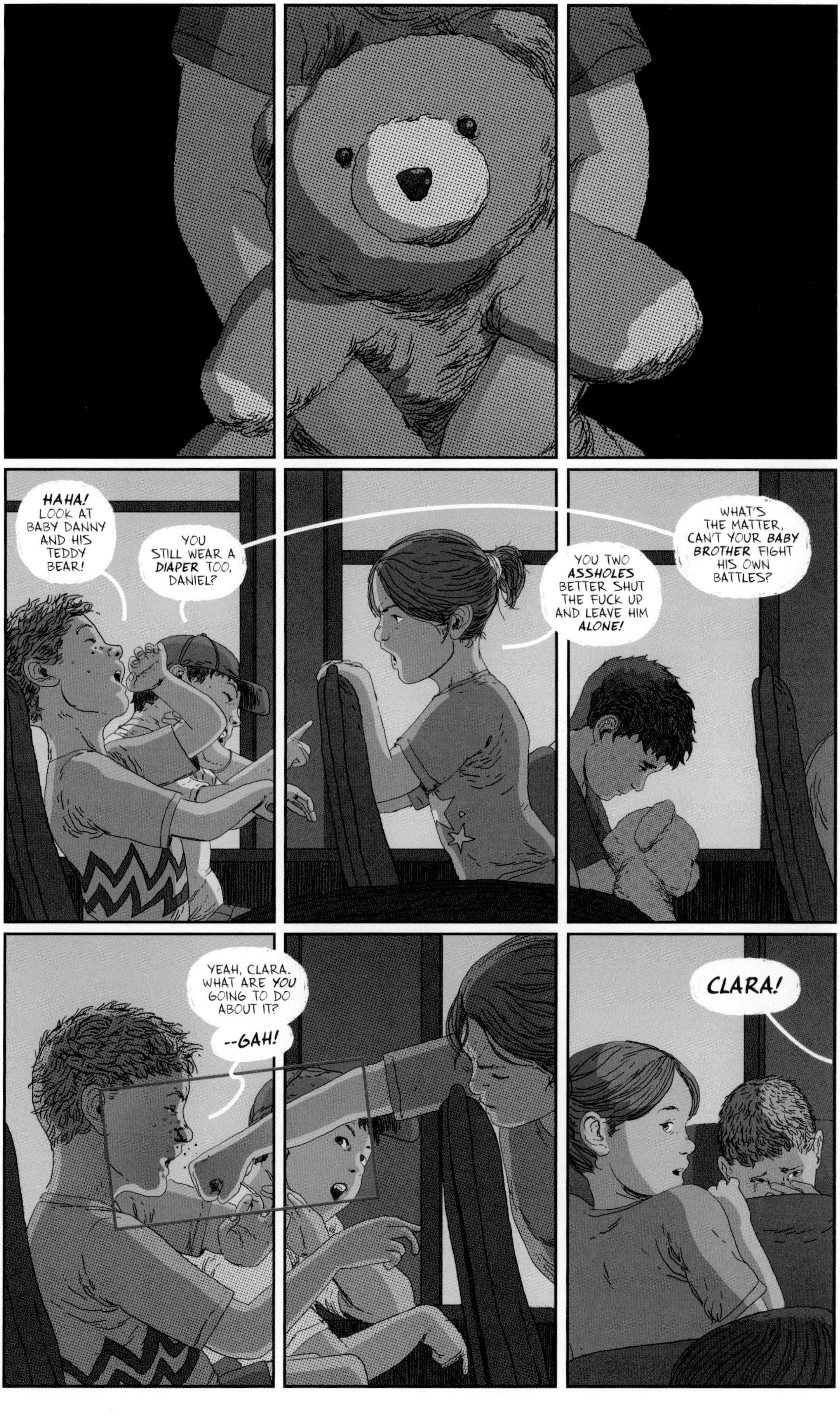
HAHA! LOOK AT BABY DANNY AND HIS TEDDY BEAR!
YOU STILL WEAR A DIAPER TOO, DANIEL?
YOU TWO ASSHOLES BETTER SHUT THE FUCK UP AND LEAVE HIM ALONE!
WHAT'S THE MATTER, CAN'T YOUR BABY BROTHER FIGHT HIS OWN BATTLES?
YEAH, CLARA. WHAT ARE YOU GOING TO DO ABOUT IT?
--GAH!
CLARA!

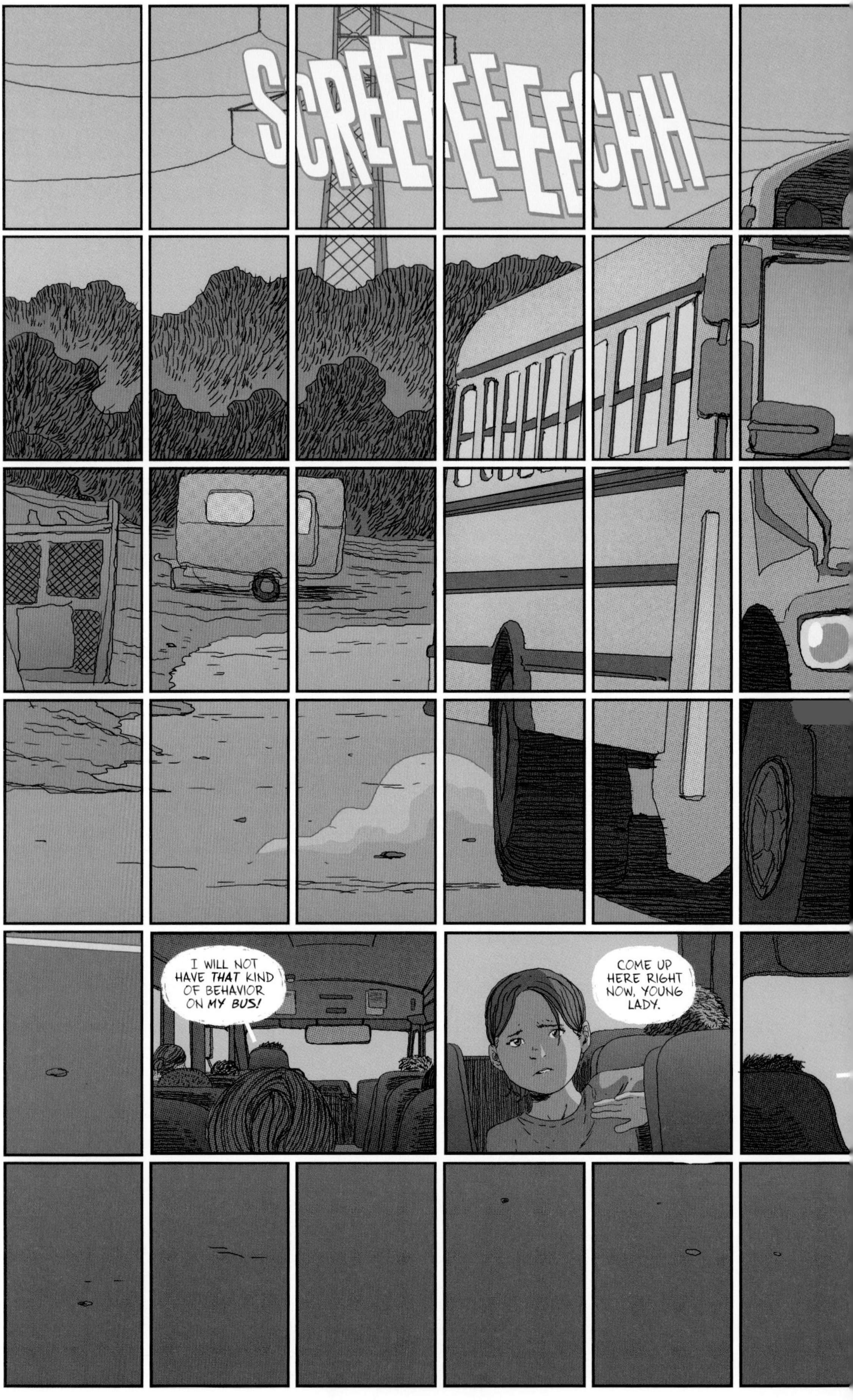
SCREEEEEEECHH
I WILL NOT HAVE THAT KIND OF BEHAVIOR ON MY BUS!
COME UP HERE RIGHT NOW, YOUNG LADY.

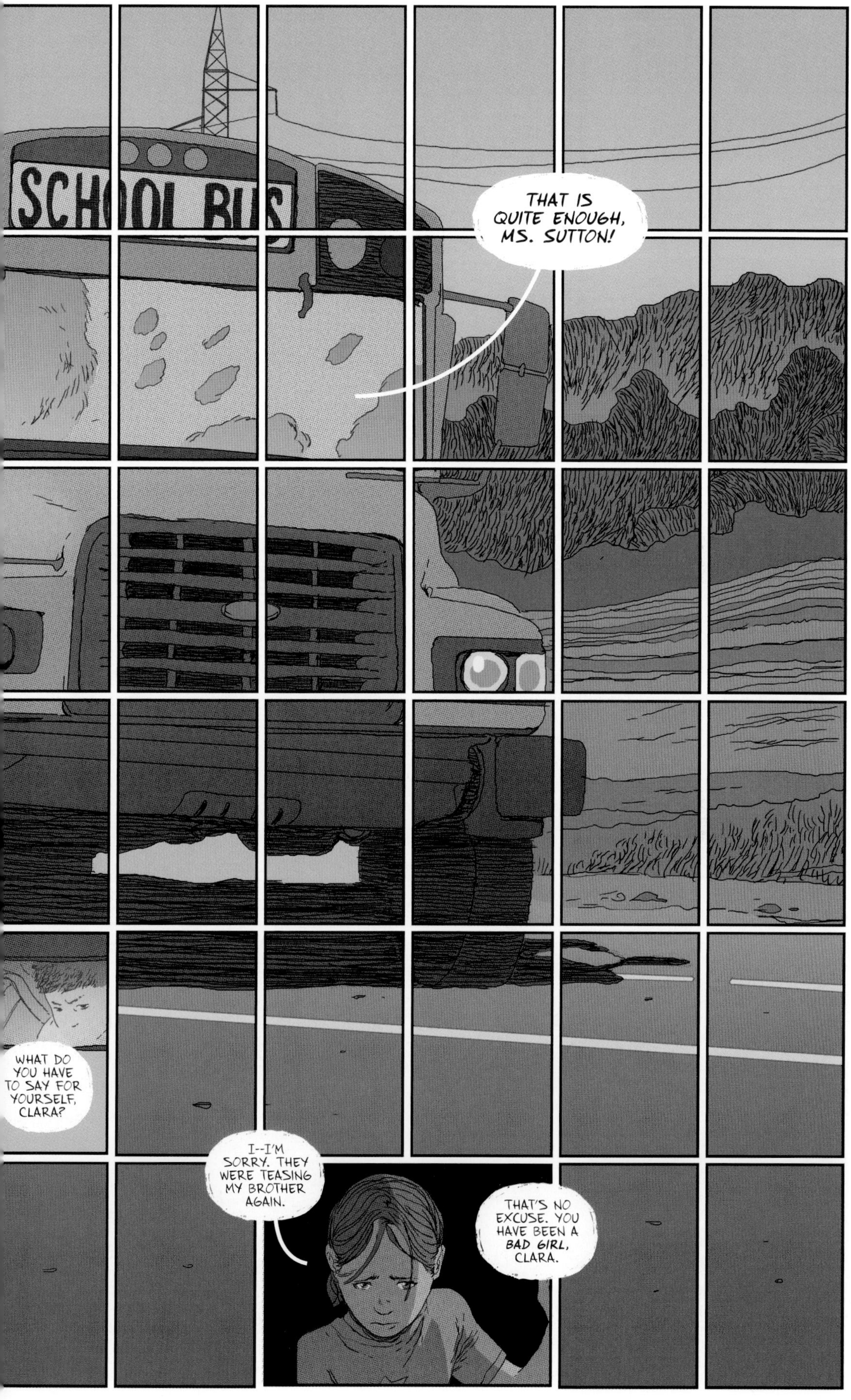
SCHOOL BUS
THAT IS QUITE ENOUGH, MS. SUTTON!
WHAT DO YOU HAVE TO SAY FOR YOURSELF, CLARA?
I--I'M SORRY. THEY WERE TEASING MY BROTHER AGAIN.
THAT'S NO EXCUSE. YOU HAVE BEEN A BAD GIRL, CLARA.

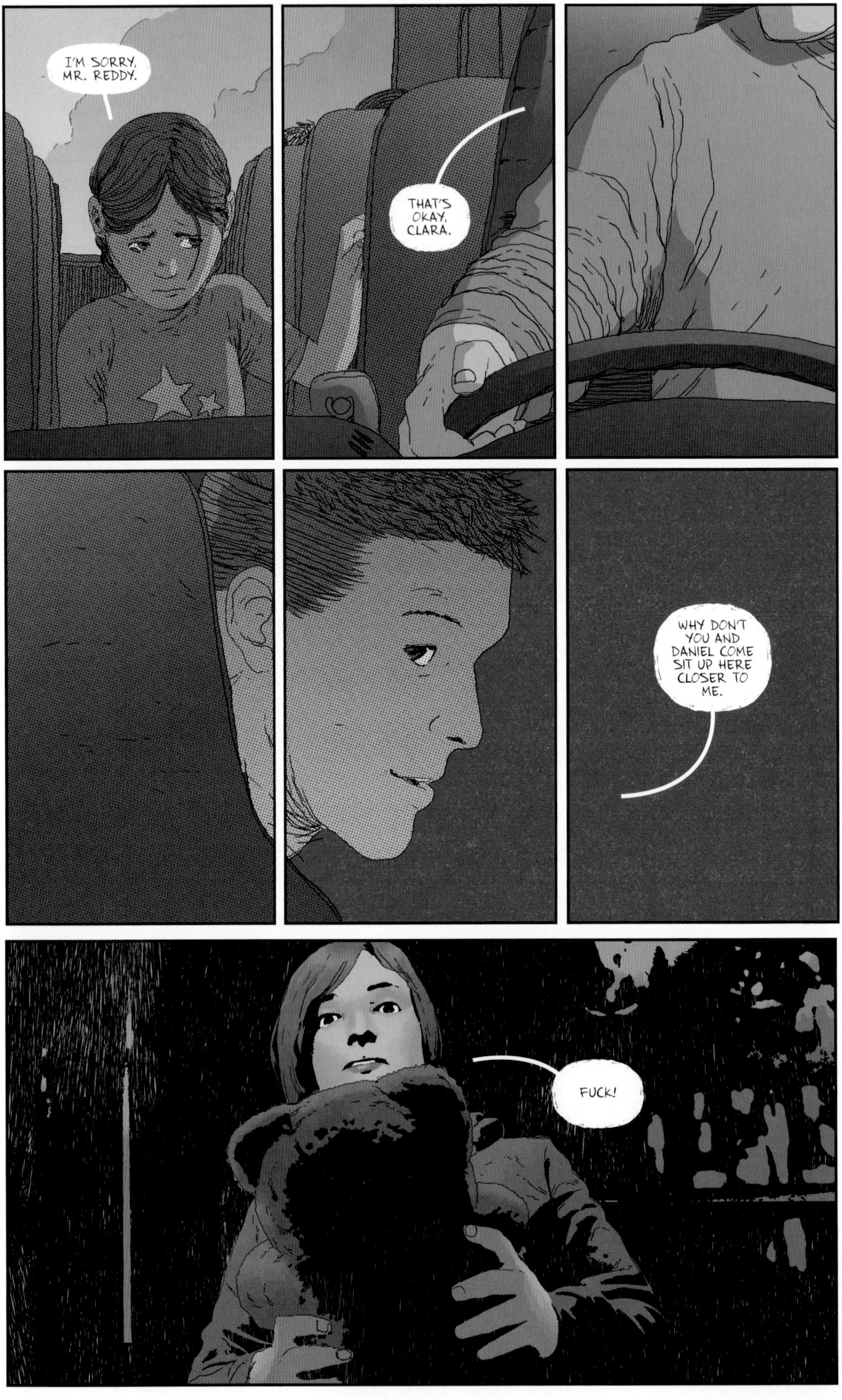
I'M SORRY, MR. REDDY.
THAT'S OKAY, CLARA.
WHY DON'T YOU AND DANIEL COME SIT UP HERE CLOSER TO ME.
FUCK!

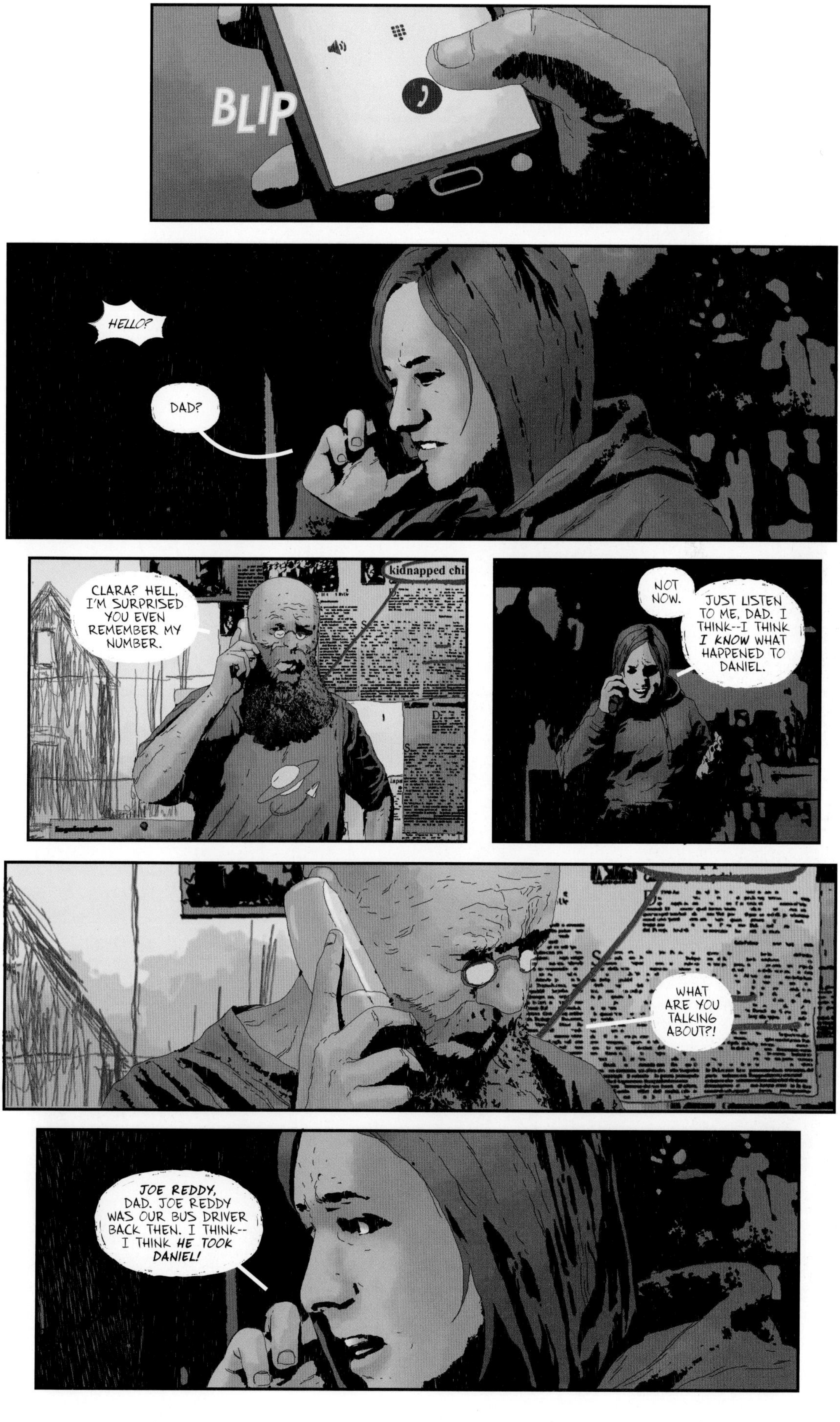
BLIP
HELLO?
DAD?
CLARA? HELL, I'M SURPRISED YOU EVEN REMEMBER MY NUMBER.
kidnapped chi
NOT NOW.
JUST LISTEN TO ME, DAD. I THINK--I THINK I KNOW WHAT HAPPENED TO DANIEL.
WHAT ARE YOU TALKING ABOUT?!
JOE REDDY, DAD. JOE REDDY WAS OUR BUS DRIVER BACK THEN. I THINK-- I THINK HE TOOK DANIEL!

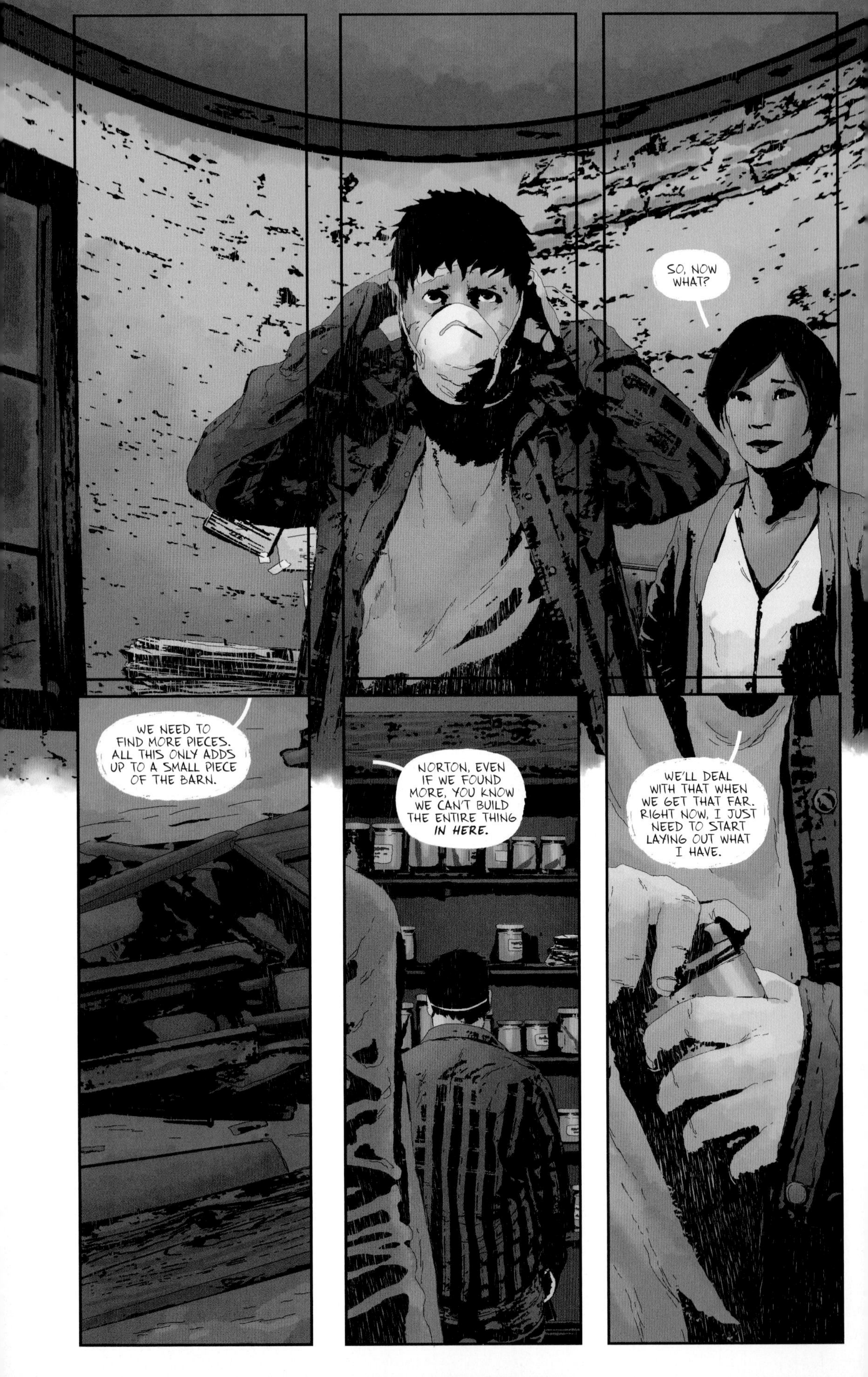
SO, NOW WHAT?
WE NEED TO FIND MORE PIECES. ALL THIS ONLY ADDS UP TO A SMALL PIECE OF THE BARN.
NORTON, EVEN IF WE FOUND MORE, YOU KNOW WE CAN'T BUILD THE ENTIRE THING IN HERE.
WE'LL DEAL WITH THAT WHEN WE GET THAT FAR. RIGHT NOW, I JUST NEED TO START LAYING OUT WHAT I HAVE.

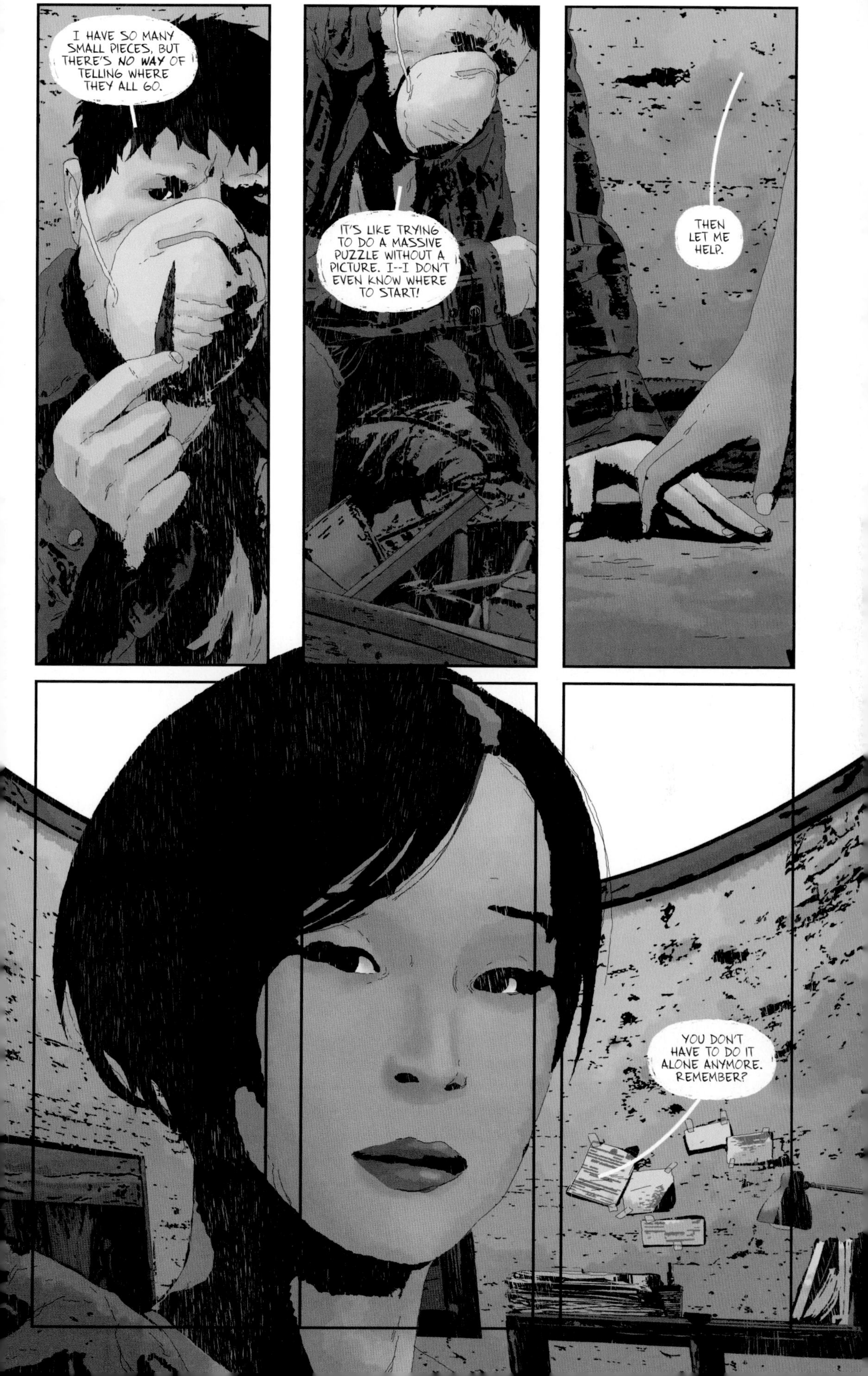
I HAVE SO MANY SMALL PIECES, BUT THERE'S **NO WAY** OF TELLING WHERE THEY ALL GO.
IT'S LIKE TRYING TO DO A MASSIVE PUZZLE WITHOUT A PICTURE. I--I DON'T EVEN KNOW WHERE TO START!
THEN LET ME HELP.
YOU DON'T HAVE TO DO IT ALONE ANYMORE. REMEMBER?

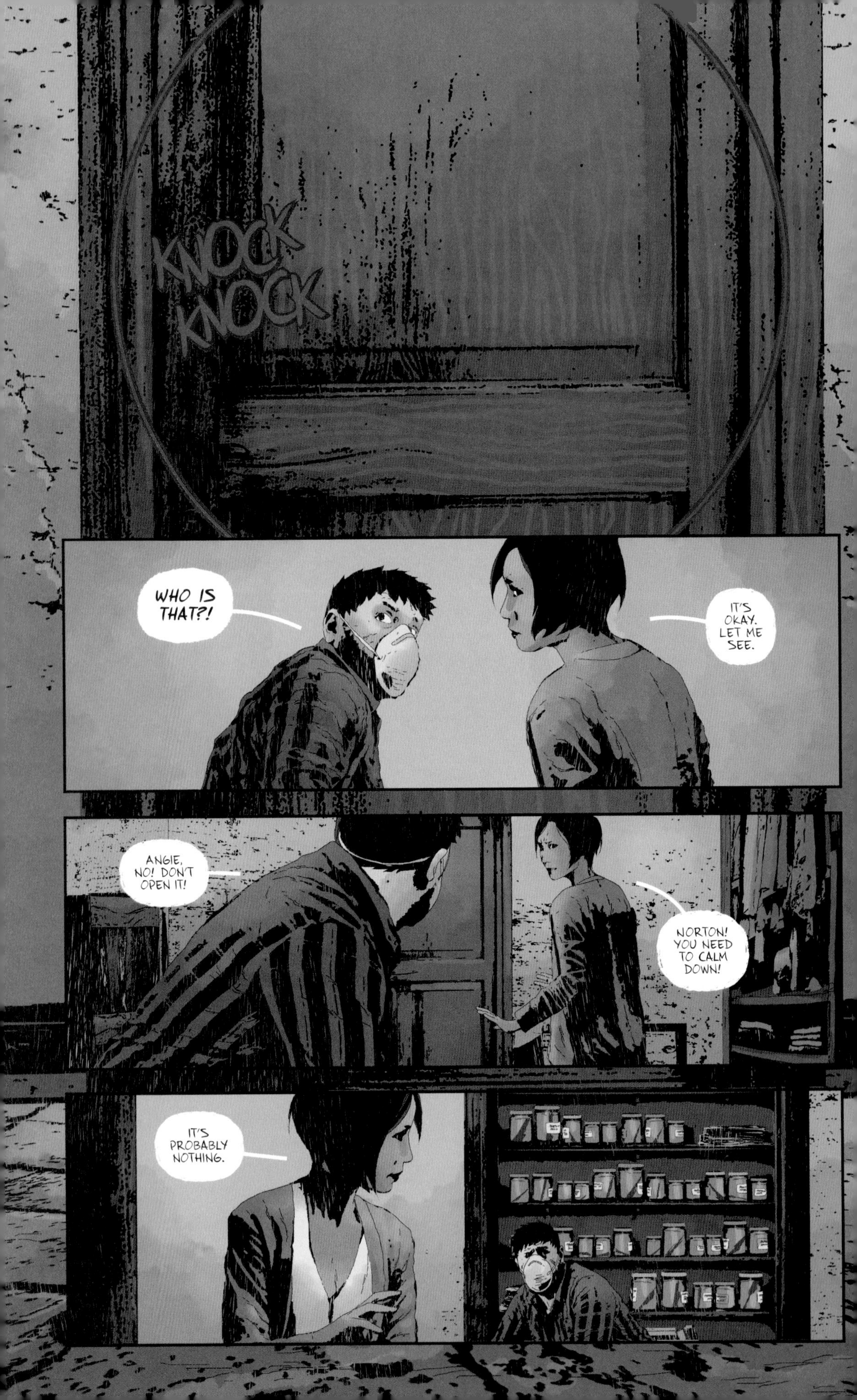
KNOCK KNOCK
WHO IS THAT?!
IT'S OKAY. LET ME SEE.
ANGIE, NO! DON'T OPEN IT!
NORTON! YOU NEED TO CALM DOWN!
IT'S PROBABLY NOTHING.

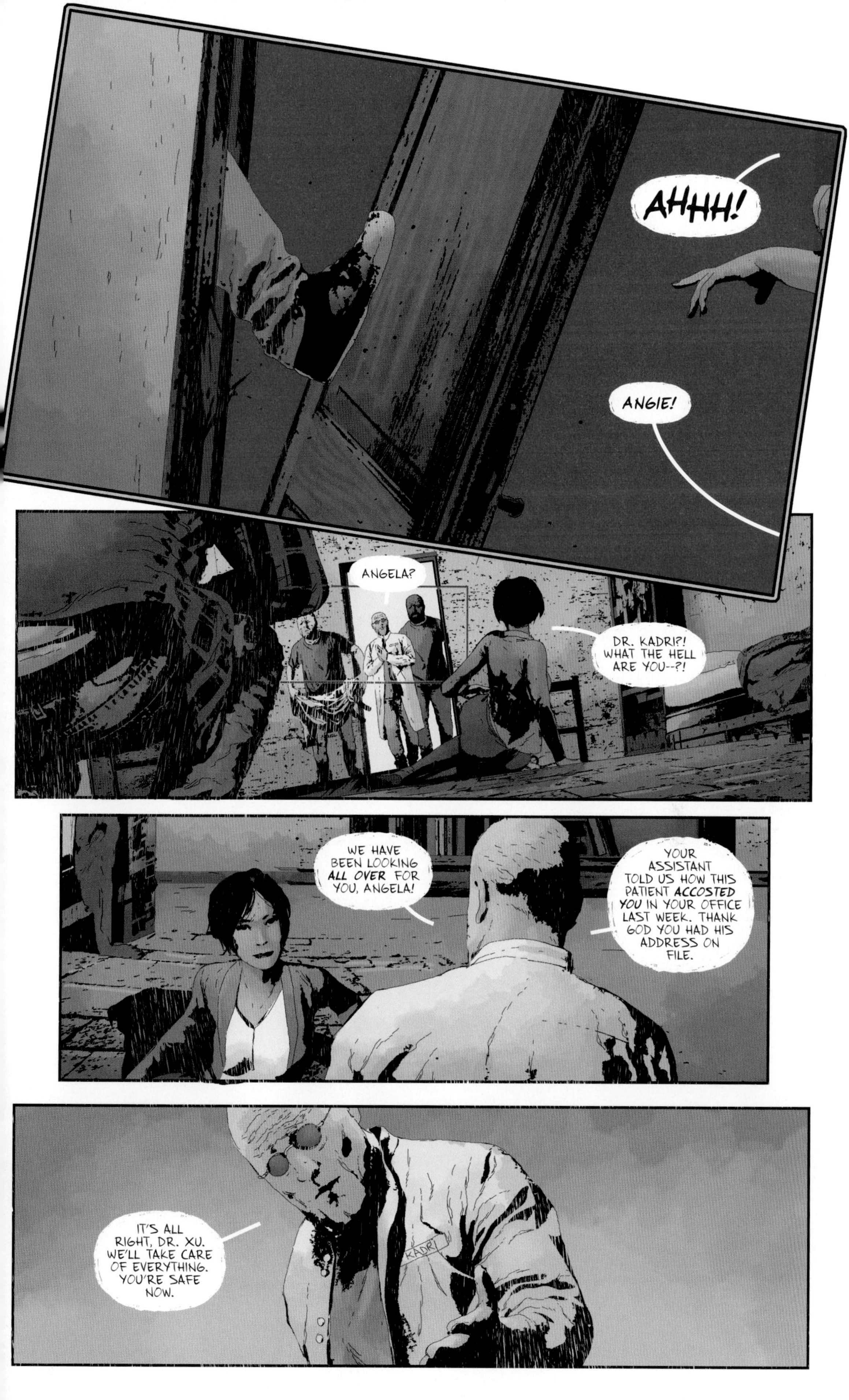
AHHH!
ANGIE!
ANGELA?
DR. KADRI?! WHAT THE HELL ARE YOU--?!
WE HAVE BEEN LOOKING ALL OVER FOR YOU, ANGELA!
YOUR ASSISTANT TOLD US HOW THIS PATIENT ACCOSTED YOU IN YOUR OFFICE LAST WEEK. THANK GOD YOU HAD HIS ADDRESS ON FILE.
IT'S ALL RIGHT, DR. XU. WE'LL TAKE CARE OF EVERYTHING. YOU'RE SAFE NOW.
KADRI

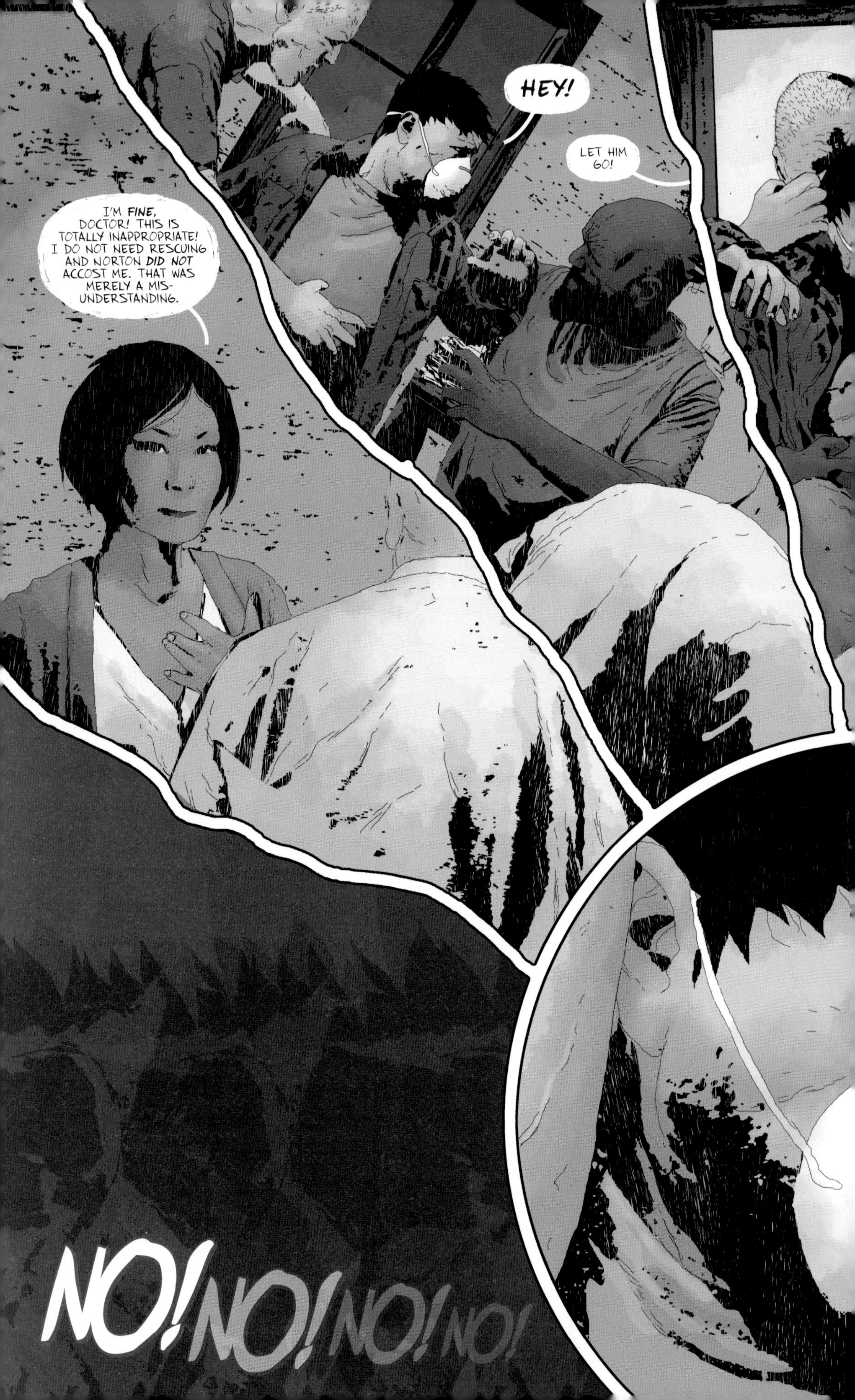
HEY!
LET HIM GO!
I'M FINE, DOCTOR! THIS IS TOTALLY INAPPROPRIATE! I DO NOT NEED RESCUING AND NORTON DID NOT ACCOST ME. THAT WAS MERELY A MIS-UNDERSTANDING.
NO! NO! NO! NO!

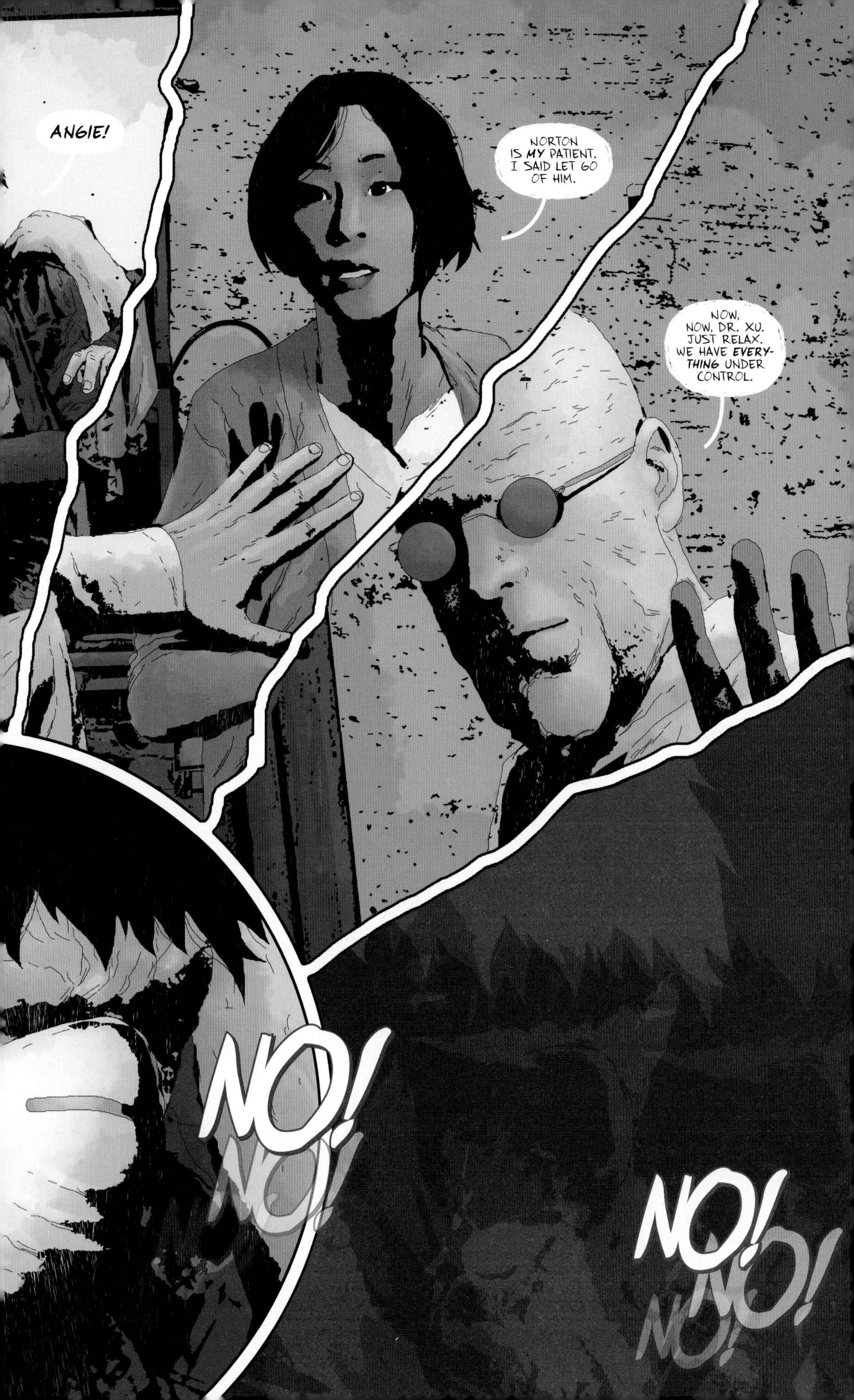
ANGIE!
NORTON IS MY PATIENT. I SAID LET GO OF HIM.
NOW, NOW, DR. XU. JUST RELAX. WE HAVE EVERYTHING UNDER CONTROL.
NO! NO!
NO! NO! NO!

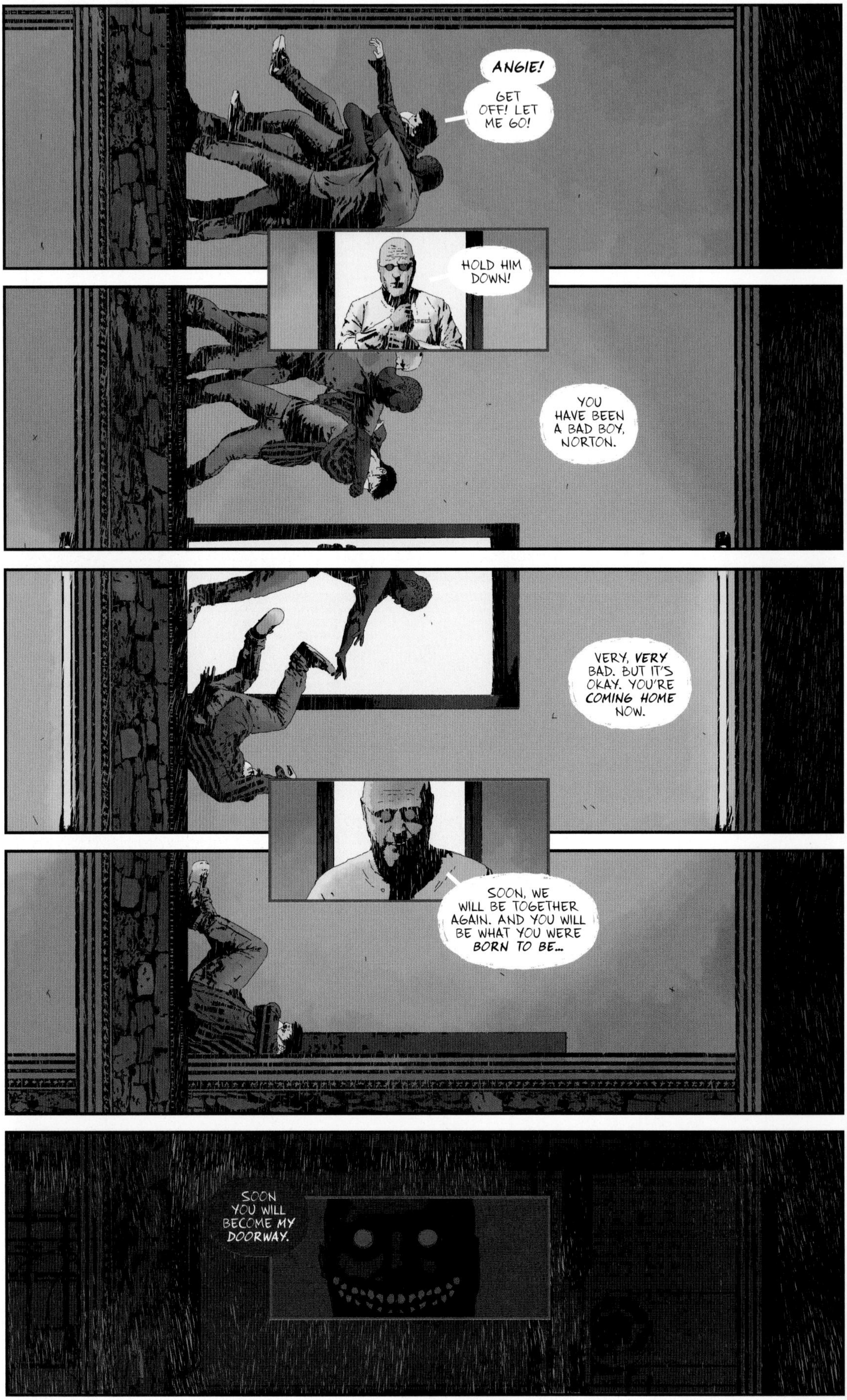
ANGIE!
GET OFF! LET ME GO!
HOLD HIM DOWN!
YOU HAVE BEEN A BAD BOY, NORTON.
VERY, VERY BAD. BUT IT'S OKAY. YOU'RE COMING HOME NOW.
SOON, WE WILL BE TOGETHER AGAIN. AND YOU WILL BE WHAT YOU WERE BORN TO BE...
SOON YOU WILL BECOME MY DOORWAY.

GIDEON
FALLS

Eight

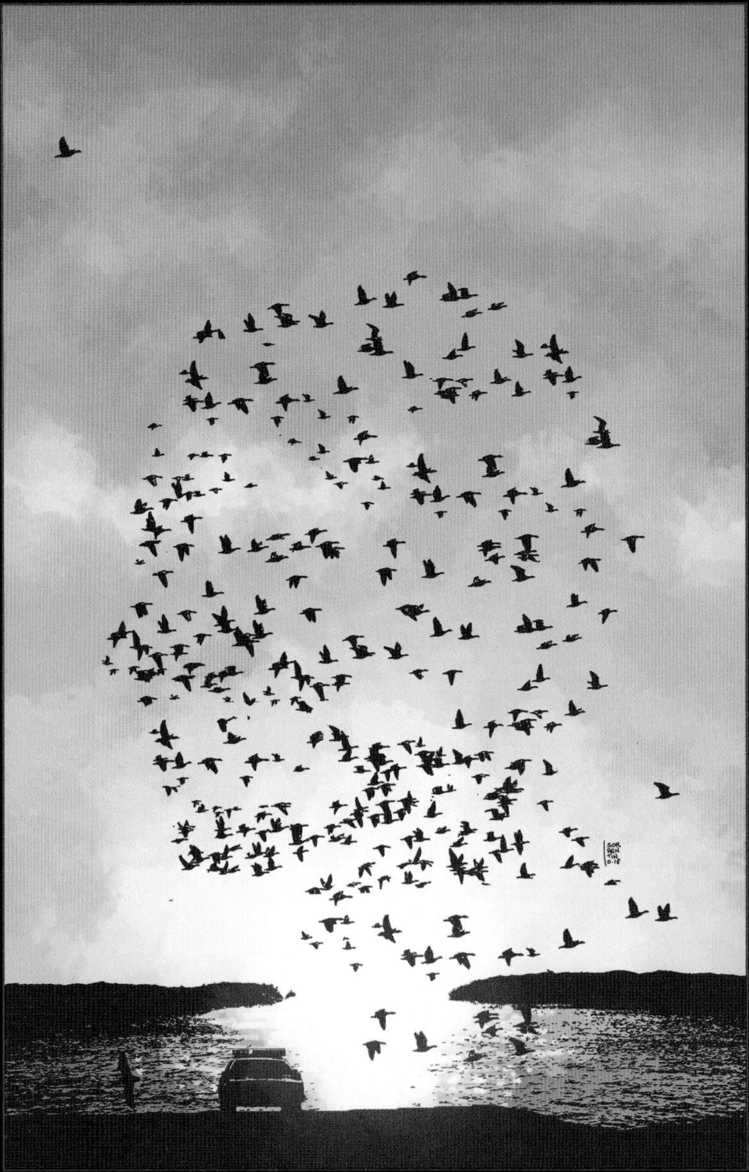

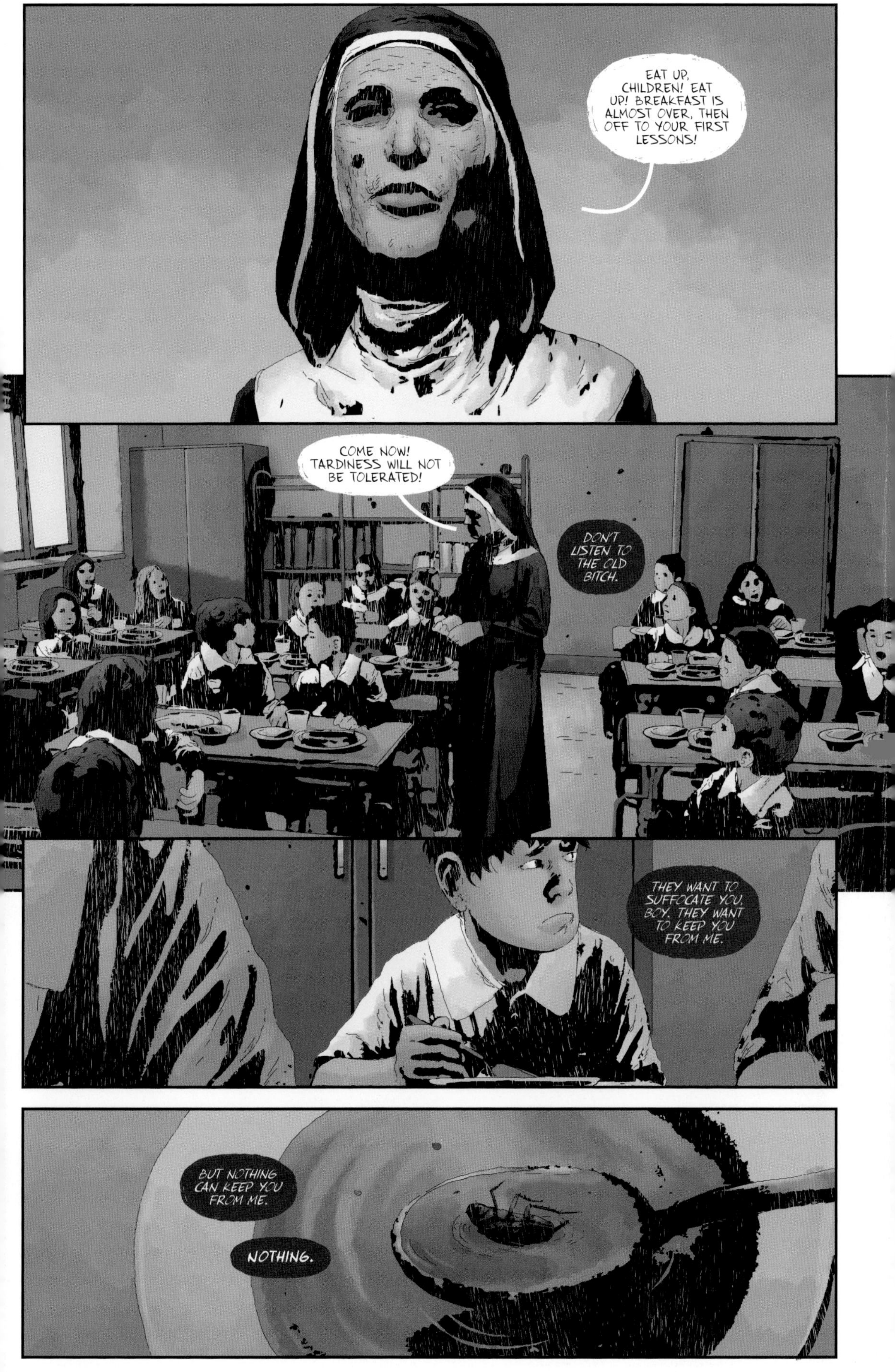
EAT UP, CHILDREN! EAT UP! BREAKFAST IS ALMOST OVER, THEN OFF TO YOUR FIRST LESSONS!
COME NOW! TARDINESS WILL NOT BE TOLERATED!
DON'T LISTEN TO THE OLD BITCH.
THEY WANT TO SUFFOCATE YOU, BOY. THEY WANT TO KEEP YOU FROM ME.
BUT NOTHING CAN KEEP YOU FROM ME.
NOTHING.

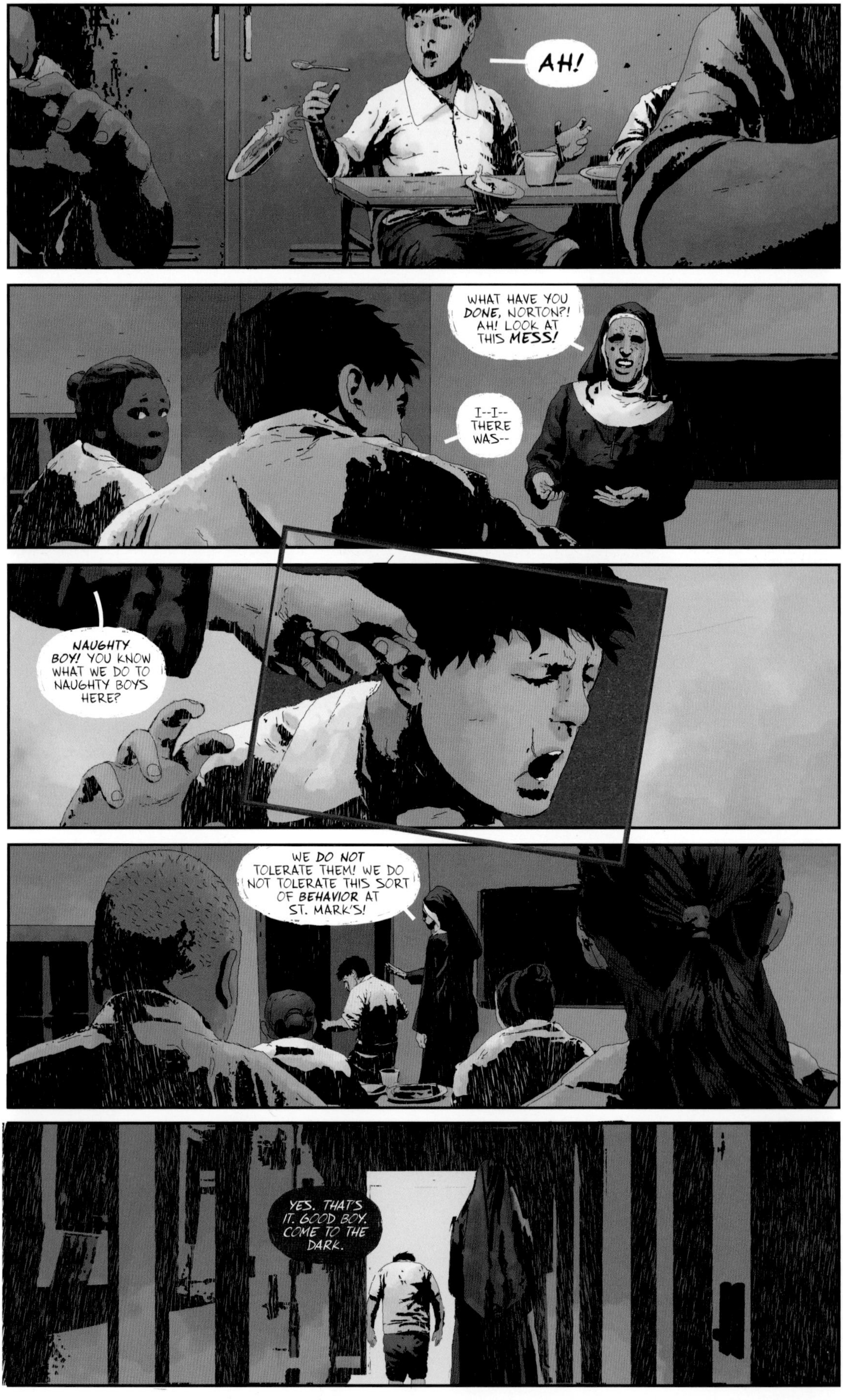
AH!
WHAT HAVE YOU DONE, NORTON?! AH! LOOK AT THIS MESS!
I--I-- THERE WAS--
NAUGHTY BOY! YOU KNOW WHAT WE DO TO NAUGHTY BOYS HERE?
WE DO NOT TOLERATE THEM! WE DO NOT TOLERATE THIS SORT OF BEHAVIOR AT ST. MARK'S!
YES. THAT'S IT. GOOD BOY. COME TO THE DARK.

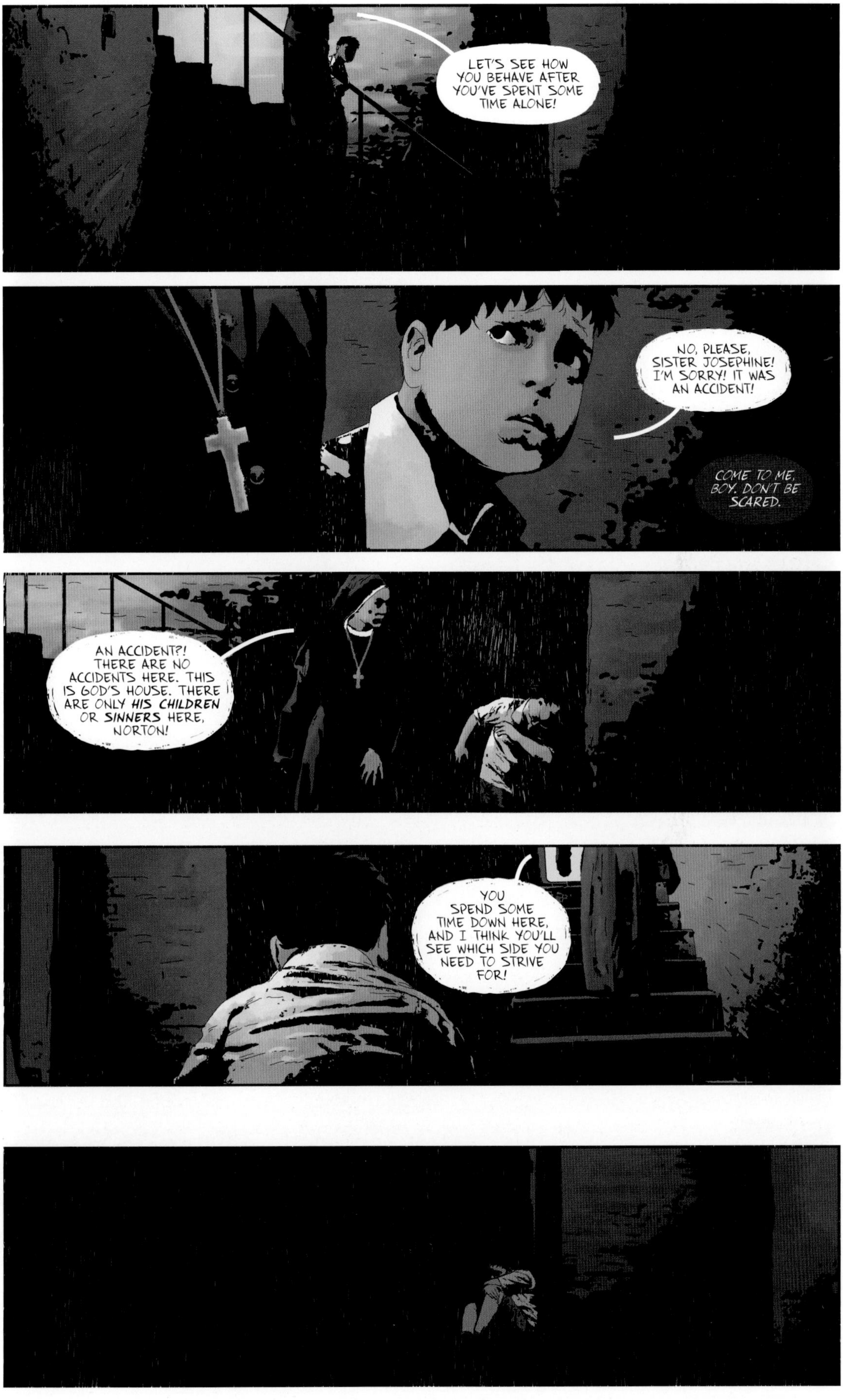
LET'S SEE HOW YOU BEHAVE AFTER YOU'VE SPENT SOME TIME ALONE!
NO, PLEASE, SISTER JOSEPHINE! I'M SORRY! IT WAS AN ACCIDENT!
COME TO ME, BOY. DON'T BE SCARED.
AN ACCIDENT?! THERE ARE NO ACCIDENTS HERE. THIS IS GOD'S HOUSE. THERE ARE ONLY HIS CHILDREN OR SINNERS HERE, NORTON!
YOU SPEND SOME TIME DOWN HERE, AND I THINK YOU'LL SEE WHICH SIDE YOU NEED TO STRIVE FOR!

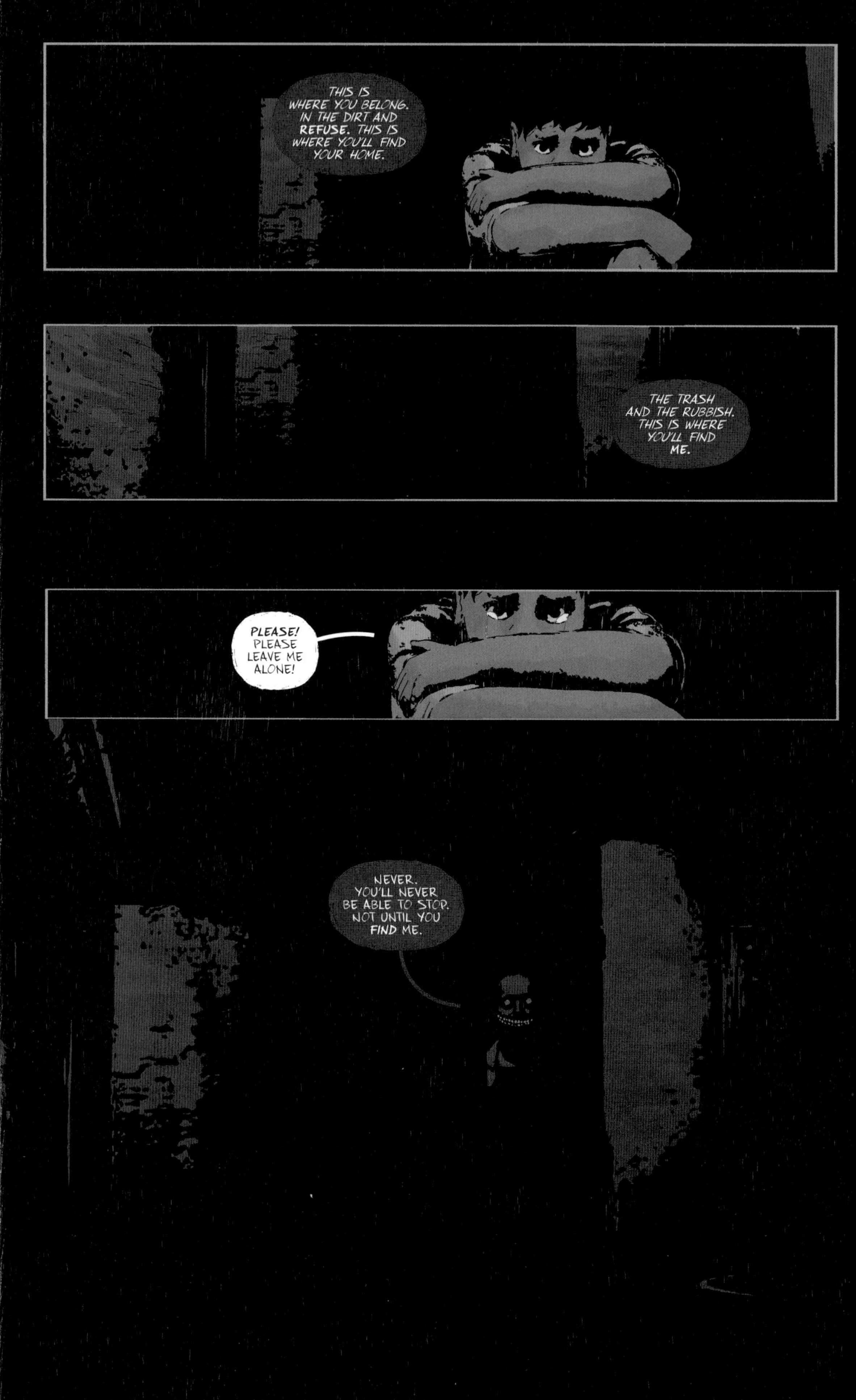
THIS IS WHERE YOU BELONG. IN THE DIRT AND REFUSE. THIS IS WHERE YOU'LL FIND YOUR HOME.
THE TRASH AND THE RUBBISH. THIS IS WHERE YOU'LL FIND ME.
PLEASE! PLEASE LEAVE ME ALONE!
NEVER. YOU'LL NEVER BE ABLE TO STOP. NOT UNTIL YOU FIND ME.

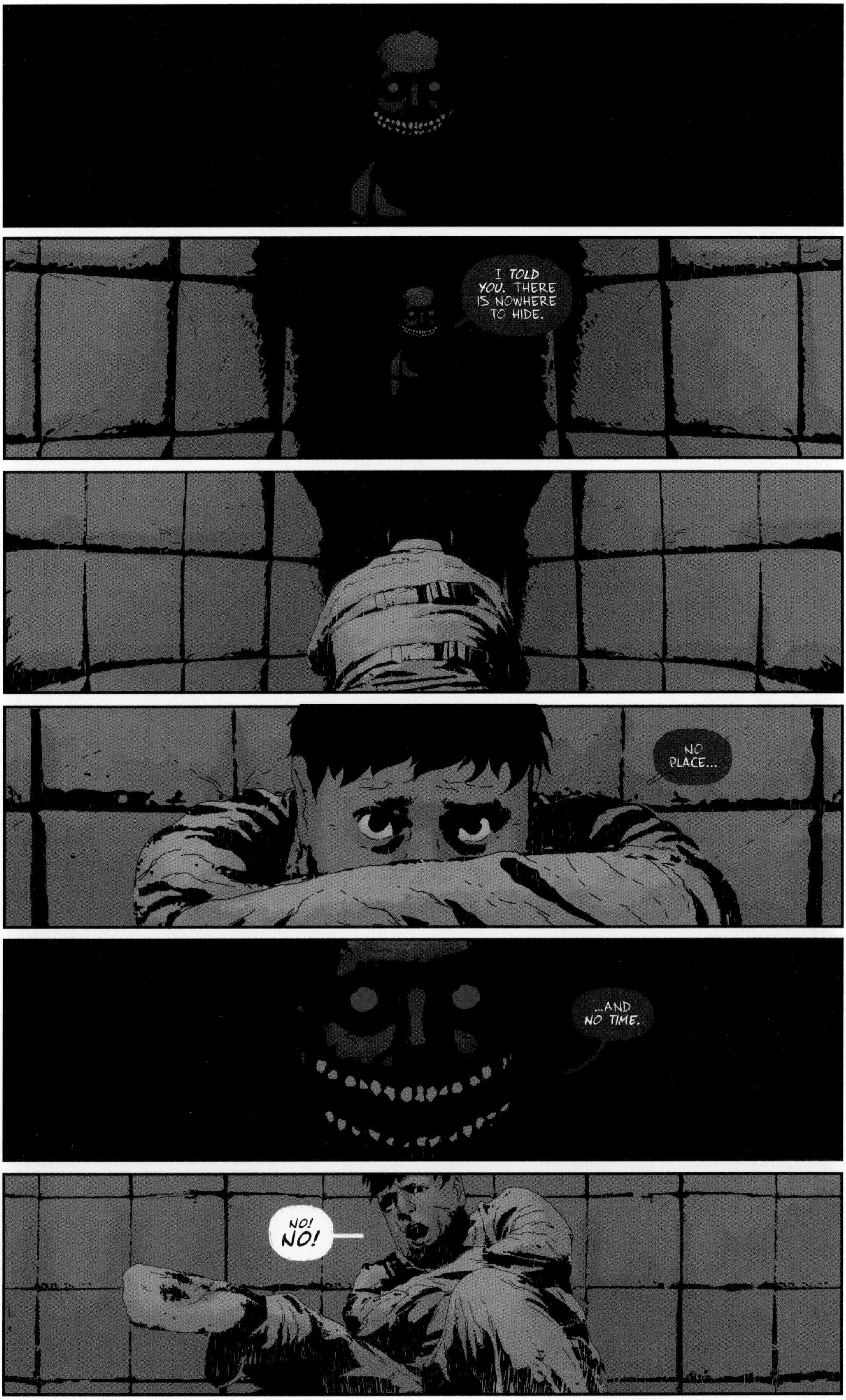
I TOLD YOU. THERE IS NOWHERE TO HIDE.
NO PLACE...
...AND NO TIME.
NO! NO!

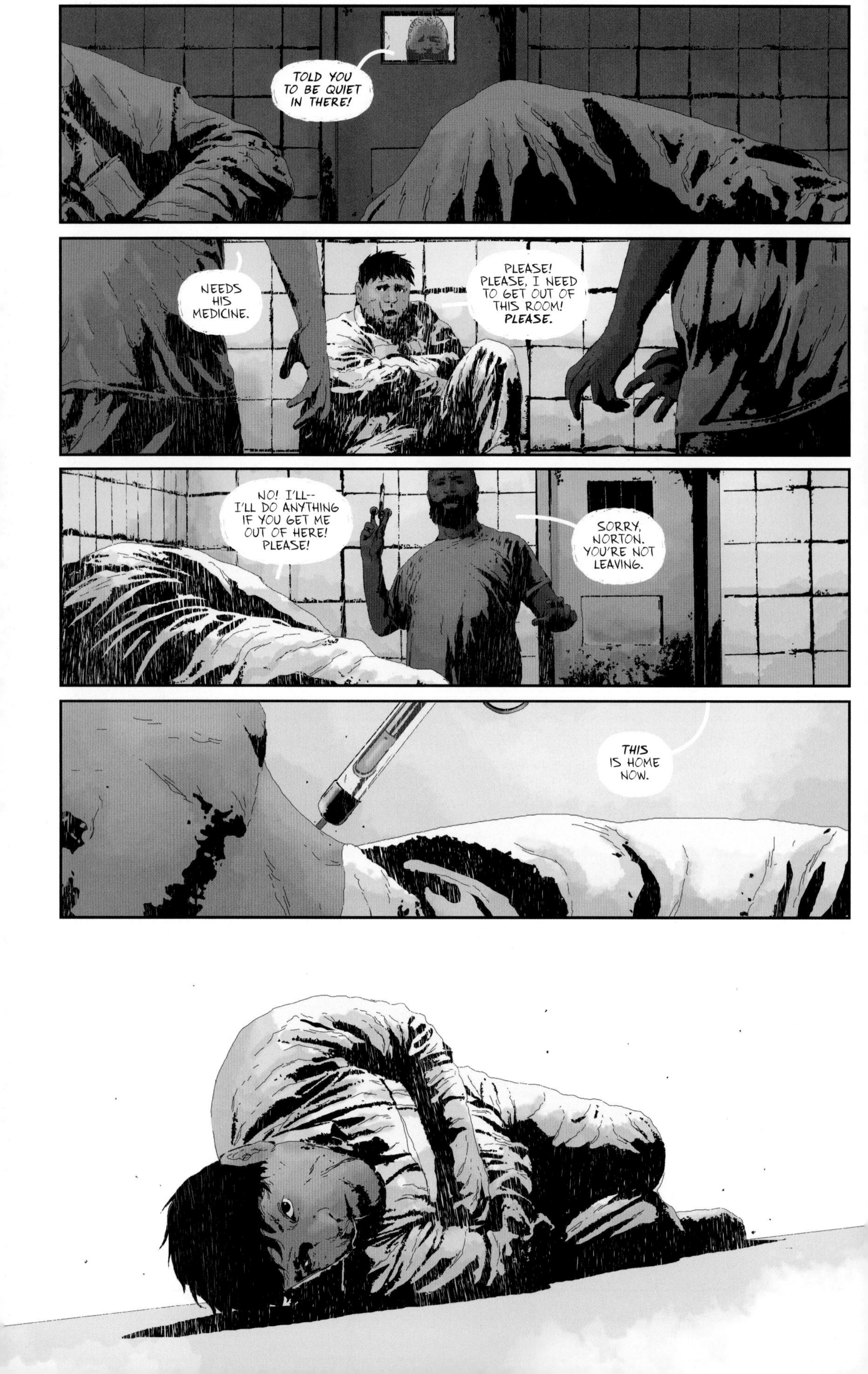
TOLD YOU TO BE QUIET IN THERE!
NEEDS HIS MEDICINE.
PLEASE! PLEASE, I NEED TO GET OUT OF THIS ROOM! **PLEASE.**
NO! I'LL-- I'LL DO ANYTHING IF YOU GET ME OUT OF HERE! PLEASE!
SORRY, NORTON. YOU'RE NOT LEAVING.
THIS IS HOME NOW.

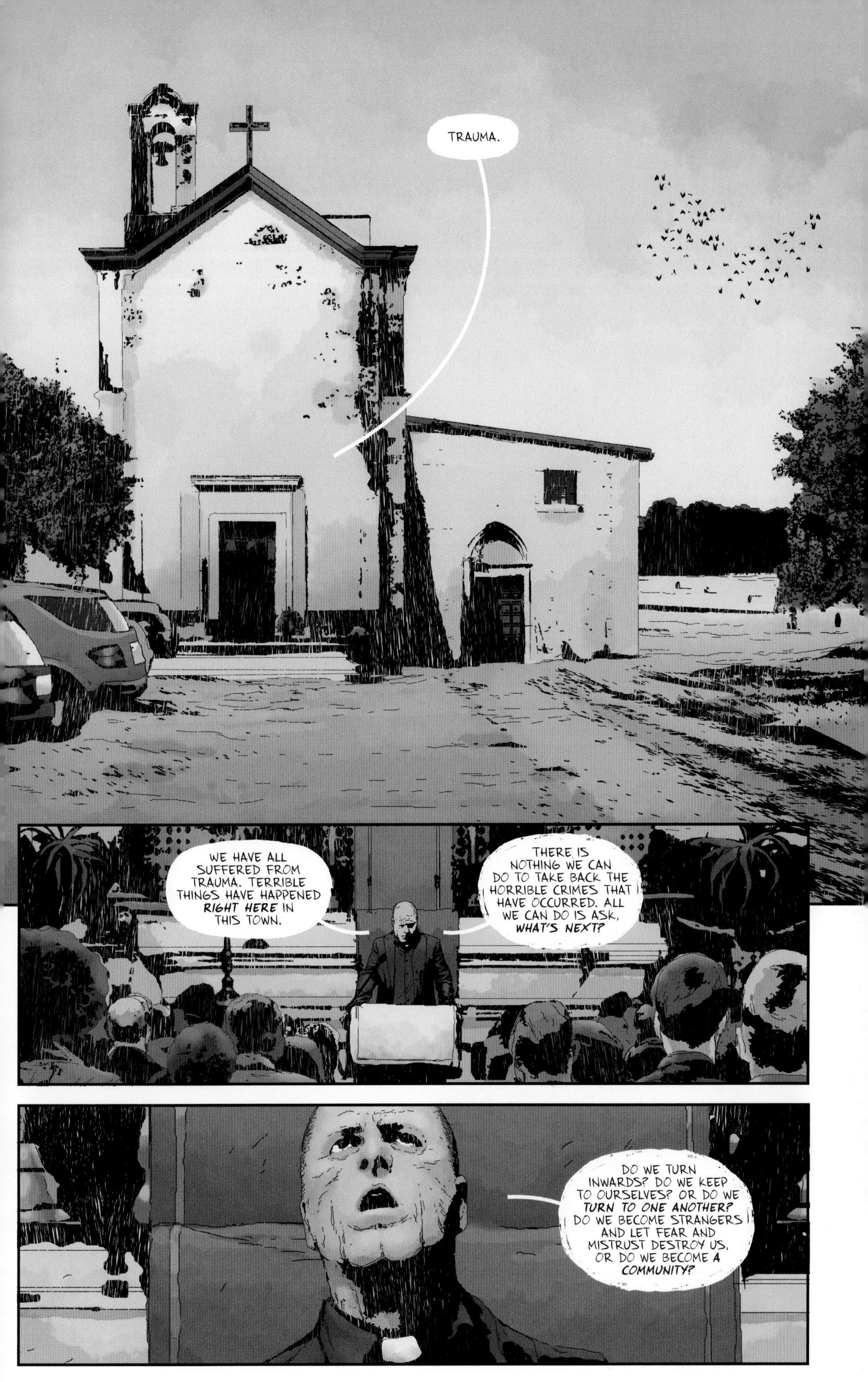
TRAUMA.
WE HAVE ALL SUFFERED FROM TRAUMA. TERRIBLE THINGS HAVE HAPPENED RIGHT HERE IN THIS TOWN.
THERE IS NOTHING WE CAN DO TO TAKE BACK THE HORRIBLE CRIMES THAT HAVE OCCURRED. ALL WE CAN DO IS ASK, WHAT'S NEXT?
DO WE TURN INWARDS? DO WE KEEP TO OURSELVES? OR DO WE TURN TO ONE ANOTHER? DO WE BECOME STRANGERS AND LET FEAR AND MISTRUST DESTROY US, OR DO WE BECOME A COMMUNITY?

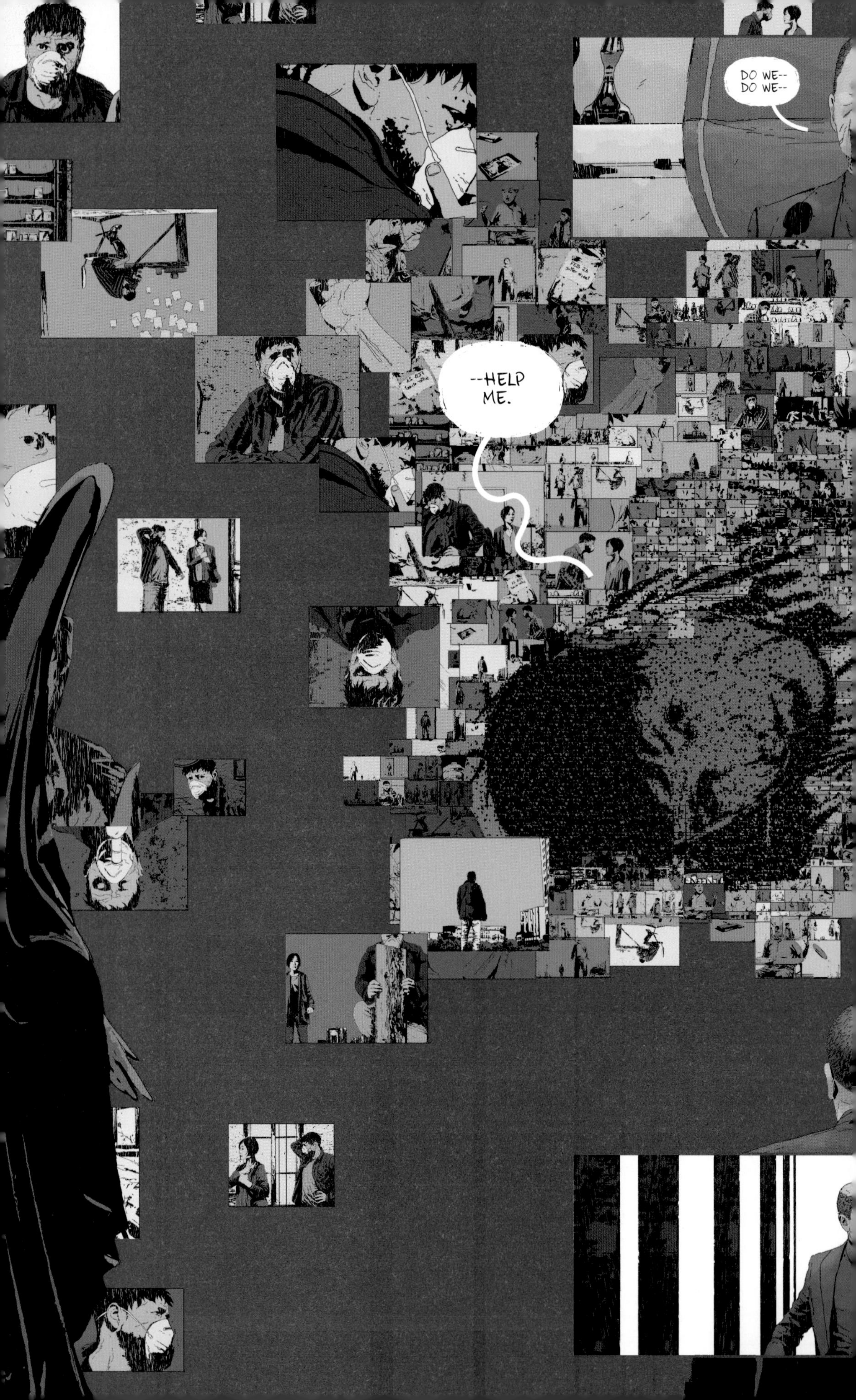
DO WE-- DO WE--
--HELP ME.

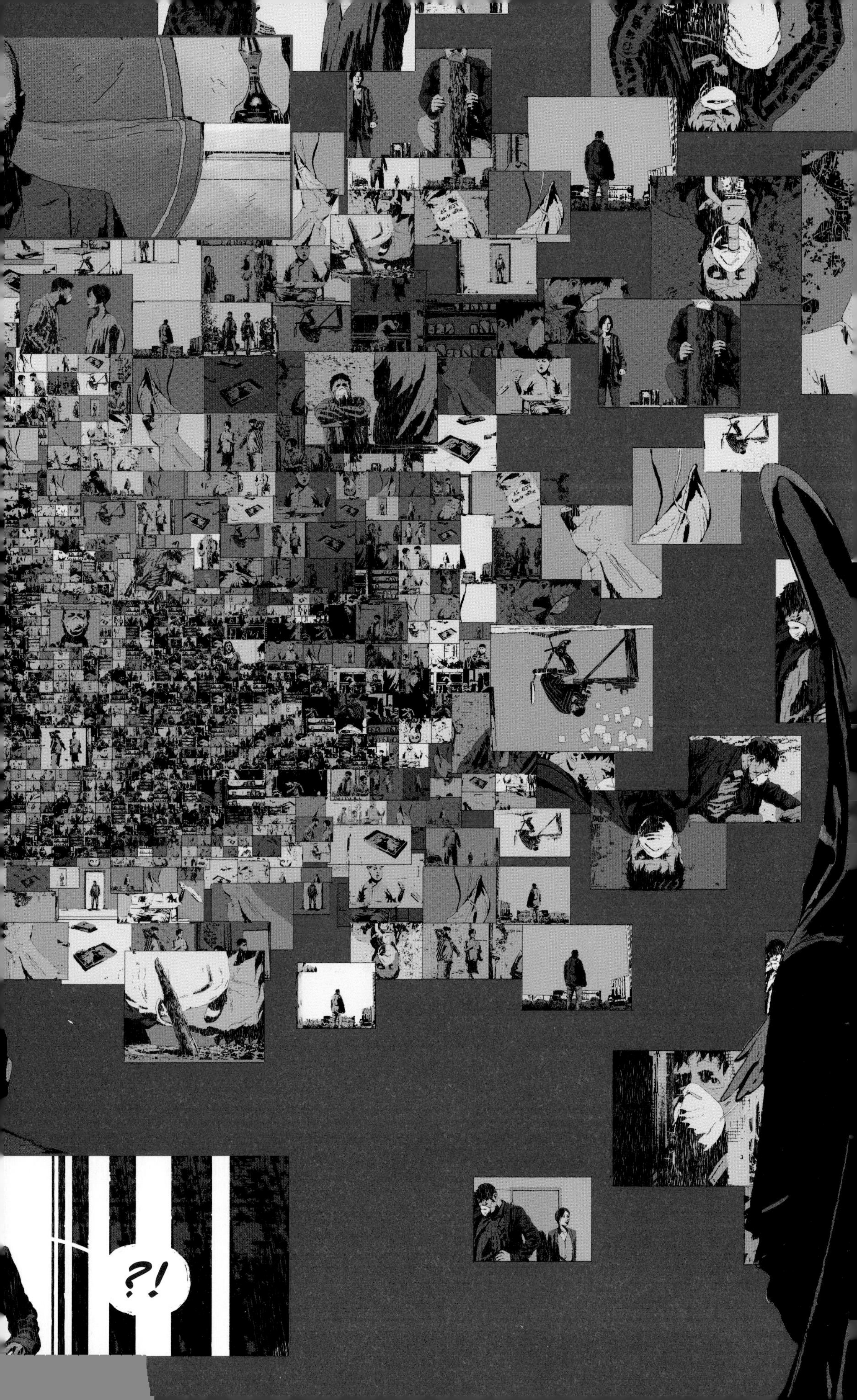
?!

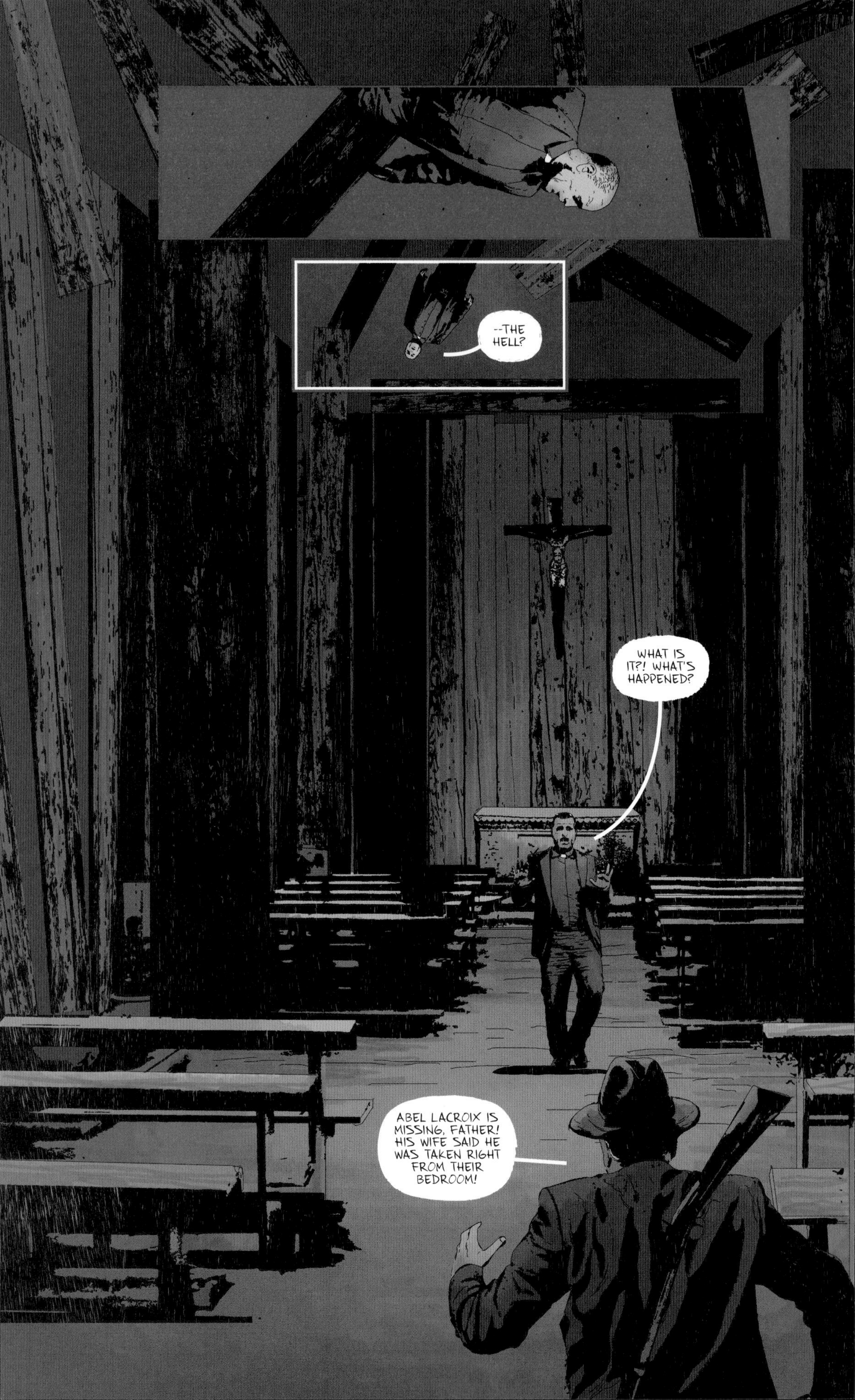
--THE HELL?
WHAT IS IT?! WHAT'S HAPPENED?
ABEL LACROIX IS MISSING, FATHER! HIS WIFE SAID HE WAS TAKEN RIGHT FROM THEIR BEDROOM!

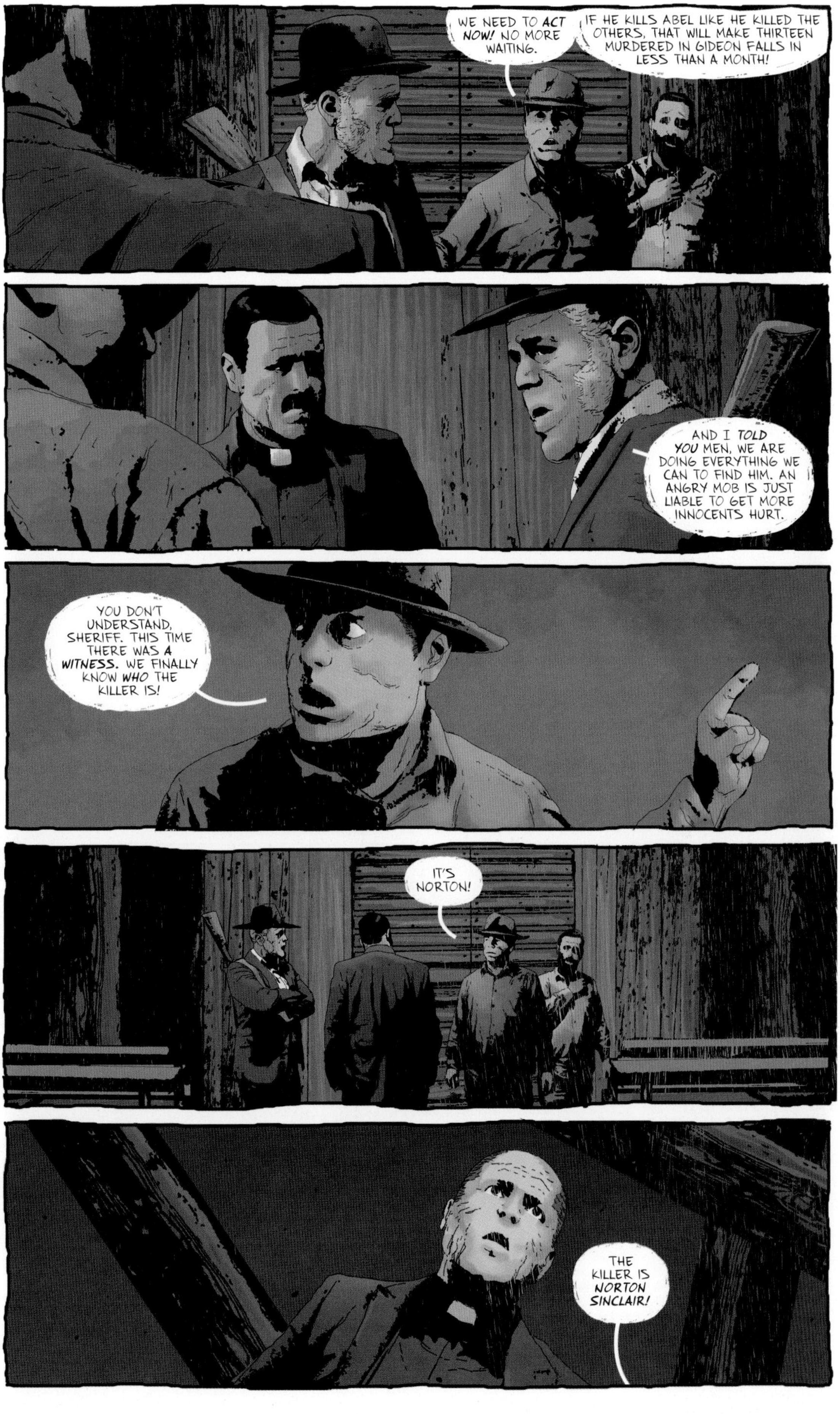
WE NEED TO **ACT NOW!** NO MORE WAITING.
IF HE KILLS ABEL LIKE HE KILLED THE OTHERS, THAT WILL MAKE THIRTEEN MURDERED IN GIDEON FALLS IN LESS THAN A MONTH!
AND I ***TOLD YOU*** MEN, WE ARE DOING EVERYTHING WE CAN TO FIND HIM. AN ANGRY MOB IS JUST LIABLE TO GET MORE INNOCENTS HURT.
YOU DON'T UNDERSTAND, SHERIFF. THIS TIME THERE WAS ***A WITNESS.*** WE FINALLY KNOW ***WHO*** THE KILLER IS!
IT'S NORTON!
THE KILLER IS ***NORTON SINCLAIR!***

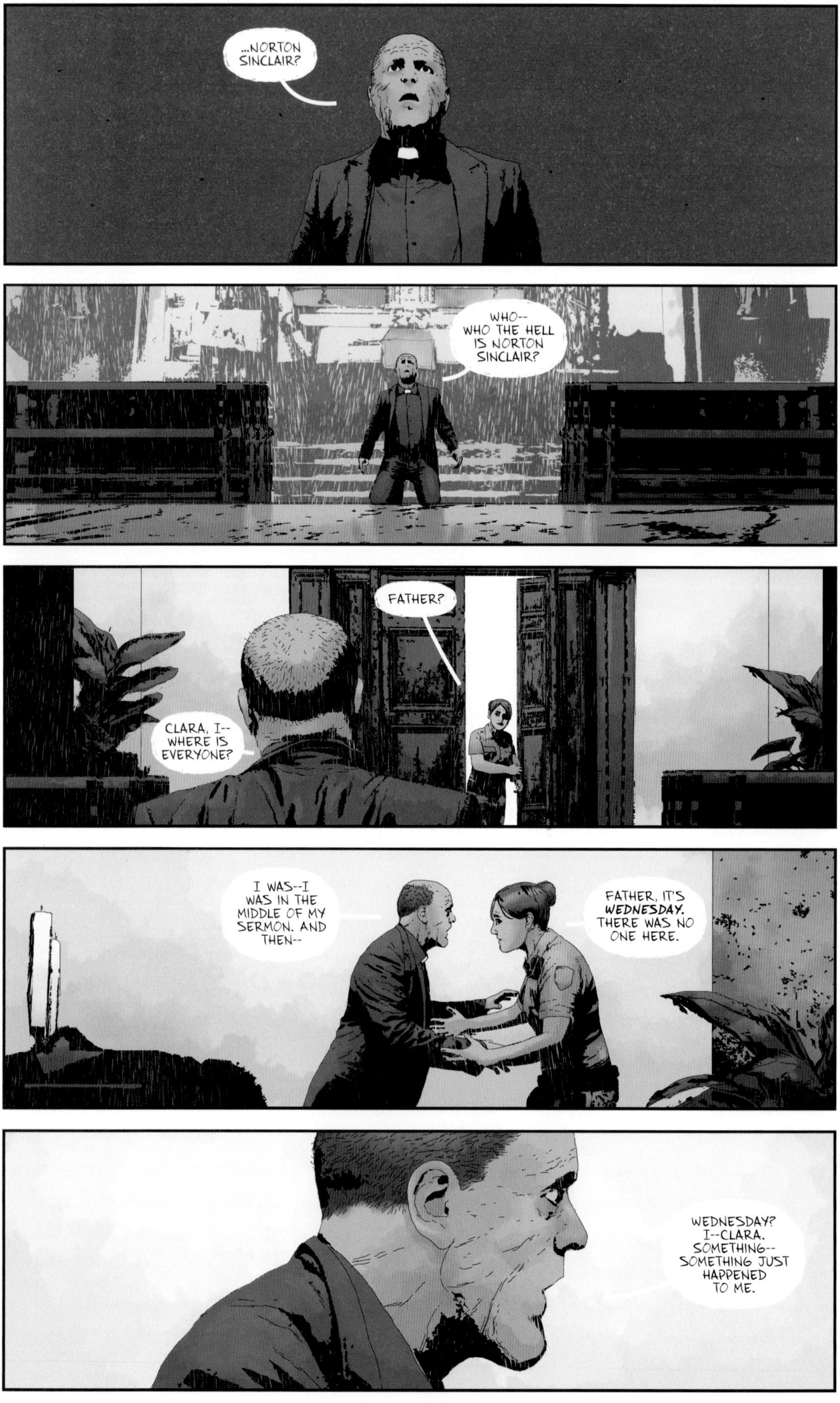

...NORTON SINCLAIR?
WHO-- WHO THE HELL IS NORTON SINCLAIR?
FATHER?
CLARA, I-- WHERE IS EVERYONE?
I WAS--I WAS IN THE MIDDLE OF MY SERMON. AND THEN--
FATHER, IT'S **WEDNESDAY.** THERE WAS NO ONE HERE.
WEDNESDAY? I--CLARA. SOMETHING-- SOMETHING JUST HAPPENED TO ME.

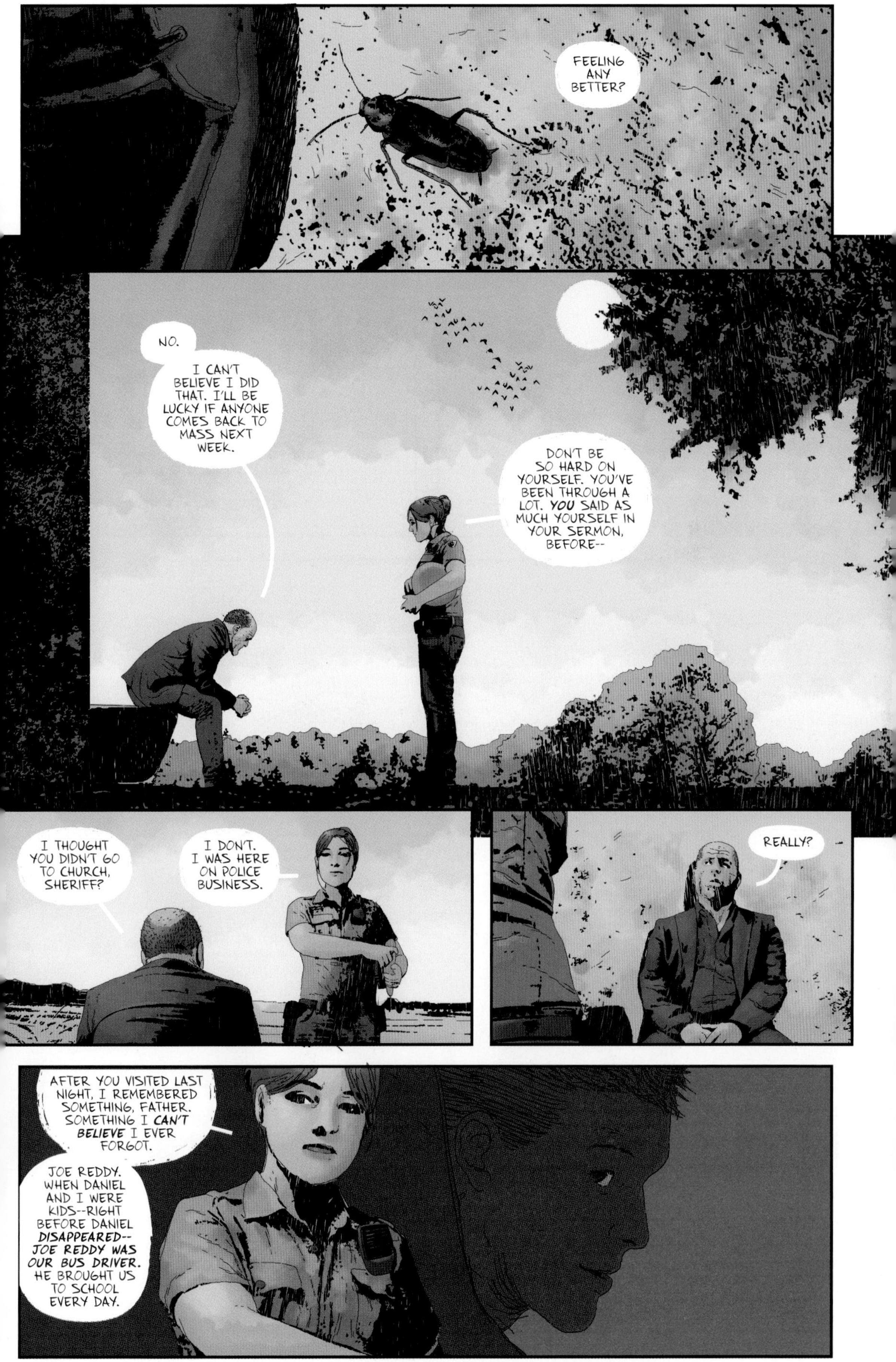
FEELING ANY BETTER?
NO.
I CAN'T BELIEVE I DID THAT. I'LL BE LUCKY IF ANYONE COMES BACK TO MASS NEXT WEEK.
DON'T BE SO HARD ON YOURSELF. YOU'VE BEEN THROUGH A LOT. **YOU** SAID AS MUCH YOURSELF IN YOUR SERMON, BEFORE--
I THOUGHT YOU DIDN'T GO TO CHURCH, SHERIFF?
I DON'T. I WAS HERE ON POLICE BUSINESS.
REALLY?
AFTER YOU VISITED LAST NIGHT, I REMEMBERED SOMETHING, FATHER. SOMETHING I **CAN'T BELIEVE** I EVER FORGOT.
JOE REDDY. WHEN DANIEL AND I WERE KIDS--RIGHT BEFORE DANIEL **DISAPPEARED--JOE REDDY WAS OUR BUS DRIVER.** HE BROUGHT US TO SCHOOL EVERY DAY.

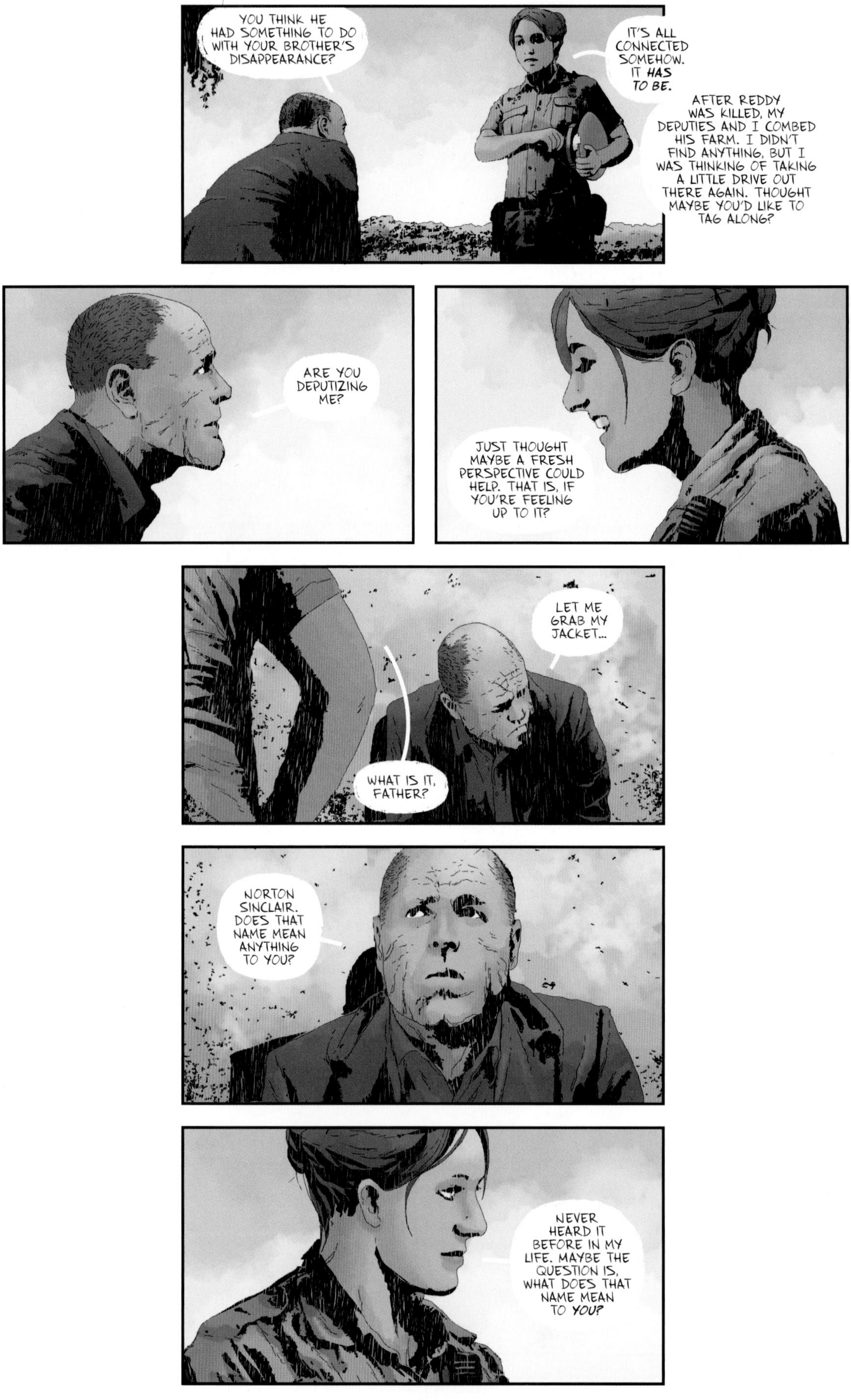
YOU THINK HE HAD SOMETHING TO DO WITH YOUR BROTHER'S DISAPPEARANCE?
IT'S ALL CONNECTED SOMEHOW. IT **HAS** TO BE.
AFTER REDDY WAS KILLED, MY DEPUTIES AND I COMBED HIS FARM. I DIDN'T FIND ANYTHING, BUT I WAS THINKING OF TAKING A LITTLE DRIVE OUT THERE AGAIN. THOUGHT MAYBE YOU'D LIKE TO TAG ALONG?
ARE YOU DEPUTIZING ME?
JUST THOUGHT MAYBE A FRESH PERSPECTIVE COULD HELP. THAT IS, IF YOU'RE FEELING UP TO IT?
LET ME GRAB MY JACKET...
WHAT IS IT, FATHER?
NORTON SINCLAIR. DOES THAT NAME MEAN ANYTHING TO YOU?
NEVER HEARD IT BEFORE IN MY LIFE. MAYBE THE QUESTION IS, WHAT DOES THAT NAME MEAN TO *YOU?*

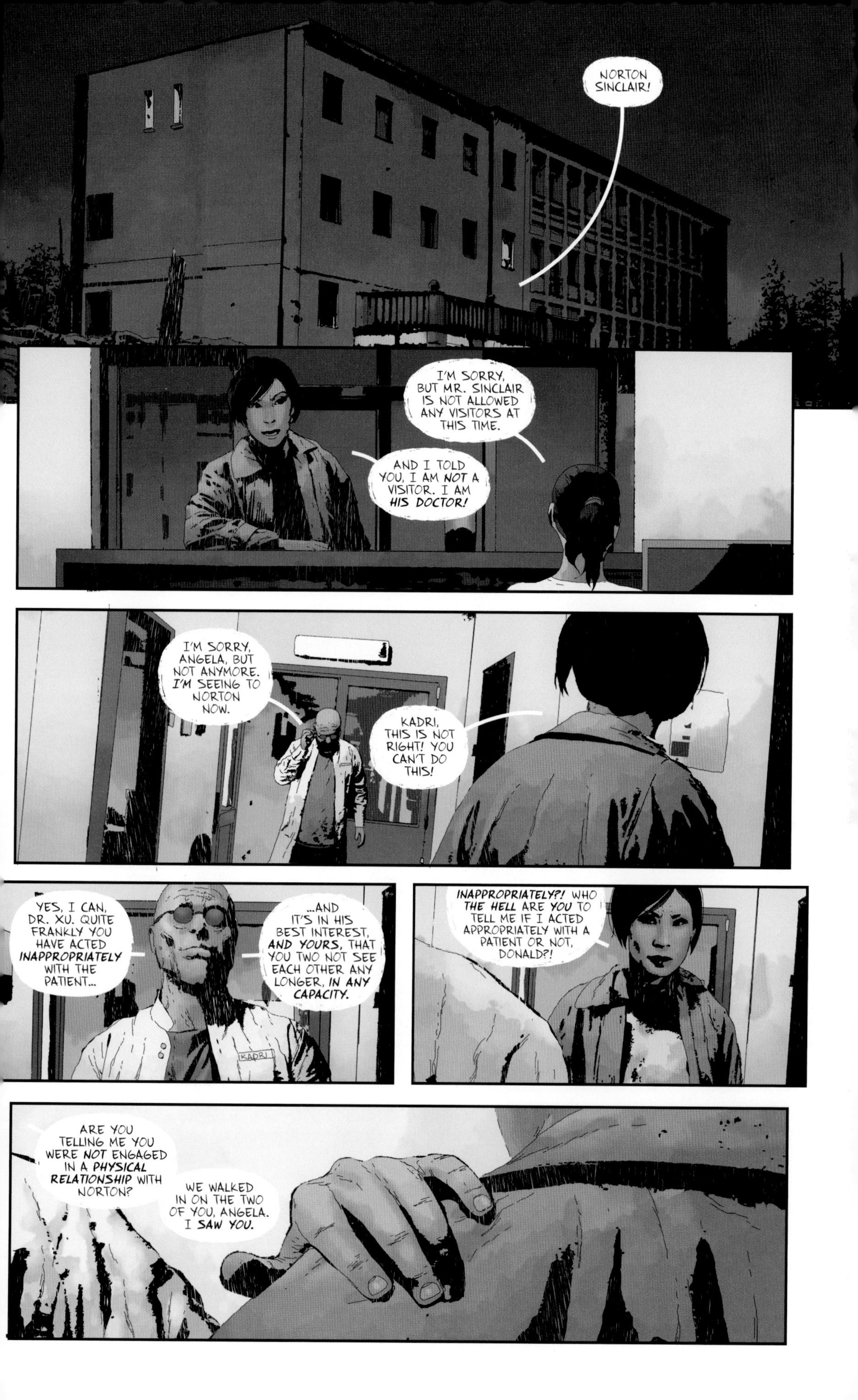
NORTON SINCLAIR!
I'M SORRY, BUT MR. SINCLAIR IS NOT ALLOWED ANY VISITORS AT THIS TIME.
AND I TOLD YOU, I AM **NOT** A VISITOR. I AM **HIS DOCTOR!**
I'M SORRY, ANGELA, BUT NOT ANYMORE. ***I'M*** SEEING TO NORTON NOW.
KADRI, THIS IS NOT RIGHT! YOU CAN'T DO THIS!
YES, I CAN, DR. XU. QUITE FRANKLY YOU HAVE ACTED ***INAPPROPRIATELY*** WITH THE PATIENT...
...AND IT'S IN HIS BEST INTEREST, ***AND YOURS***, THAT YOU TWO NOT SEE EACH OTHER ANY LONGER, ***IN ANY CAPACITY.***
KADRI
INAPPROPRIATELY?! WHO ***THE HELL*** ARE ***YOU*** TO TELL ME IF I ACTED APPROPRIATELY WITH A PATIENT OR NOT, DONALD?!
ARE YOU TELLING ME YOU WERE ***NOT*** ENGAGED IN A ***PHYSICAL RELATIONSHIP*** WITH NORTON?
WE WALKED IN ON THE TWO OF YOU, ANGELA. I ***SAW YOU.***

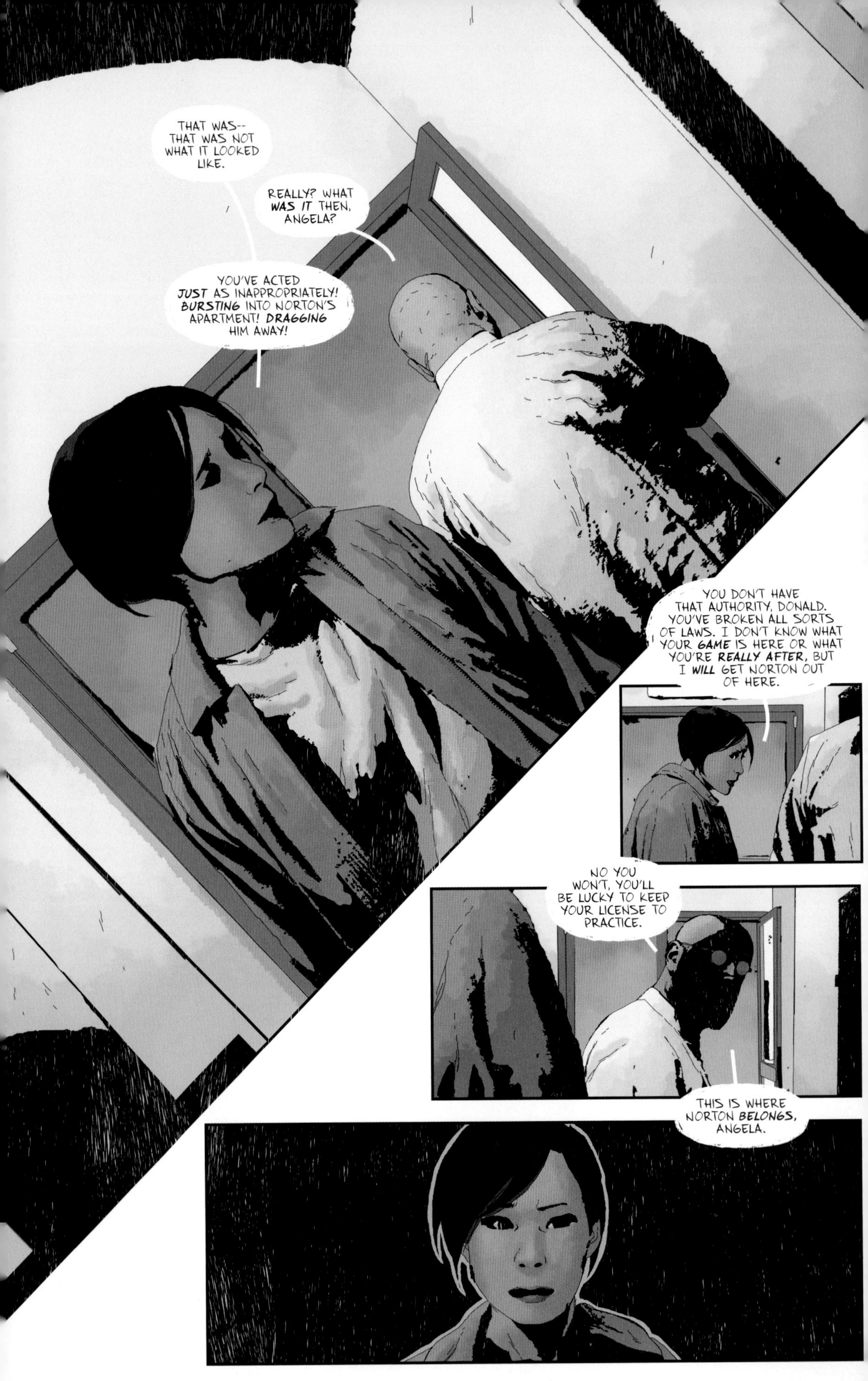
THAT WAS-- THAT WAS NOT WHAT IT LOOKED LIKE.
REALLY? WHAT WAS IT THEN, ANGELA?
YOU'VE ACTED JUST AS INAPPROPRIATELY! BURSTING INTO NORTON'S APARTMENT! DRAGGING HIM AWAY!
YOU DON'T HAVE THAT AUTHORITY, DONALD. YOU'VE BROKEN ALL SORTS OF LAWS. I DON'T KNOW WHAT YOUR GAME IS HERE OR WHAT YOU'RE REALLY AFTER, BUT I WILL GET NORTON OUT OF HERE.
NO YOU WON'T, YOU'LL BE LUCKY TO KEEP YOUR LICENSE TO PRACTICE.
THIS IS WHERE NORTON BELONGS, ANGELA.

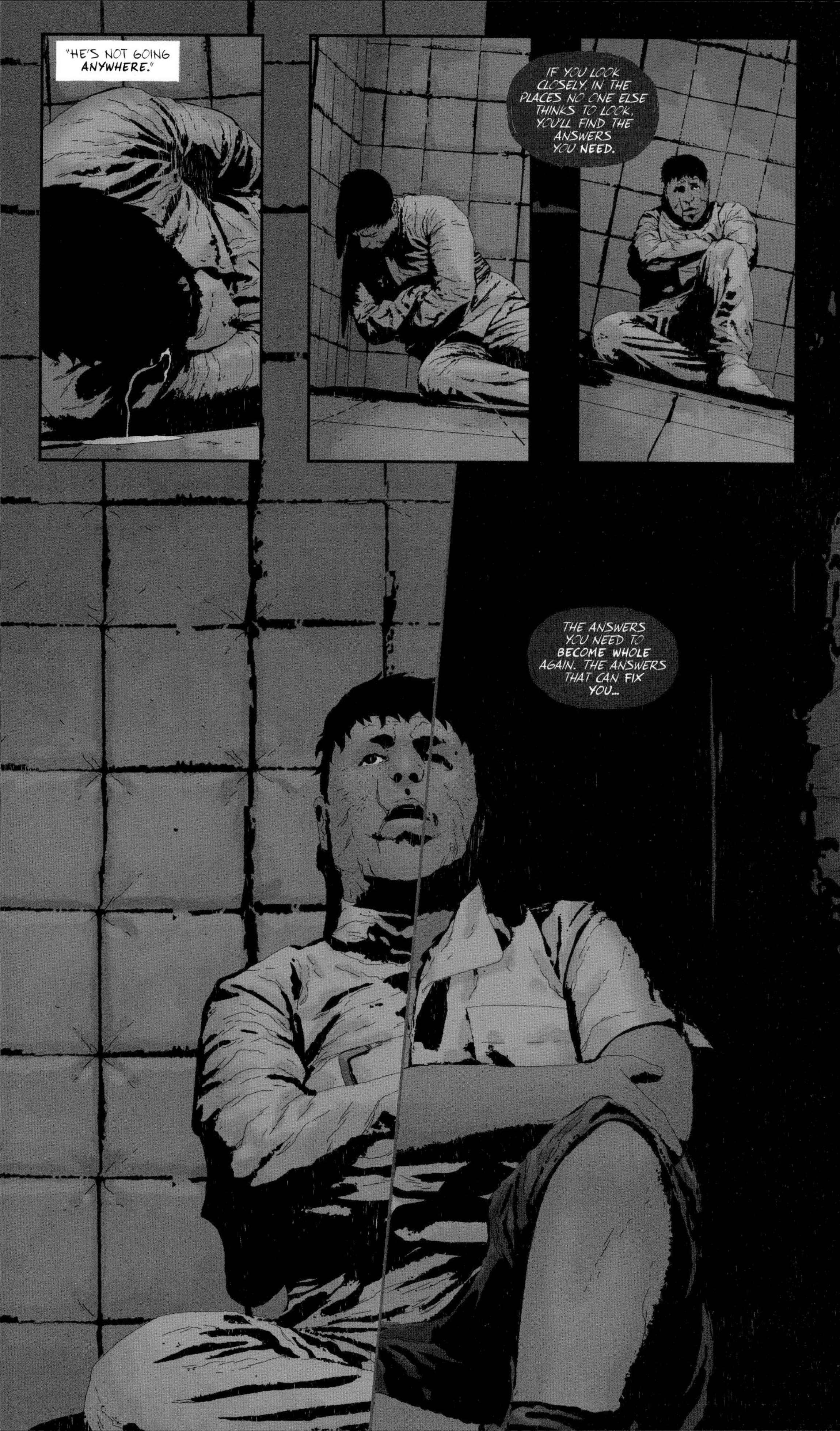
"HE'S NOT GOING ANYWHERE."
IF YOU LOOK CLOSELY, IN THE PLACES NO ONE ELSE THINKS TO LOOK, YOU'LL FIND THE ANSWERS YOU NEED.
THE ANSWERS YOU NEED TO BECOME WHOLE AGAIN. THE ANSWERS THAT CAN FIX YOU...

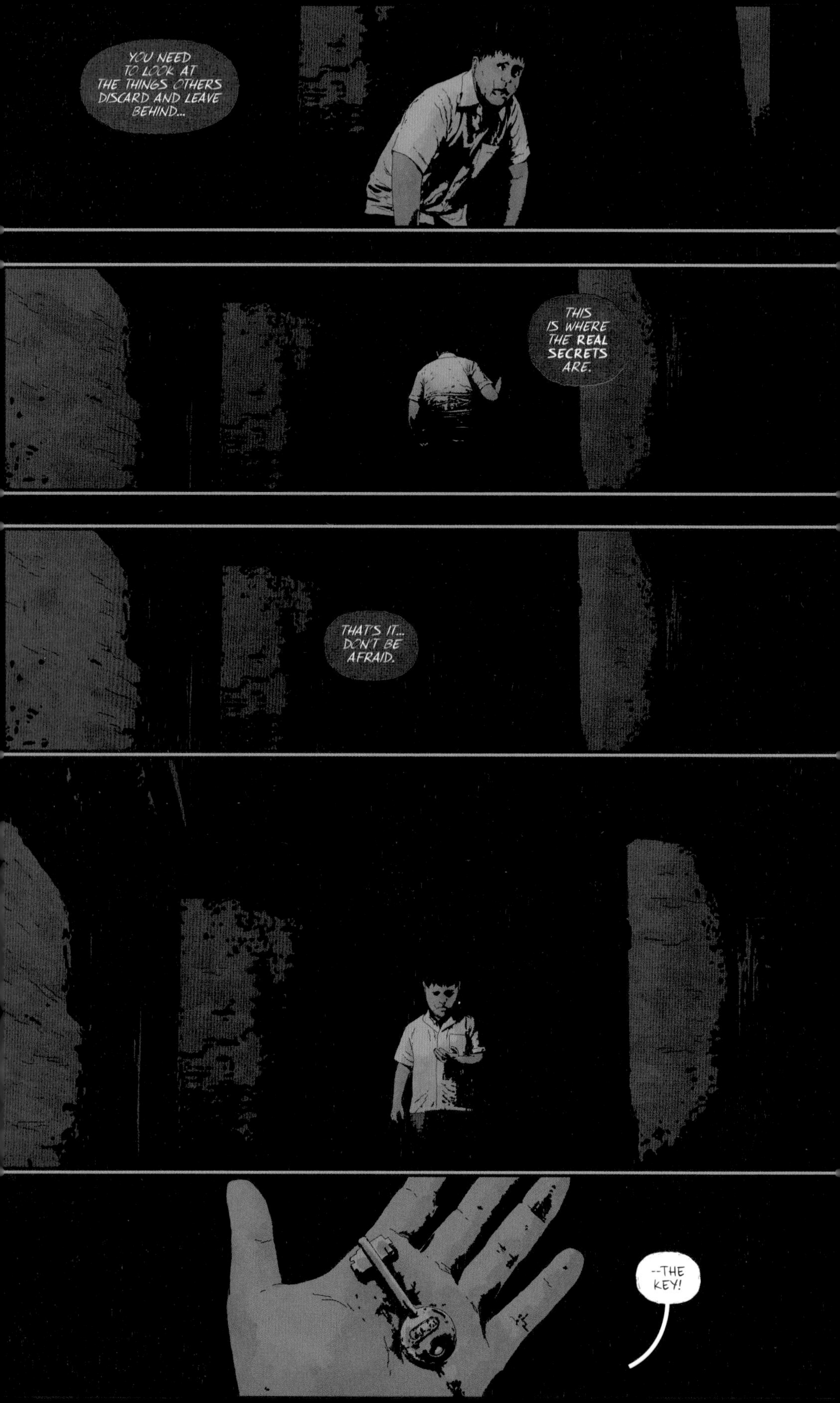
YOU NEED TO LOOK AT THE THINGS OTHERS DISCARD AND LEAVE BEHIND...
THIS IS WHERE THE **REAL SECRETS** ARE.
THAT'S IT... DON'T BE AFRAID.
--THE KEY!

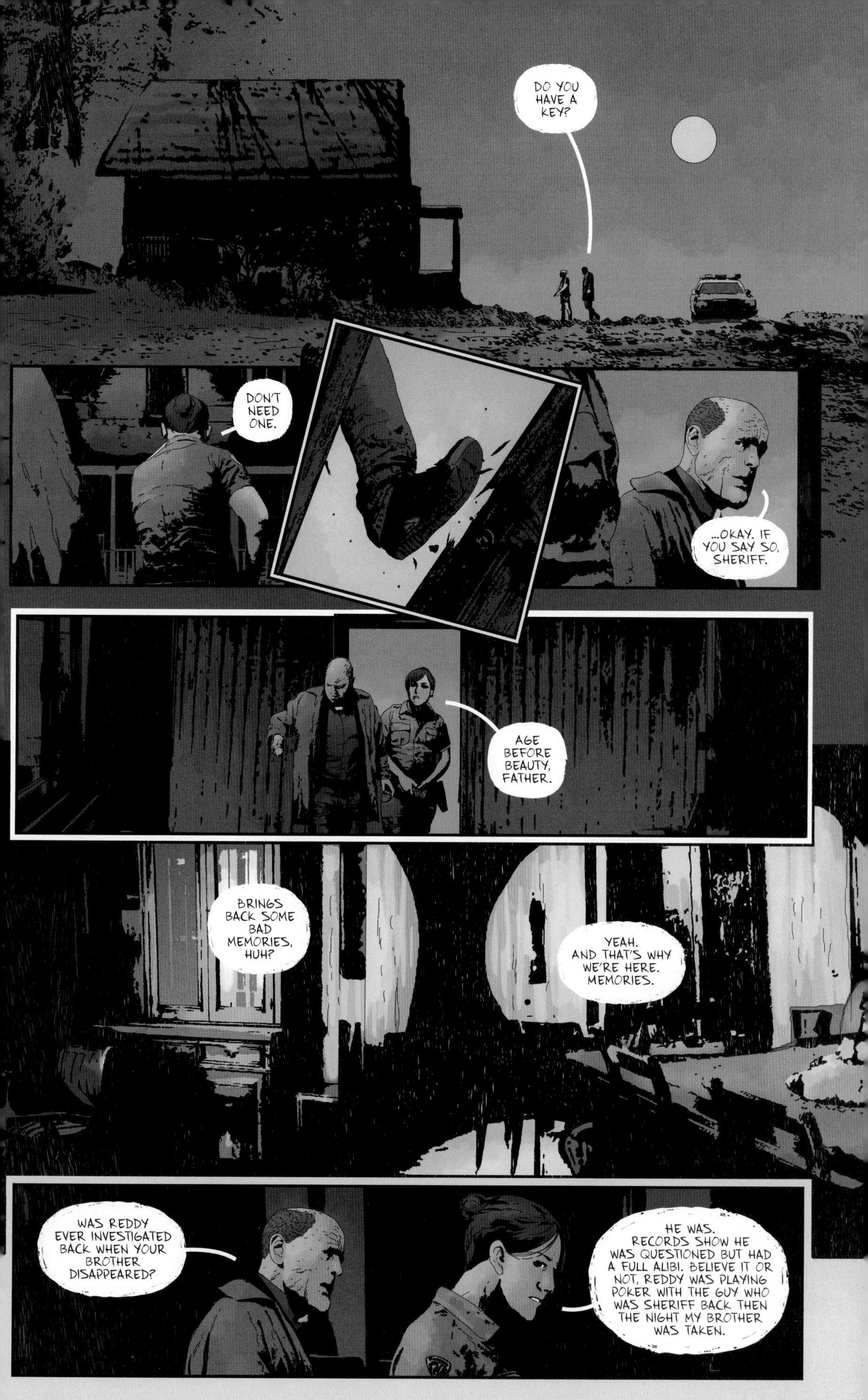
DO YOU HAVE A KEY?
DON'T NEED ONE.
...OKAY. IF YOU SAY SO, SHERIFF.
AGE BEFORE BEAUTY, FATHER.
BRINGS BACK SOME BAD MEMORIES, HUH?
YEAH. AND THAT'S WHY WE'RE HERE. MEMORIES.
WAS REDDY EVER INVESTIGATED BACK WHEN YOUR BROTHER DISAPPEARED?
HE WAS. RECORDS SHOW HE WAS QUESTIONED BUT HAD A FULL ALIBI. BELIEVE IT OR NOT, REDDY WAS PLAYING POKER WITH THE GUY WHO WAS SHERIFF BACK THEN THE NIGHT MY BROTHER WAS TAKEN.

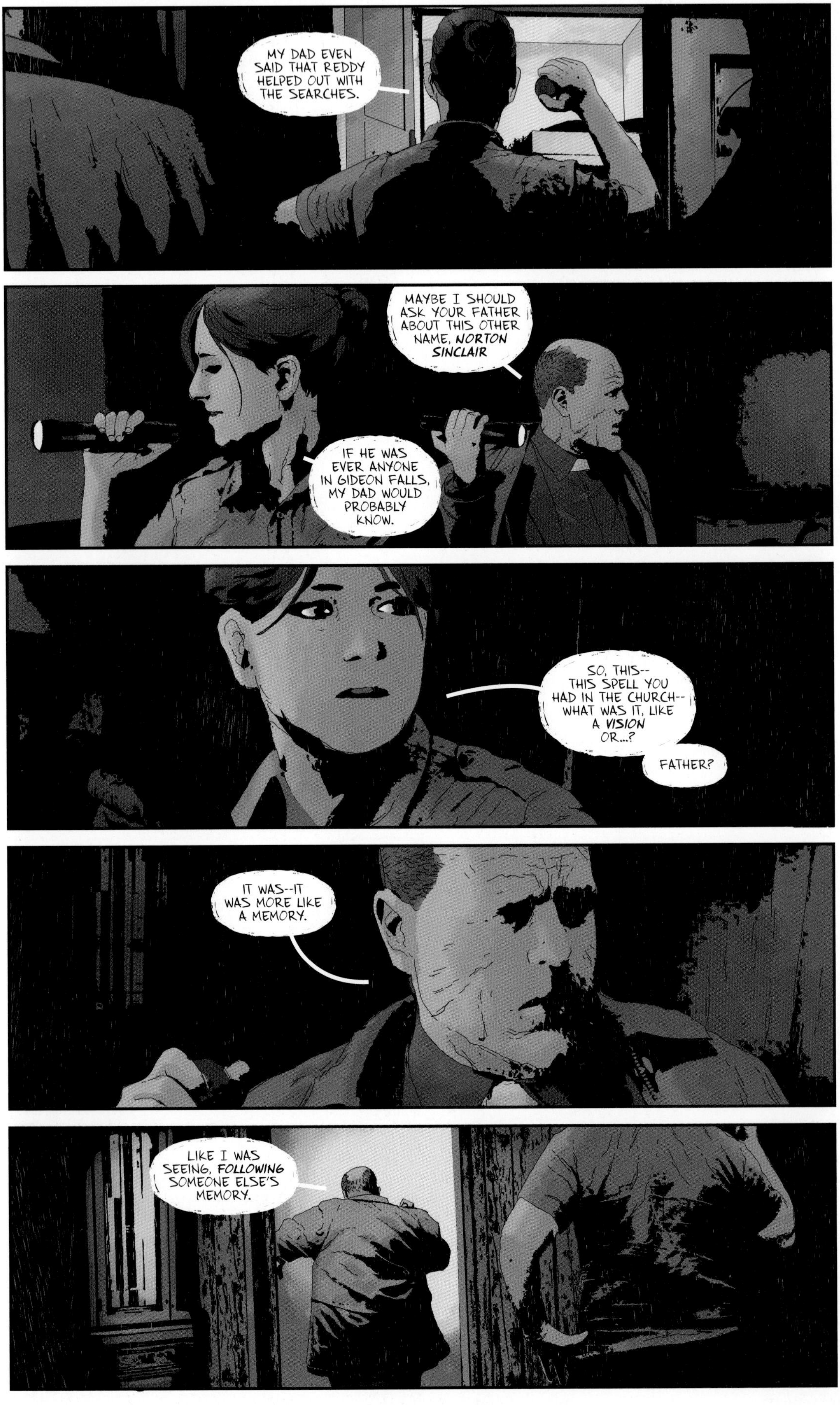
MY DAD EVEN SAID THAT REDDY HELPED OUT WITH THE SEARCHES.
MAYBE I SHOULD ASK YOUR FATHER ABOUT THIS OTHER NAME, NORTON SINCLAIR
IF HE WAS EVER ANYONE IN GIDEON FALLS, MY DAD WOULD PROBABLY KNOW.
SO, THIS-- THIS SPELL YOU HAD IN THE CHURCH-- WHAT WAS IT, LIKE A VISION OR...?
FATHER?
IT WAS--IT WAS MORE LIKE A MEMORY.
LIKE I WAS SEEING, FOLLOWING SOMEONE ELSE'S MEMORY.

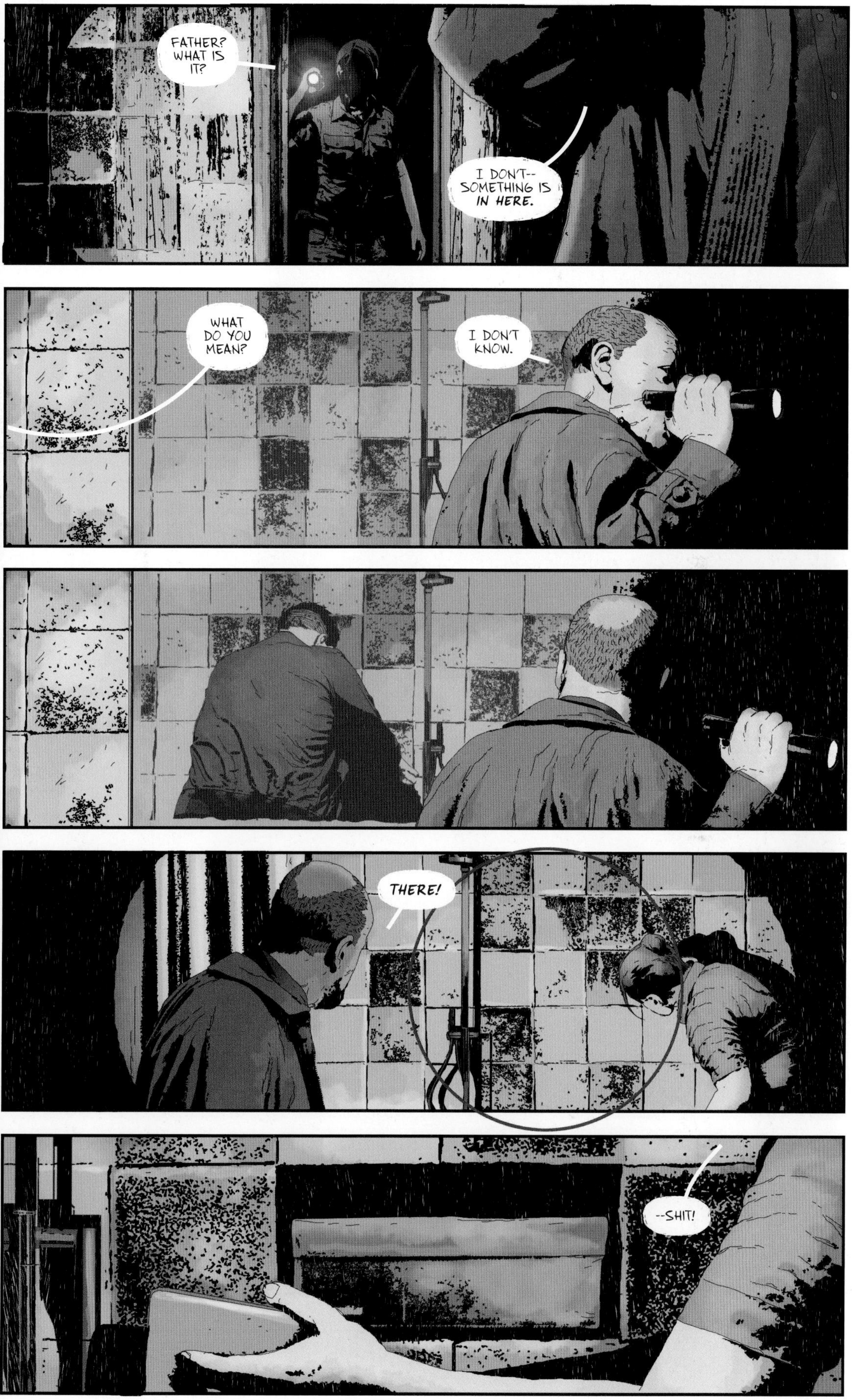
FATHER? WHAT IS IT?
I DON'T-- SOMETHING IS IN HERE.
WHAT DO YOU MEAN?
I DON'T KNOW.
THERE!
--SHIT!

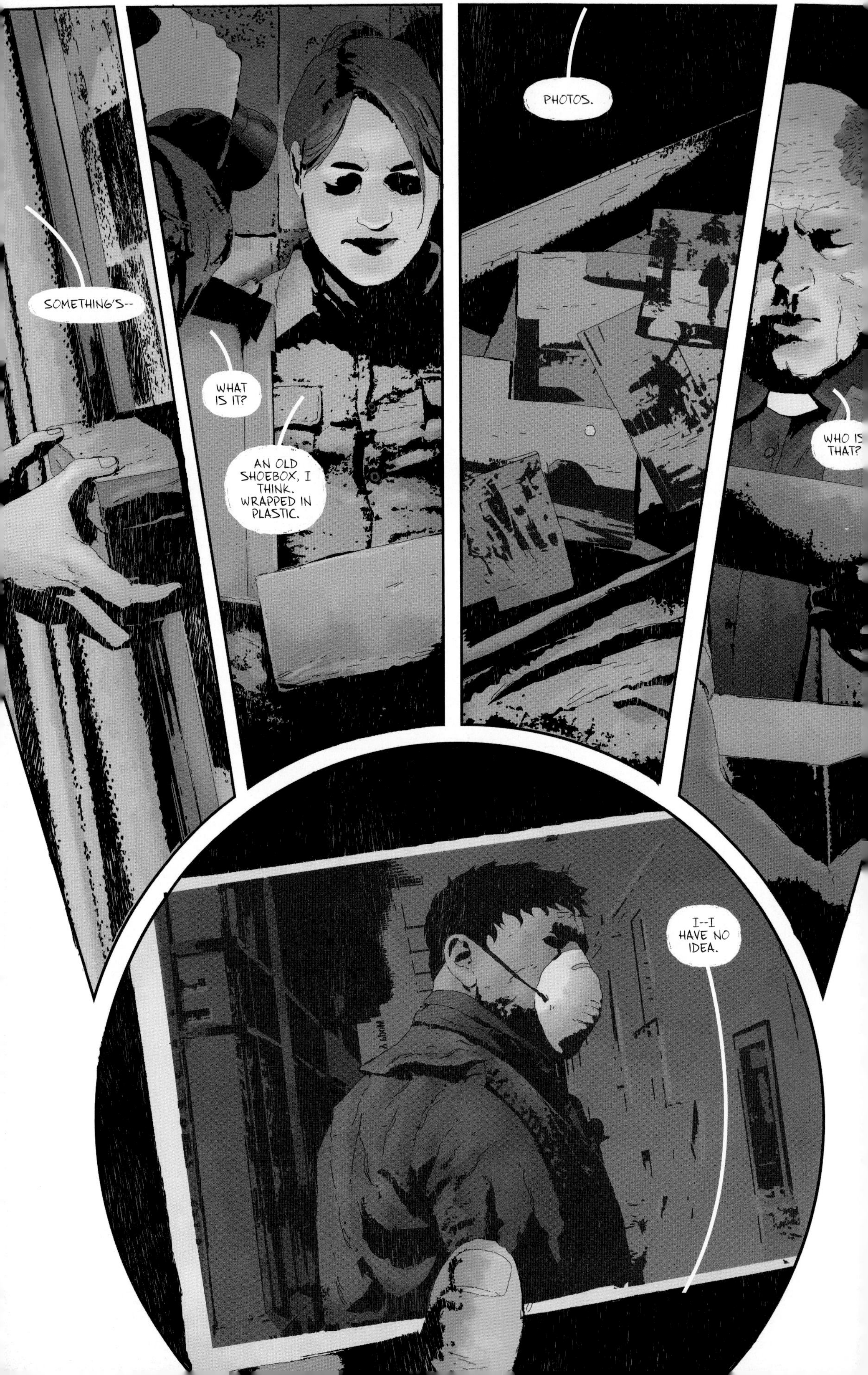
SOMETHING'S--
WHAT IS IT?
AN OLD SHOEBOX, I THINK. WRAPPED IN PLASTIC.
PHOTOS.
WHO IS THAT?
I--I HAVE NO IDEA.

GIDEON
FALLS

Nine

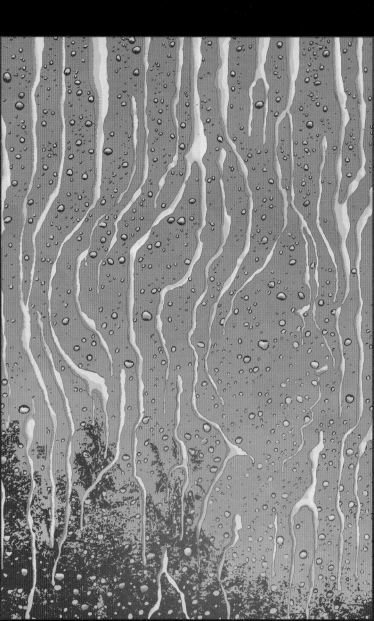

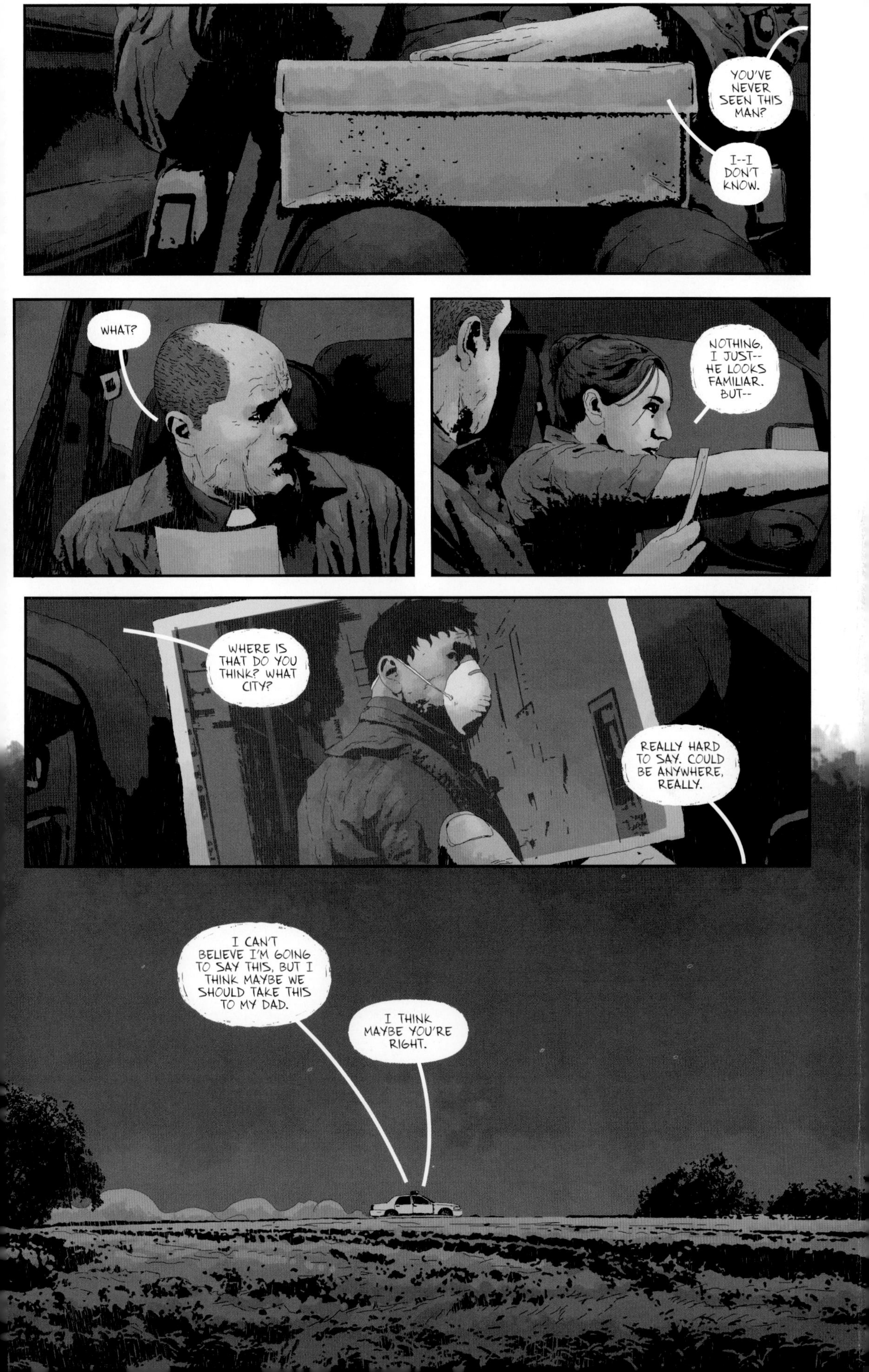
YOU'VE NEVER SEEN THIS MAN?
I--I DON'T KNOW.
WHAT?
NOTHING, I JUST-- HE LOOKS FAMILIAR. BUT--
WHERE IS THAT DO YOU THINK? WHAT CITY?
REALLY HARD TO SAY. COULD BE ANYWHERE, REALLY.
I CAN'T BELIEVE I'M GOING TO SAY THIS, BUT I THINK MAYBE WE SHOULD TAKE THIS TO MY DAD.
I THINK MAYBE YOU'RE RIGHT.

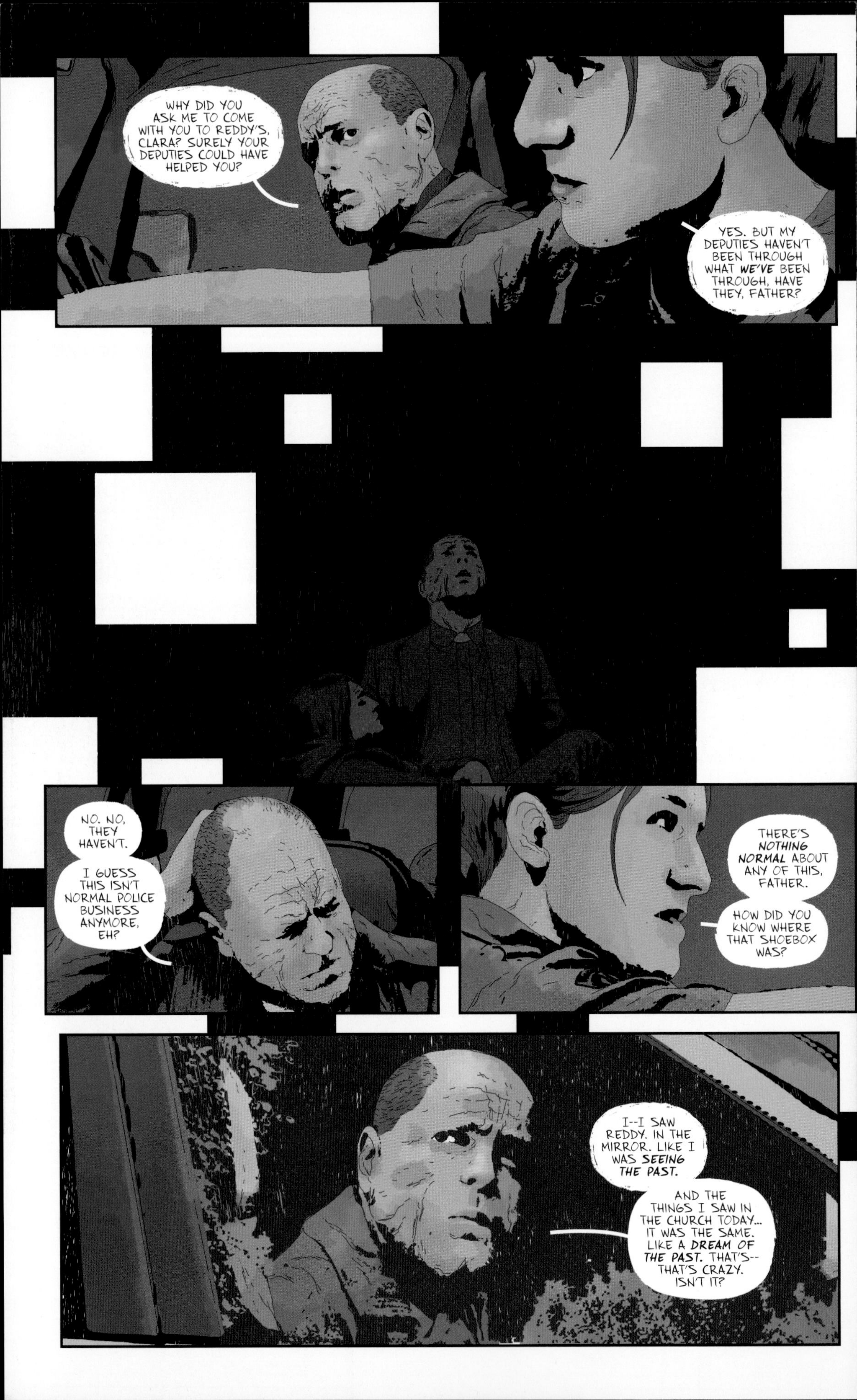
WHY DID YOU ASK ME TO COME WITH YOU TO REDDY'S, CLARA? SURELY YOUR DEPUTIES COULD HAVE HELPED YOU?
YES. BUT MY DEPUTIES HAVEN'T BEEN THROUGH WHAT **WE'VE** BEEN THROUGH, HAVE THEY, FATHER?
NO. NO, THEY HAVEN'T.
I GUESS THIS ISN'T NORMAL POLICE BUSINESS ANYMORE, EH?
THERE'S **NOTHING NORMAL** ABOUT ANY OF THIS, FATHER.
HOW DID YOU KNOW WHERE THAT SHOEBOX WAS?
I--I SAW REDDY. IN THE MIRROR. LIKE I WAS **SEEING THE PAST.**
AND THE THINGS I SAW IN THE CHURCH TODAY... IT WAS THE SAME. LIKE A **DREAM OF THE PAST.** THAT'S-- THAT'S CRAZY. ISN'T IT?

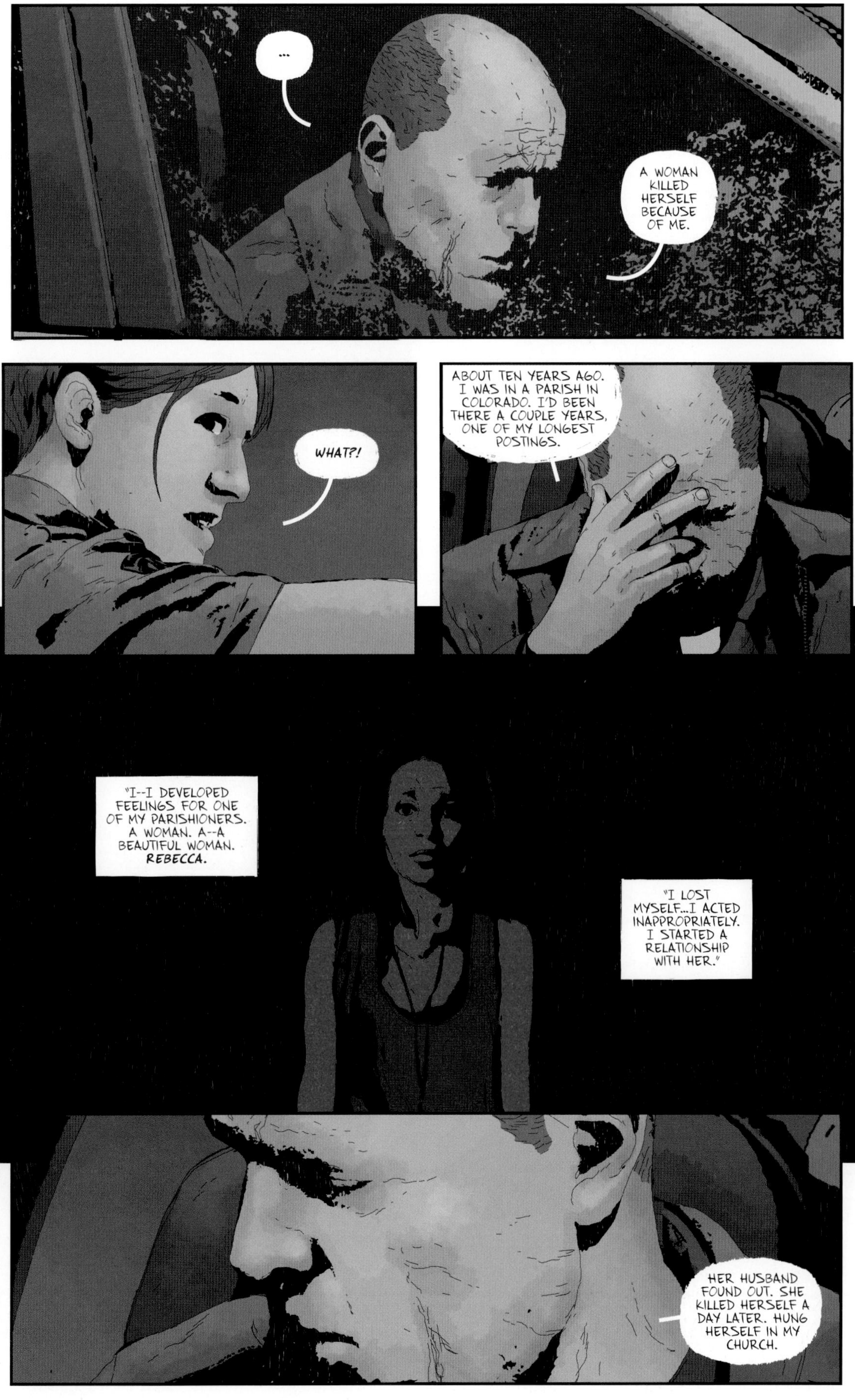
...
A WOMAN KILLED HERSELF BECAUSE OF ME.
WHAT?!
ABOUT TEN YEARS AGO. I WAS IN A PARISH IN COLORADO. I'D BEEN THERE A COUPLE YEARS, ONE OF MY LONGEST POSTINGS.
"I--I DEVELOPED FEELINGS FOR ONE OF MY PARISHIONERS. A WOMAN. A--A BEAUTIFUL WOMAN. REBECCA.
"I LOST MYSELF...I ACTED INAPPROPRIATELY. I STARTED A RELATIONSHIP WITH HER."
HER HUSBAND FOUND OUT. SHE KILLED HERSELF A DAY LATER. HUNG HERSELF IN MY CHURCH.

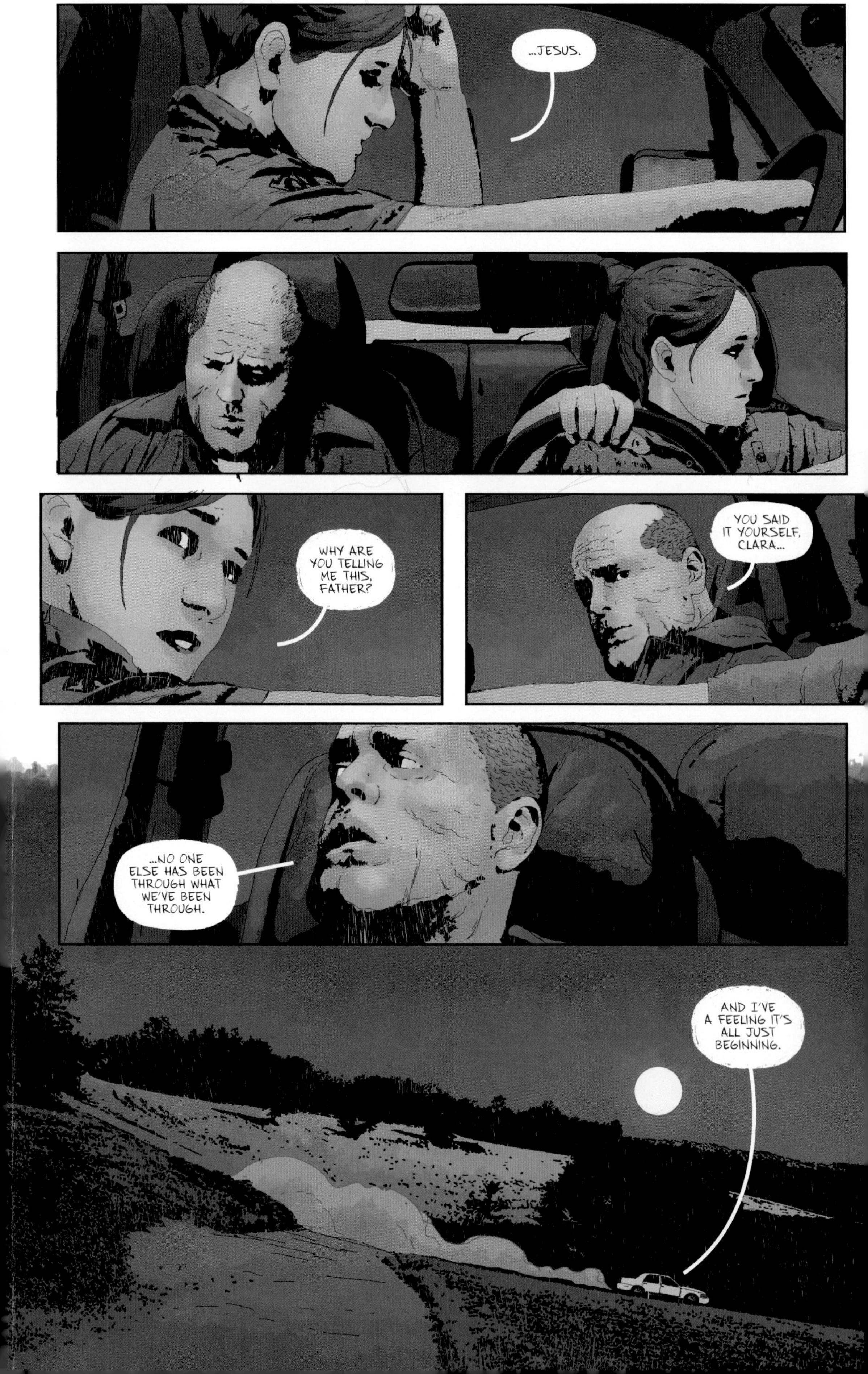
...JESUS.
WHY ARE YOU TELLING ME THIS, FATHER?
YOU SAID IT YOURSELF, CLARA...
...NO ONE ELSE HAS BEEN THROUGH WHAT WE'VE BEEN THROUGH.
AND I'VE A FEELING IT'S ALL JUST BEGINNING.

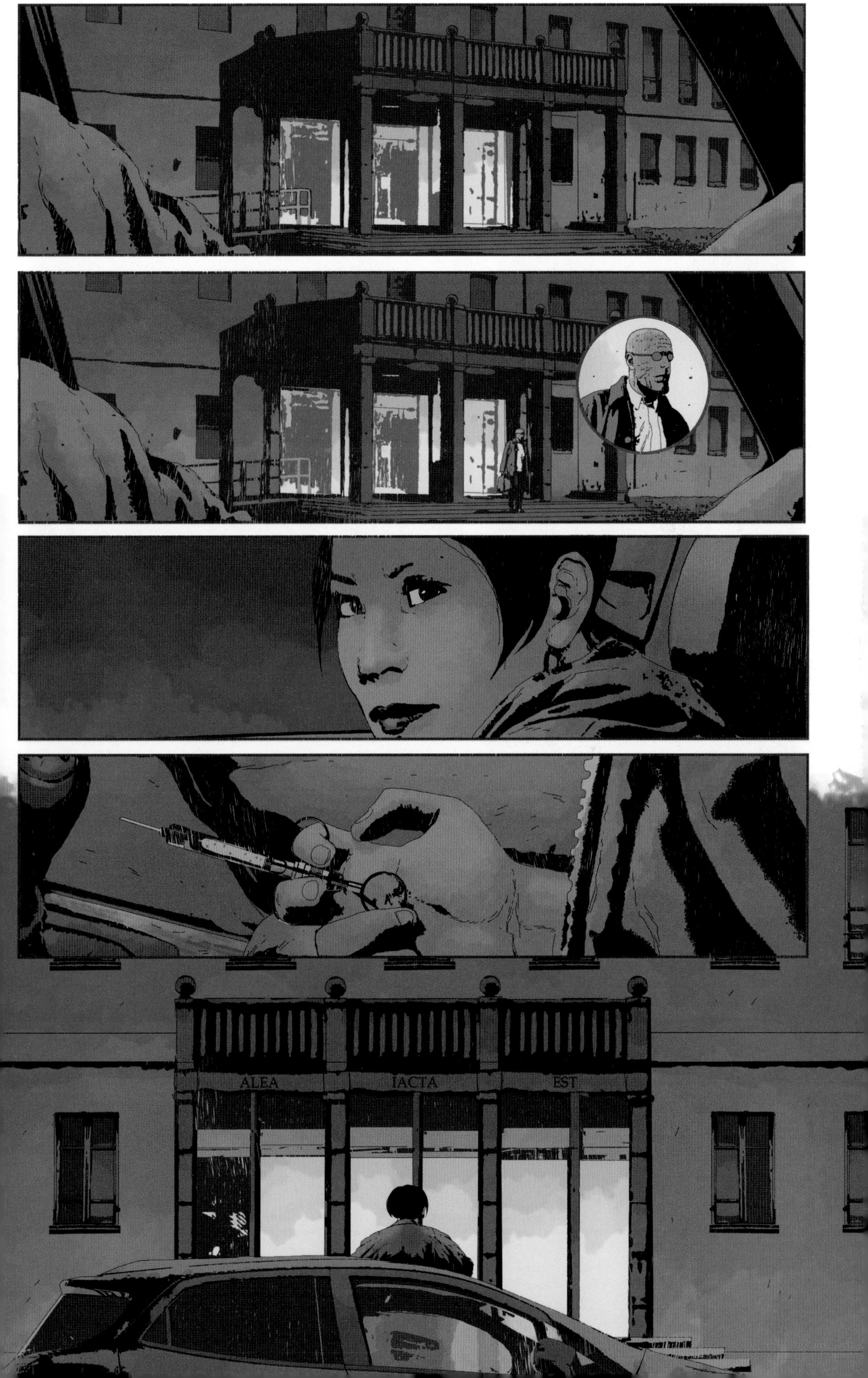
ALEA IACTA EST

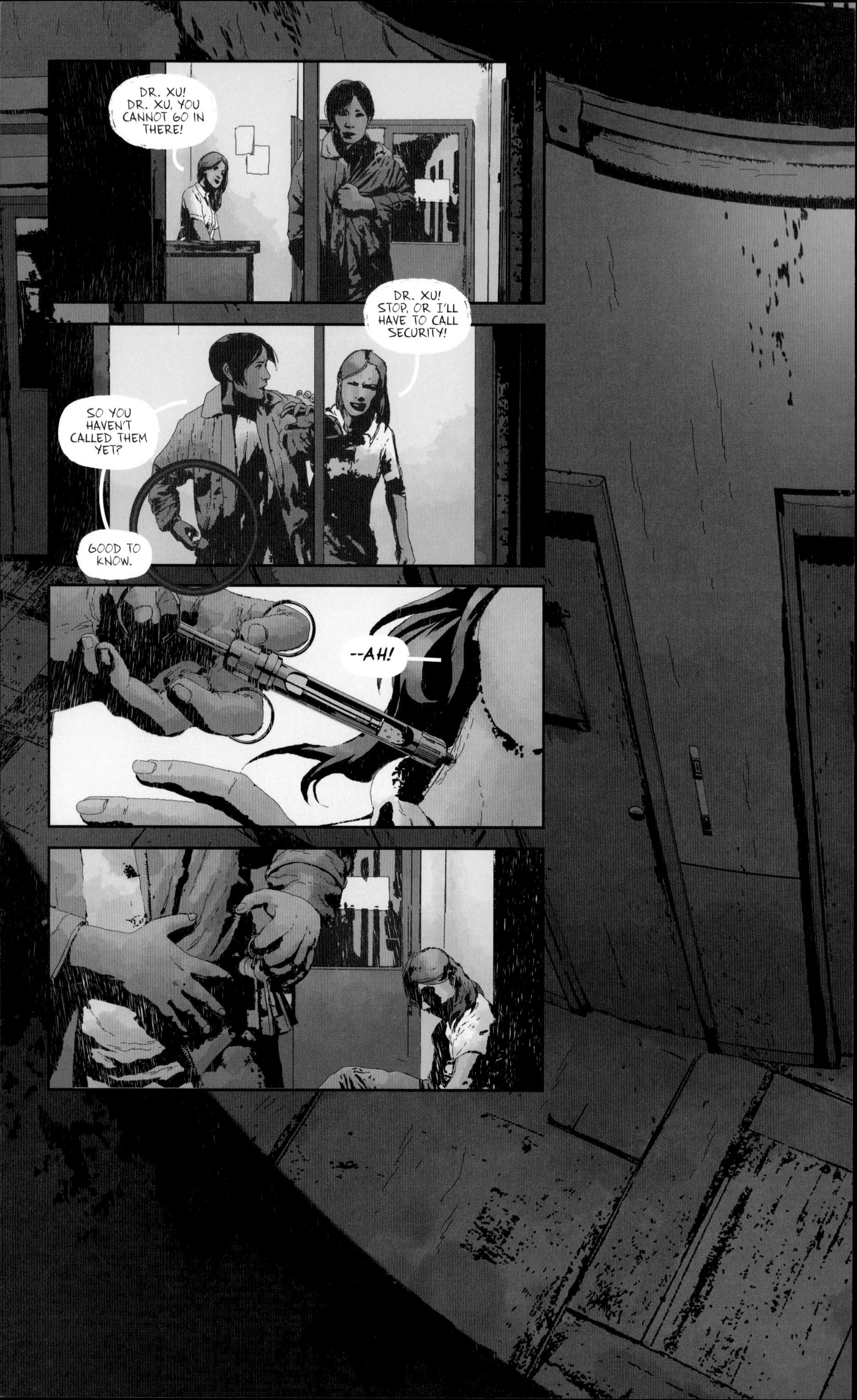
DR. XU! DR. XU, YOU CANNOT GO IN THERE!
DR. XU! STOP, OR I'LL HAVE TO CALL SECURITY!
SO YOU HAVEN'T CALLED THEM YET?
GOOD TO KNOW.
--AH!

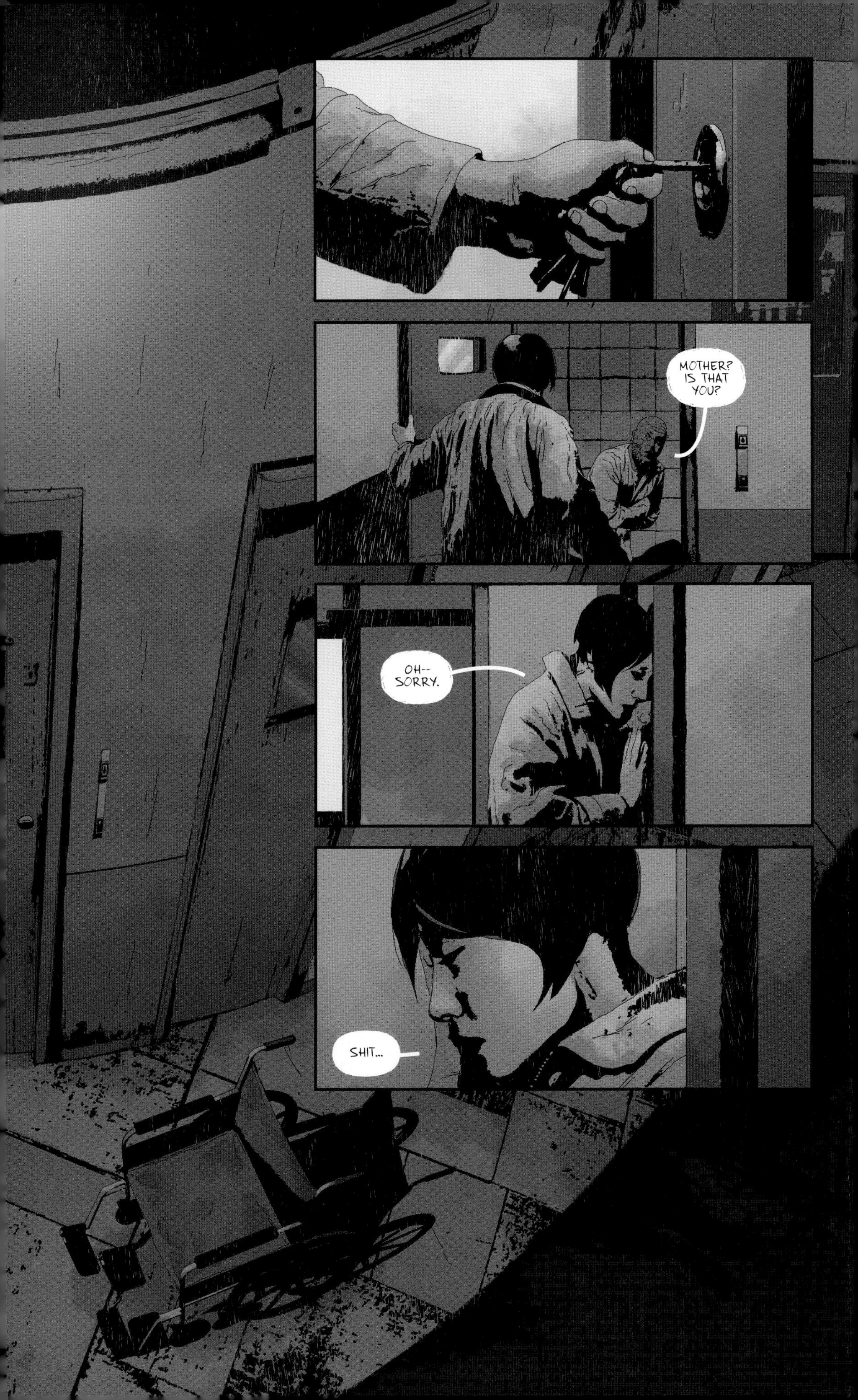

MOTHER? IS THAT YOU?
OH-- SORRY.
SHIT...

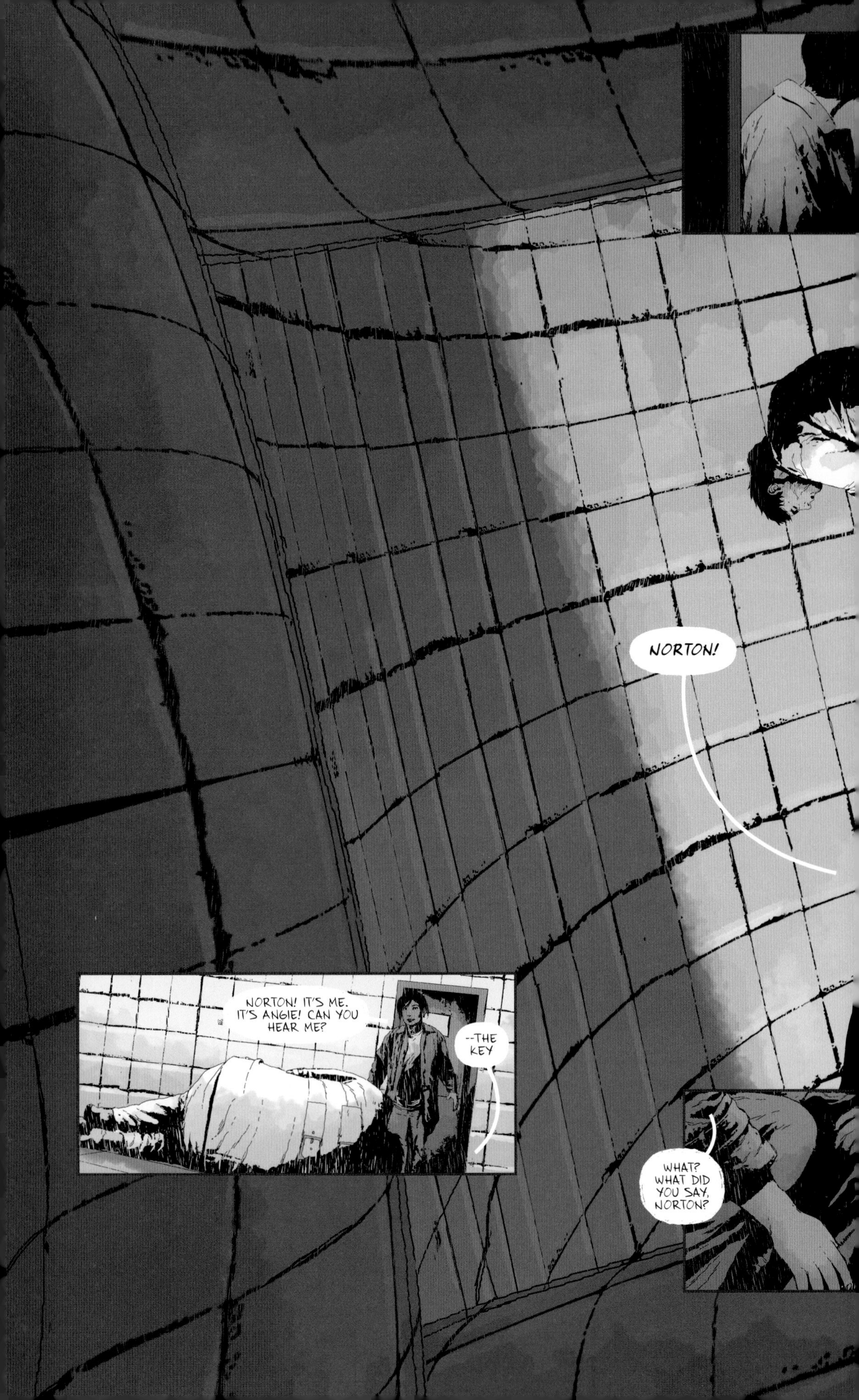
NORTON!
NORTON! IT'S ME. IT'S ANGIE! CAN YOU HEAR ME?
--THE KEY
WHAT? WHAT DID YOU SAY, NORTON?

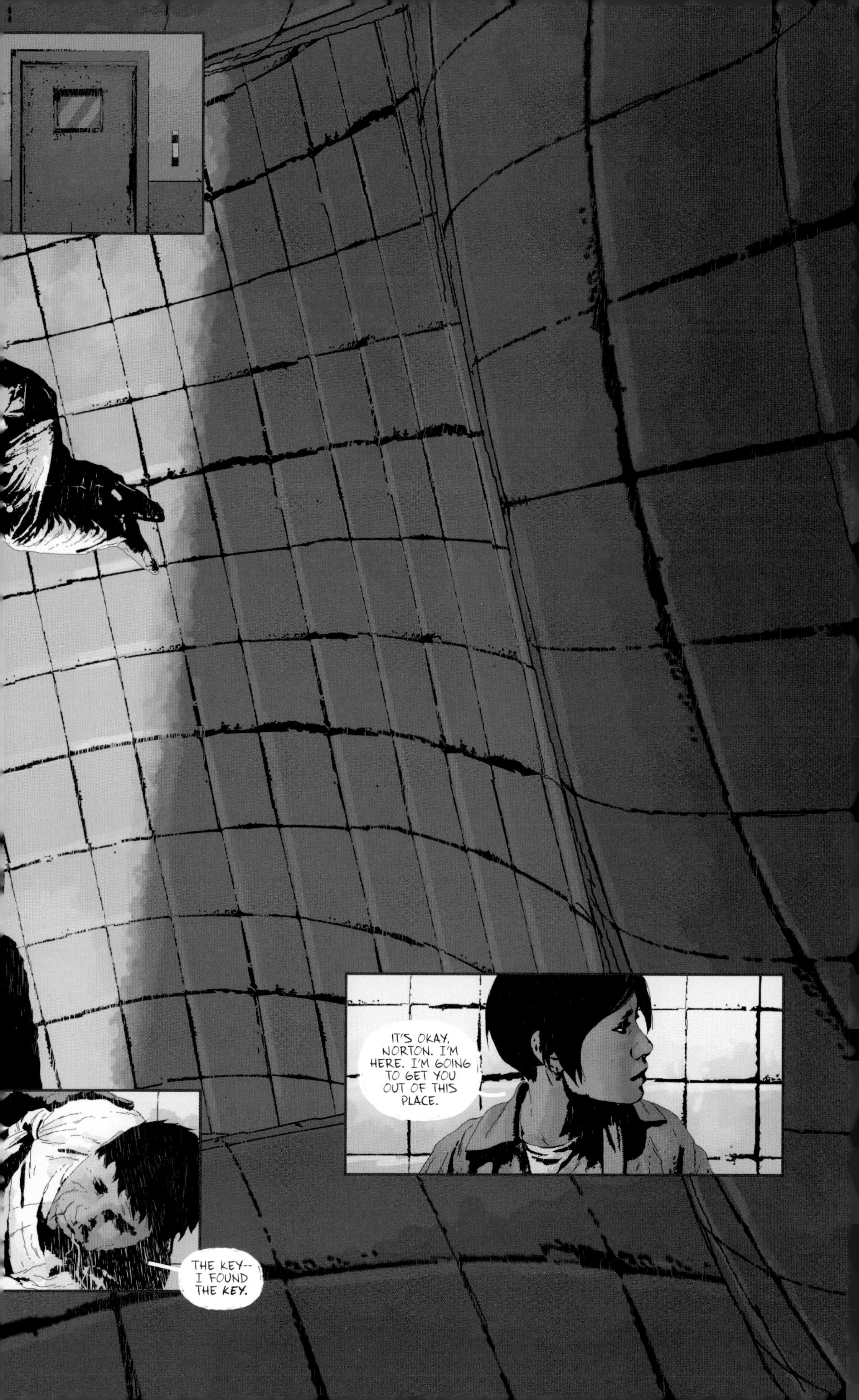
IT'S OKAY, NORTON. I'M HERE. I'M GOING TO GET YOU OUT OF THIS PLACE.
THE KEY-- I FOUND THE KEY.

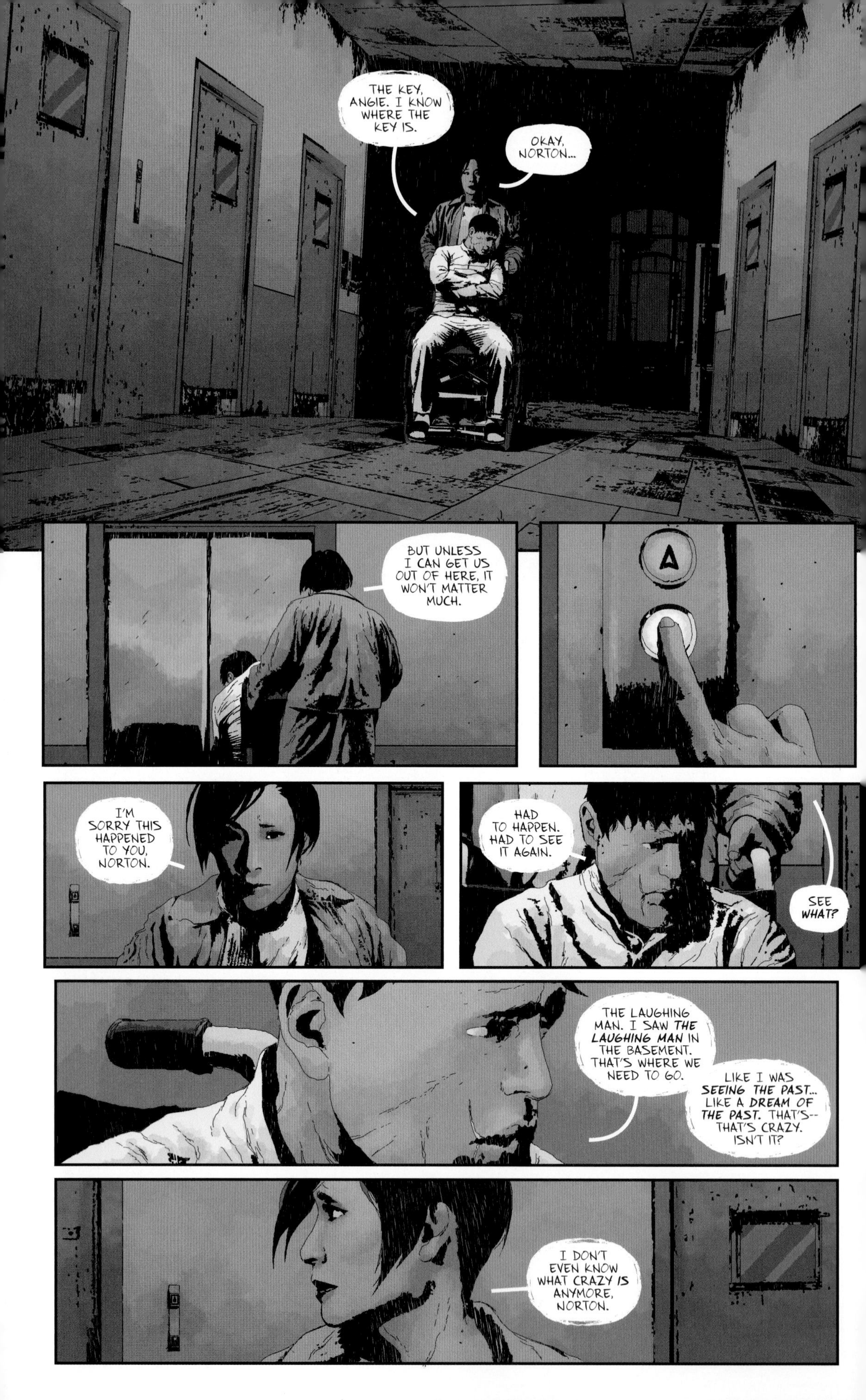
THE KEY, ANGIE. I KNOW WHERE THE KEY IS.
OKAY, NORTON...
BUT UNLESS I CAN GET US OUT OF HERE, IT WON'T MATTER MUCH.
I'M SORRY THIS HAPPENED TO YOU, NORTON.
HAD TO HAPPEN. HAD TO SEE IT AGAIN.
SEE WHAT?
THE LAUGHING MAN. I SAW THE LAUGHING MAN IN THE BASEMENT. THAT'S WHERE WE NEED TO GO.
LIKE I WAS SEEING THE PAST... LIKE A DREAM OF THE PAST. THAT'S-- THAT'S CRAZY. ISN'T IT?
I DON'T EVEN KNOW WHAT CRAZY IS ANYMORE, NORTON.

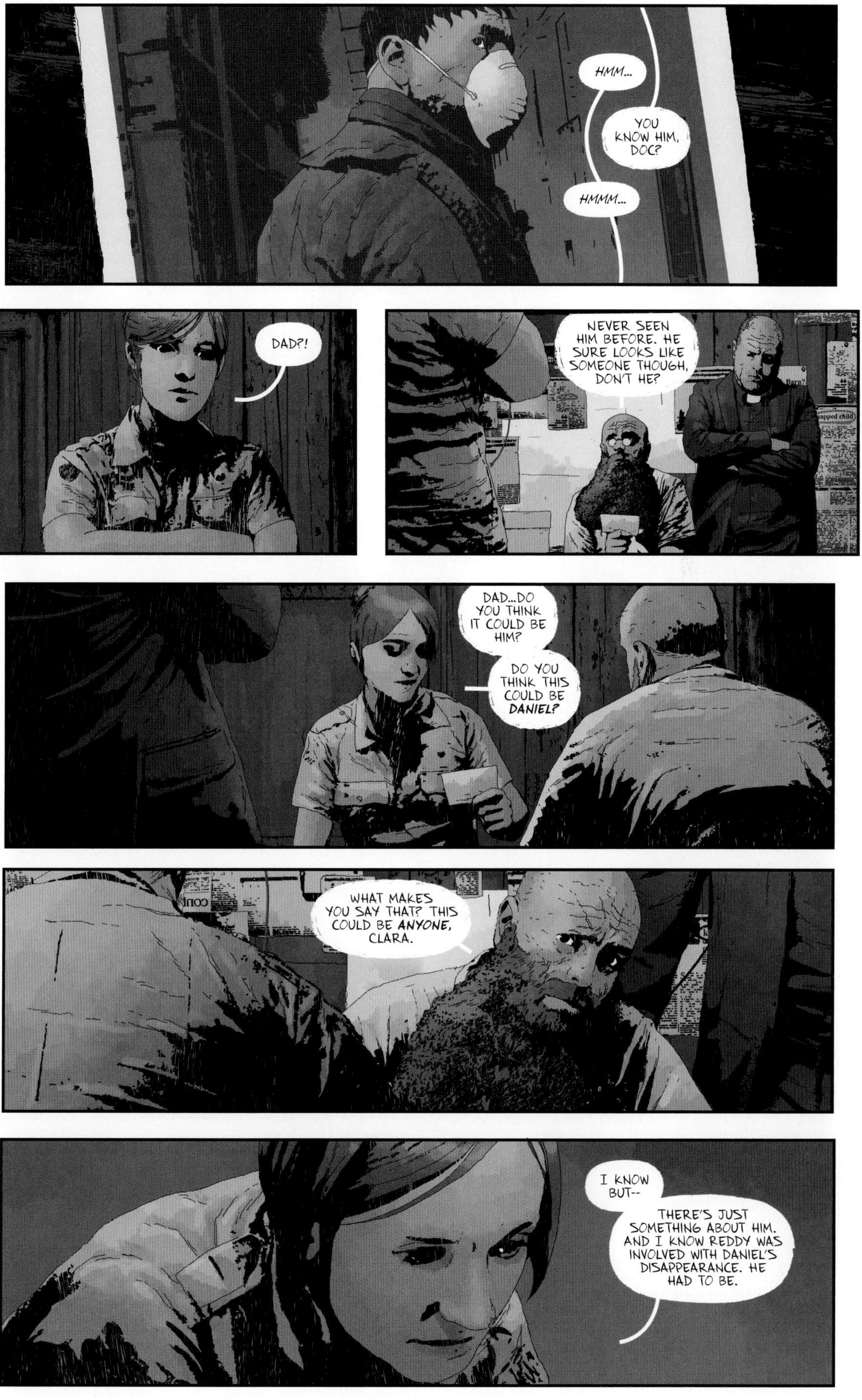
HMM...
YOU KNOW HIM, DOC?
HMMM...
DAD?!
NEVER SEEN HIM BEFORE. HE SURE LOOKS LIKE SOMEONE THOUGH, DON'T HE?
DAD...DO YOU THINK IT COULD BE HIM?
DO YOU THINK THIS COULD BE DANIEL?
WHAT MAKES YOU SAY THAT? THIS COULD BE ANYONE, CLARA.
I KNOW BUT--
THERE'S JUST SOMETHING ABOUT HIM. AND I KNOW REDDY WAS INVOLVED WITH DANIEL'S DISAPPEARANCE. HE HAD TO BE.

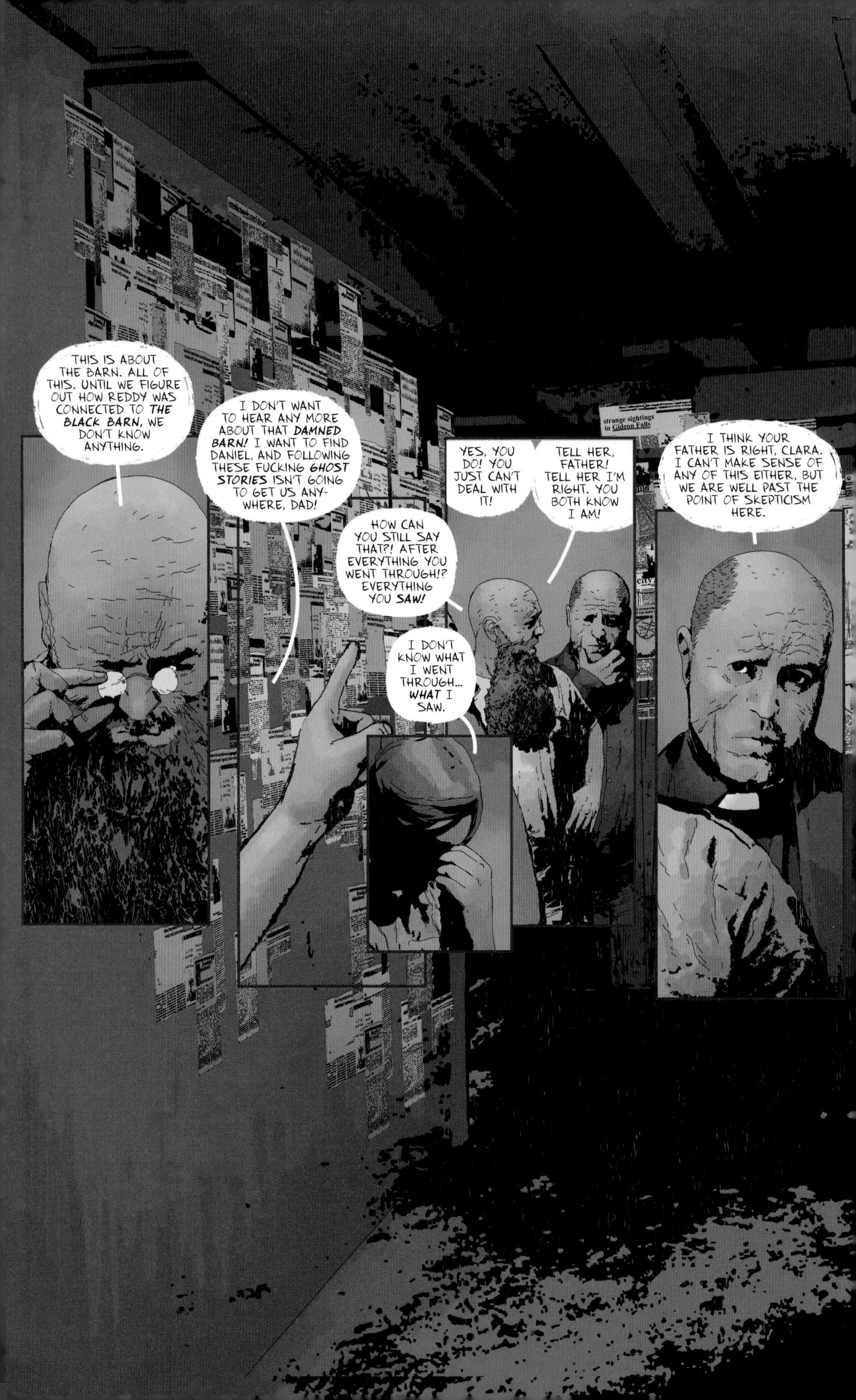
THIS IS ABOUT THE BARN. ALL OF THIS. UNTIL WE FIGURE OUT HOW REDDY WAS CONNECTED TO THE BLACK BARN, WE DON'T KNOW ANYTHING.
I DON'T WANT TO HEAR ANY MORE ABOUT THAT DAMNED BARN! I WANT TO FIND DANIEL, AND FOLLOWING THESE FUCKING GHOST STORIES ISN'T GOING TO GET US ANYWHERE, DAD!
HOW CAN YOU STILL SAY THAT?! AFTER EVERYTHING YOU WENT THROUGH!? EVERYTHING YOU SAW!
I DON'T KNOW WHAT I WENT THROUGH... WHAT I SAW.
YES, YOU DO! YOU JUST CAN'T DEAL WITH IT!
TELL HER, FATHER! TELL HER I'M RIGHT. YOU BOTH KNOW I AM!
strange sightings in Gideon Falls
I THINK YOUR FATHER IS RIGHT, CLARA. I CAN'T MAKE SENSE OF ANY OF THIS EITHER, BUT WE ARE WELL PAST THE POINT OF SKEPTICISM HERE.

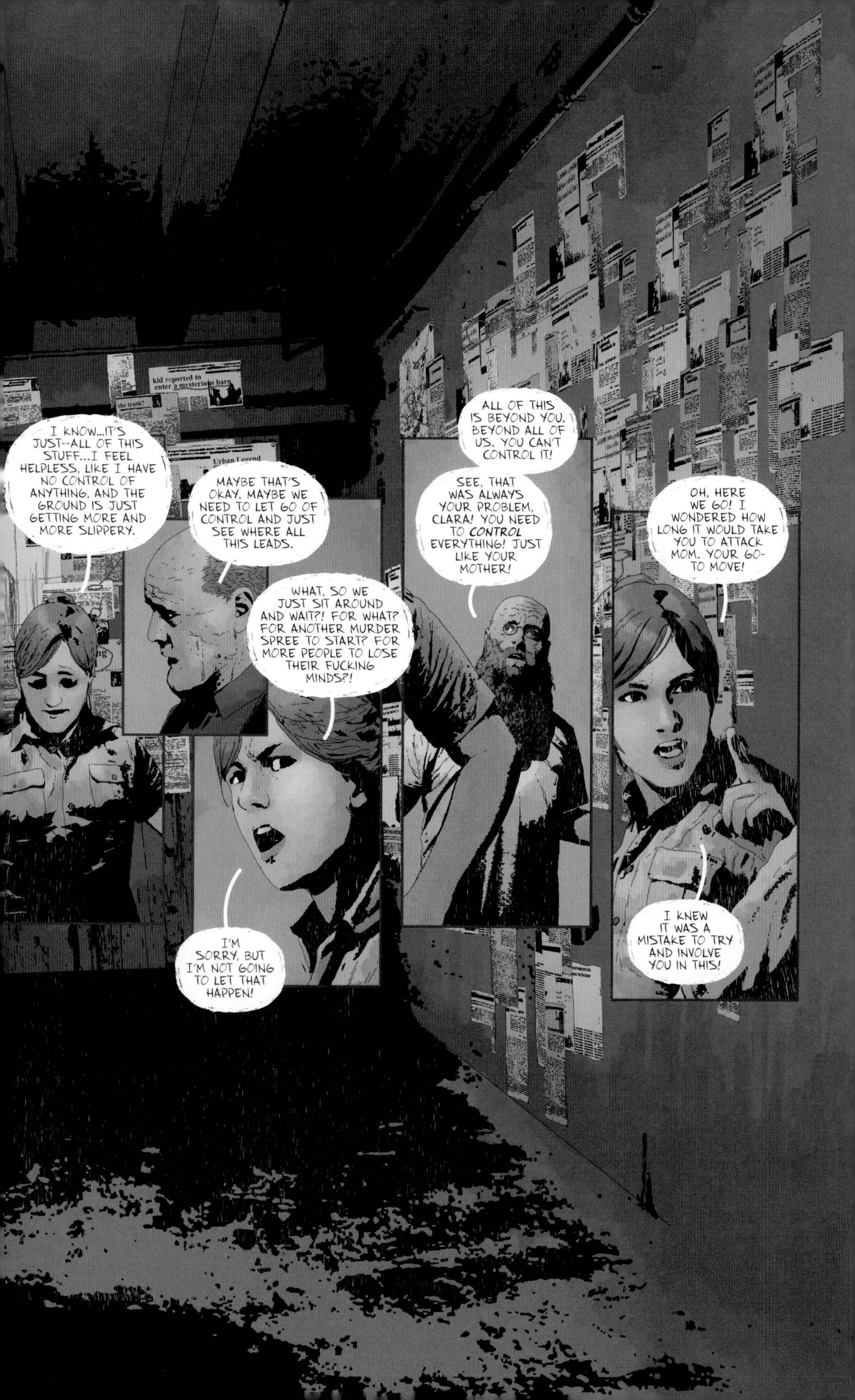
the truth?
Urban Legend
I KNOW...IT'S JUST--ALL OF THIS STUFF...I FEEL HELPLESS, LIKE I HAVE NO CONTROL OF ANYTHING, AND THE GROUND IS JUST GETTING MORE AND MORE SLIPPERY.
MAYBE THAT'S OKAY. MAYBE WE NEED TO LET GO OF CONTROL AND JUST SEE WHERE ALL THIS LEADS.
WHAT, SO WE JUST SIT AROUND AND WAIT?! FOR WHAT? FOR ANOTHER MURDER SPREE TO START? FOR MORE PEOPLE TO LOSE THEIR FUCKING MINDS?!
I'M SORRY, BUT I'M NOT GOING TO LET THAT HAPPEN!
ALL OF THIS IS BEYOND YOU. BEYOND ALL OF US. YOU CAN'T CONTROL IT!
SEE, THAT WAS ALWAYS YOUR PROBLEM, CLARA! YOU NEED TO **CONTROL** EVERYTHING! JUST LIKE YOUR MOTHER!
OH, HERE WE GO! I WONDERED HOW LONG IT WOULD TAKE YOU TO ATTACK MOM. YOUR GO-TO MOVE!
I KNEW IT WAS A MISTAKE TO TRY AND INVOLVE YOU IN THIS!

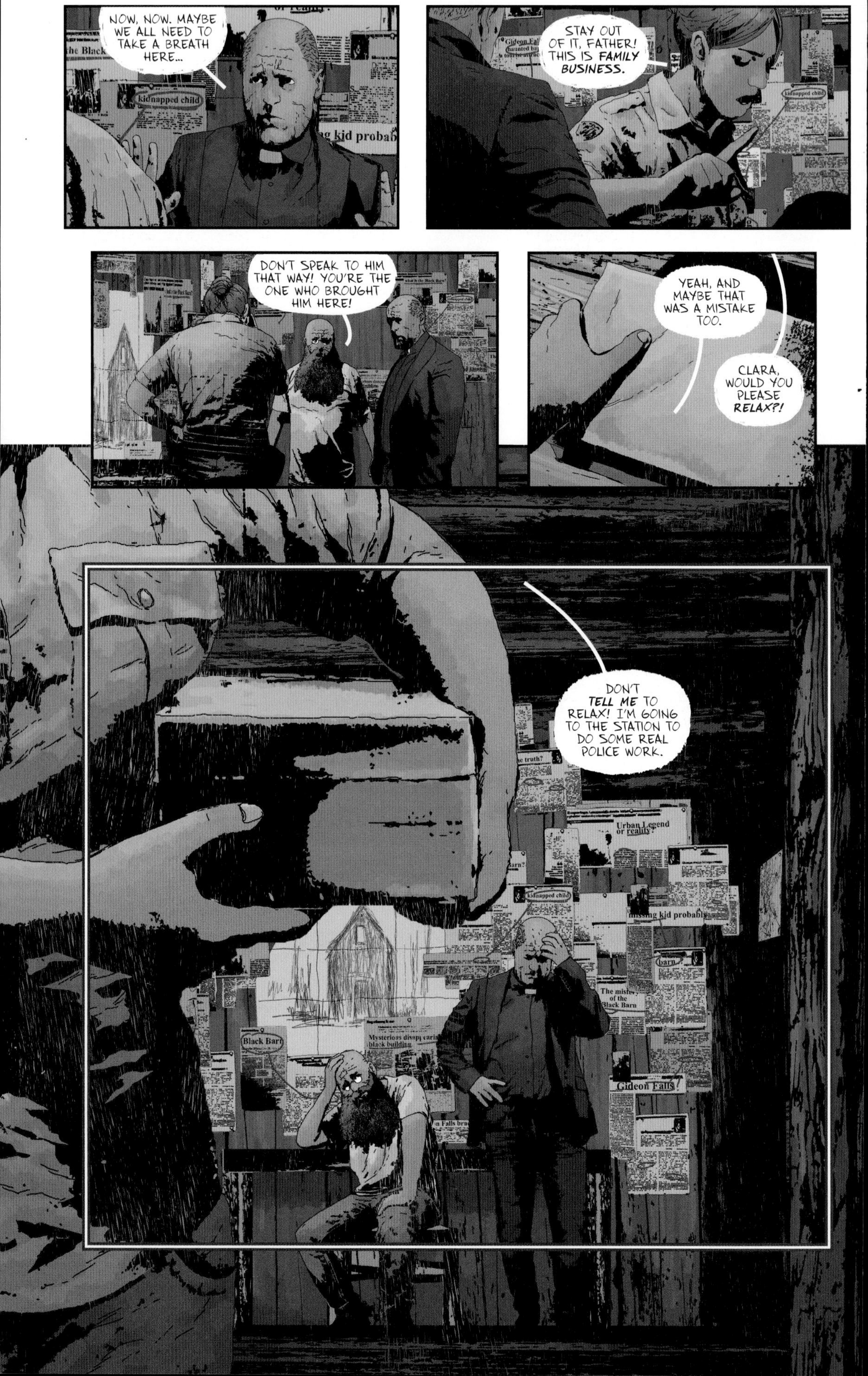
NOW, NOW. MAYBE WE ALL NEED TO TAKE A BREATH HERE...
STAY OUT OF IT, FATHER! THIS IS FAMILY BUSINESS.
DON'T SPEAK TO HIM THAT WAY! YOU'RE THE ONE WHO BROUGHT HIM HERE!
YEAH, AND MAYBE THAT WAS A MISTAKE TOO.
CLARA, WOULD YOU PLEASE RELAX?!
DON'T TELL ME TO RELAX! I'M GOING TO THE STATION TO DO SOME REAL POLICE WORK.

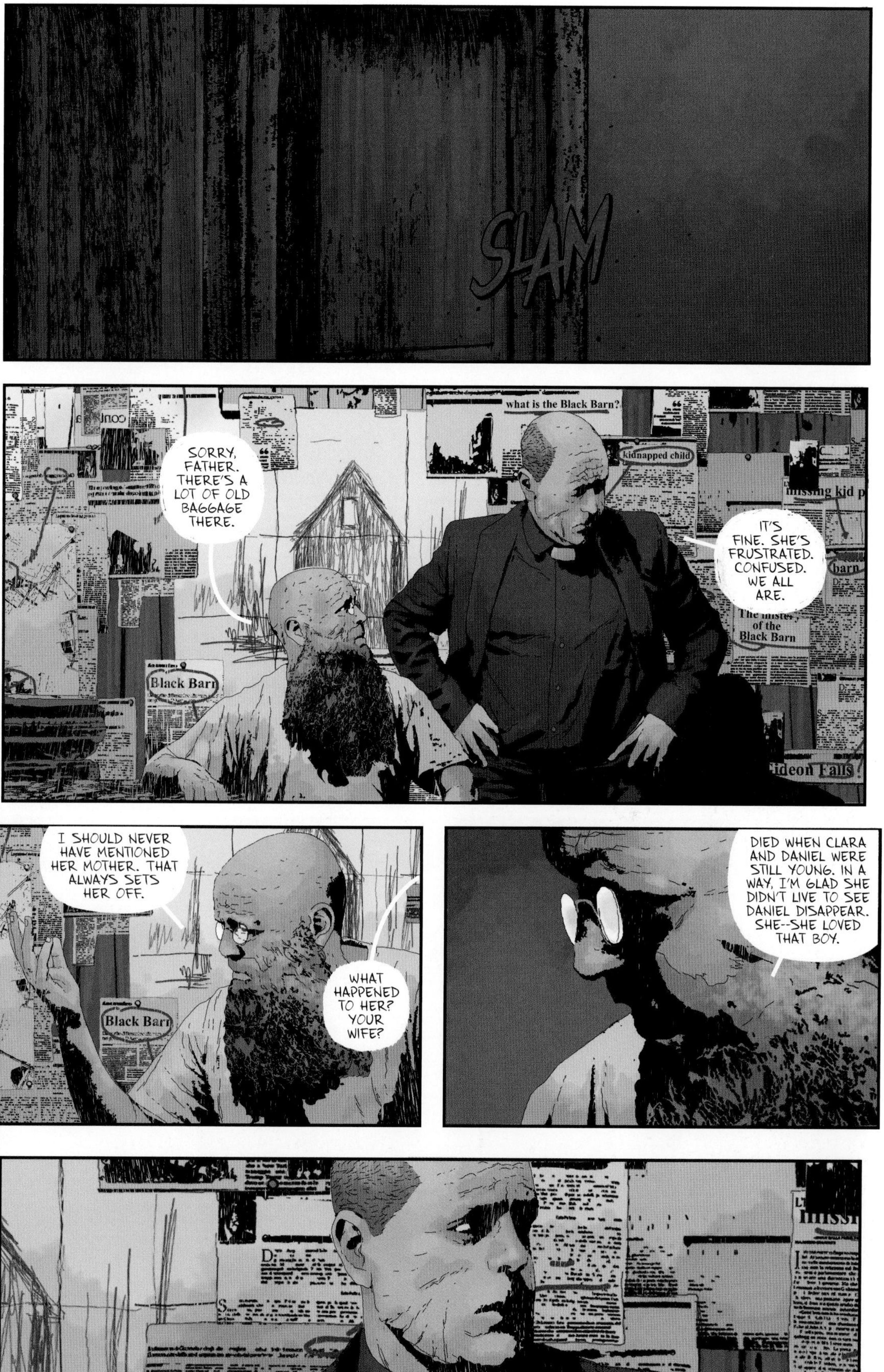
SLAM
SORRY, FATHER. THERE'S A LOT OF OLD BAGGAGE THERE.
IT'S FINE. SHE'S FRUSTRATED. CONFUSED. WE ALL ARE.
I SHOULD NEVER HAVE MENTIONED HER MOTHER. THAT ALWAYS SETS HER OFF.
WHAT HAPPENED TO HER? YOUR WIFE?
DIED WHEN CLARA AND DANIEL WERE STILL YOUNG. IN A WAY, I'M GLAD SHE DIDN'T LIVE TO SEE DANIEL DISAPPEAR. SHE--SHE LOVED THAT BOY.

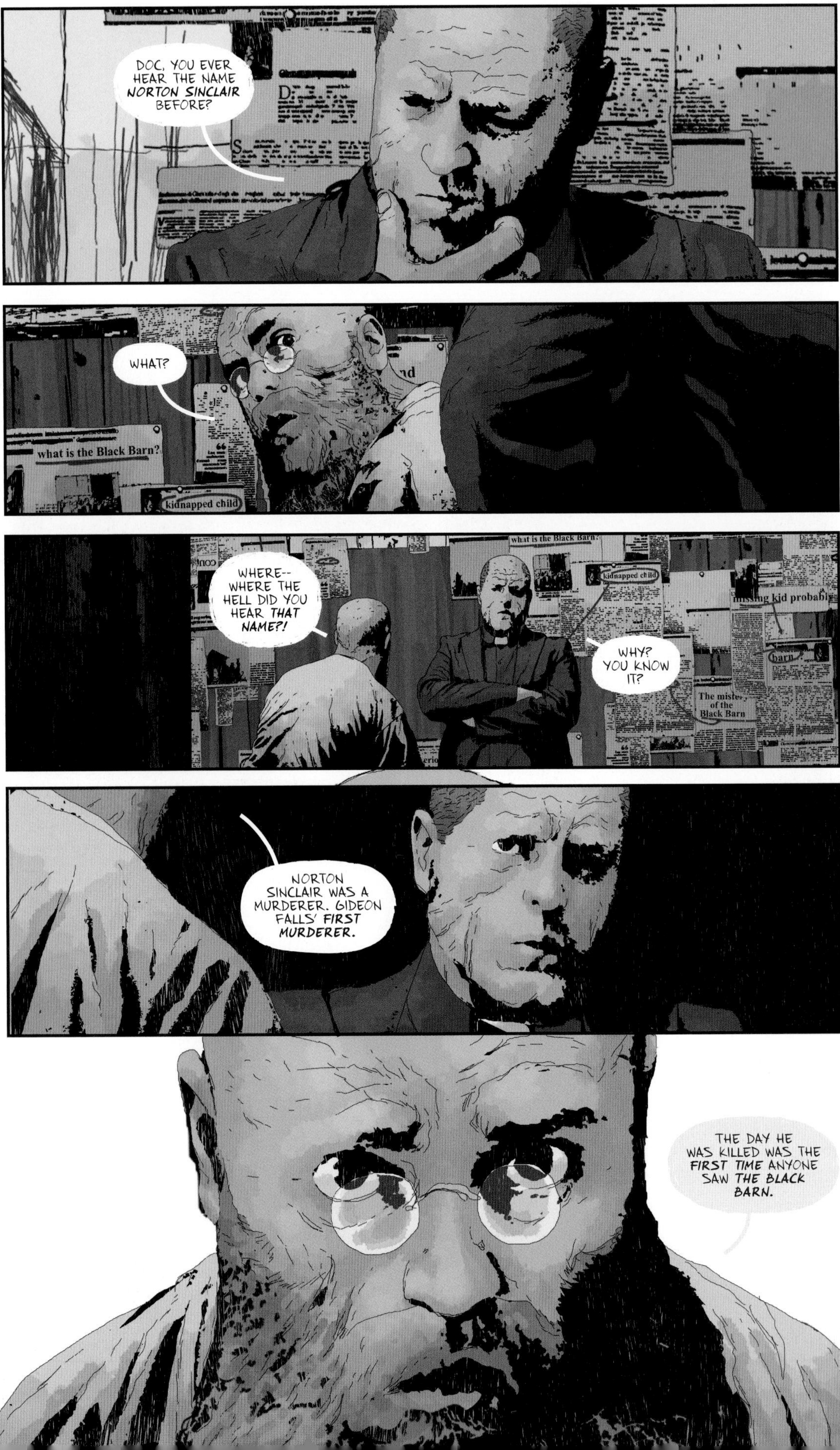
DOC, YOU EVER HEAR THE NAME NORTON SINCLAIR BEFORE?
WHAT?
what is the Black Barn?
kidnapped child
WHERE-- WHERE THE HELL DID YOU HEAR THAT NAME?!
WHY? YOU KNOW IT?
NORTON SINCLAIR WAS A MURDERER. GIDEON FALLS' FIRST MURDERER.
THE DAY HE WAS KILLED WAS THE FIRST TIME ANYONE SAW THE BLACK BARN.

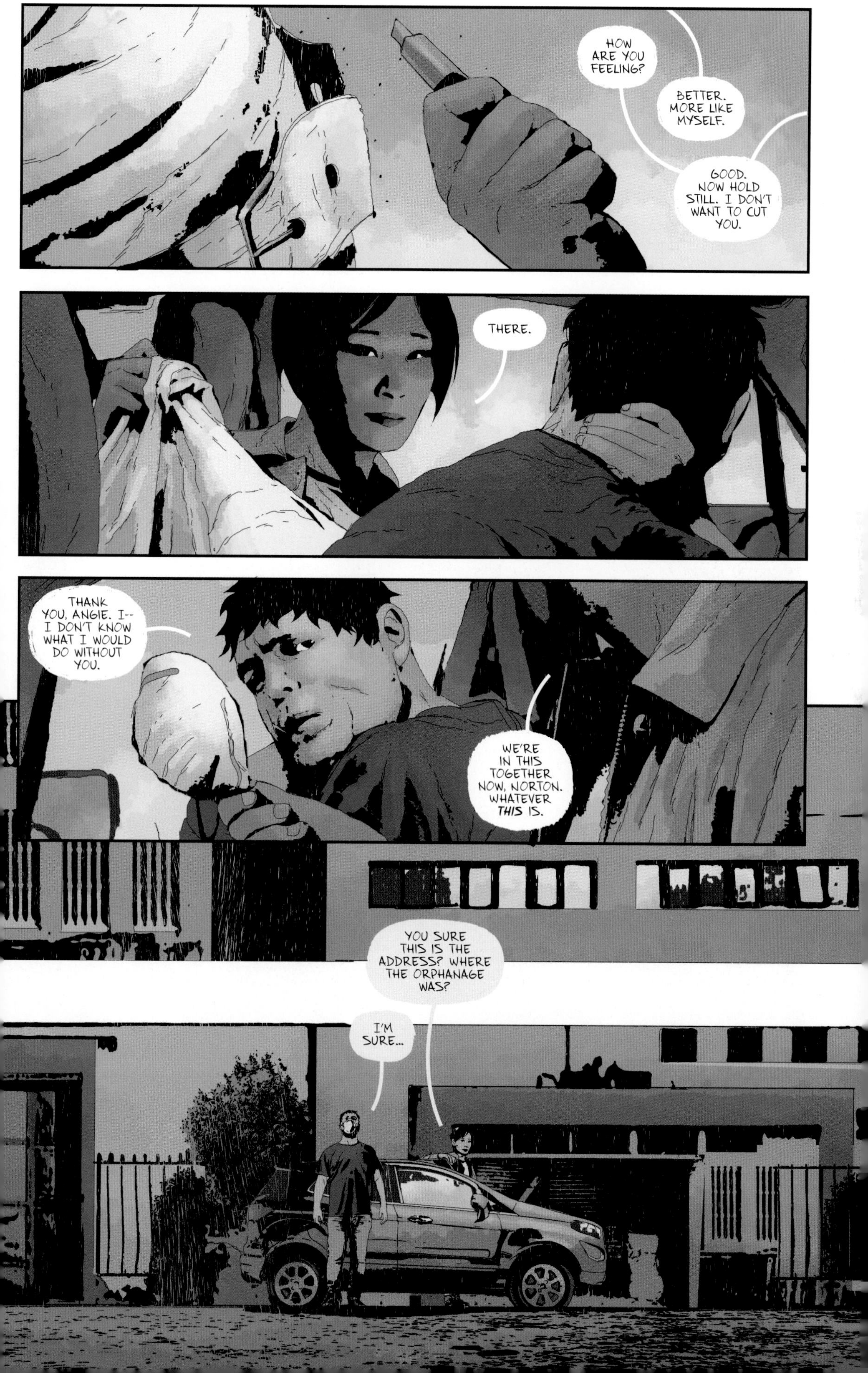
HOW ARE YOU FEELING?
BETTER. MORE LIKE MYSELF.
GOOD. NOW HOLD STILL. I DON'T WANT TO CUT YOU.
THERE.
THANK YOU, ANGIE. I-- I DON'T KNOW WHAT I WOULD DO WITHOUT YOU.
WE'RE IN THIS TOGETHER NOW, NORTON. WHATEVER *THIS* IS.
YOU SURE THIS IS THE ADDRESS? WHERE THE ORPHANAGE WAS?
I'M SURE...

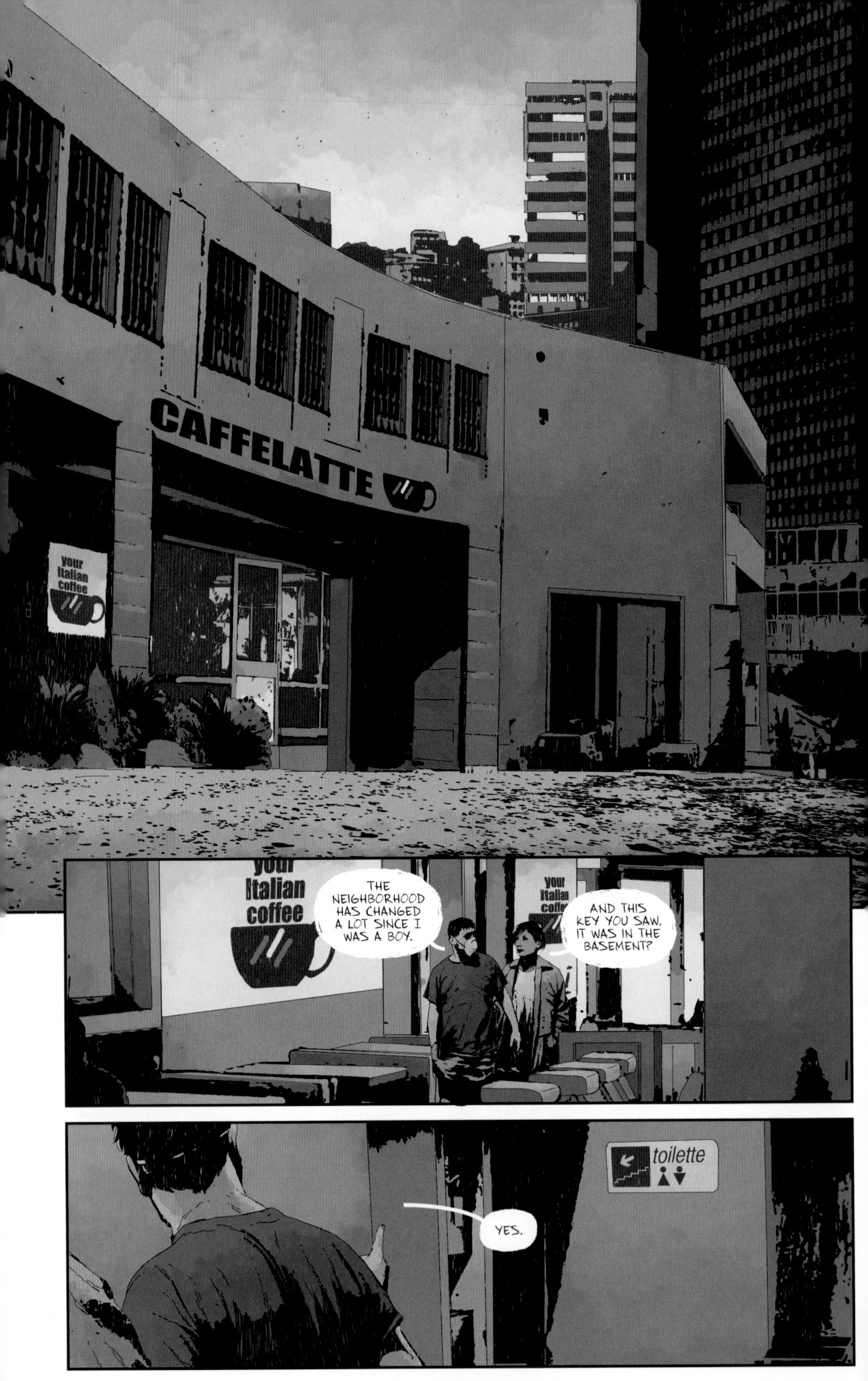
CAFFELATTE
your Italian coffee
your Italian coffee
THE NEIGHBORHOOD HAS CHANGED A LOT SINCE I WAS A BOY.
AND THIS KEY YOU SAW, IT WAS IN THE BASEMENT?
toilette
YES.

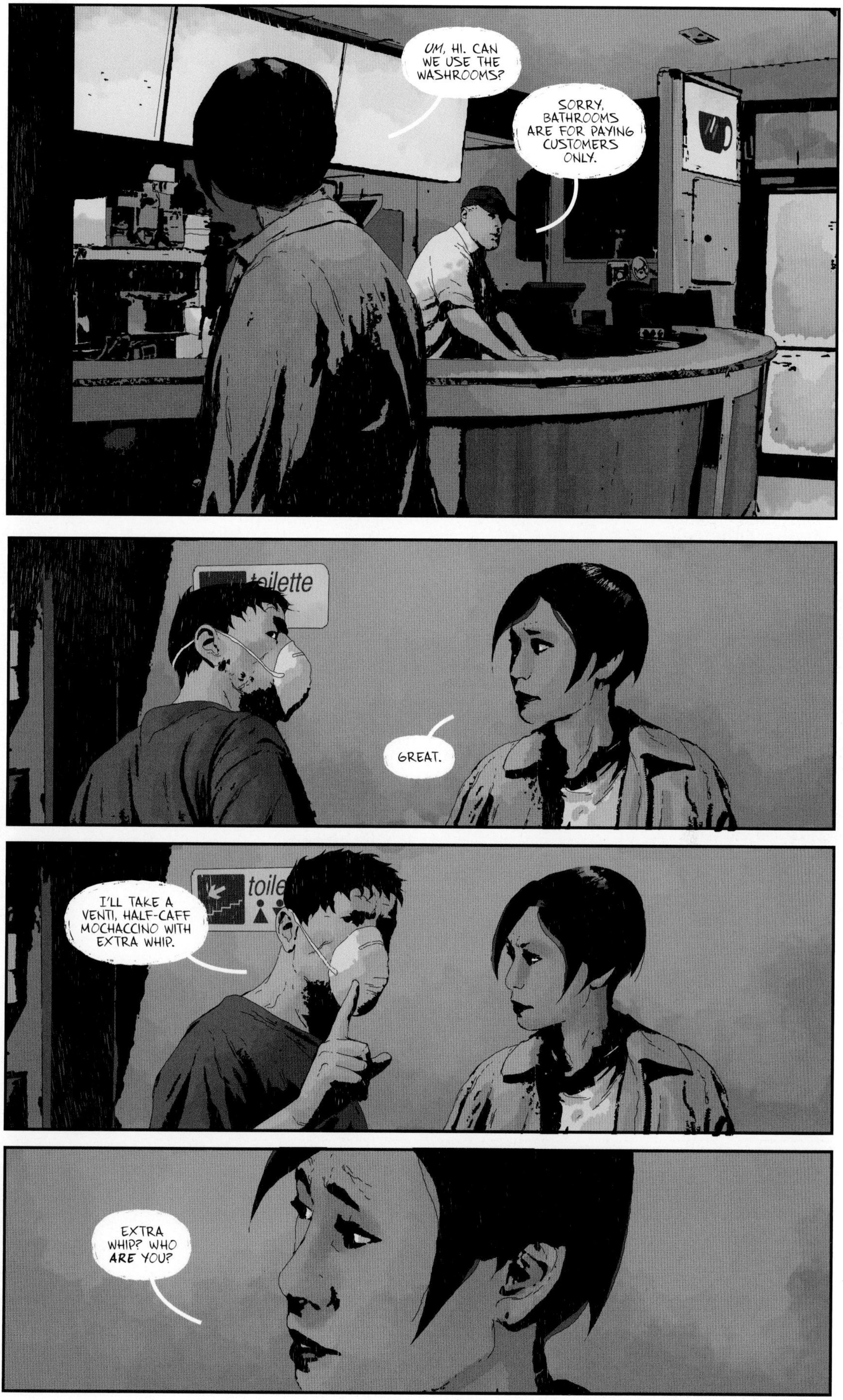
UM, HI. CAN WE USE THE WASHROOMS?
SORRY, BATHROOMS ARE FOR PAYING CUSTOMERS ONLY.
toilette
GREAT.
I'LL TAKE A VENTI, HALF-CAFF MOCHACCINO WITH EXTRA WHIP.
EXTRA WHIP? WHO **ARE** YOU?

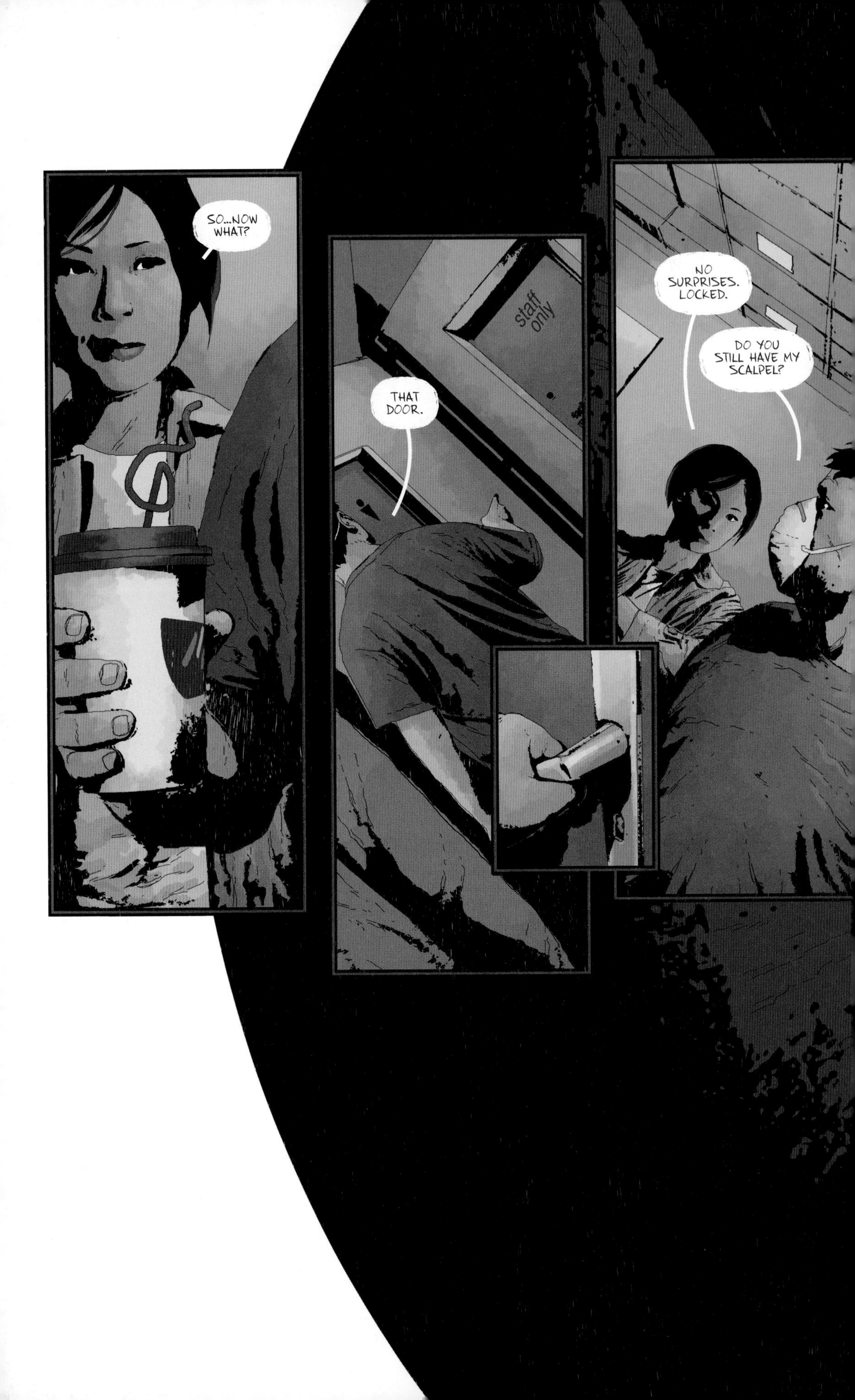
SO...NOW WHAT?
staff only
THAT DOOR.
NO SURPRISES. LOCKED.
DO YOU STILL HAVE MY SCALPEL?

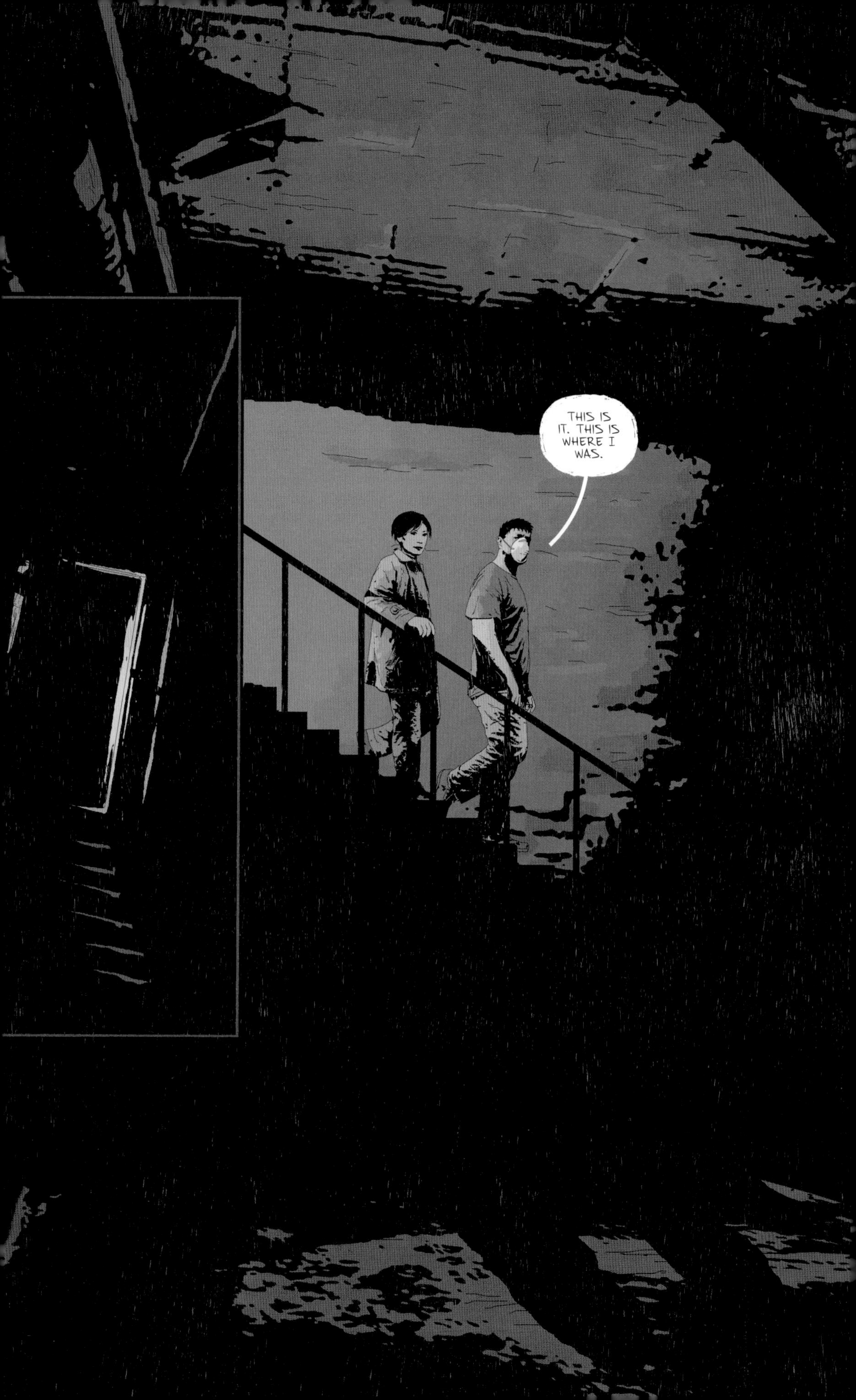
THIS IS IT. THIS IS WHERE I WAS.

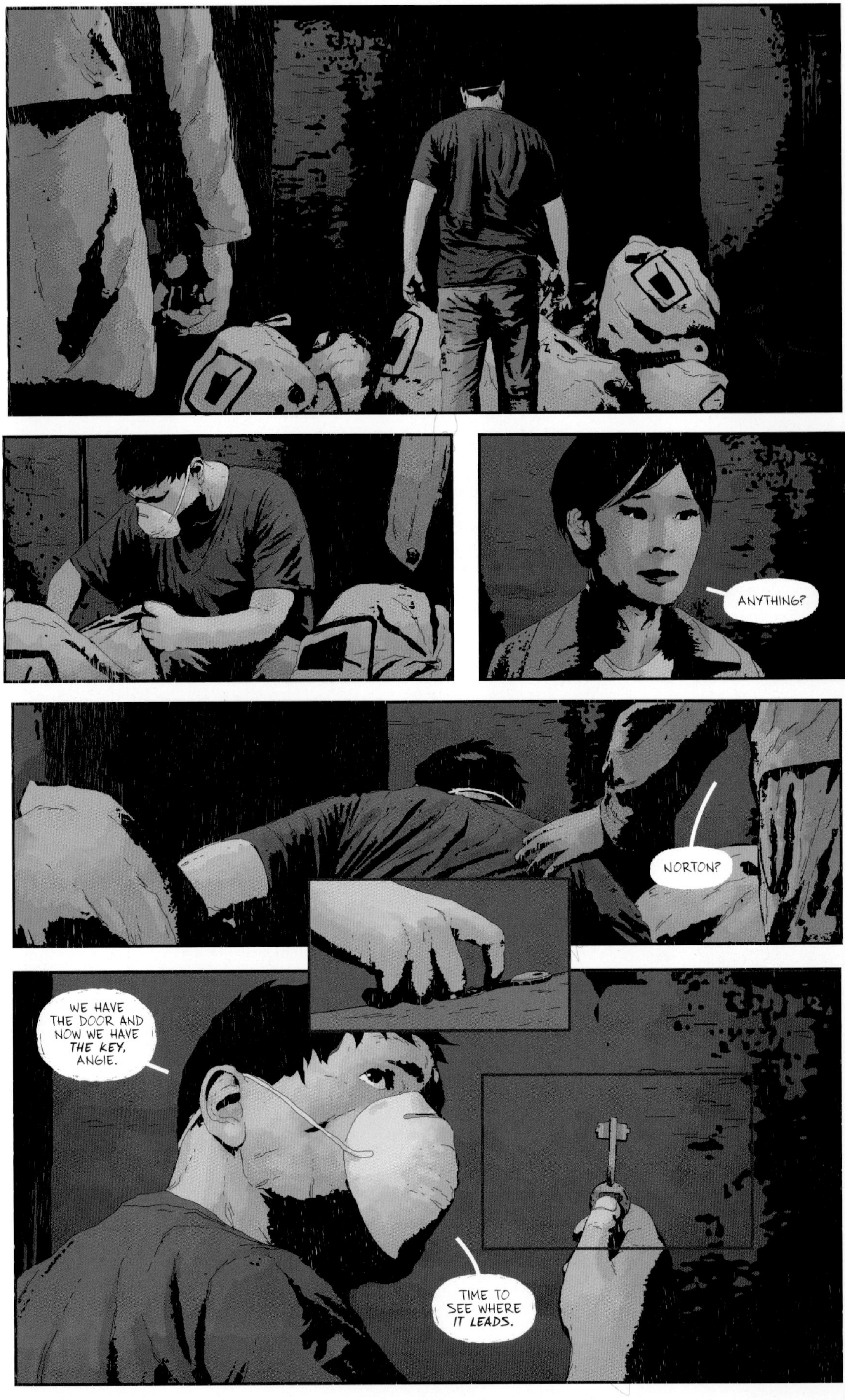
ANYTHING?
NORTON?
WE HAVE THE DOOR AND NOW WE HAVE THE KEY, ANGIE.
TIME TO SEE WHERE IT LEADS.

GIDEON
FALLS

Ten

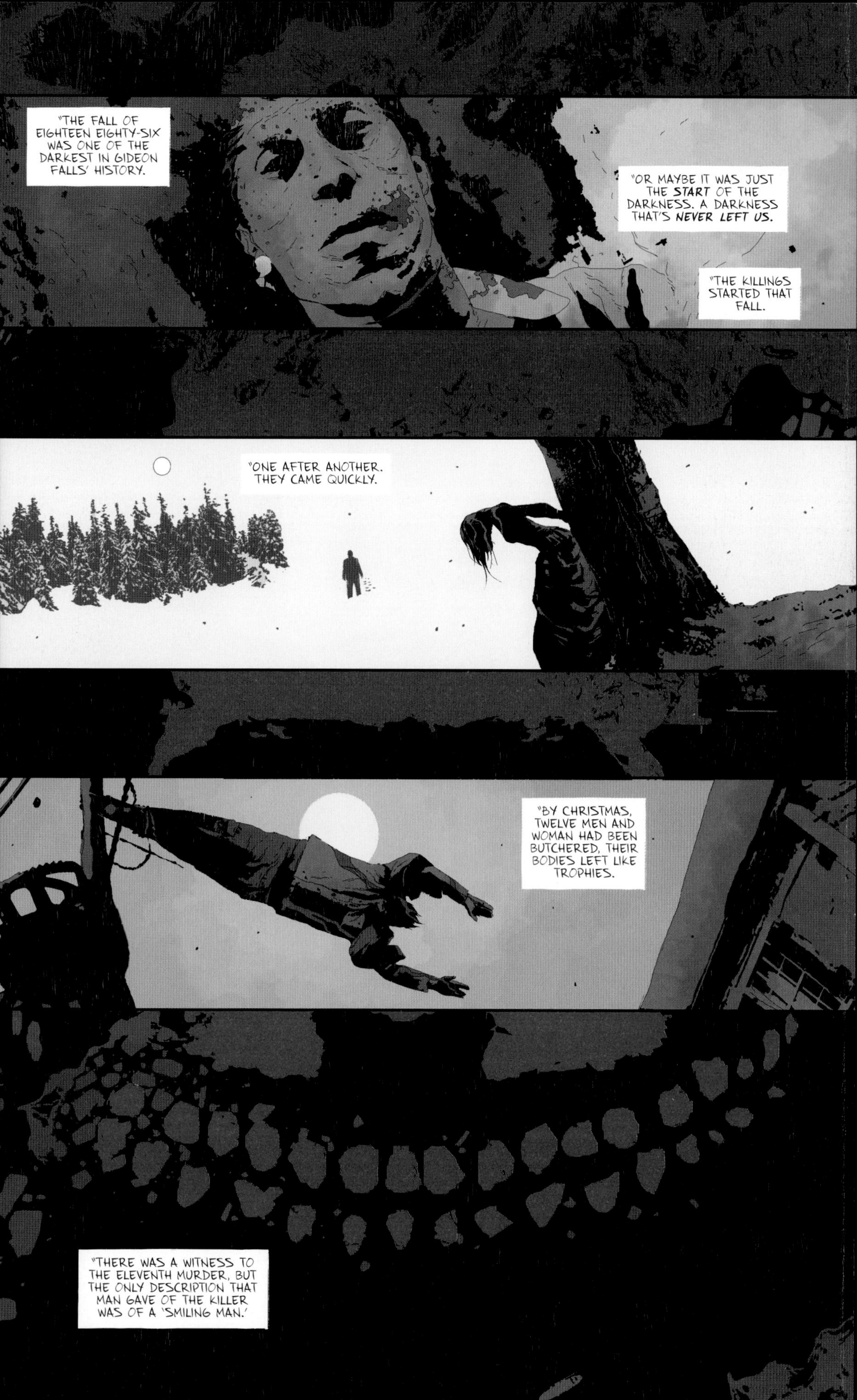
"THE FALL OF EIGHTEEN EIGHTY-SIX WAS ONE OF THE DARKEST IN GIDEON FALLS' HISTORY.
"OR MAYBE IT WAS JUST THE START OF THE DARKNESS. A DARKNESS THAT'S NEVER LEFT US.
"THE KILLINGS STARTED THAT FALL.
"ONE AFTER ANOTHER. THEY CAME QUICKLY.
"BY CHRISTMAS, TWELVE MEN AND WOMAN HAD BEEN BUTCHERED, THEIR BODIES LEFT LIKE TROPHIES.
"THERE WAS A WITNESS TO THE ELEVENTH MURDER, BUT THE ONLY DESCRIPTION THAT MAN GAVE OF THE KILLER WAS OF A 'SMILING MAN.'

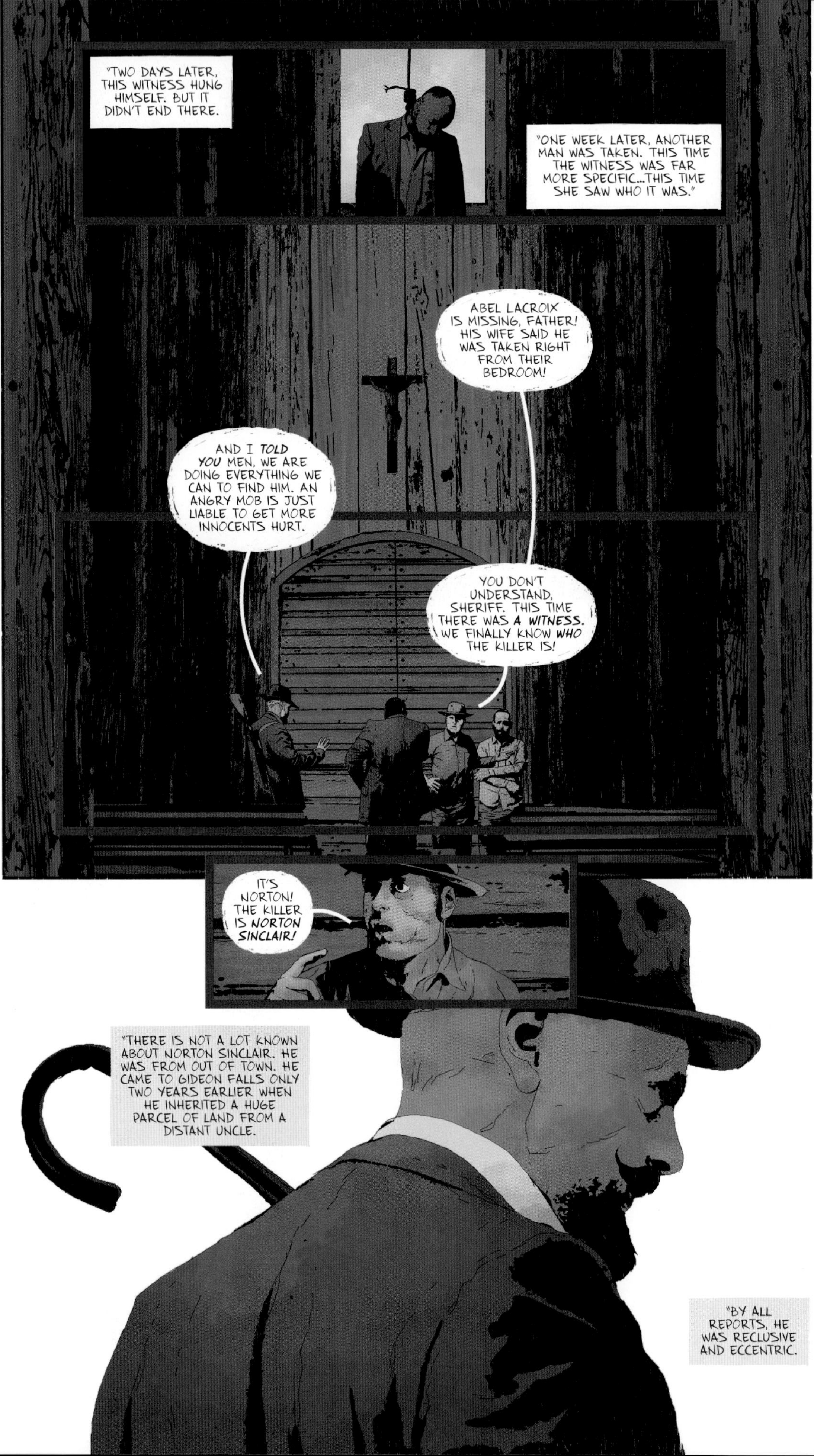
"TWO DAYS LATER, THIS WITNESS HUNG HIMSELF. BUT IT DIDN'T END THERE.
"ONE WEEK LATER, ANOTHER MAN WAS TAKEN. THIS TIME THE WITNESS WAS FAR MORE SPECIFIC...THIS TIME SHE SAW WHO IT WAS."
ABEL LACROIX IS MISSING, FATHER! HIS WIFE SAID HE WAS TAKEN RIGHT FROM THEIR BEDROOM!
AND I *TOLD YOU* MEN, WE ARE DOING EVERYTHING WE CAN TO FIND HIM. AN ANGRY MOB IS JUST LIABLE TO GET MORE INNOCENTS HURT.
YOU DON'T UNDERSTAND, SHERIFF. THIS TIME THERE WAS **A WITNESS.** WE FINALLY KNOW **WHO** THE KILLER IS!
IT'S NORTON! THE KILLER IS ***NORTON SINCLAIR!***
"THERE IS NOT A LOT KNOWN ABOUT NORTON SINCLAIR. HE WAS FROM OUT OF TOWN. HE CAME TO GIDEON FALLS ONLY TWO YEARS EARLIER WHEN HE INHERITED A HUGE PARCEL OF LAND FROM A DISTANT UNCLE.
"BY ALL REPORTS, HE WAS RECLUSIVE AND ECCENTRIC.

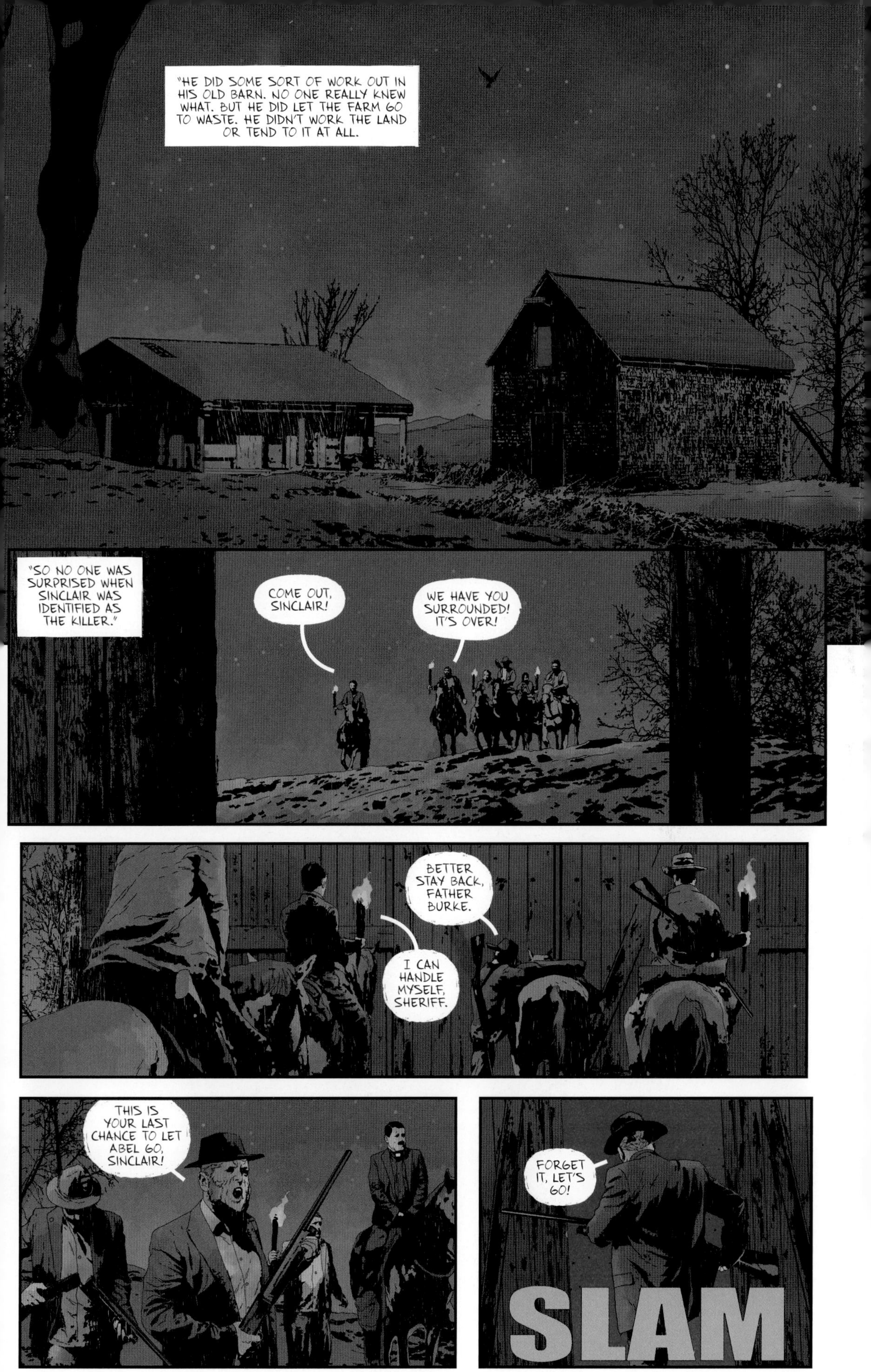
"HE DID SOME SORT OF WORK OUT IN HIS OLD BARN. NO ONE REALLY KNEW WHAT. BUT HE DID LET THE FARM GO TO WASTE. HE DIDN'T WORK THE LAND OR TEND TO IT AT ALL.
"SO NO ONE WAS SURPRISED WHEN SINCLAIR WAS IDENTIFIED AS THE KILLER."
COME OUT, SINCLAIR!
WE HAVE YOU SURROUNDED! IT'S OVER!
BETTER STAY BACK, FATHER BURKE.
I CAN HANDLE MYSELF, SHERIFF.
THIS IS YOUR LAST CHANCE TO LET ABEL GO, SINCLAIR!
FORGET IT, LET'S GO!
SLAM

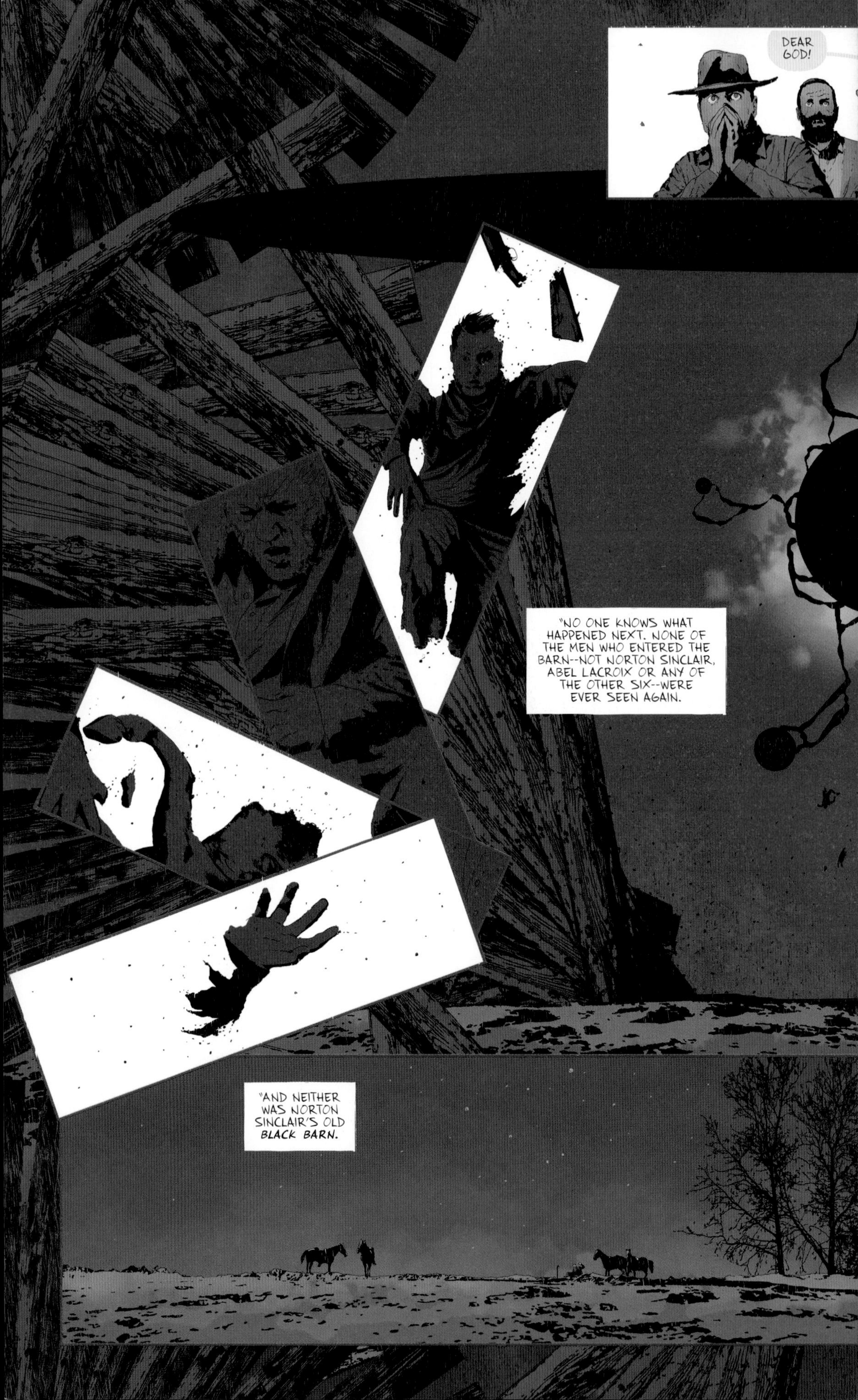
DEAR GOD!
"NO ONE KNOWS WHAT HAPPENED NEXT. NONE OF THE MEN WHO ENTERED THE BARN--NOT NORTON SINCLAIR, ABEL LACROIX OR ANY OF THE OTHER SIX--WERE EVER SEEN AGAIN.
"AND NEITHER WAS NORTON SINCLAIR'S OLD BLACK BARN.

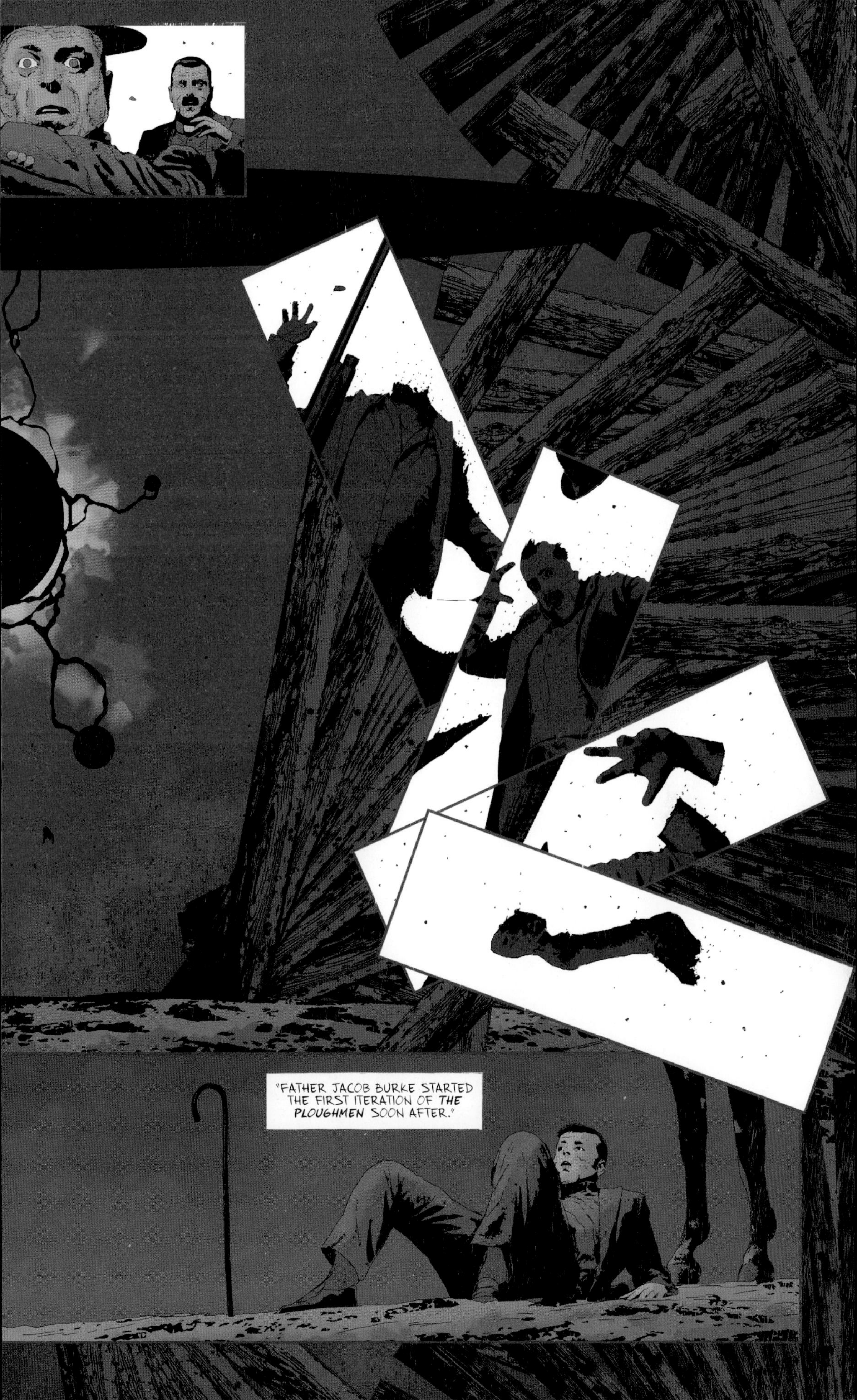

"FATHER JACOB BURKE STARTED THE FIRST ITERATION OF *THE PLOUGHMEN* SOON AFTER."

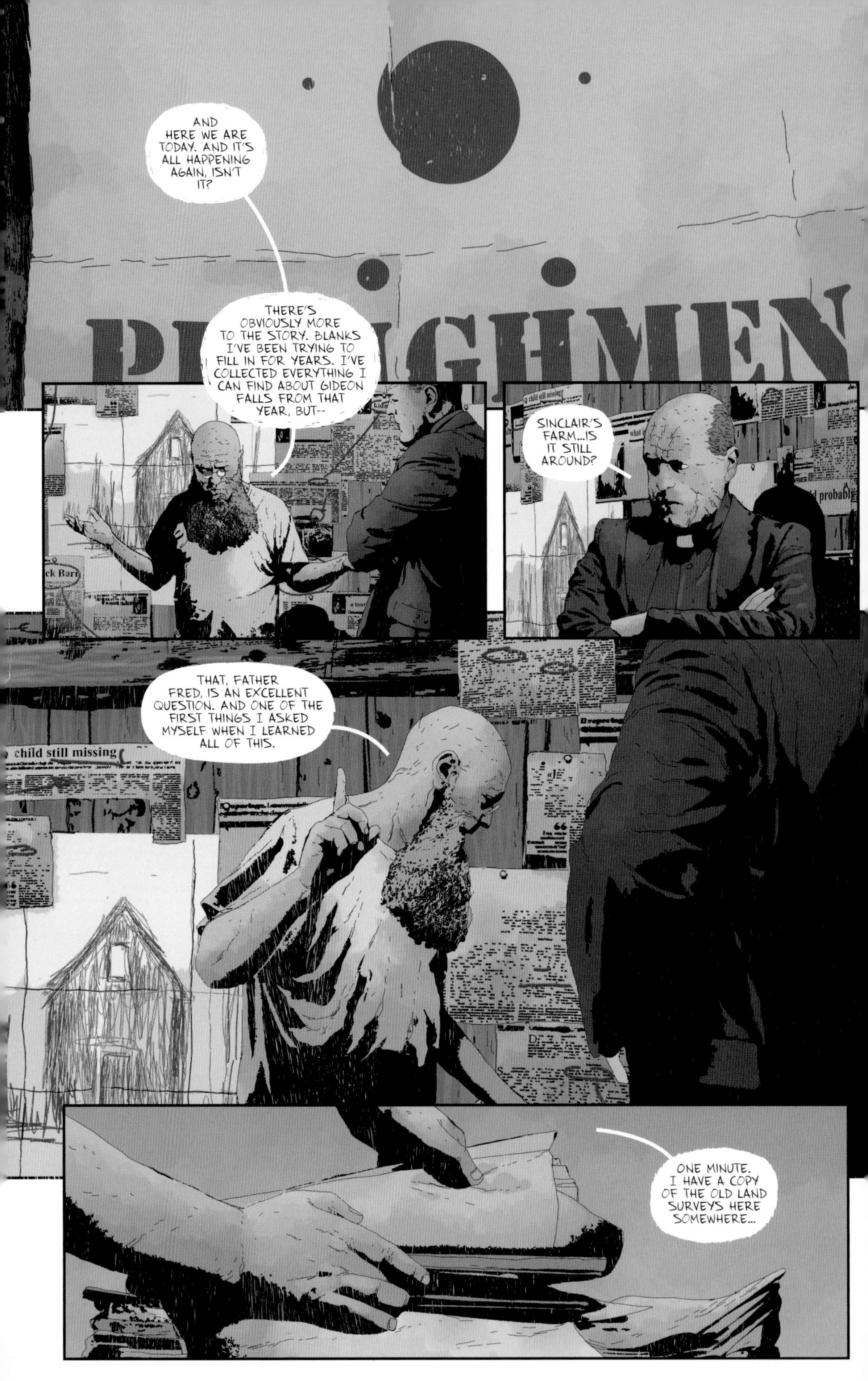
AND HERE WE ARE TODAY. AND IT'S ALL HAPPENING AGAIN, ISN'T IT?
THERE'S OBVIOUSLY MORE TO THE STORY. BLANKS I'VE BEEN TRYING TO FILL IN FOR YEARS. I'VE COLLECTED EVERYTHING I CAN FIND ABOUT GIDEON FALLS FROM THAT YEAR, BUT--
SINCLAIR'S FARM...IS IT STILL AROUND?
THAT, FATHER FRED, IS AN EXCELLENT QUESTION. AND ONE OF THE FIRST THINGS I ASKED MYSELF WHEN I LEARNED ALL OF THIS.
ONE MINUTE. I HAVE A COPY OF THE OLD LAND SURVEYS HERE SOMEWHERE...

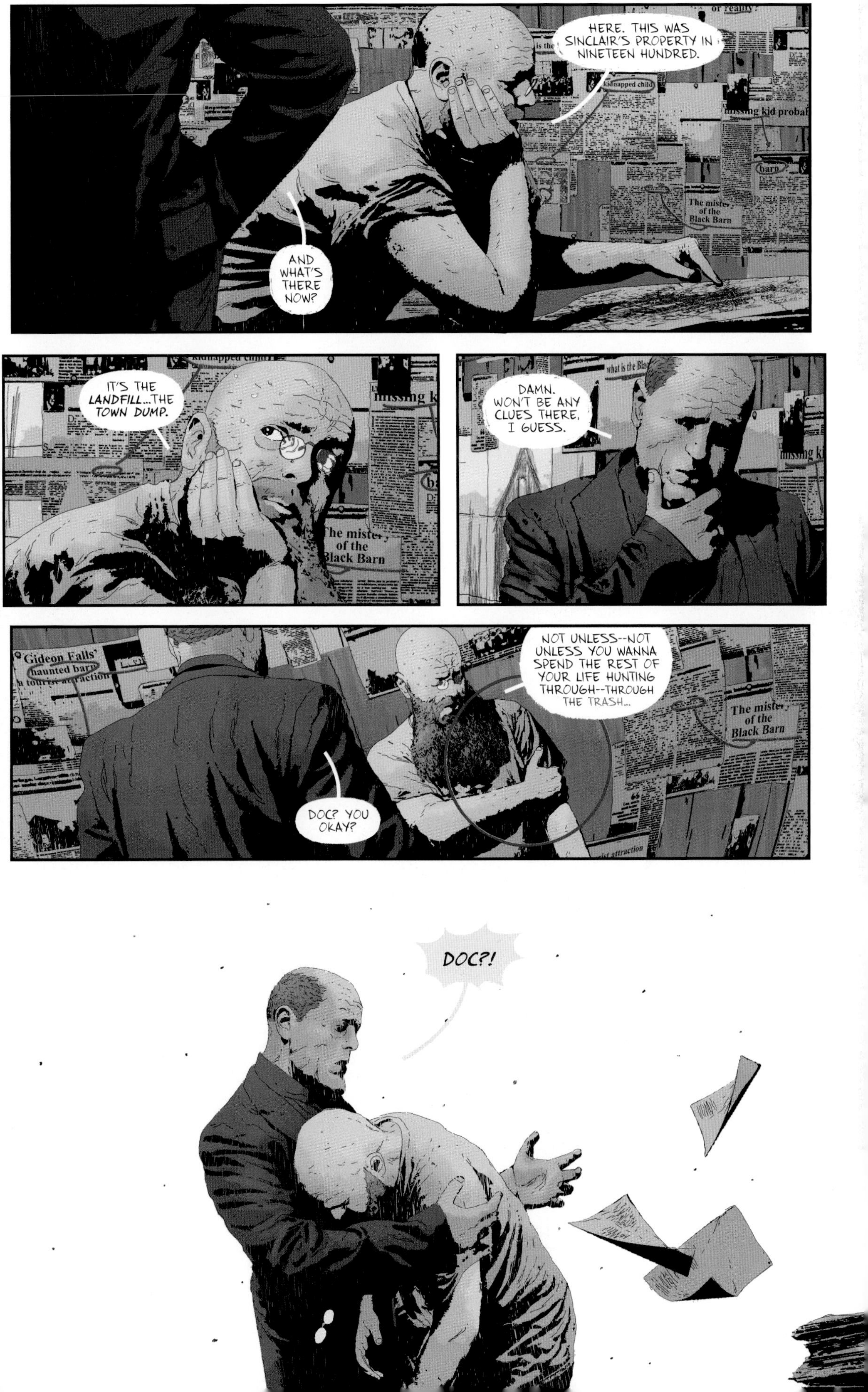
HERE. THIS WAS SINCLAIR'S PROPERTY IN NINETEEN HUNDRED.
AND WHAT'S THERE NOW?
IT'S THE LANDFILL...THE TOWN DUMP.
DAMN. WON'T BE ANY CLUES THERE, I GUESS.
NOT UNLESS--NOT UNLESS YOU WANNA SPEND THE REST OF YOUR LIFE HUNTING THROUGH--THROUGH THE TRASH...
DOC? YOU OKAY?
DOC?!

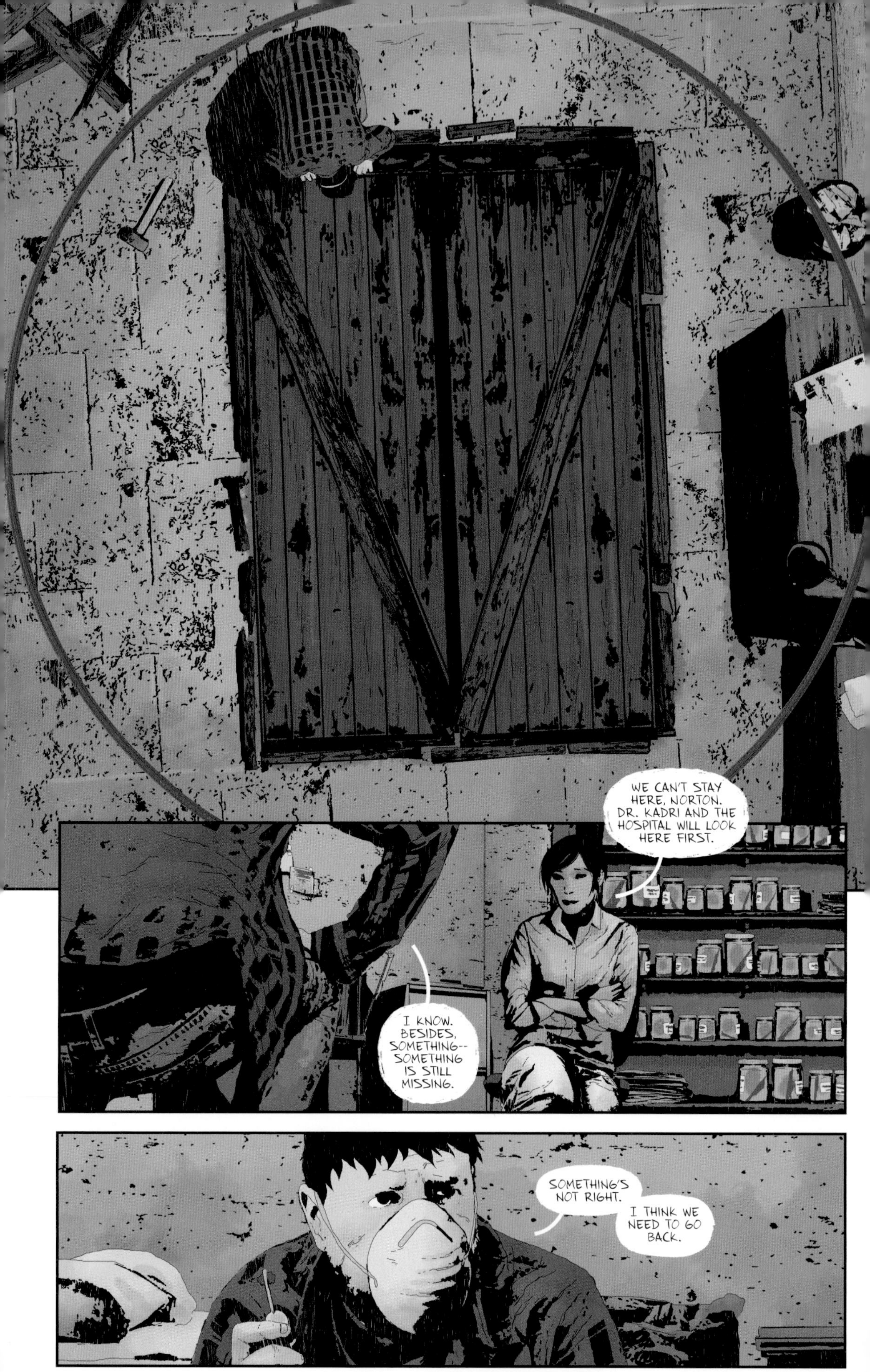
WE CAN'T STAY HERE, NORTON. DR. KADRI AND THE HOSPITAL WILL LOOK HERE FIRST.
I KNOW. BESIDES, SOMETHING-- SOMETHING IS STILL MISSING.
SOMETHING'S NOT RIGHT.
I THINK WE NEED TO GO BACK.

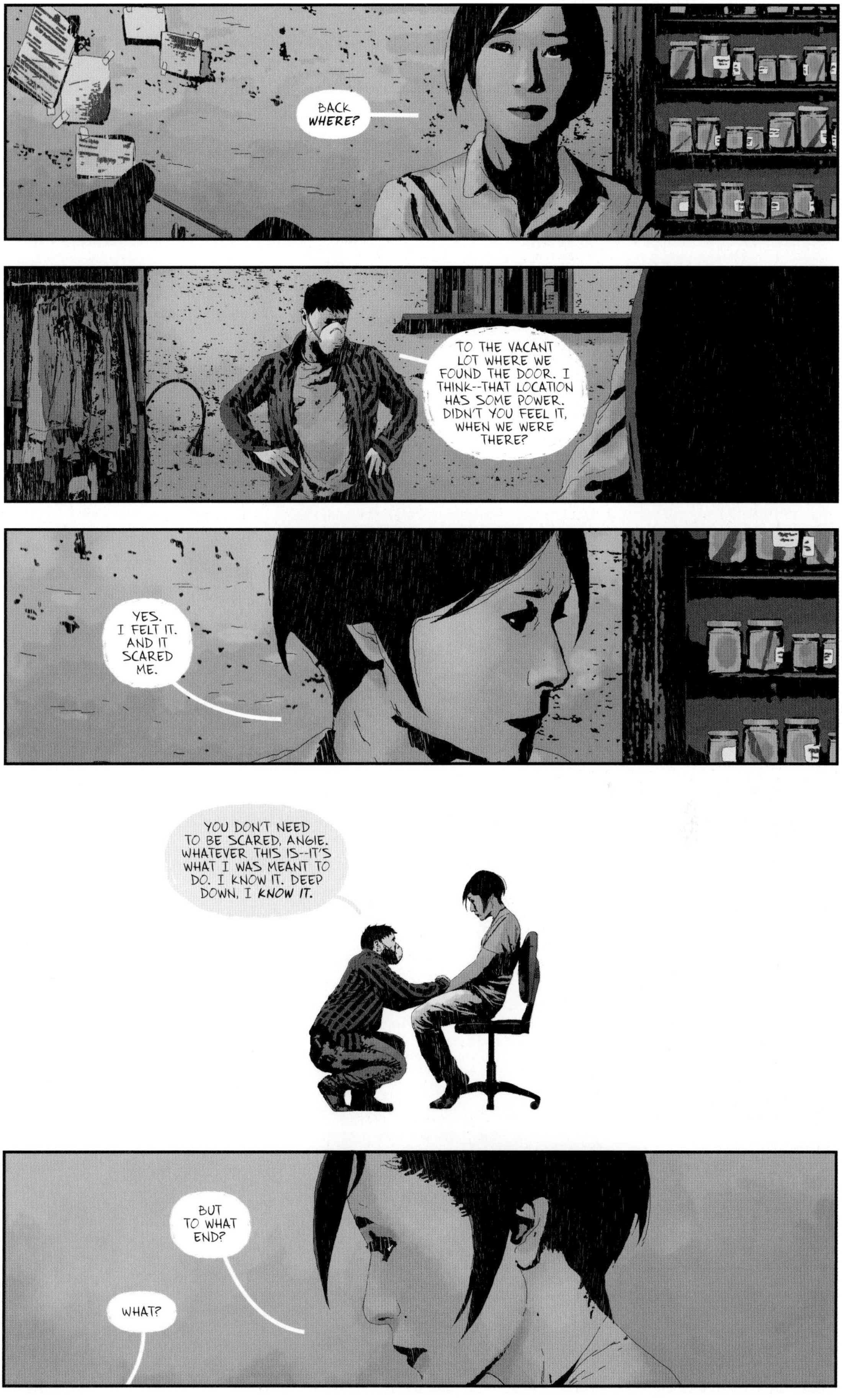
BACK WHERE?
TO THE VACANT LOT WHERE WE FOUND THE DOOR. I THINK--THAT LOCATION HAS SOME POWER. DIDN'T YOU FEEL IT, WHEN WE WERE THERE?
YES. I FELT IT. AND IT SCARED ME.
YOU DON'T NEED TO BE SCARED, ANGIE. WHATEVER THIS IS--IT'S WHAT I WAS MEANT TO DO. I KNOW IT. DEEP DOWN, I KNOW IT.
BUT TO WHAT END?
WHAT?

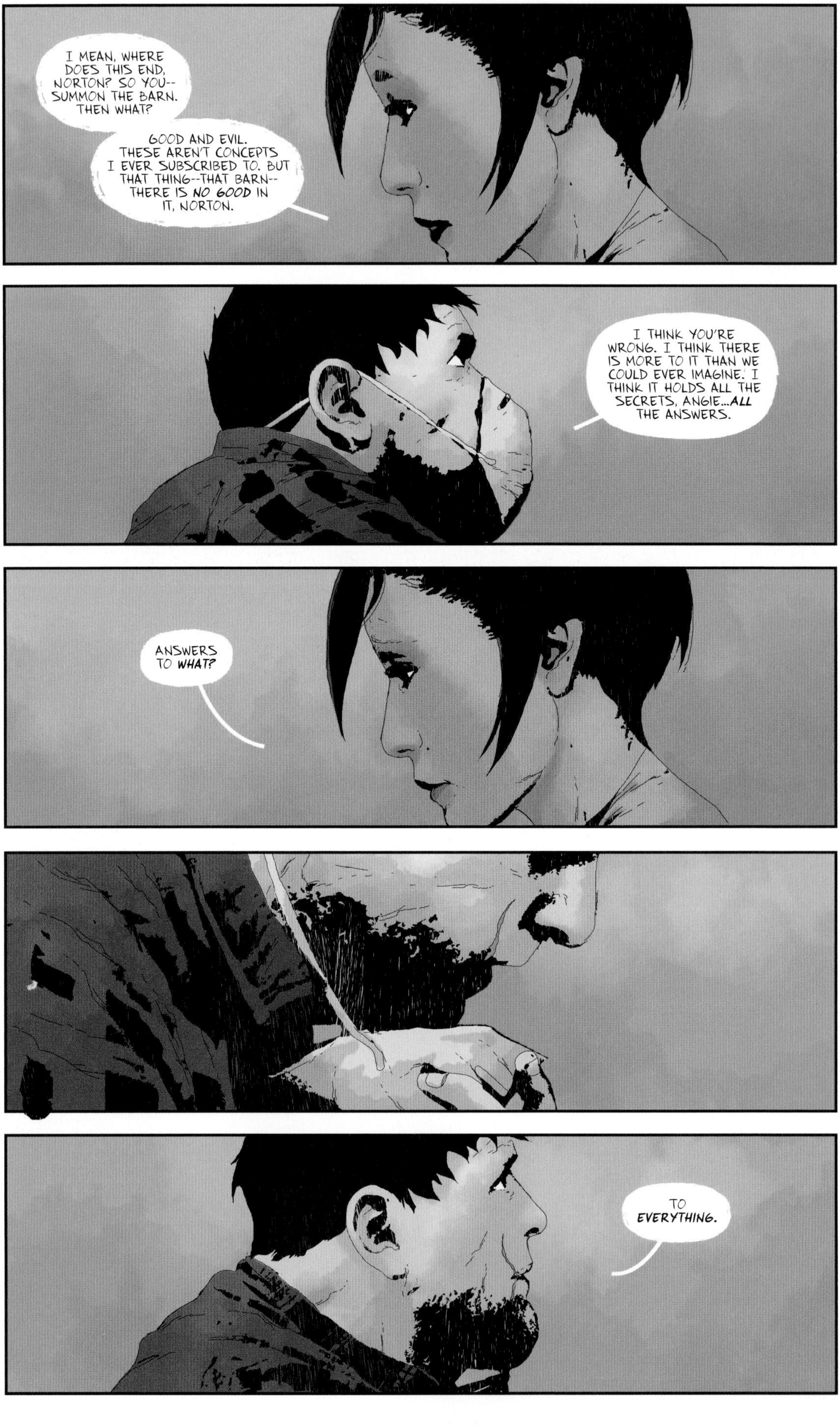
I MEAN, WHERE DOES THIS END, NORTON? SO YOU--SUMMON THE BARN. THEN WHAT?
GOOD AND EVIL. THESE AREN'T CONCEPTS I EVER SUBSCRIBED TO. BUT THAT THING--THAT BARN--THERE IS NO GOOD IN IT, NORTON.
I THINK YOU'RE WRONG. I THINK THERE IS MORE TO IT THAN WE COULD EVER IMAGINE. I THINK IT HOLDS ALL THE SECRETS, ANGIE...ALL THE ANSWERS.
ANSWERS TO WHAT?
TO EVERYTHING.

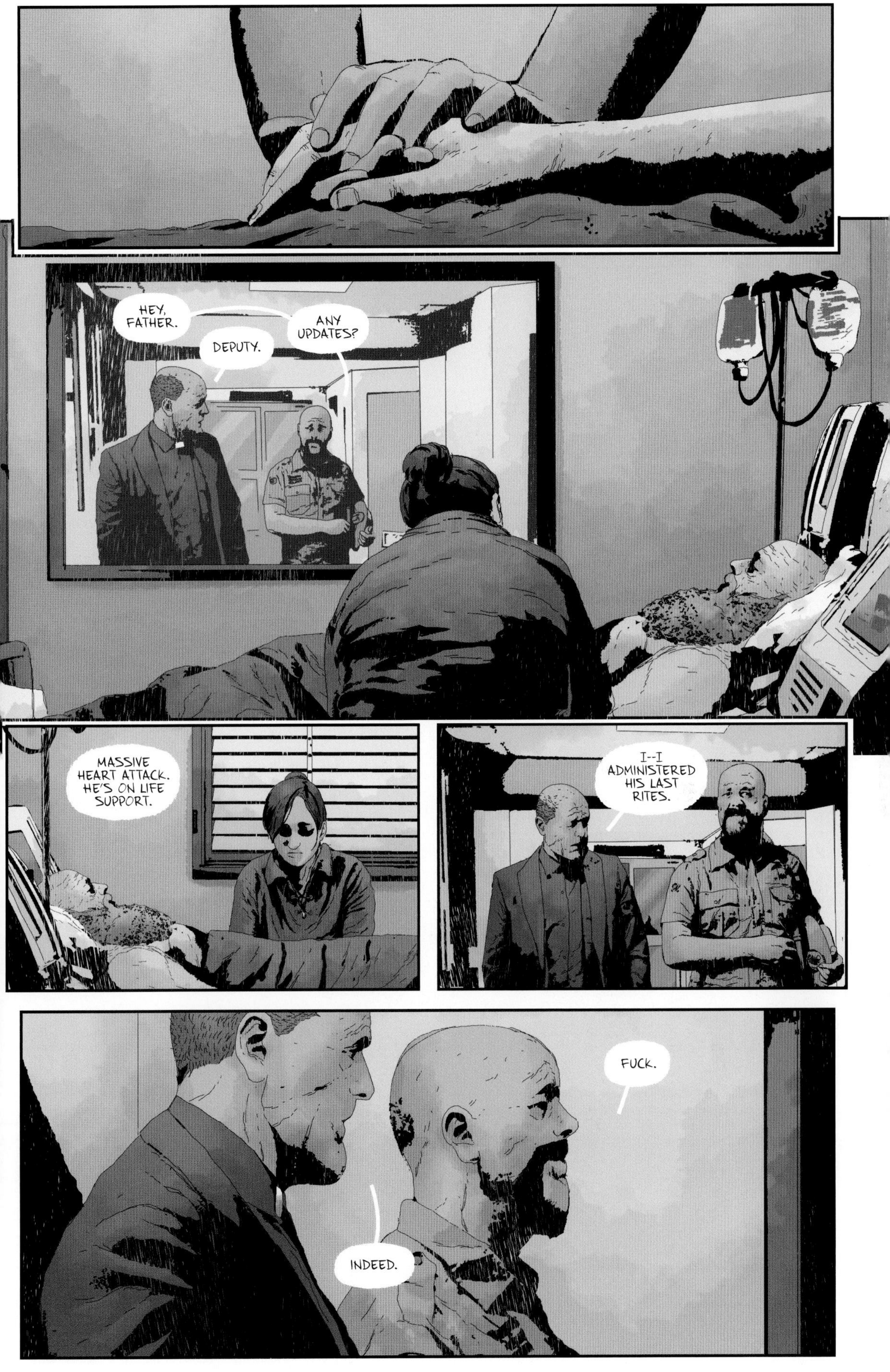

HEY, FATHER.
DEPUTY.
ANY UPDATES?
MASSIVE HEART ATTACK. HE'S ON LIFE SUPPORT.
I--I ADMINISTERED HIS LAST RITES.
FUCK.
INDEED.

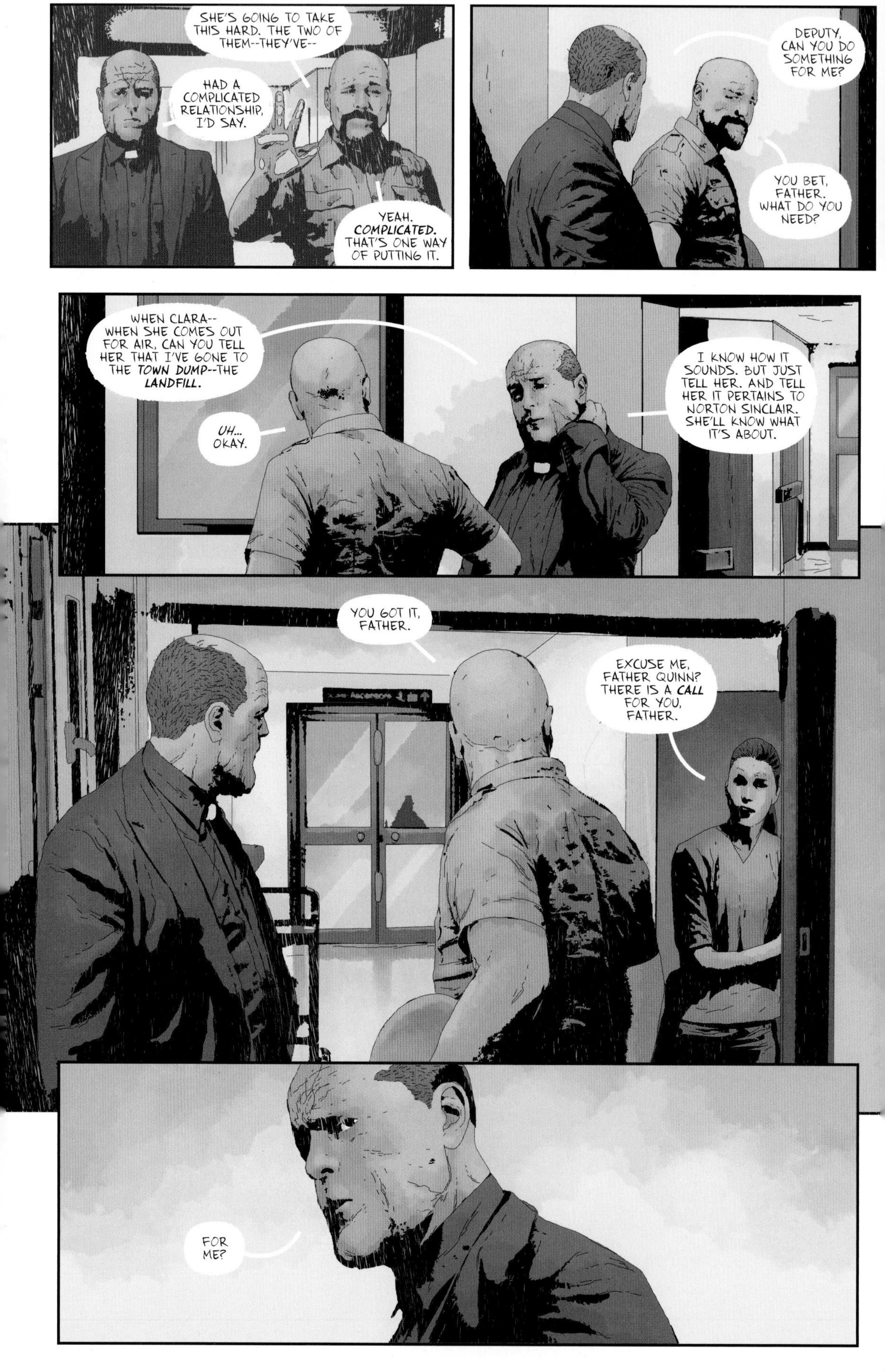
SHE'S GOING TO TAKE THIS HARD. THE TWO OF THEM--THEY'VE--
HAD A COMPLICATED RELATIONSHIP, I'D SAY.
YEAH. COMPLICATED. THAT'S ONE WAY OF PUTTING IT.
DEPUTY, CAN YOU DO SOMETHING FOR ME?
YOU BET, FATHER. WHAT DO YOU NEED?
WHEN CLARA-- WHEN SHE COMES OUT FOR AIR, CAN YOU TELL HER THAT I'VE GONE TO THE TOWN DUMP--THE LANDFILL.
UH... OKAY.
I KNOW HOW IT SOUNDS. BUT JUST TELL HER. AND TELL HER IT PERTAINS TO NORTON SINCLAIR. SHE'LL KNOW WHAT IT'S ABOUT.
YOU GOT IT, FATHER.
EXCUSE ME, FATHER QUINN? THERE IS A CALL FOR YOU, FATHER.
FOR ME?

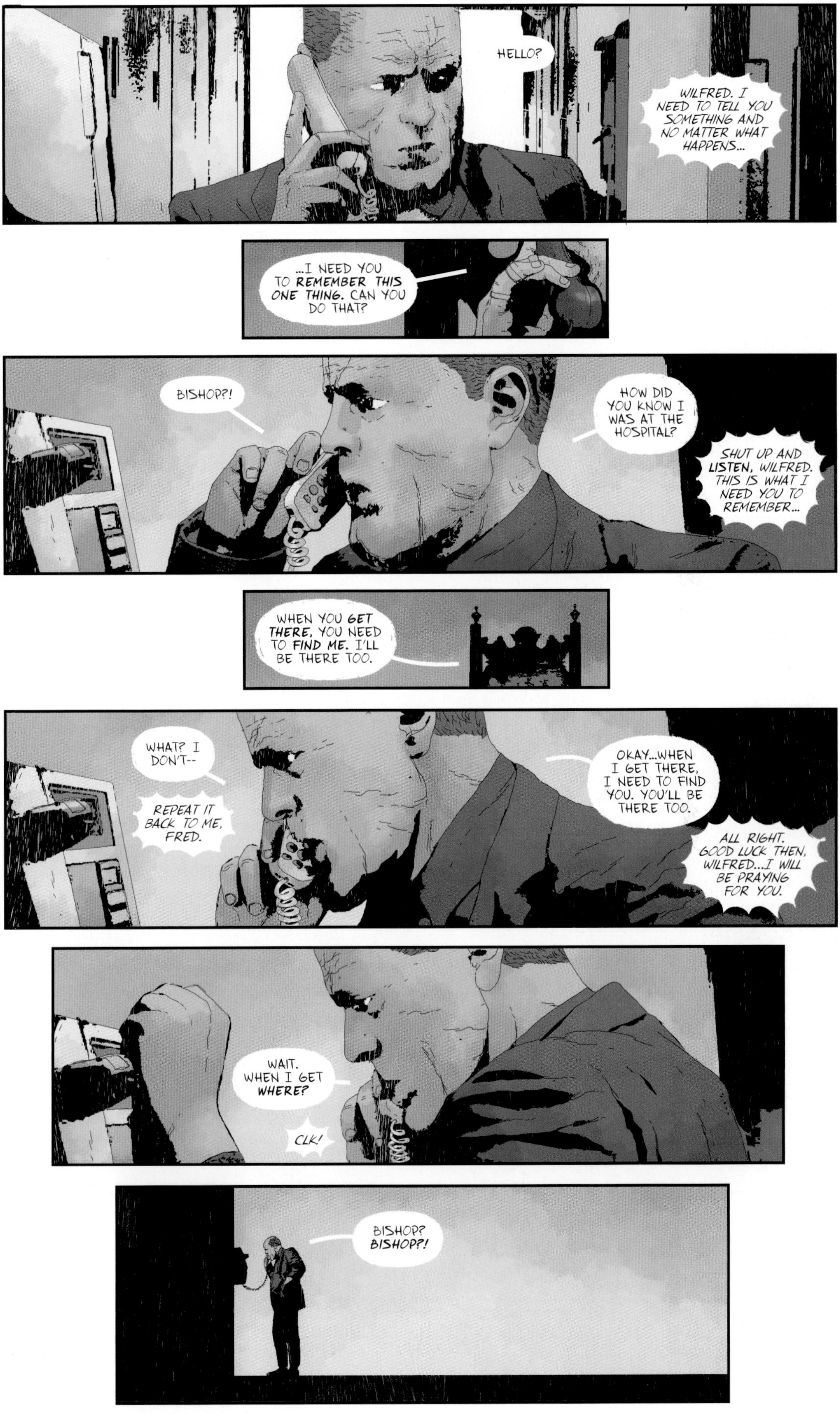
HELLO?
WILFRED. I NEED TO TELL YOU SOMETHING AND NO MATTER WHAT HAPPENS...
...I NEED YOU TO REMEMBER THIS ONE THING. CAN YOU DO THAT?
BISHOP?!
HOW DID YOU KNOW I WAS AT THE HOSPITAL?
SHUT UP AND LISTEN, WILFRED. THIS IS WHAT I NEED YOU TO REMEMBER...
WHEN YOU GET THERE, YOU NEED TO FIND ME. I'LL BE THERE TOO.
WHAT? I DON'T--
REPEAT IT BACK TO ME, FRED.
OKAY...WHEN I GET THERE, I NEED TO FIND YOU. YOU'LL BE THERE TOO.
ALL RIGHT. GOOD LUCK THEN, WILFRED...I WILL BE PRAYING FOR YOU.
WAIT. WHEN I GET WHERE?
CLK!
BISHOP? BISHOP?!

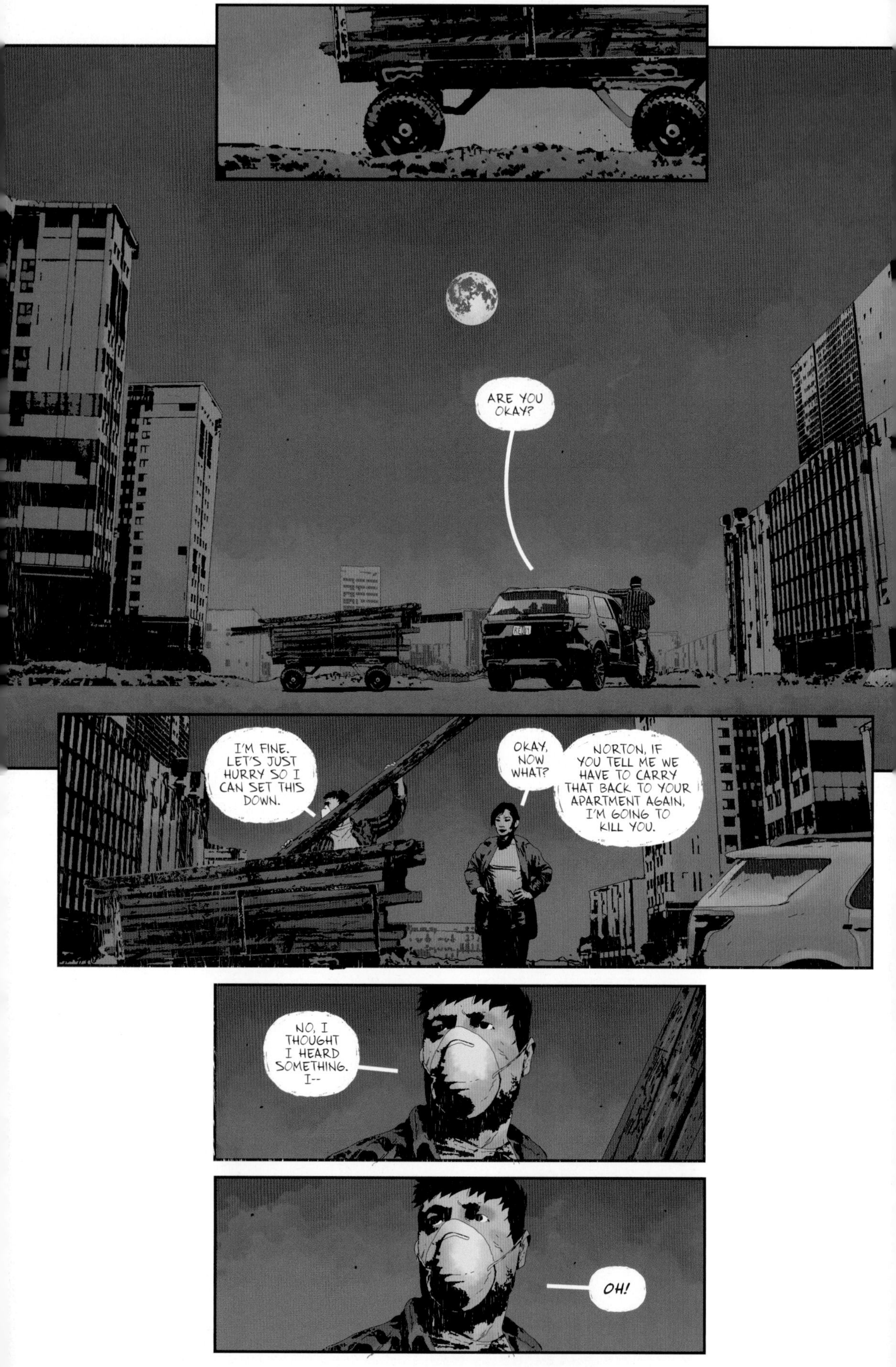
ARE YOU OKAY?
I'M FINE. LET'S JUST HURRY SO I CAN SET THIS DOWN.
OKAY, NOW WHAT?
NORTON, IF YOU TELL ME WE HAVE TO CARRY THAT BACK TO YOUR APARTMENT AGAIN, I'M GOING TO KILL YOU.
NO, I THOUGHT I HEARD SOMETHING. I--
OH!

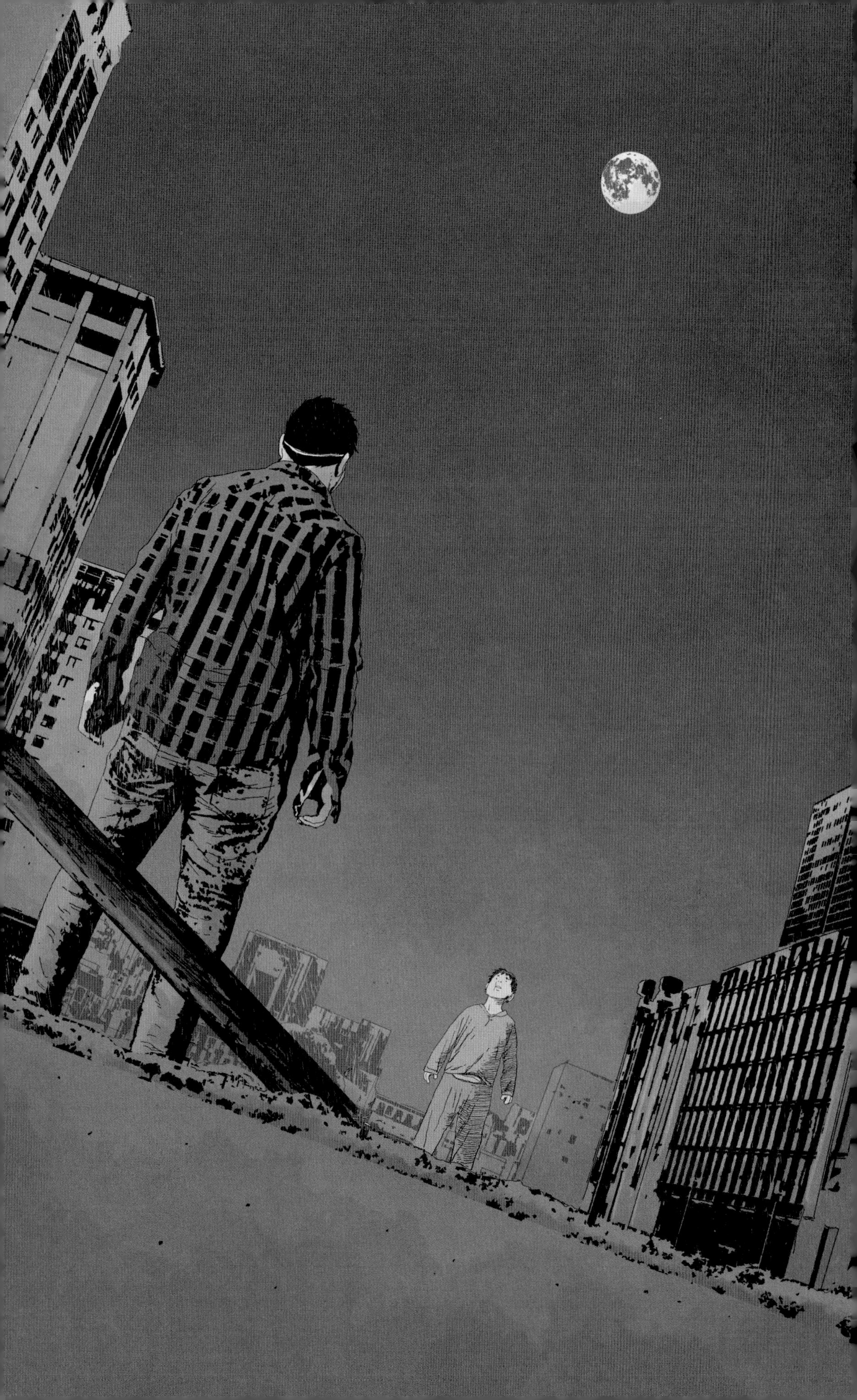

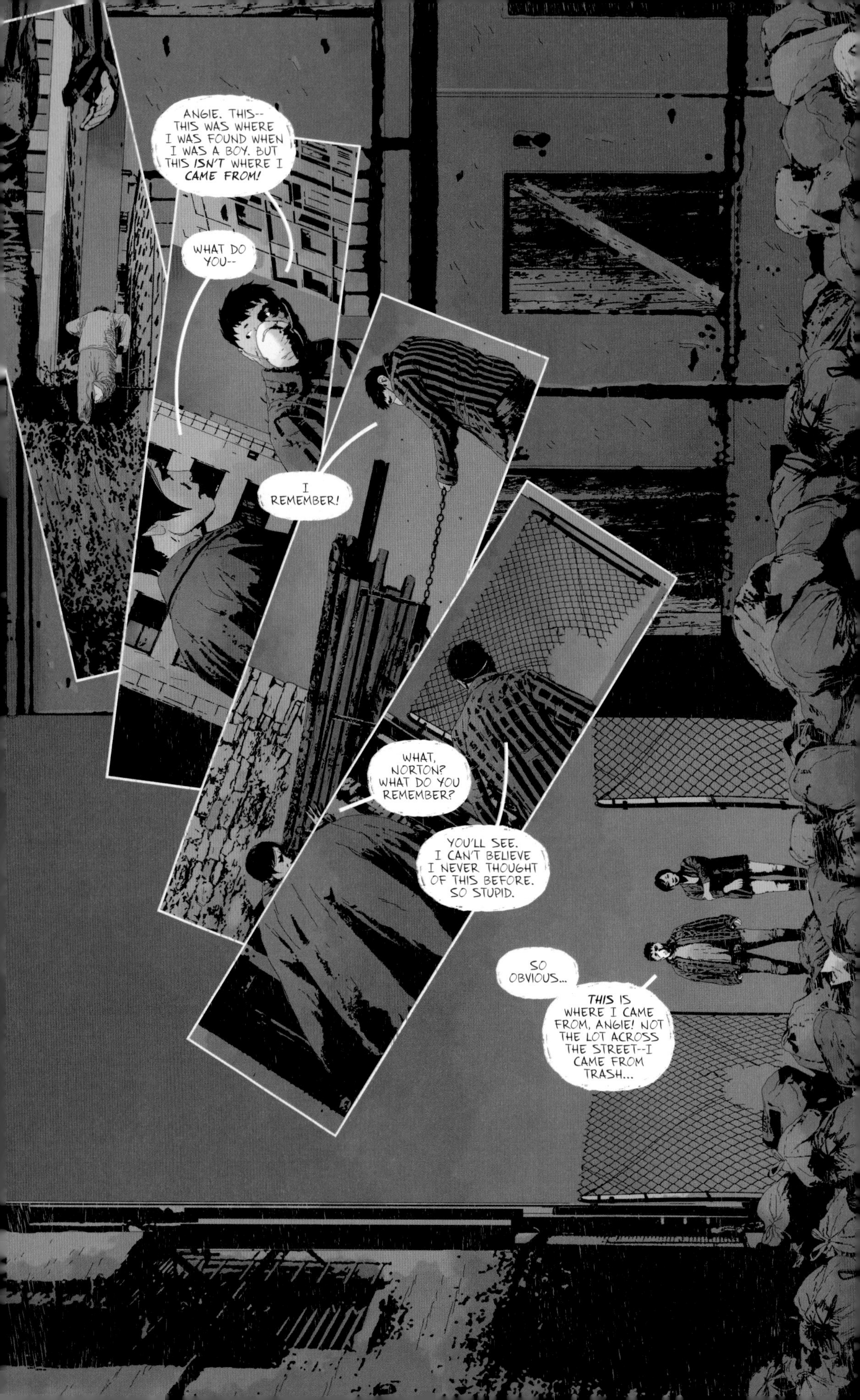
ANGIE. THIS-- THIS WAS WHERE I WAS FOUND WHEN I WAS A BOY. BUT THIS ISN'T WHERE I CAME FROM!
WHAT DO YOU--
I REMEMBER!
WHAT, NORTON? WHAT DO YOU REMEMBER?
YOU'LL SEE. I CAN'T BELIEVE I NEVER THOUGHT OF THIS BEFORE. SO STUPID.
SO OBVIOUS...
THIS IS WHERE I CAME FROM, ANGIE! NOT THE LOT ACROSS THE STREET--I CAME FROM TRASH...

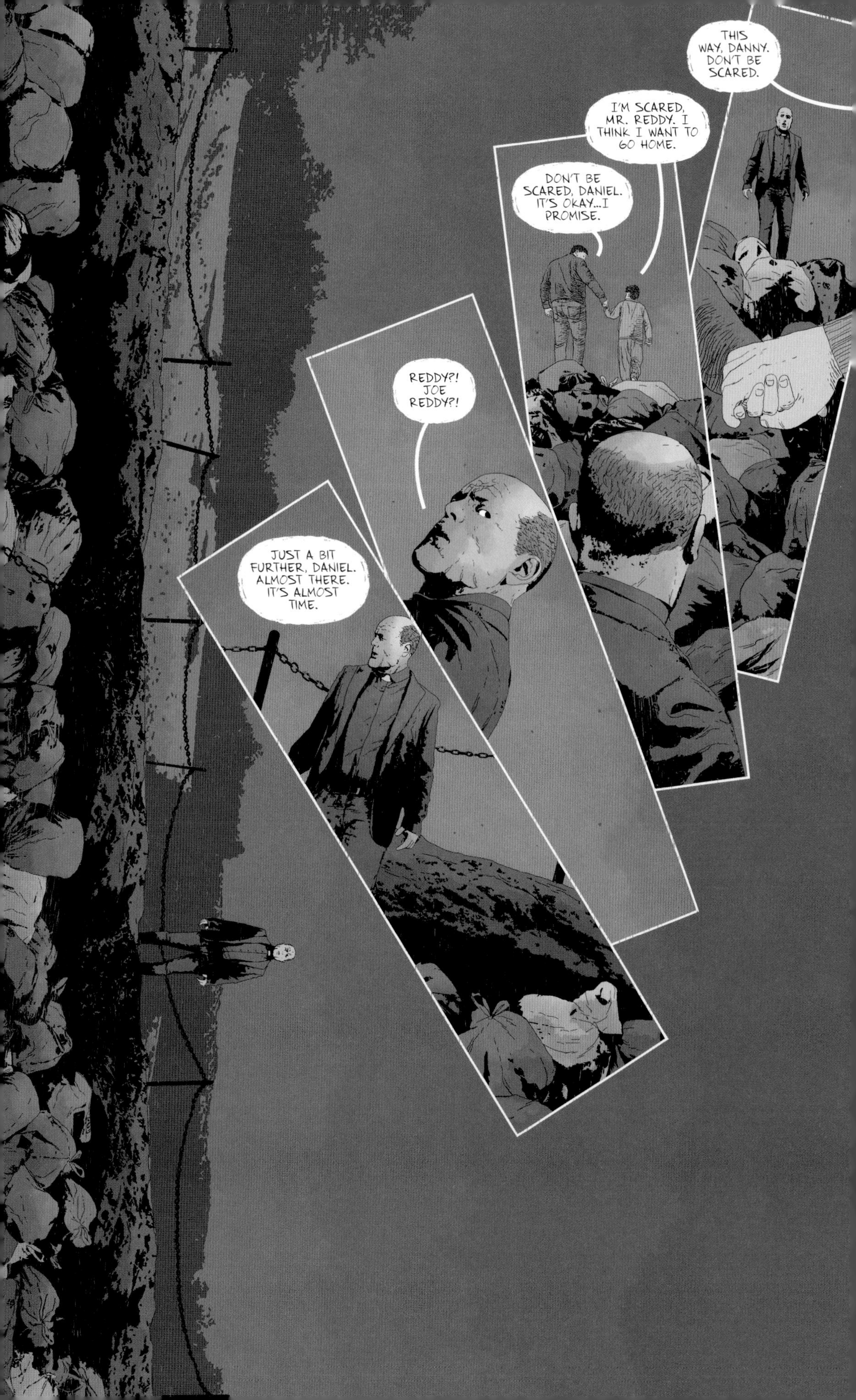
THIS WAY, DANNY. DON'T BE SCARED.
I'M SCARED, MR. REDDY. I THINK I WANT TO GO HOME.
DON'T BE SCARED, DANIEL. IT'S OKAY...I PROMISE.
REDDY?! JOE REDDY?!
JUST A BIT FURTHER, DANIEL. ALMOST THERE. IT'S ALMOST TIME.

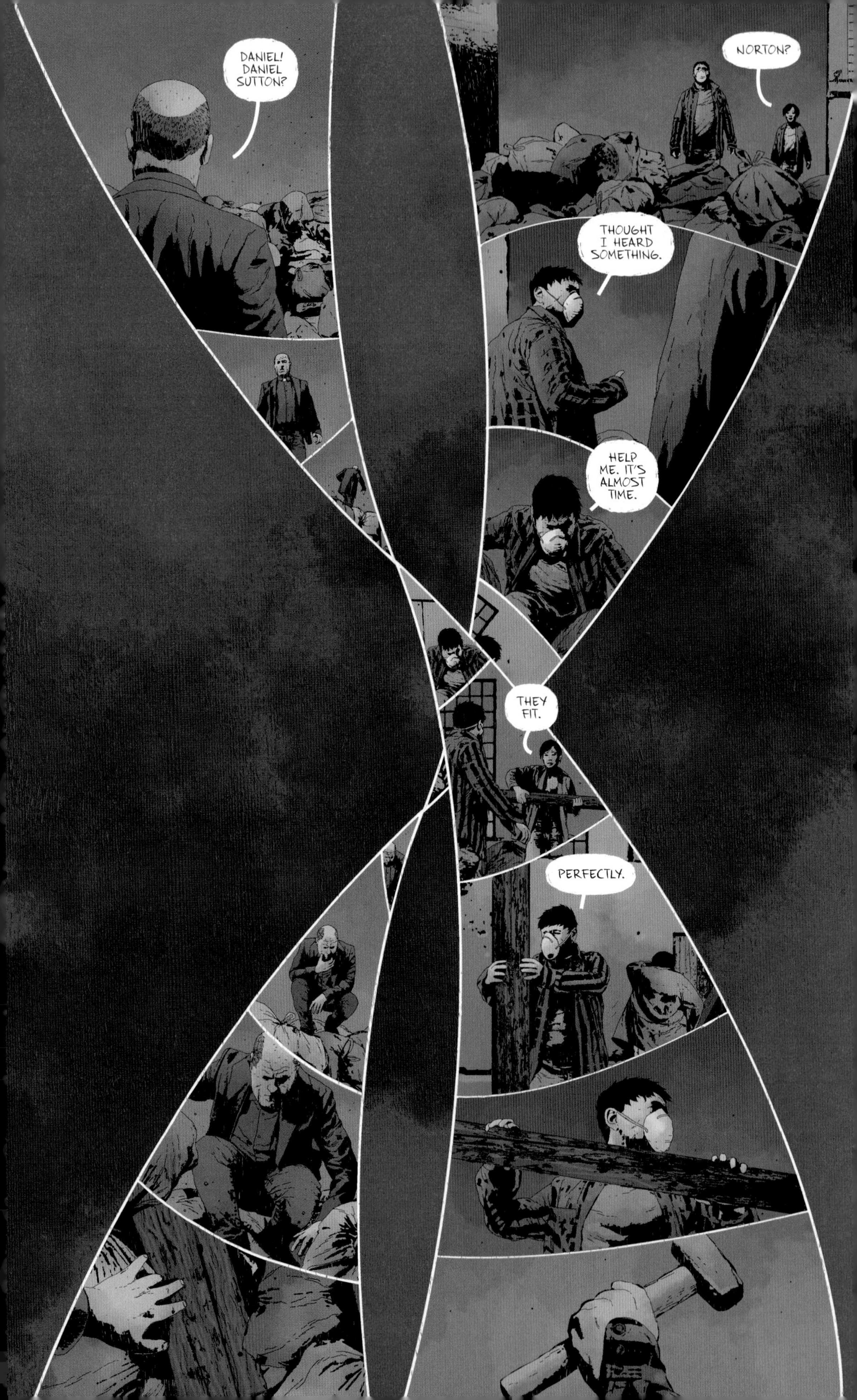
DANIEL! DANIEL SUTTON?
NORTON?
THOUGHT I HEARD SOMETHING.
HELP ME. IT'S ALMOST TIME.
THEY FIT.
PERFECTLY.

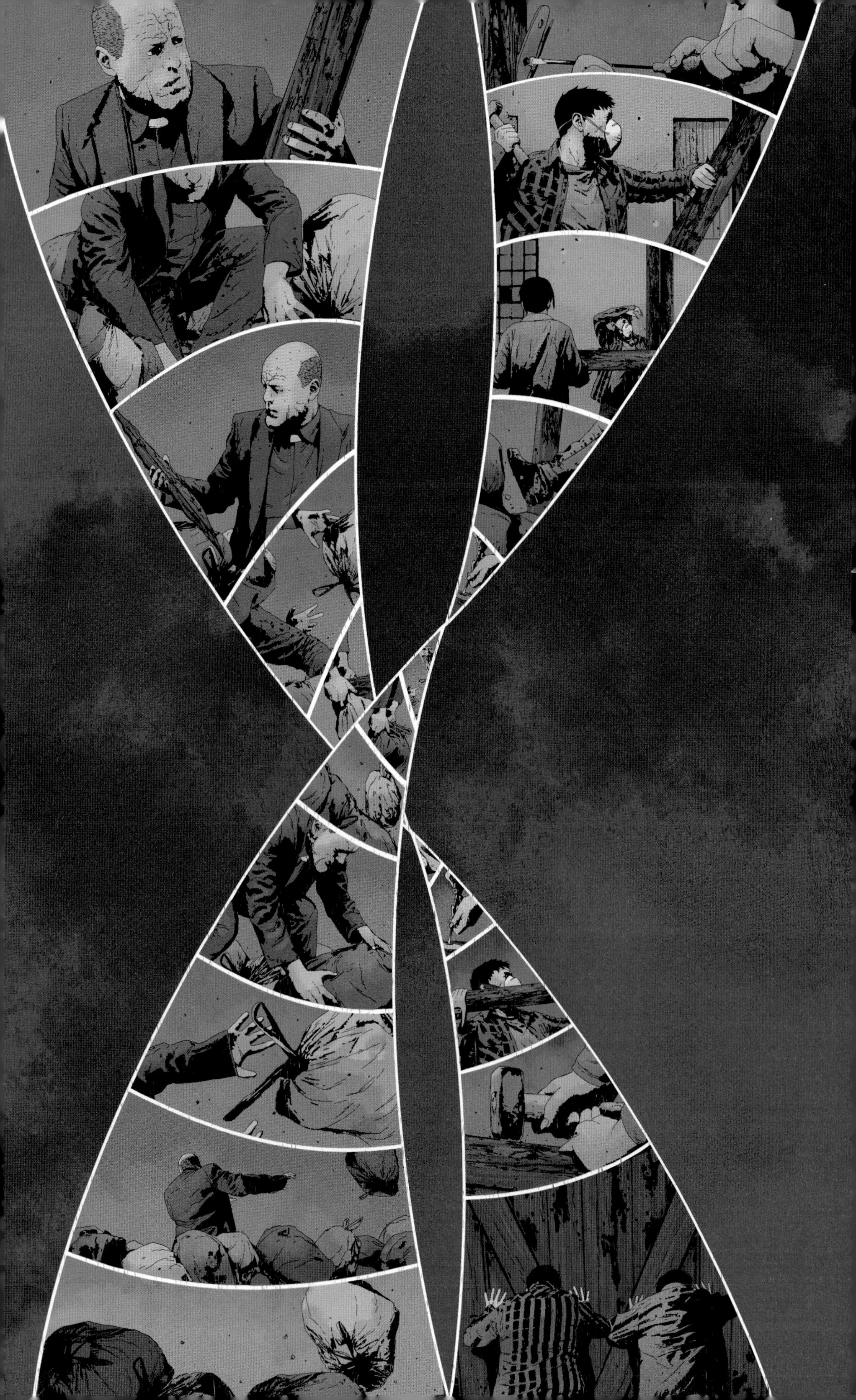

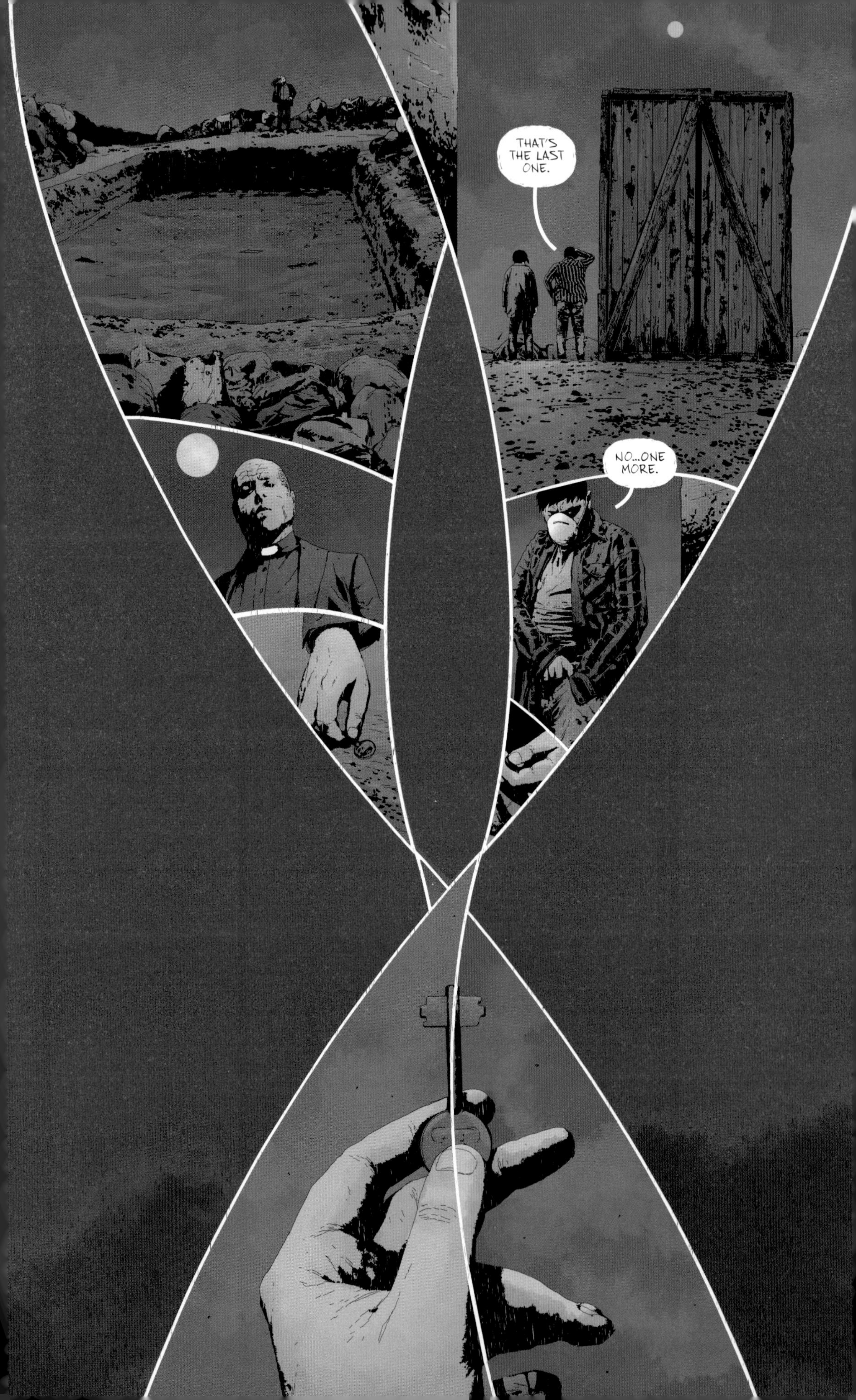
THAT'S THE LAST ONE.
NO...ONE MORE.

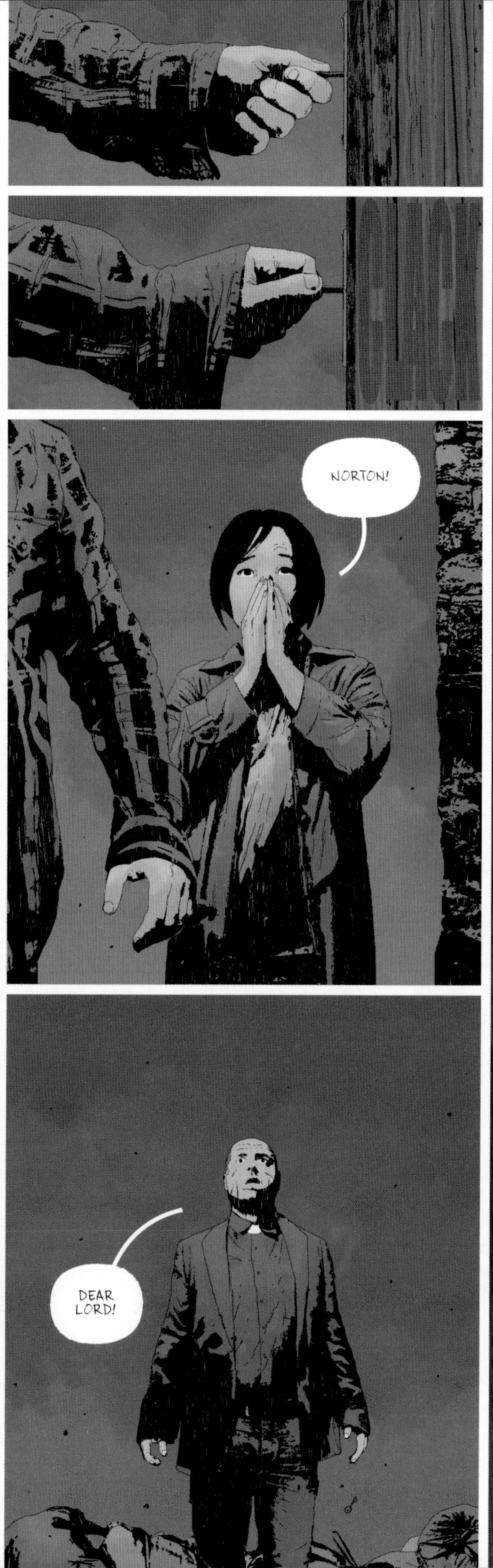
NORTON!
DEAR LORD!

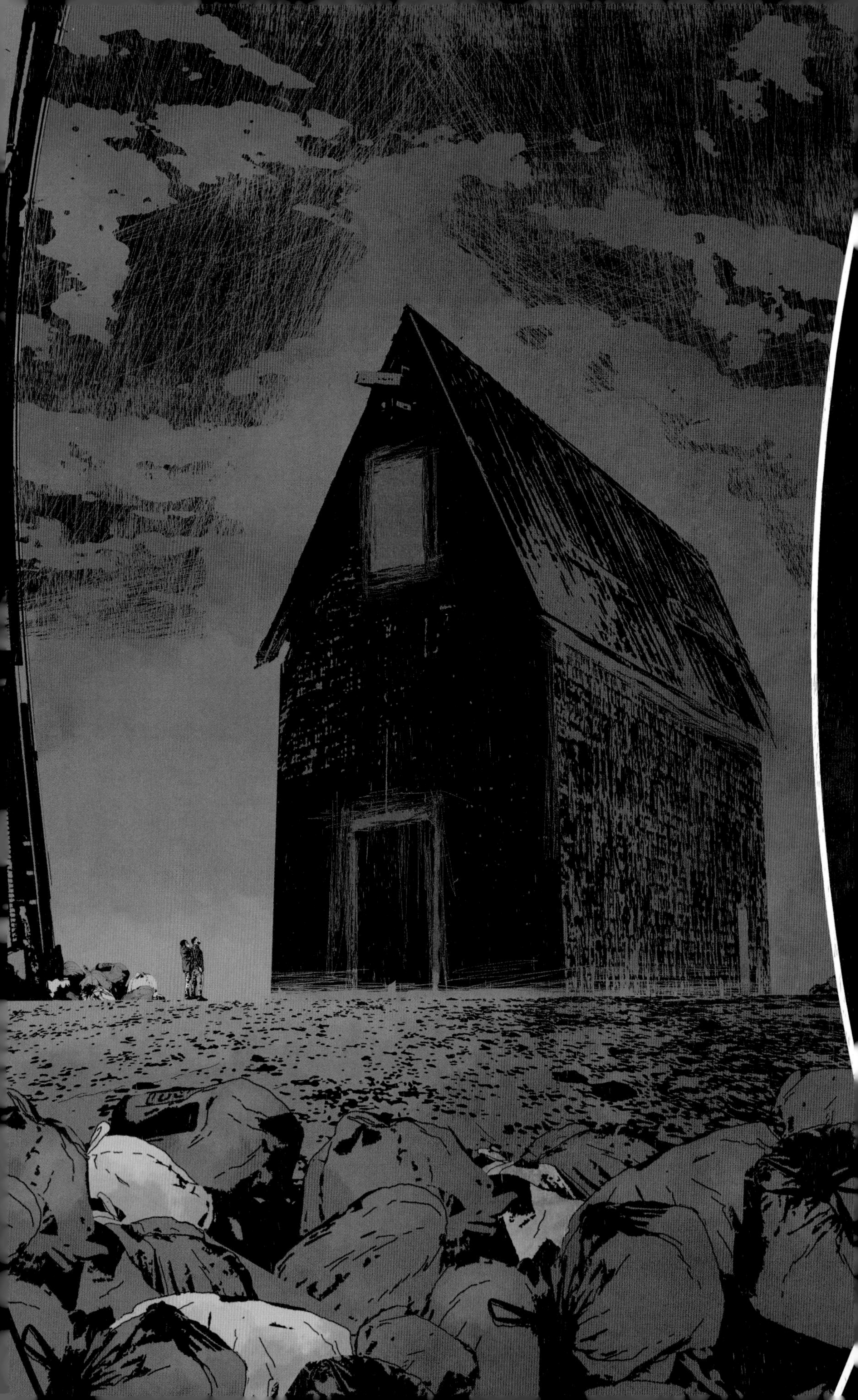

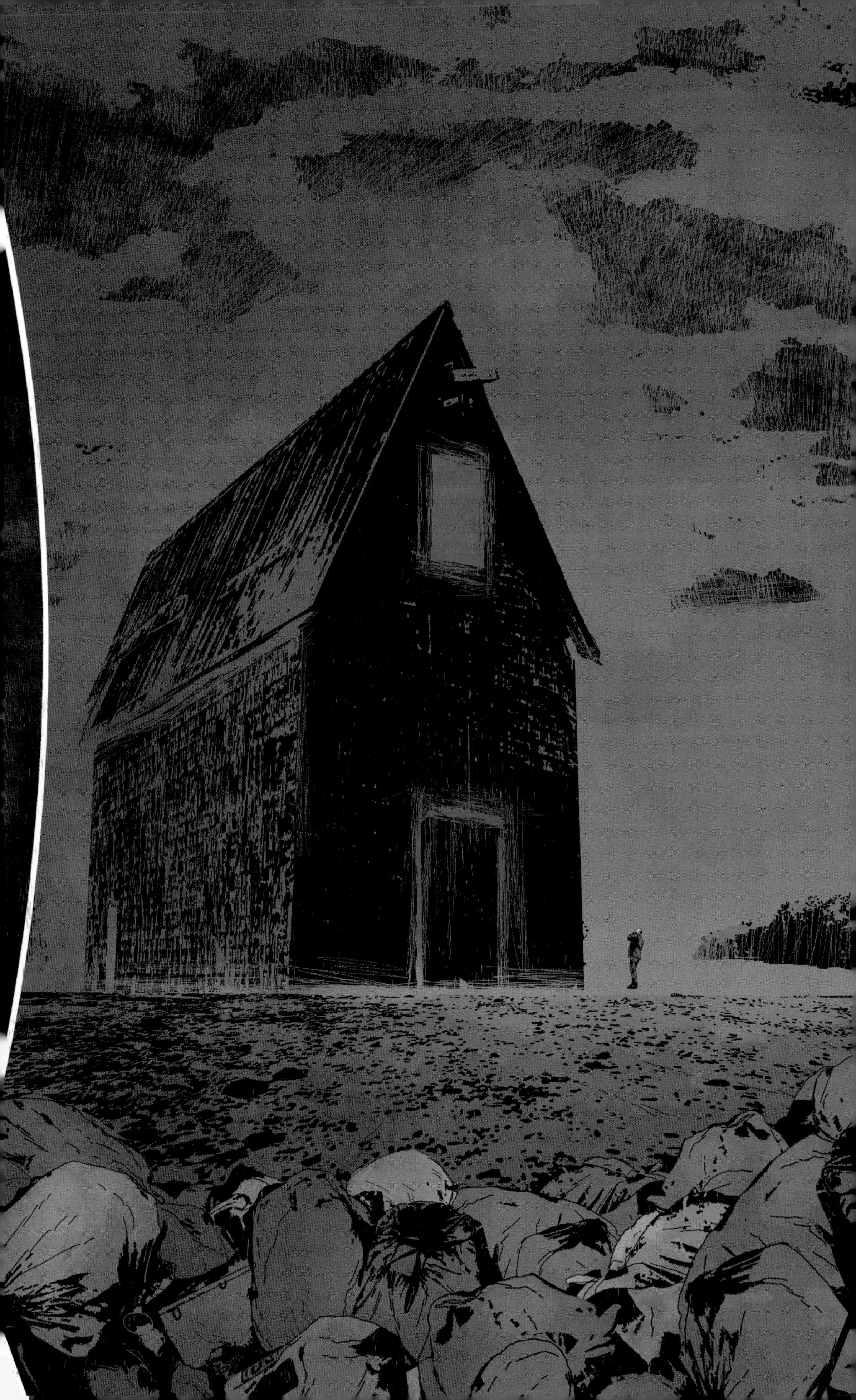

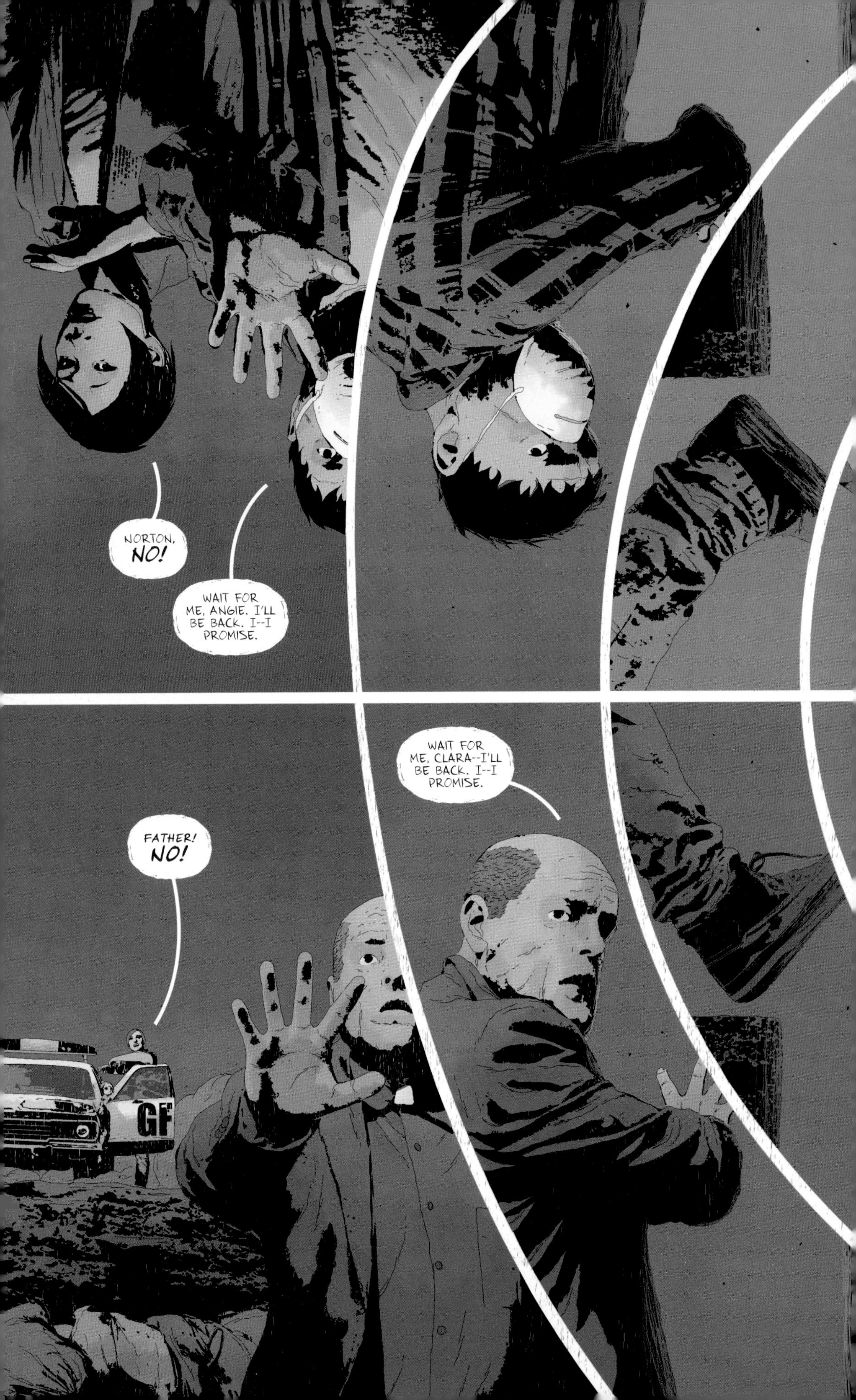
NORTON, NO!
WAIT FOR ME, ANGIE. I'LL BE BACK. I--I PROMISE.
WAIT FOR ME, CLARA--I'LL BE BACK. I--I PROMISE.
FATHER! NO!
GF

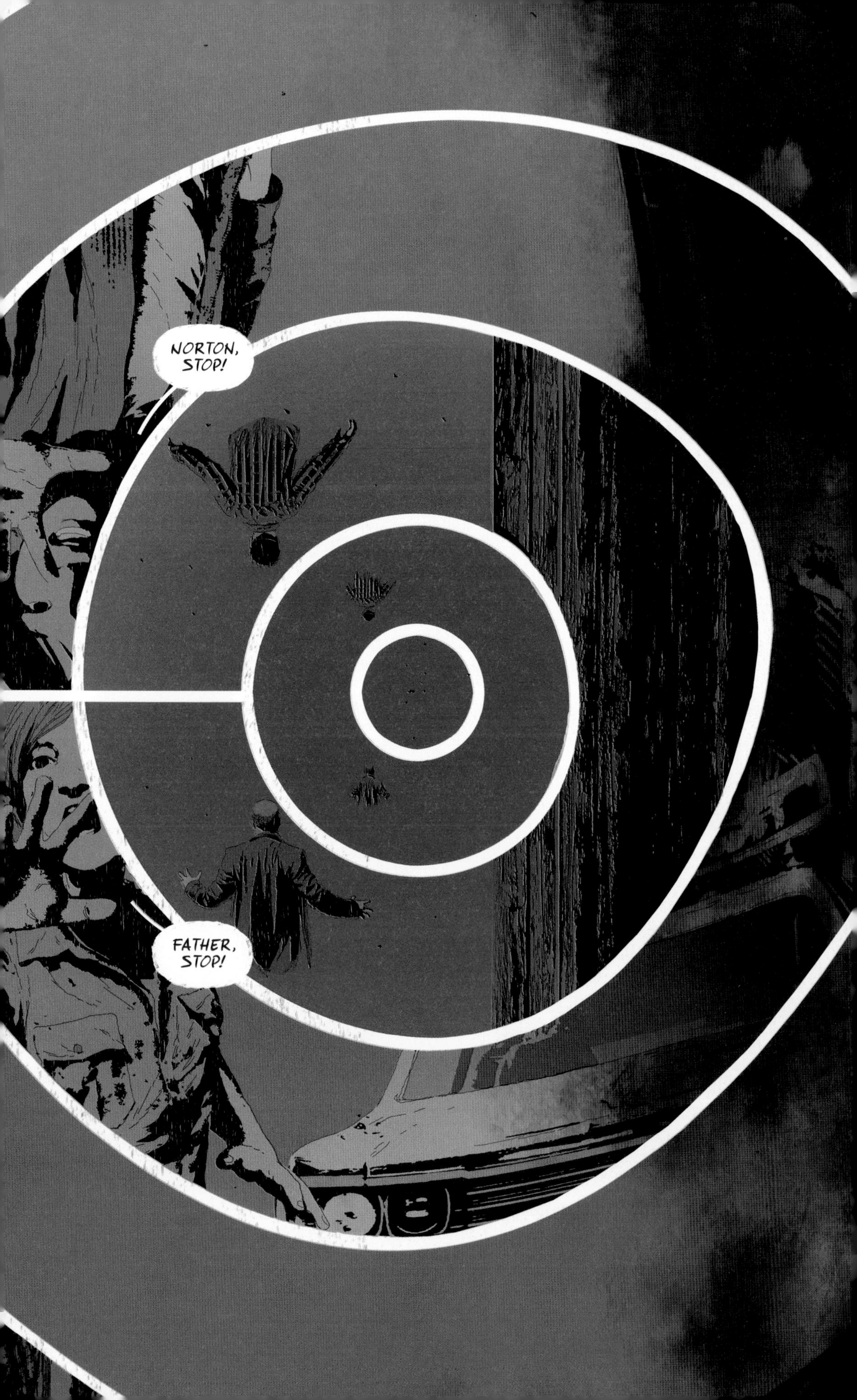
NORTON, STOP!
FATHER, STOP!

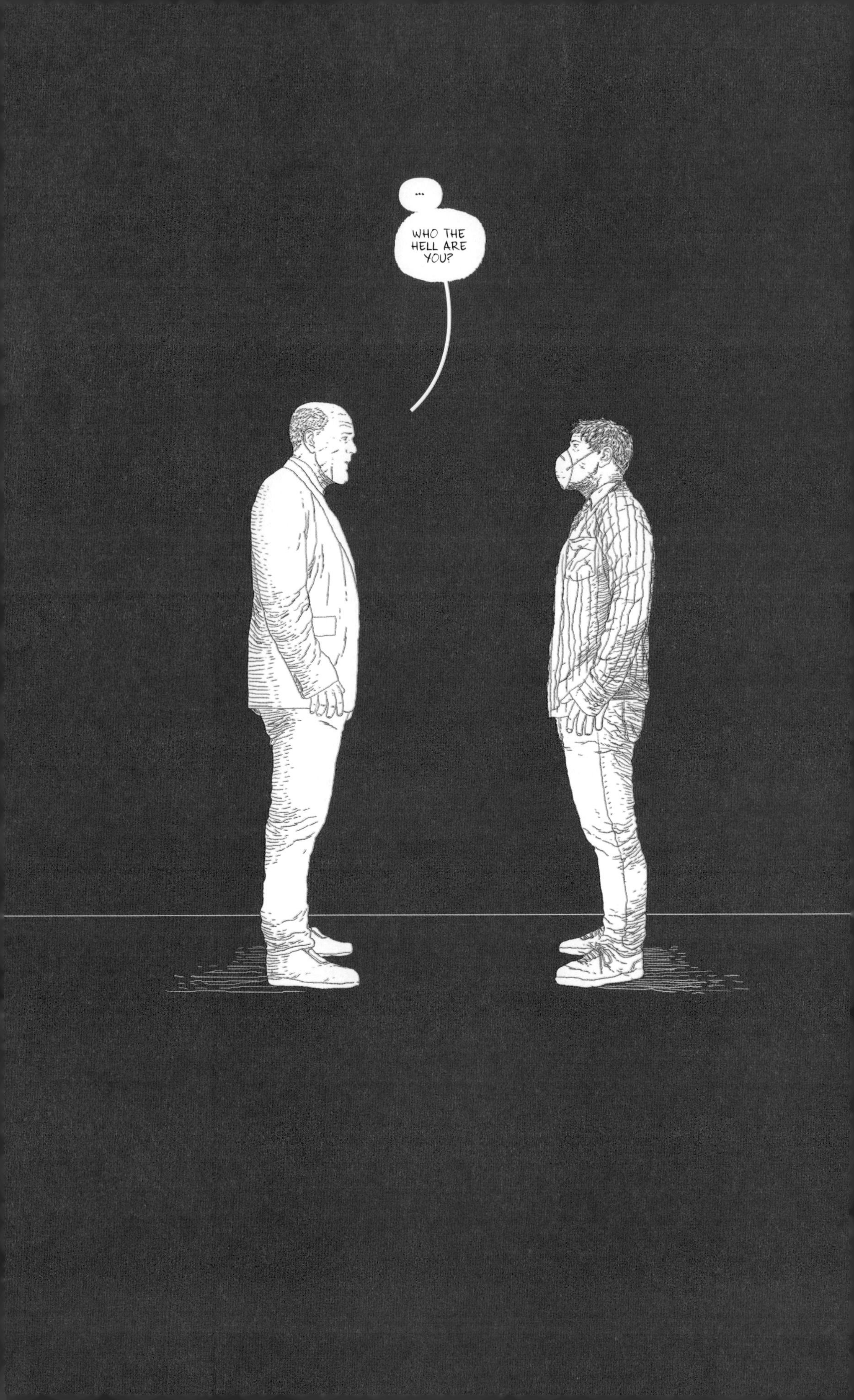
...
WHO THE HELL ARE YOU?

GIDEON
FALLS

Eleven

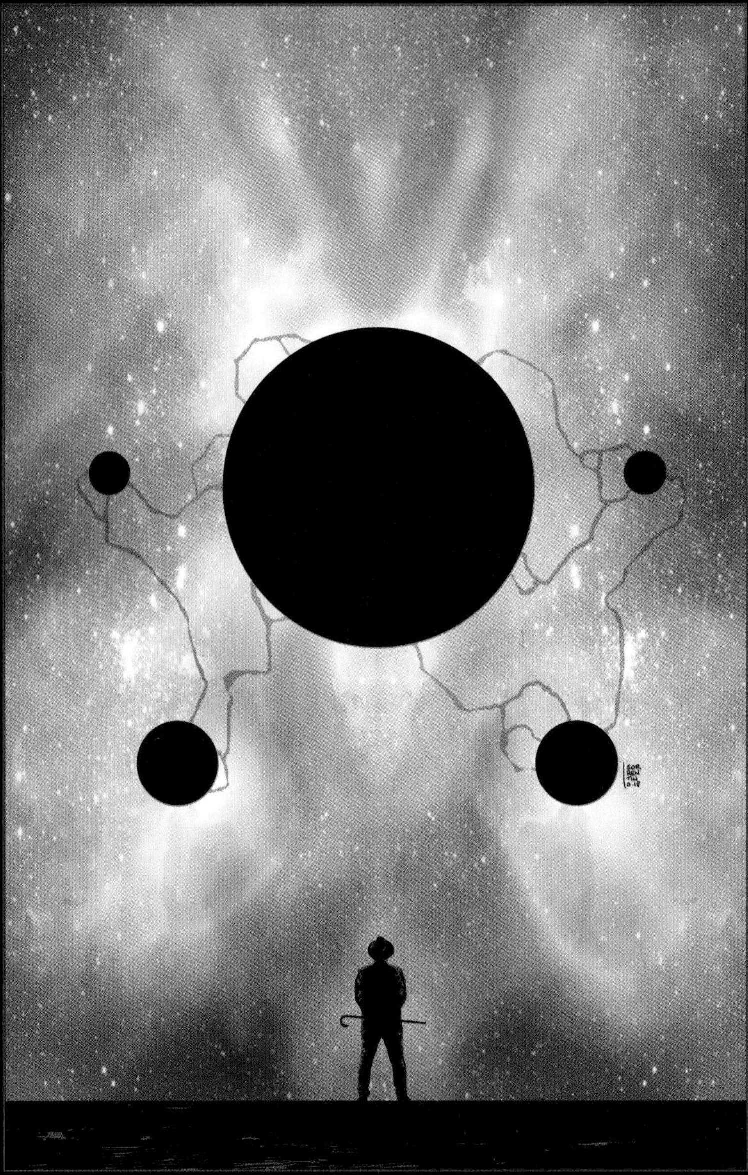

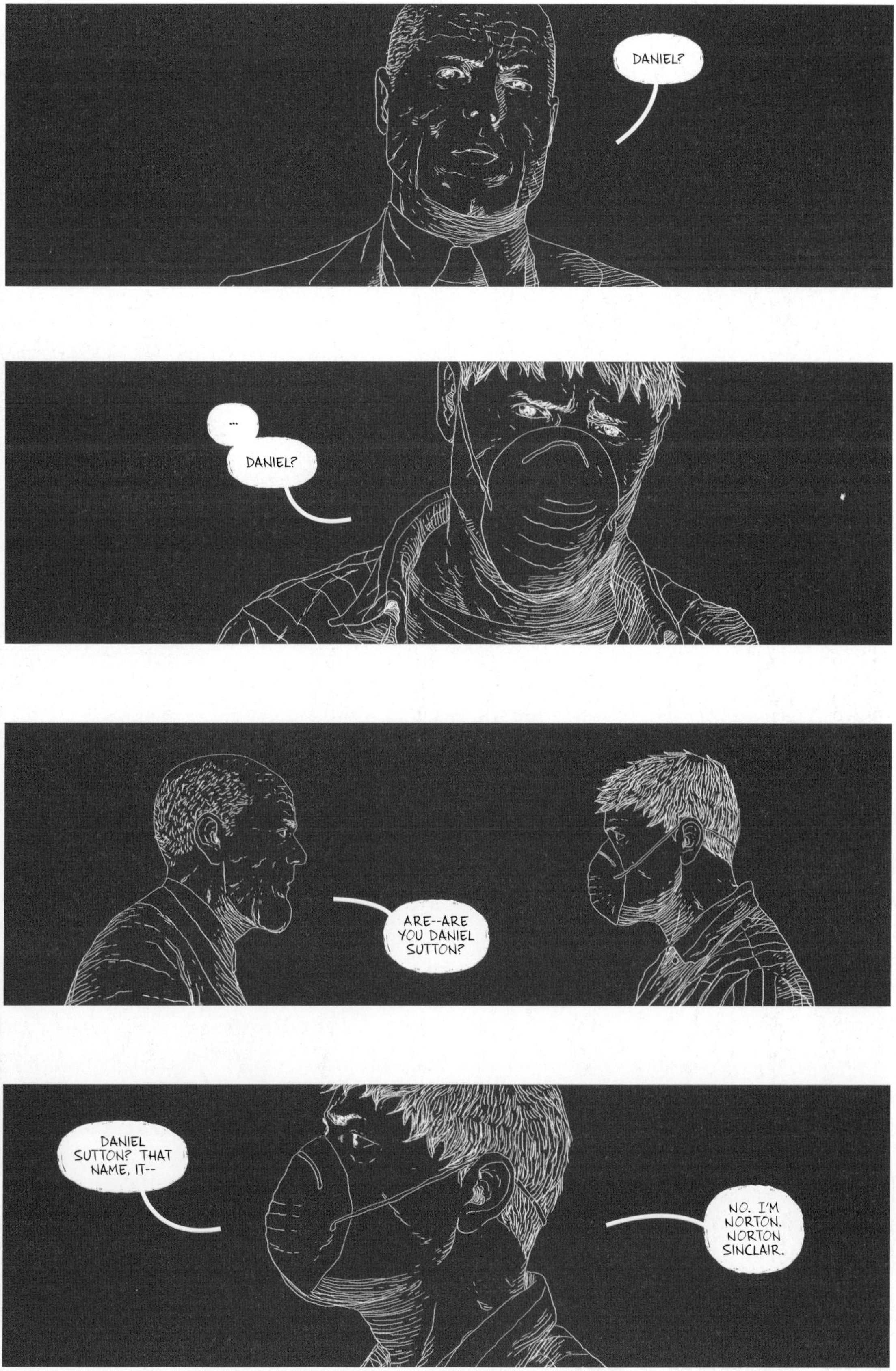
DANIEL?
...
DANIEL?
ARE--ARE YOU DANIEL SUTTON?
DANIEL SUTTON? THAT NAME, IT--
NO. I'M NORTON. NORTON SINCLAIR.

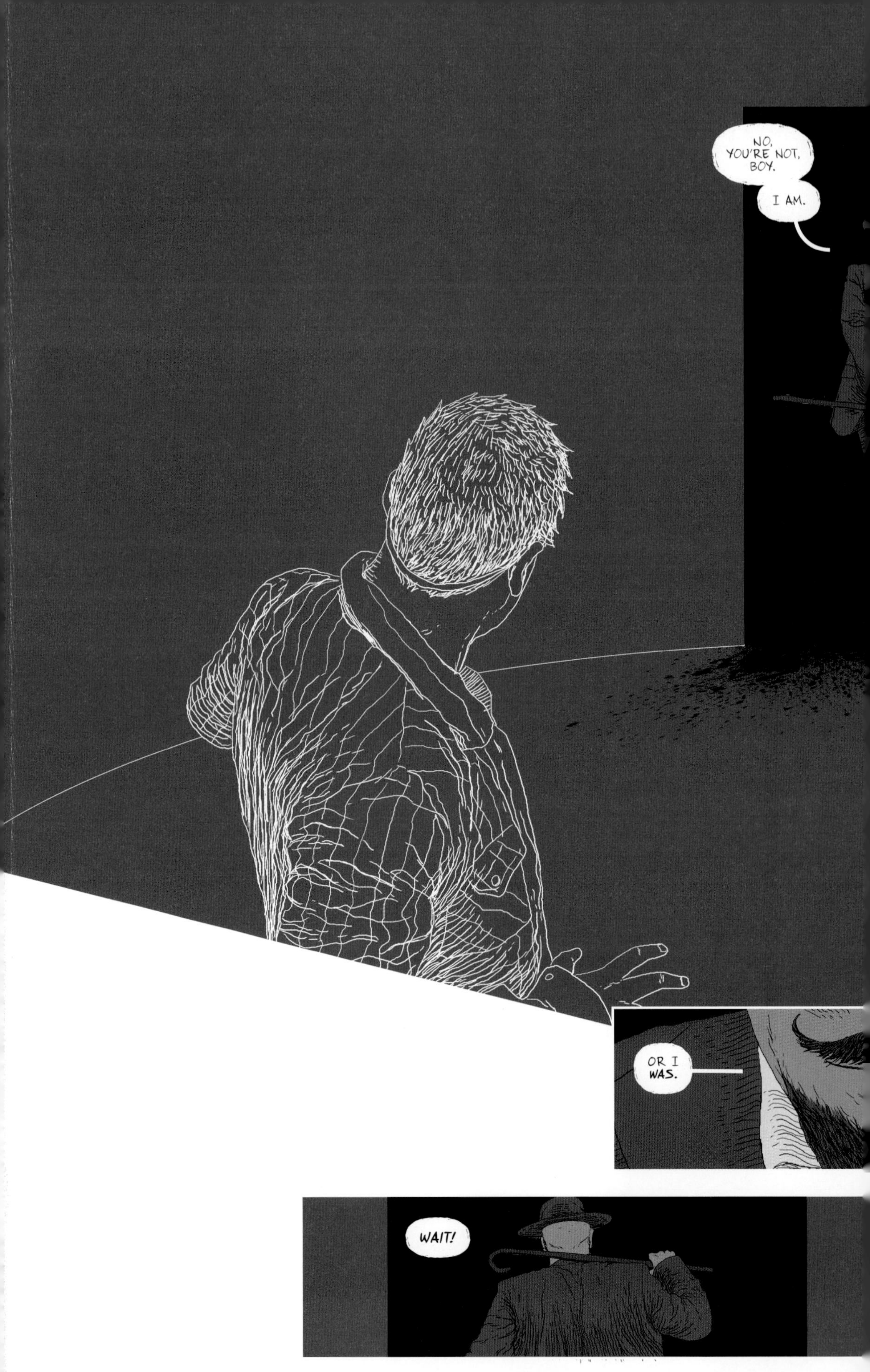
NO, YOU'RE NOT, BOY.
I AM.
OR I WAS.
WAIT!

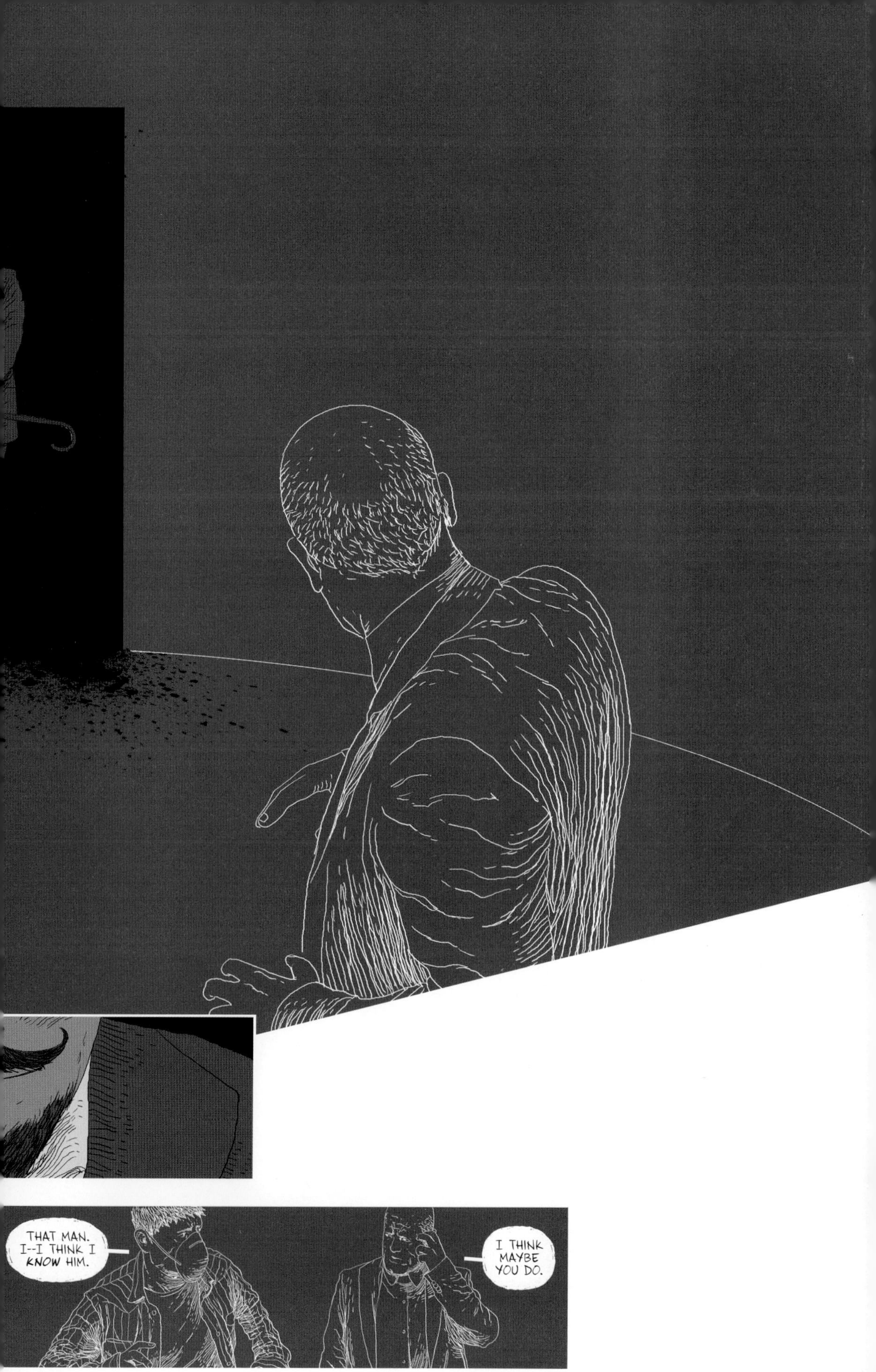
THAT MAN. I--I THINK I KNOW HIM.
I THINK MAYBE YOU DO.

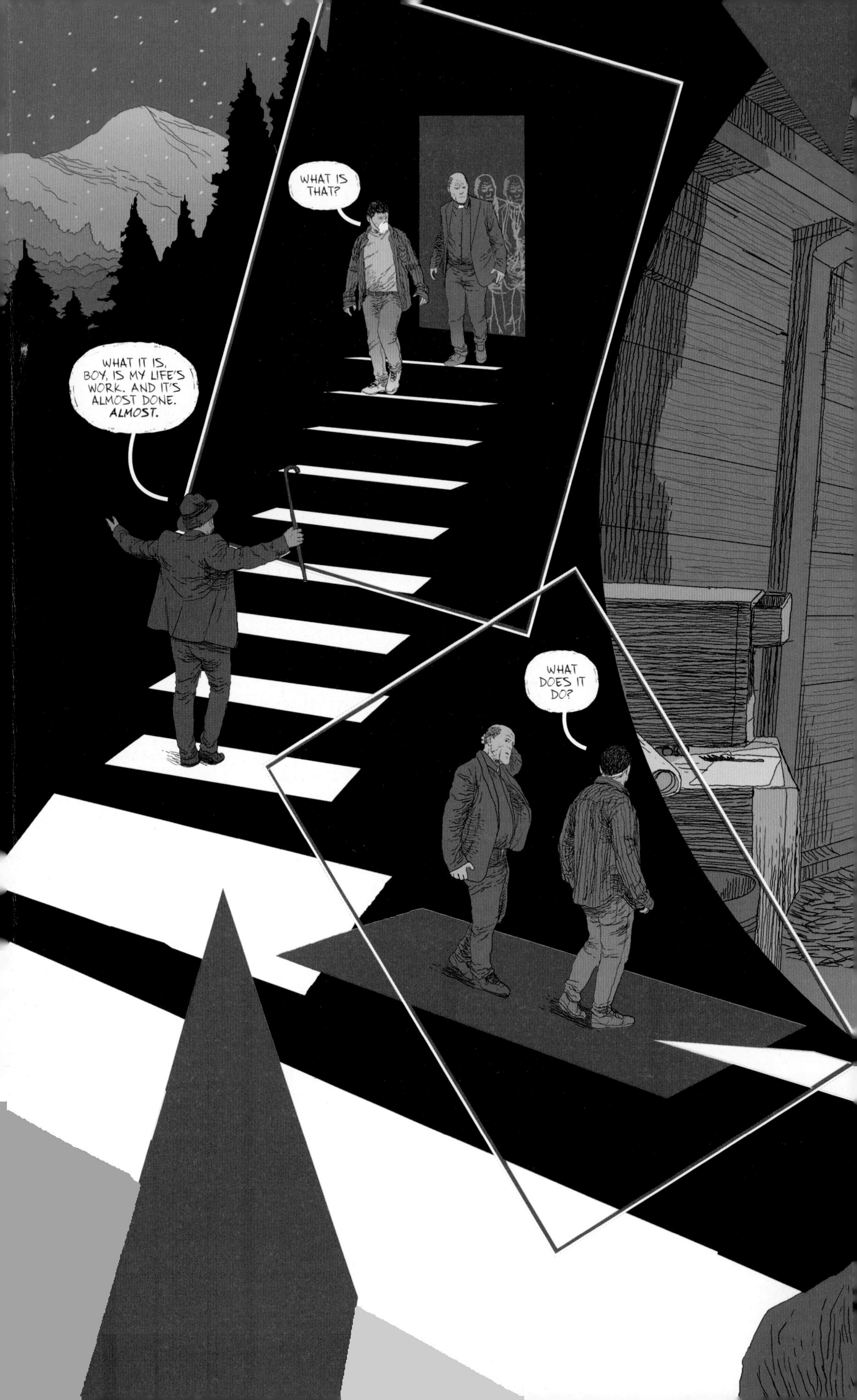
WHAT IS THAT?
WHAT IT IS, BOY, IS MY LIFE'S WORK. AND IT'S ALMOST DONE. **ALMOST.**
WHAT DOES IT DO?

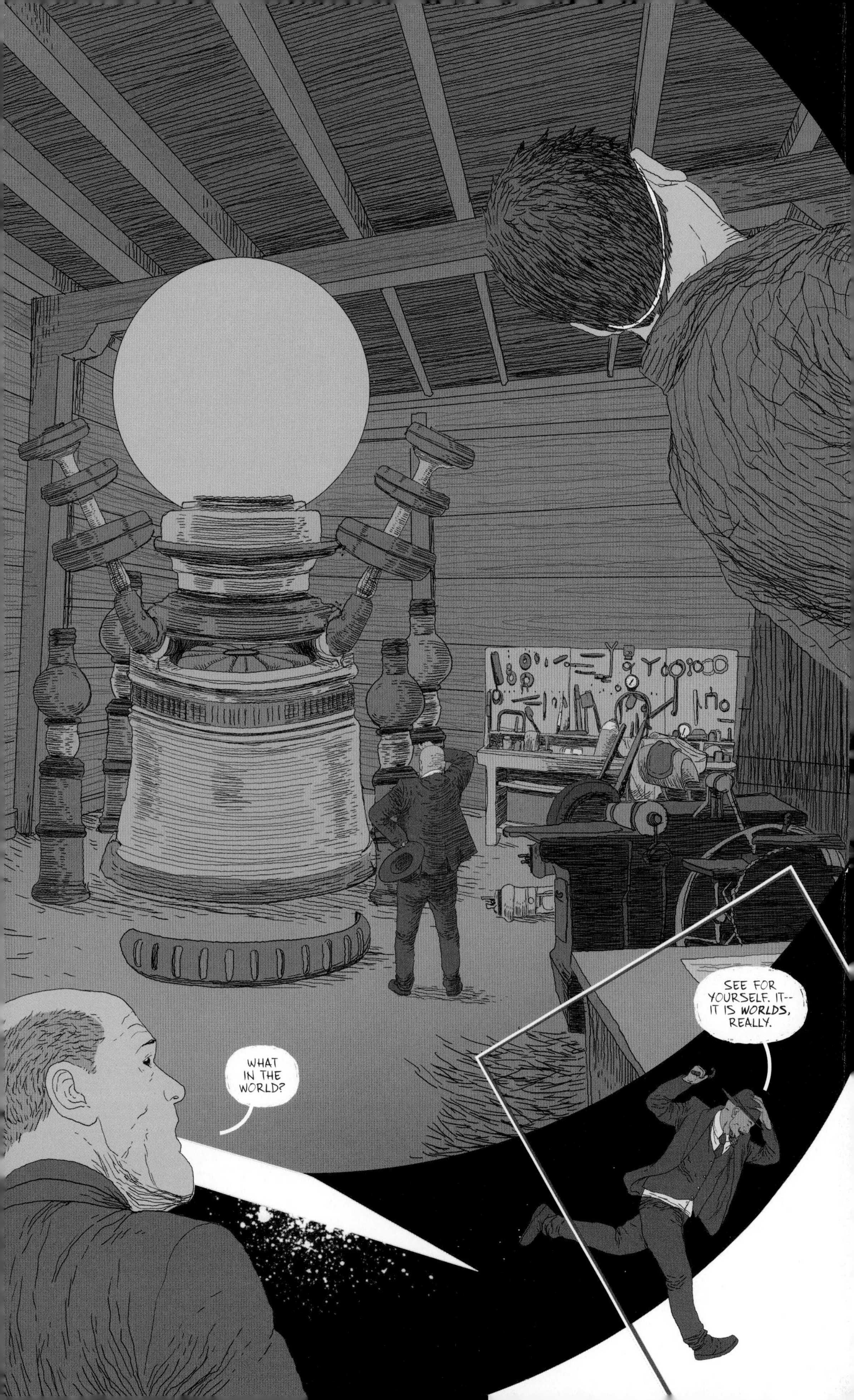
WHAT IN THE WORLD?
SEE FOR YOURSELF. IT-- IT IS WORLDS, REALLY.

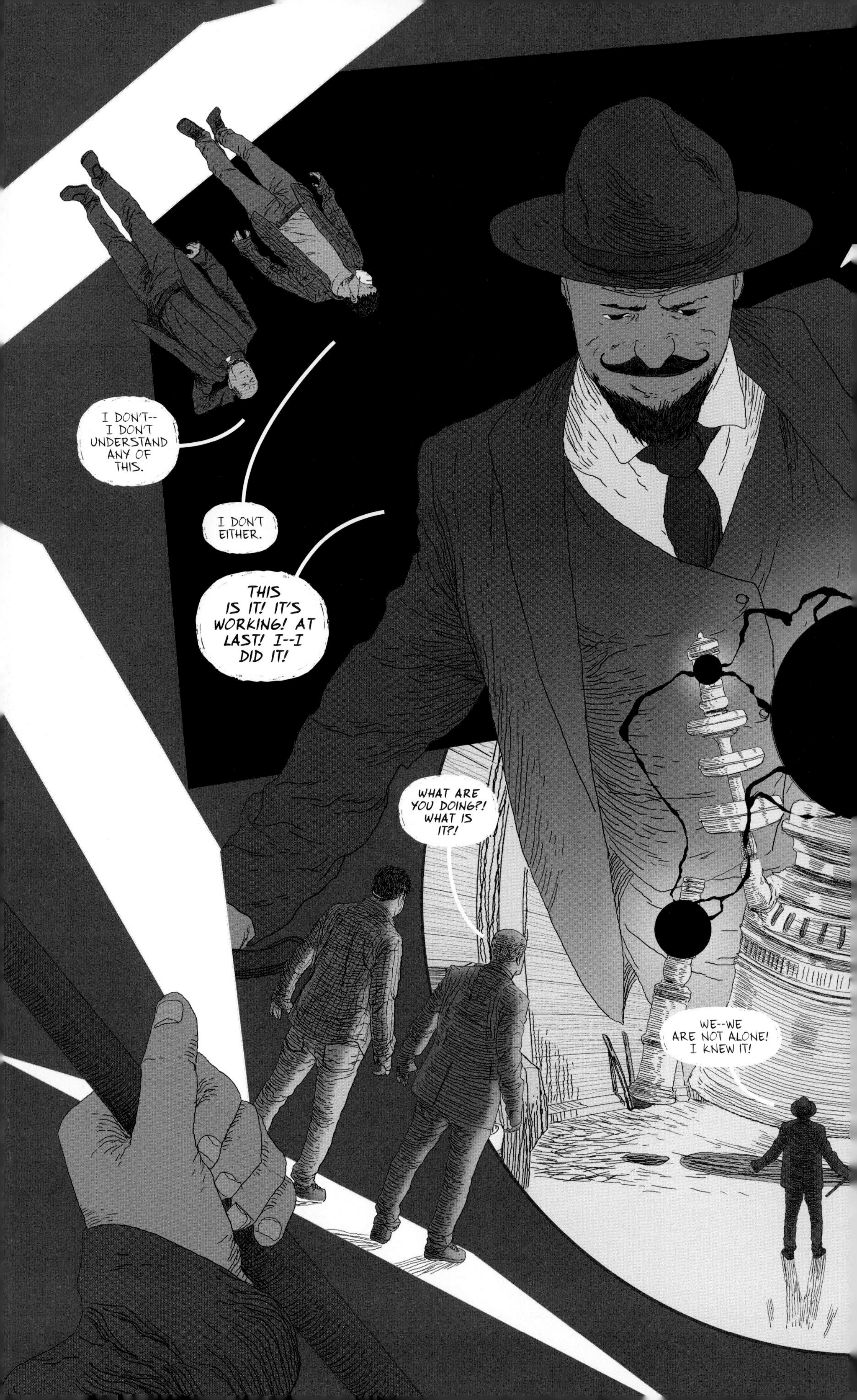
I DON'T-- I DON'T UNDERSTAND ANY OF THIS.
I DON'T EITHER.
THIS IS IT! IT'S WORKING! AT LAST! I--I DID IT!
WHAT ARE YOU DOING?! WHAT IS IT?!
WE--WE ARE NOT ALONE! I KNEW IT!

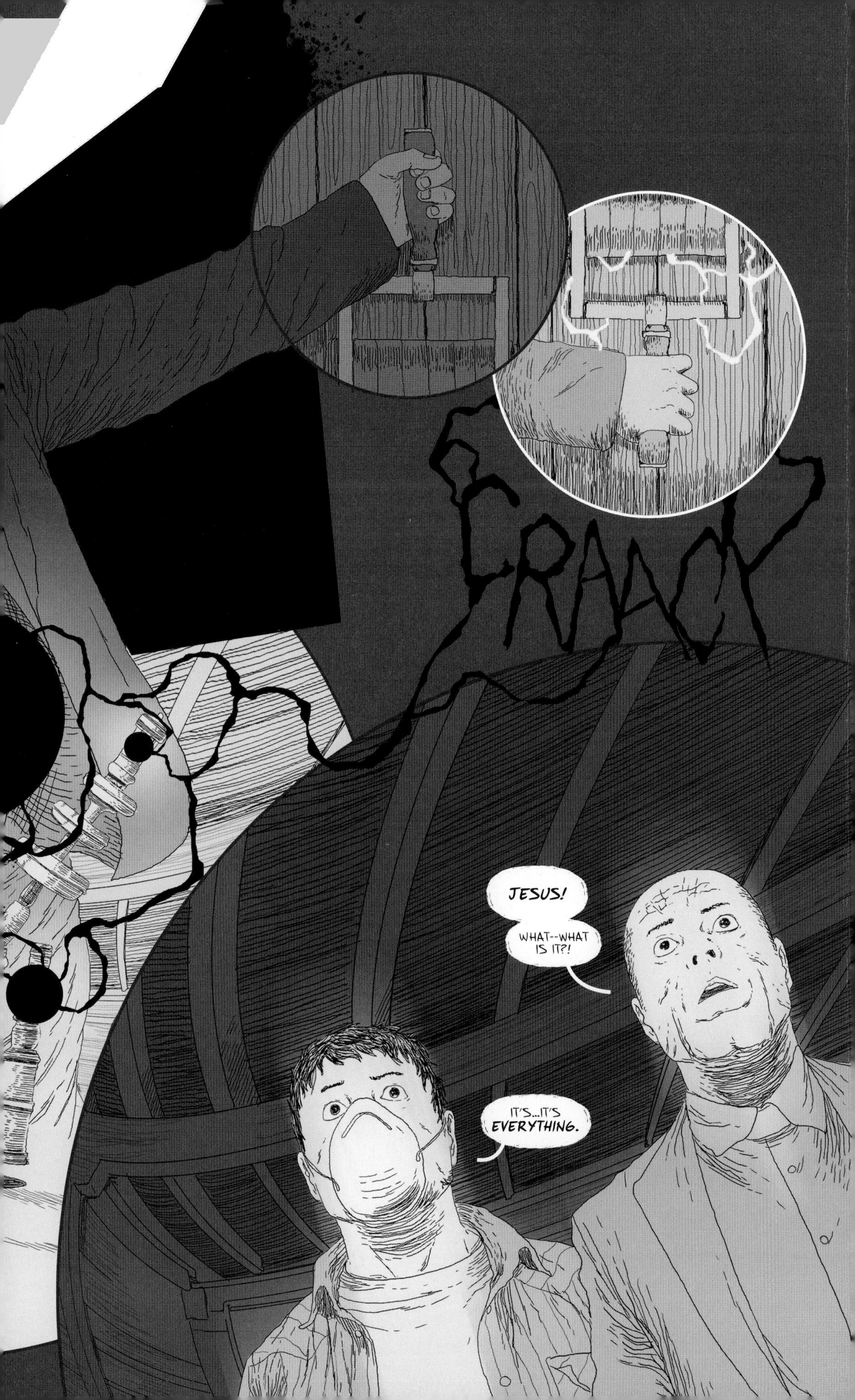
CRAACK
JESUS!
WHAT--WHAT IS IT?!
IT'S...IT'S EVERYTHING.

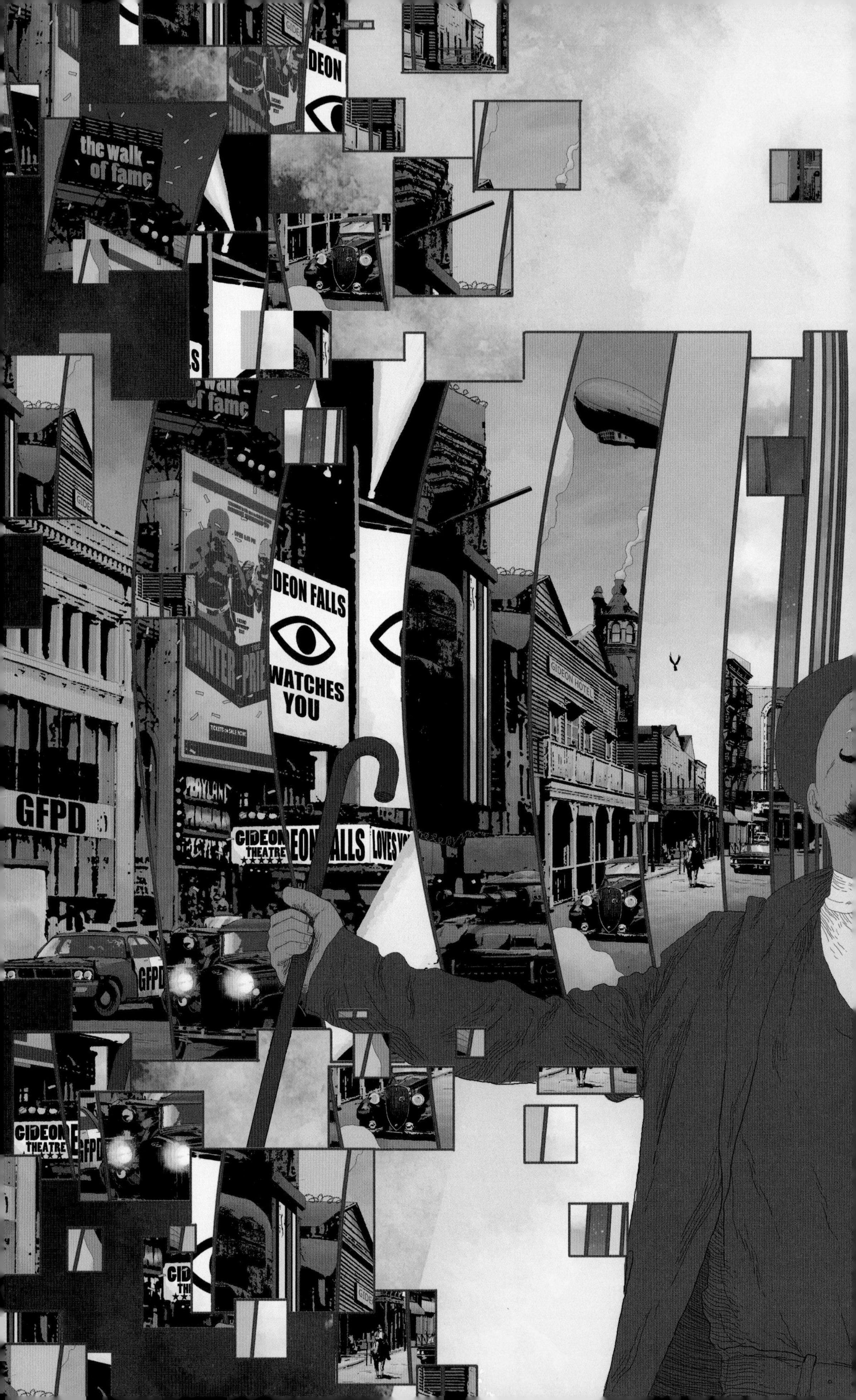

DEON
the walk of fame
DEON FALLS
WATCHES YOU
HUNTER
TICKETS ON SALE NOW!
GFPD
GIDEON THEATRE
EON FALLS
GIDEON HOTEL
GFPD
GIDEON THEATRE

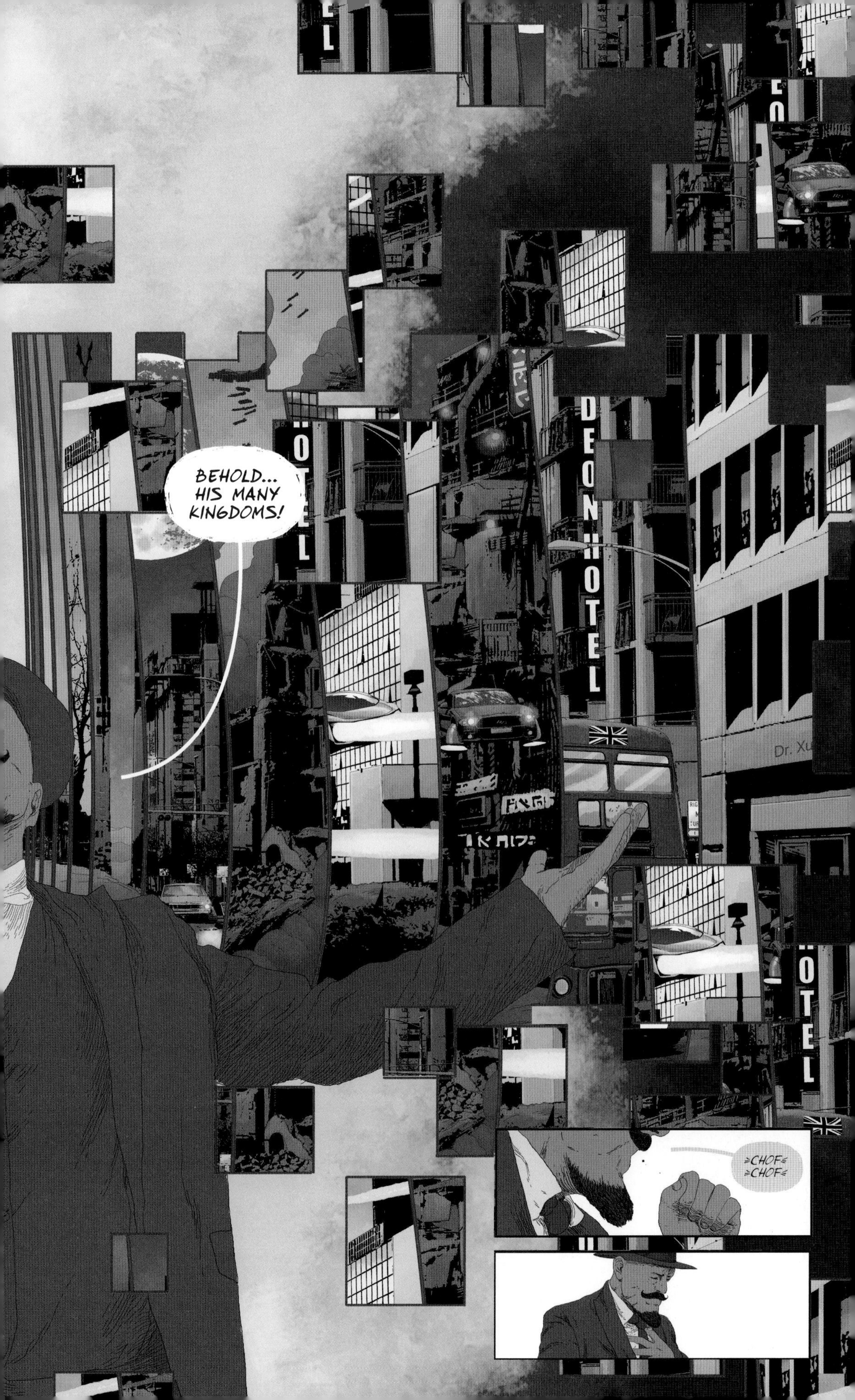
BEHOLD... HIS MANY KINGDOMS!
HOTEL
DEON HOTEL
HOTEL
CHOF CHOF

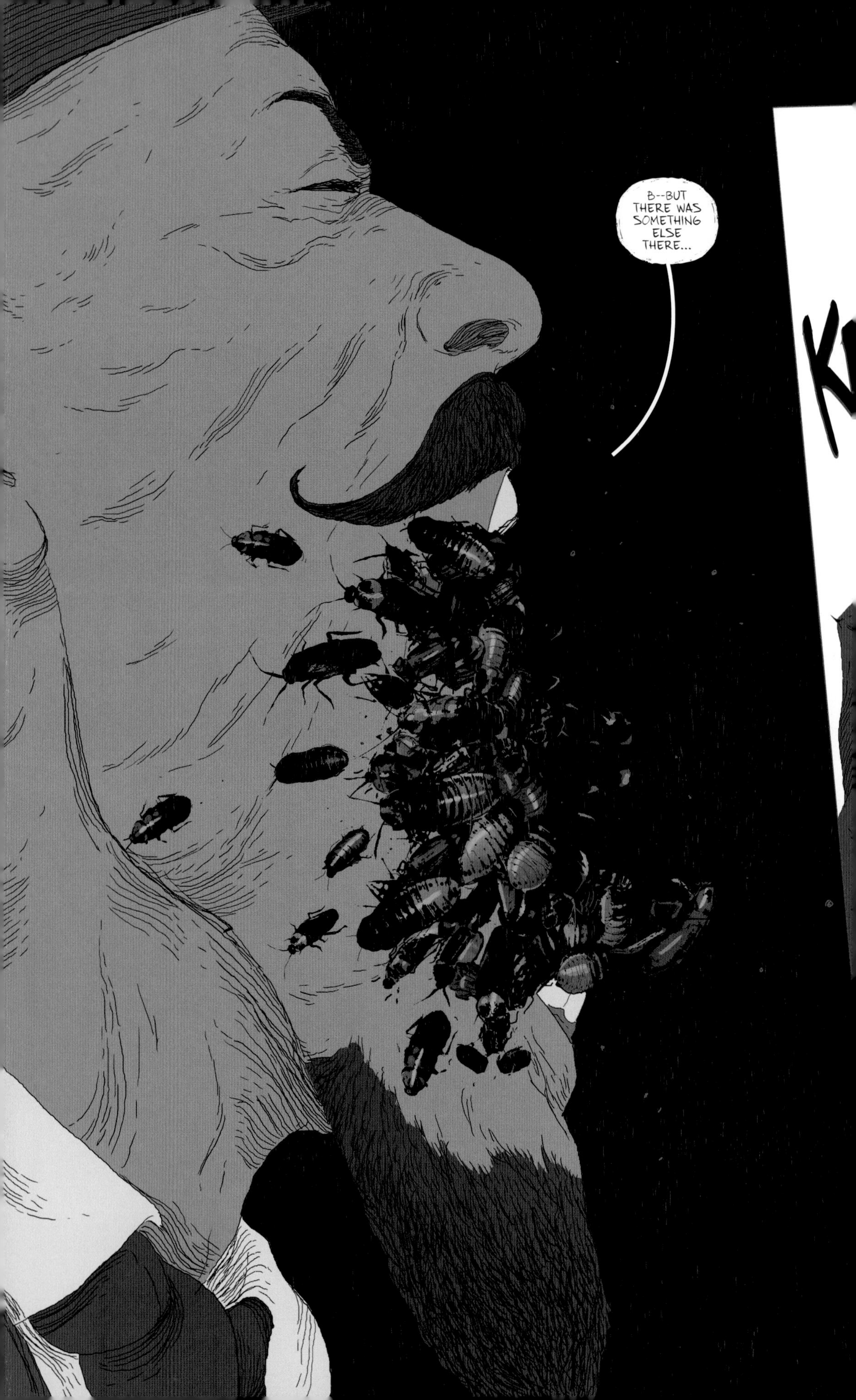
B--BUT THERE WAS SOMETHING ELSE THERE...

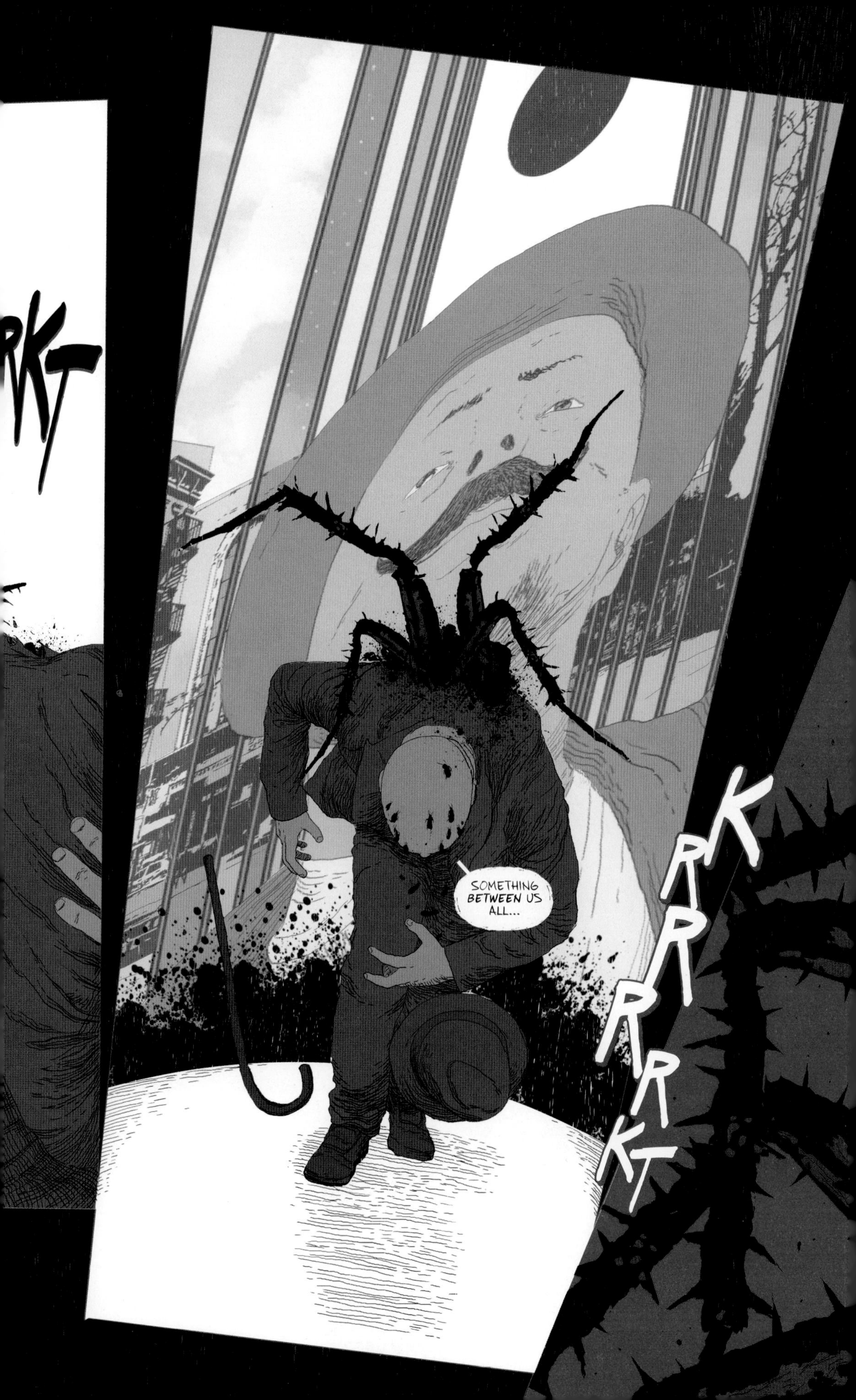
RKT
SOMETHING BETWEEN US ALL...
KRRRRRKT

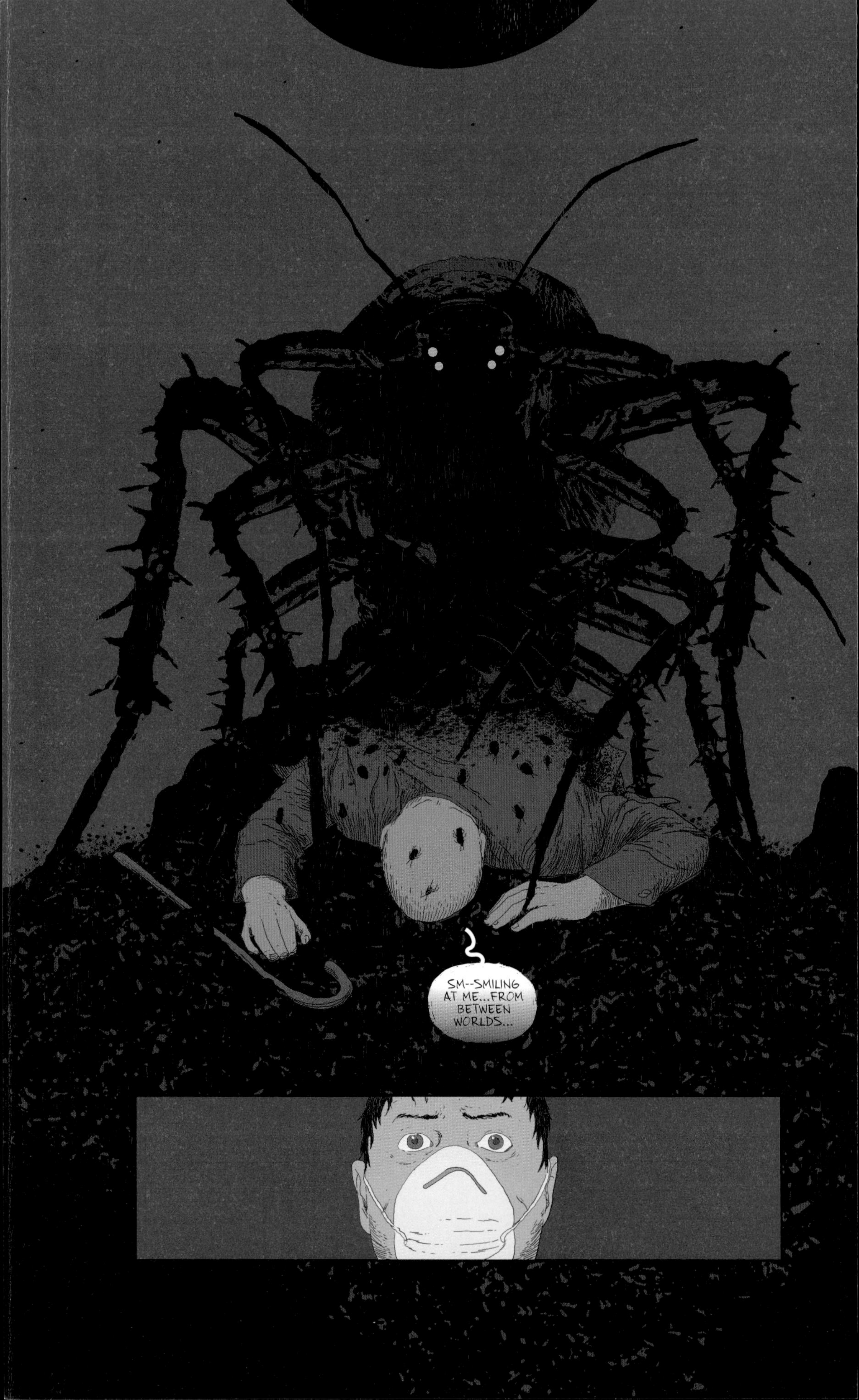
SM--SMILING AT ME...FROM BETWEEN WORLDS...

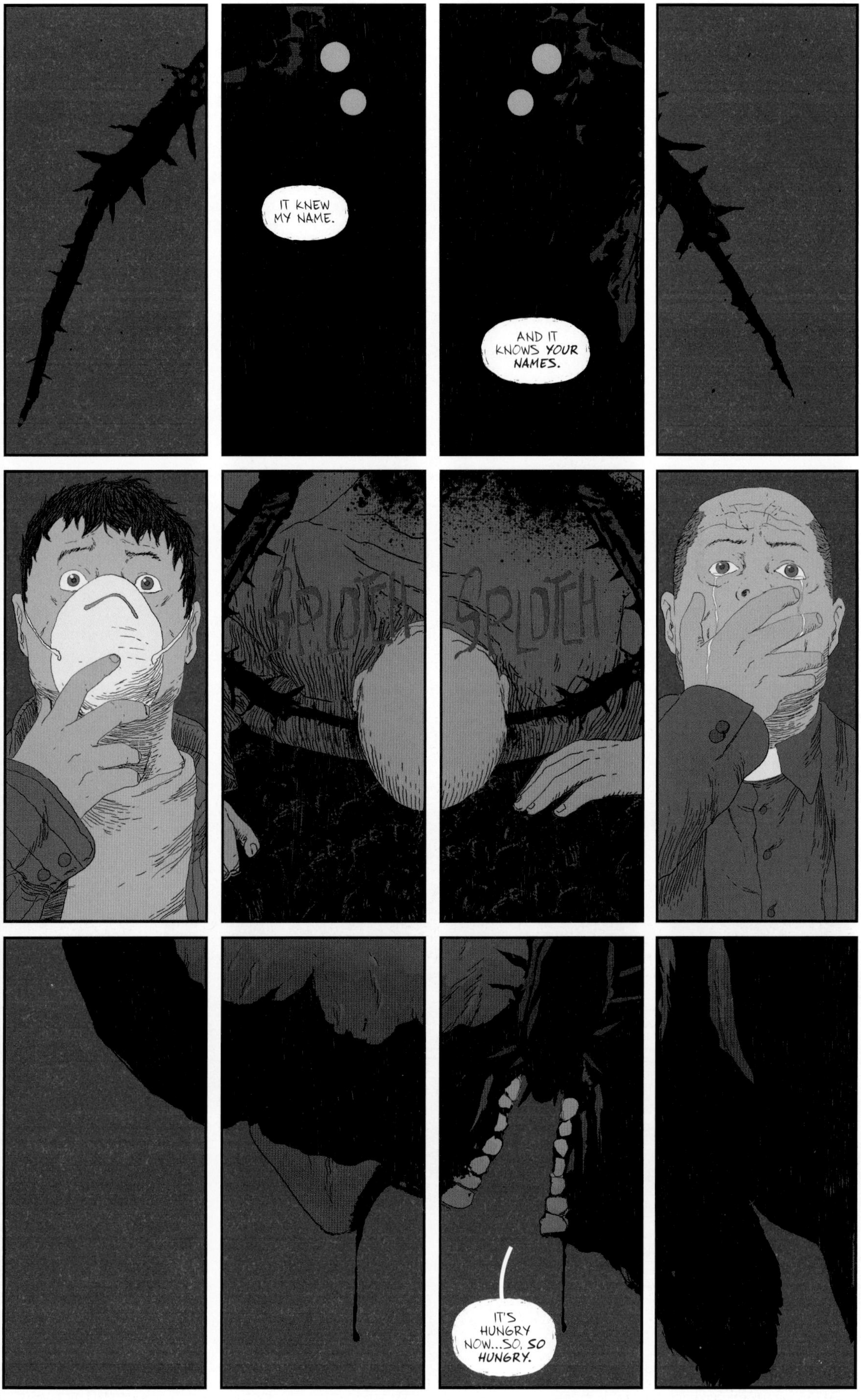
IT KNEW MY NAME.
AND IT KNOWS YOUR NAMES.
SPLOTCH
SPLOTCH
IT'S HUNGRY NOW...SO, SO HUNGRY.

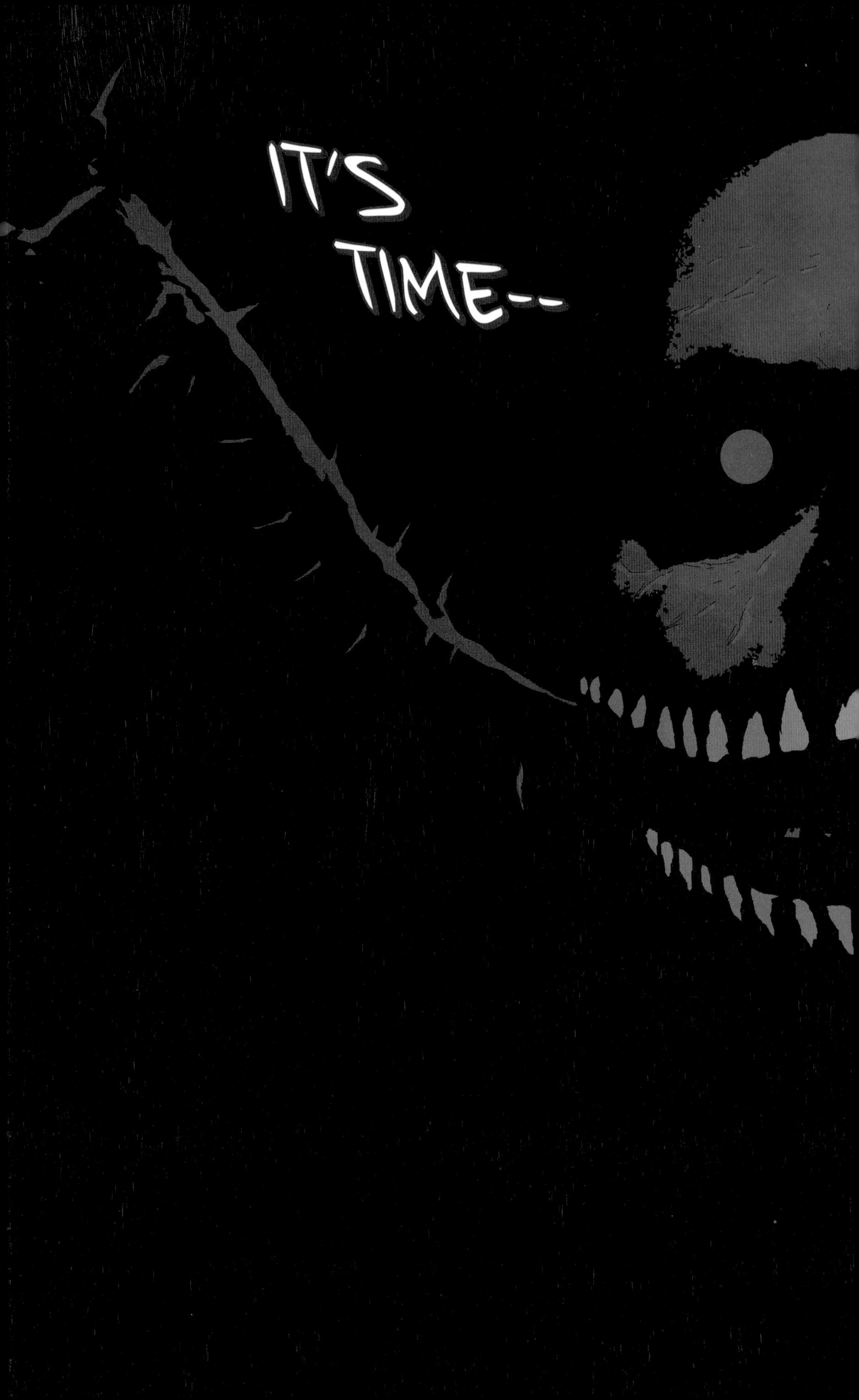
IT'S TIME--

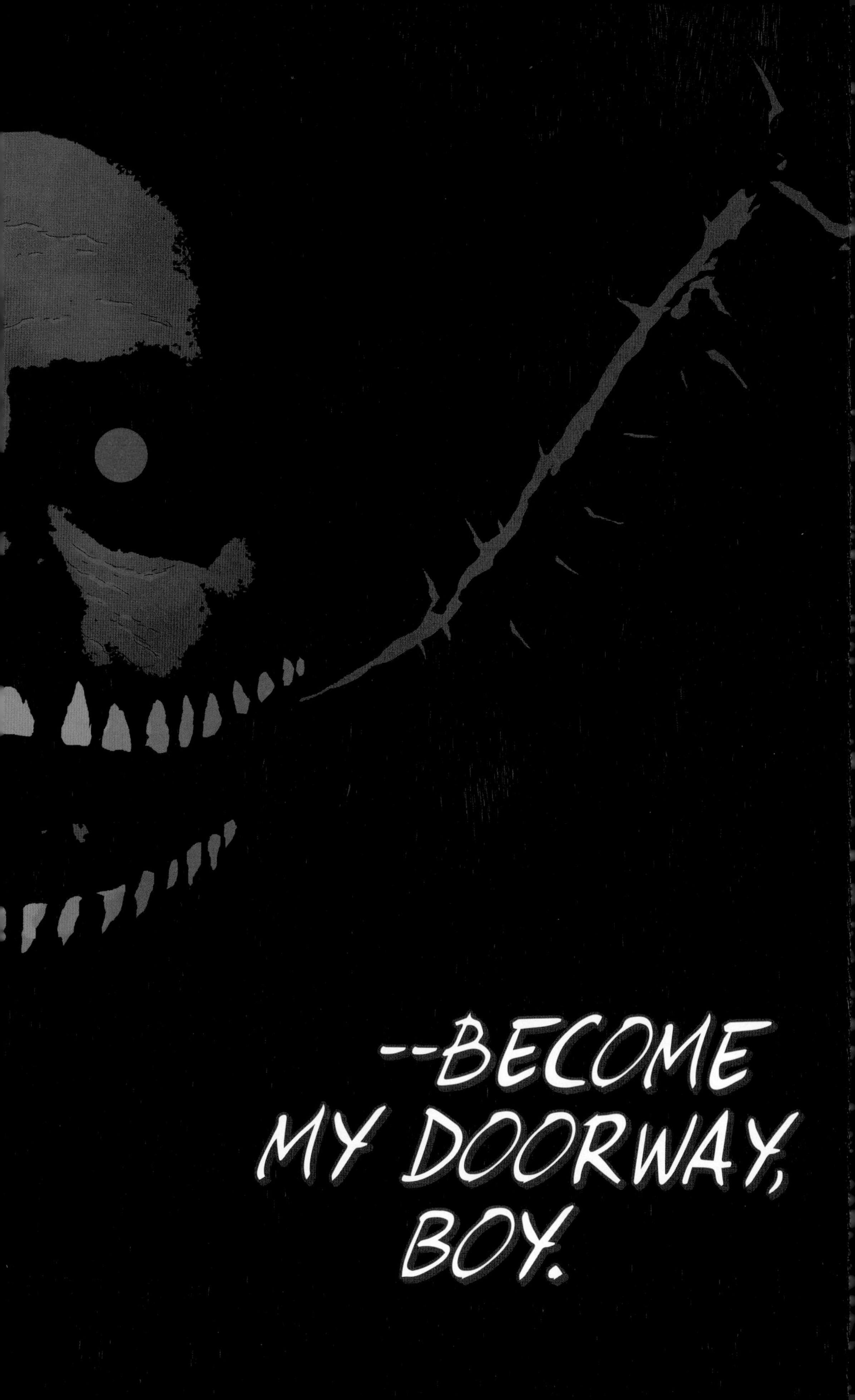
--BECOME MY DOORWAY, BOY.

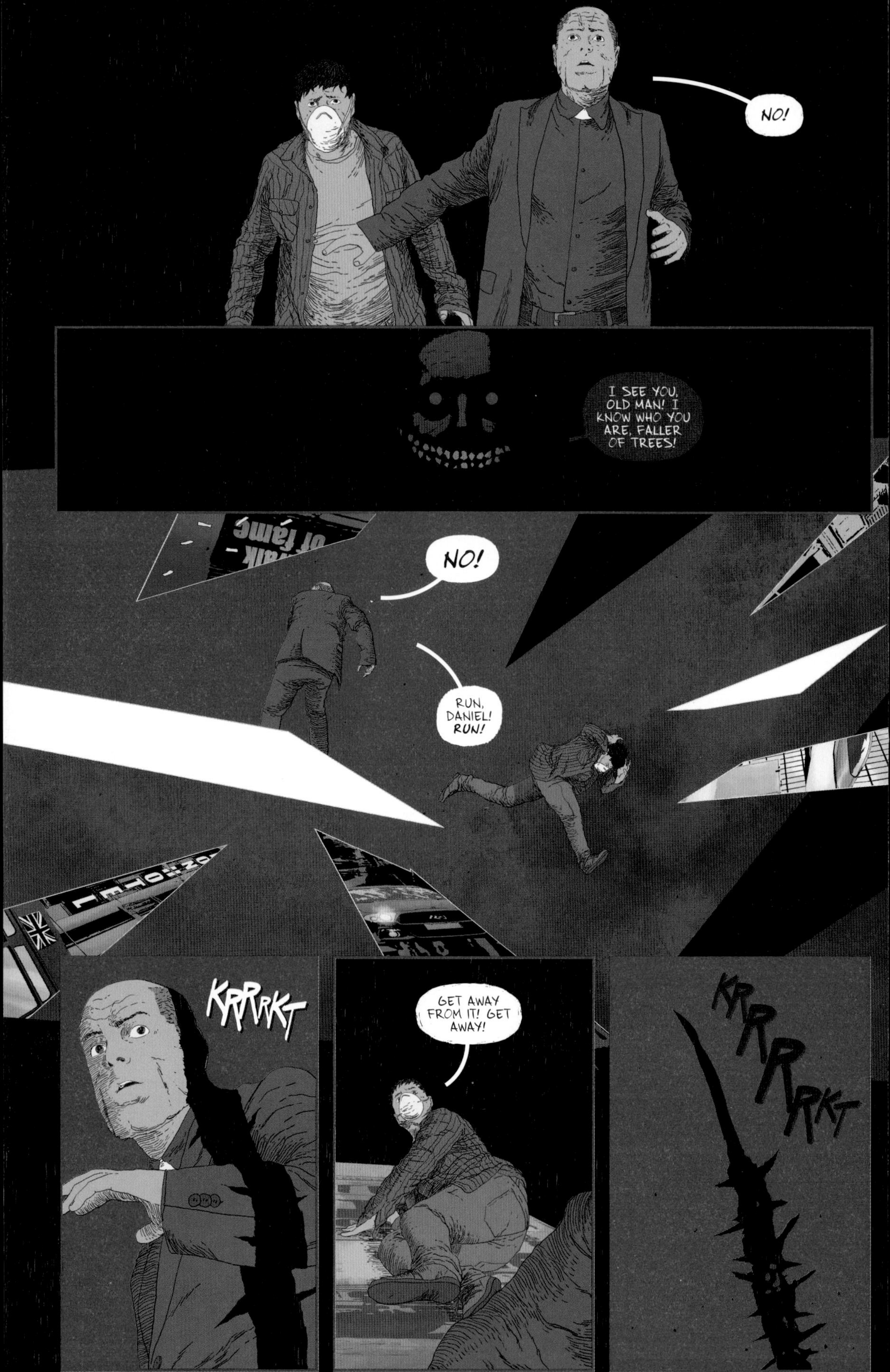
NO!
I SEE YOU, OLD MAN! I KNOW WHO YOU ARE, FALLER OF TREES!
NO!
RUN, DANIEL! RUN!
KRRRKT
GET AWAY FROM IT! GET AWAY!
KRRRRKT

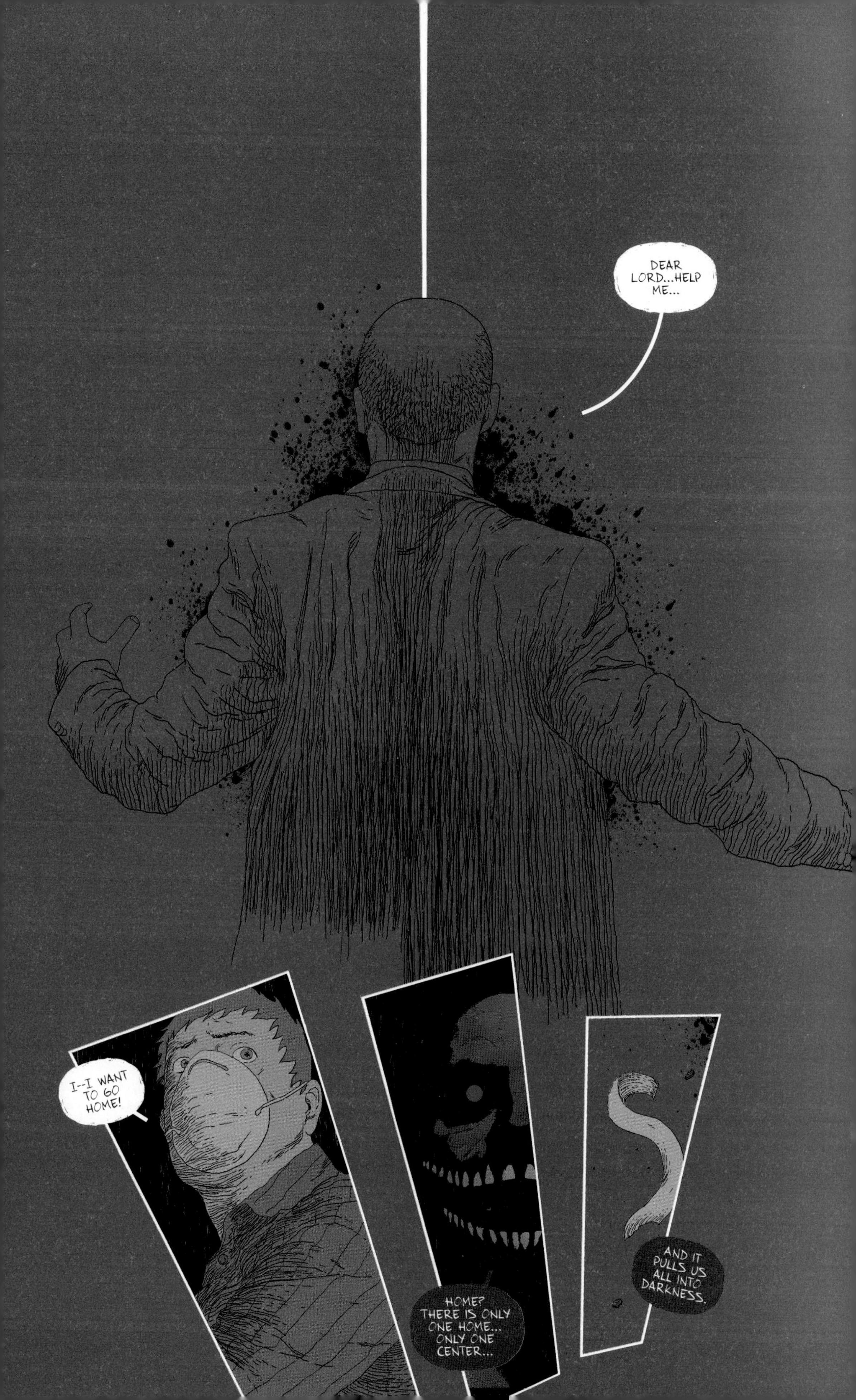
DEAR LORD...HELP ME...
I--I WANT TO GO HOME!
HOME? THERE IS ONLY ONE HOME... ONLY ONE CENTER...
AND IT PULLS US ALL INTO DARKNESS.

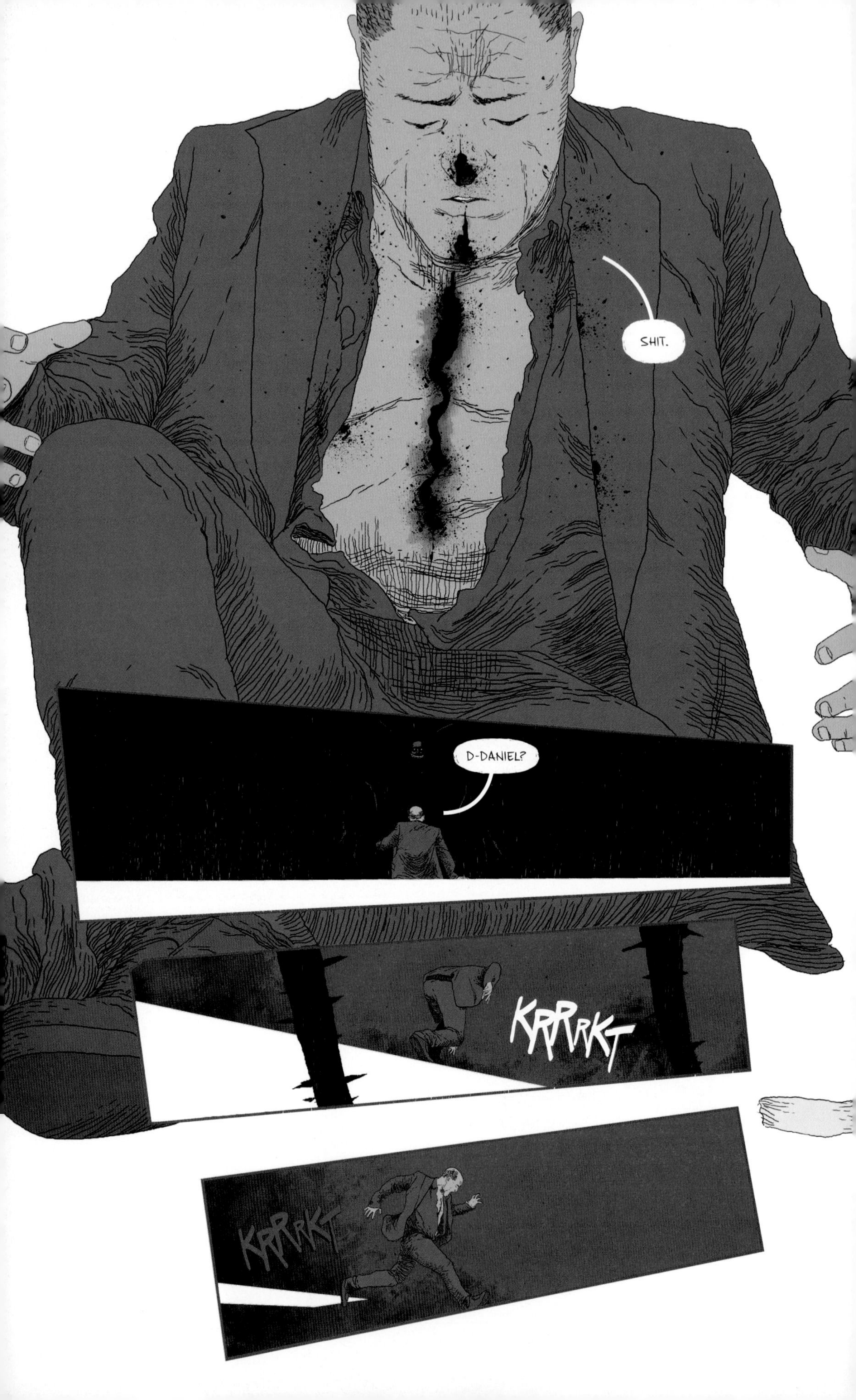
SHIT.
D-DANIEL?
KRRRKT
KRRRKT

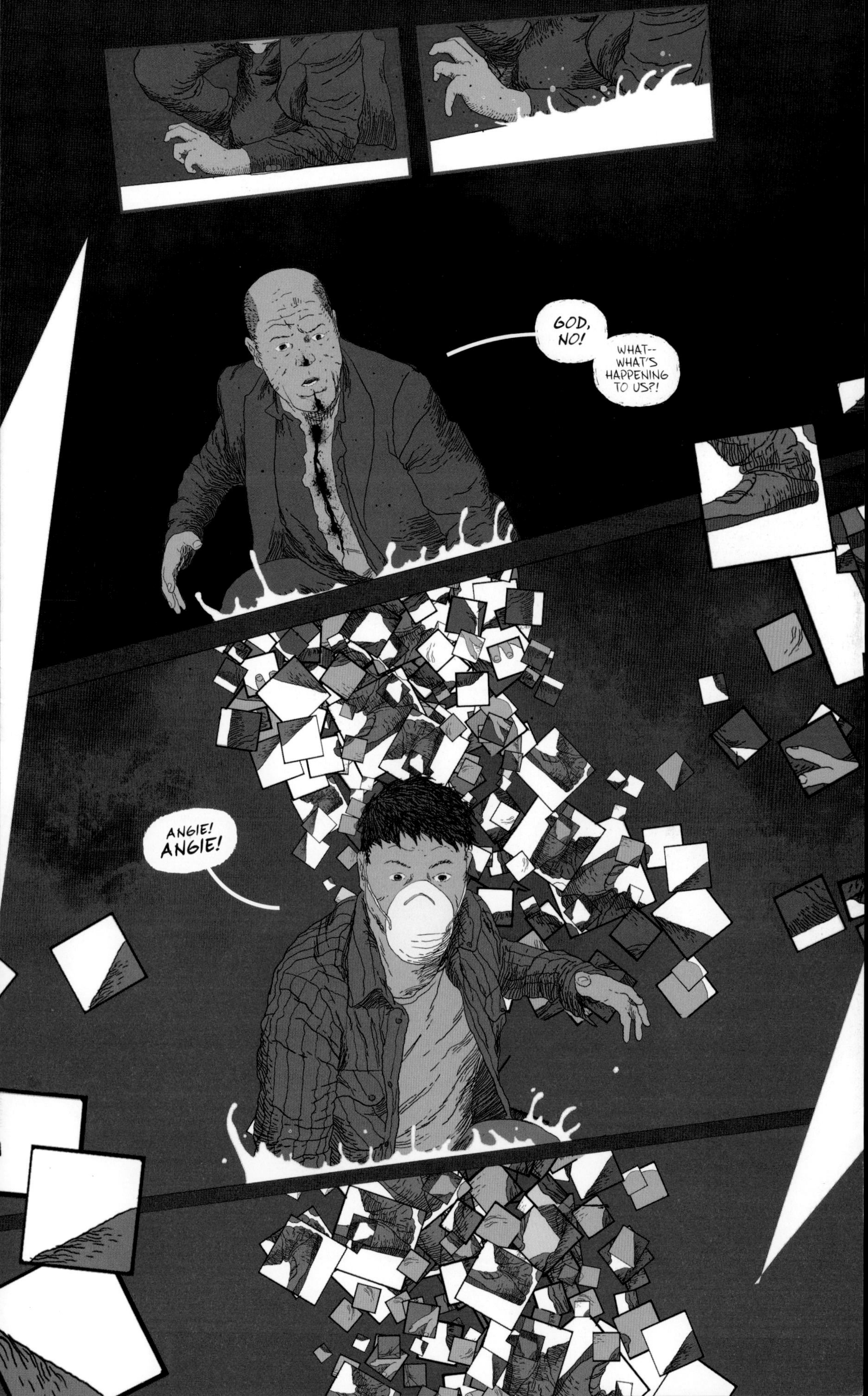
GOD, NO!
WHAT-- WHAT'S HAPPENING TO US?!
ANGIE! ANGIE!

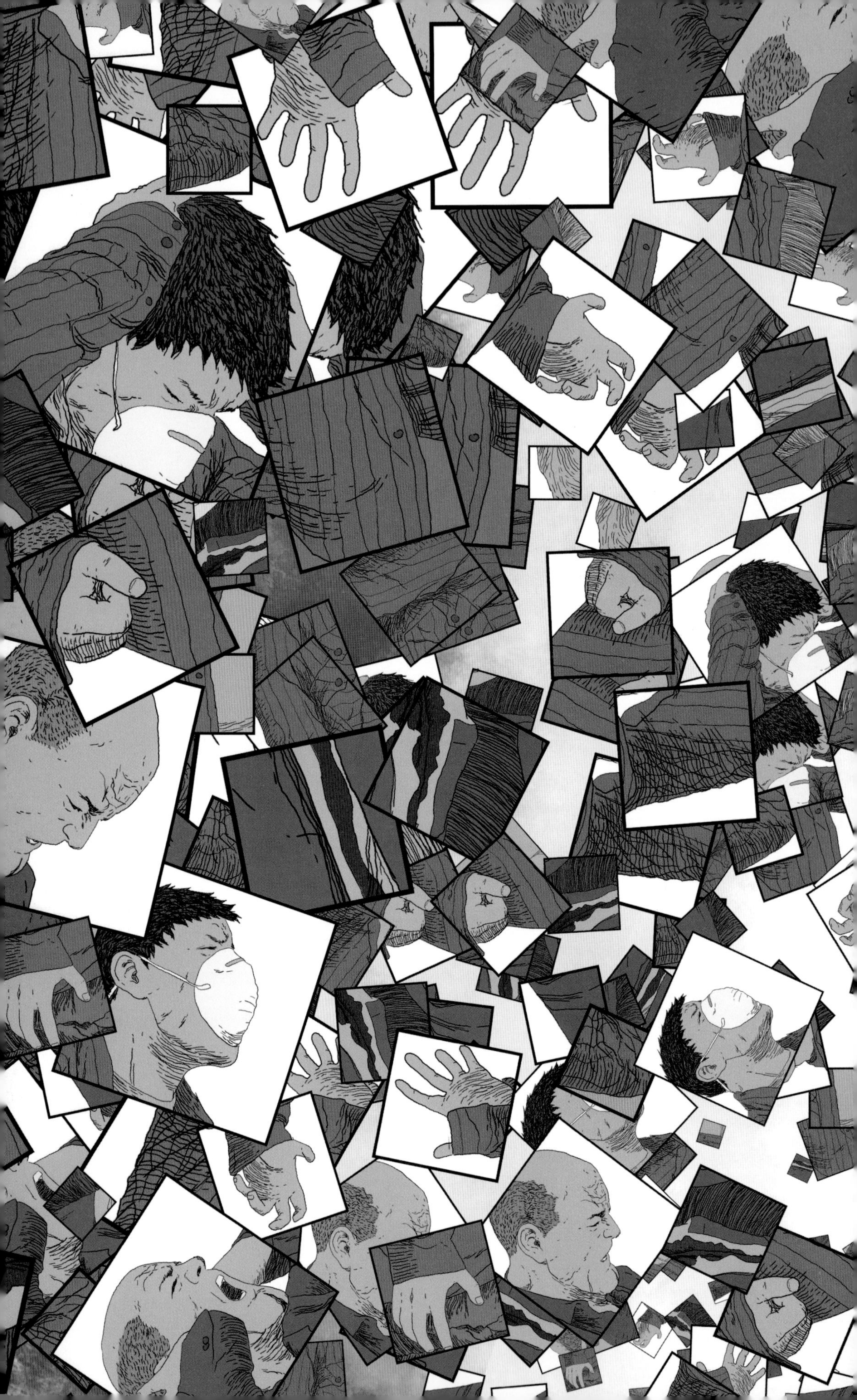

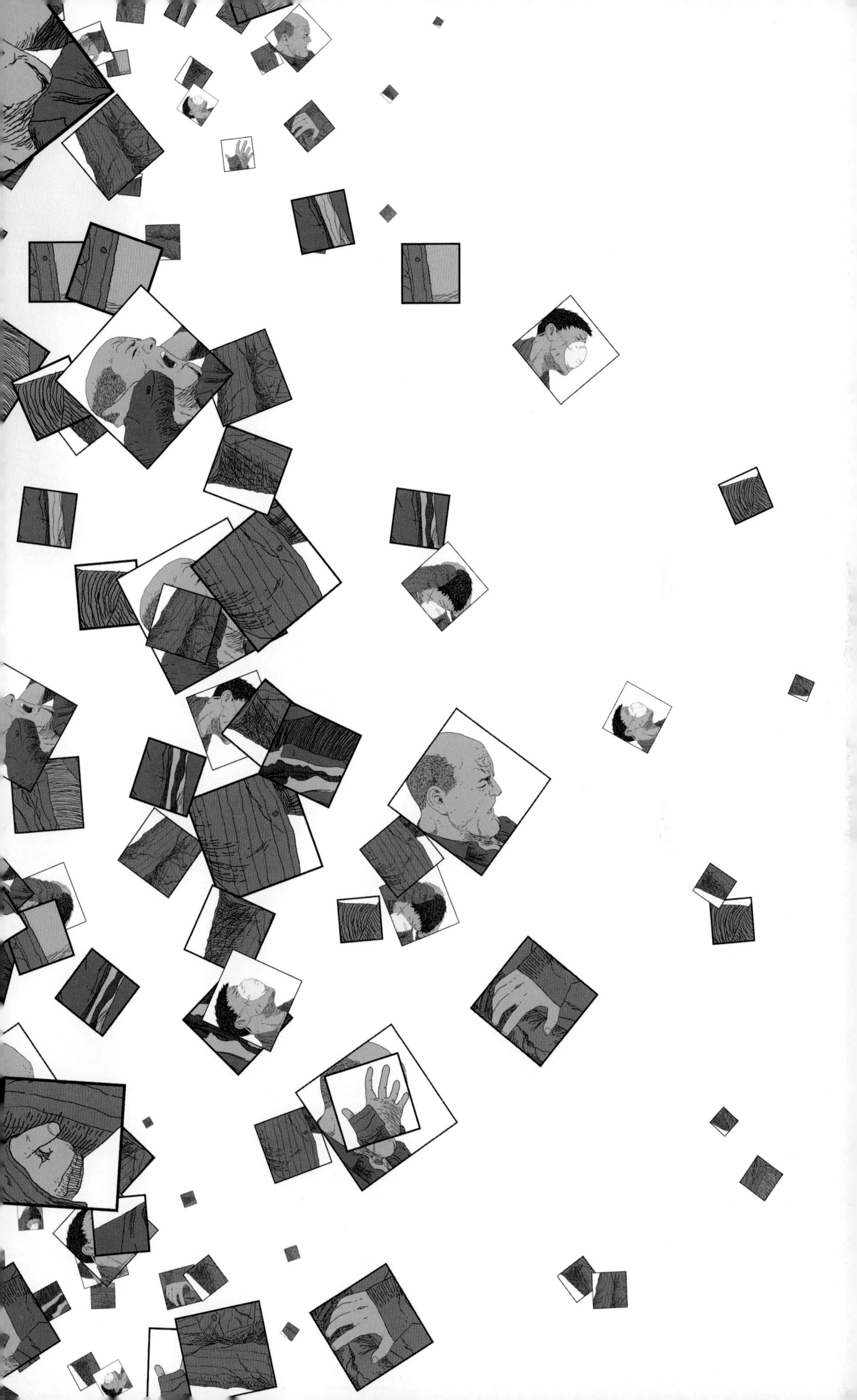

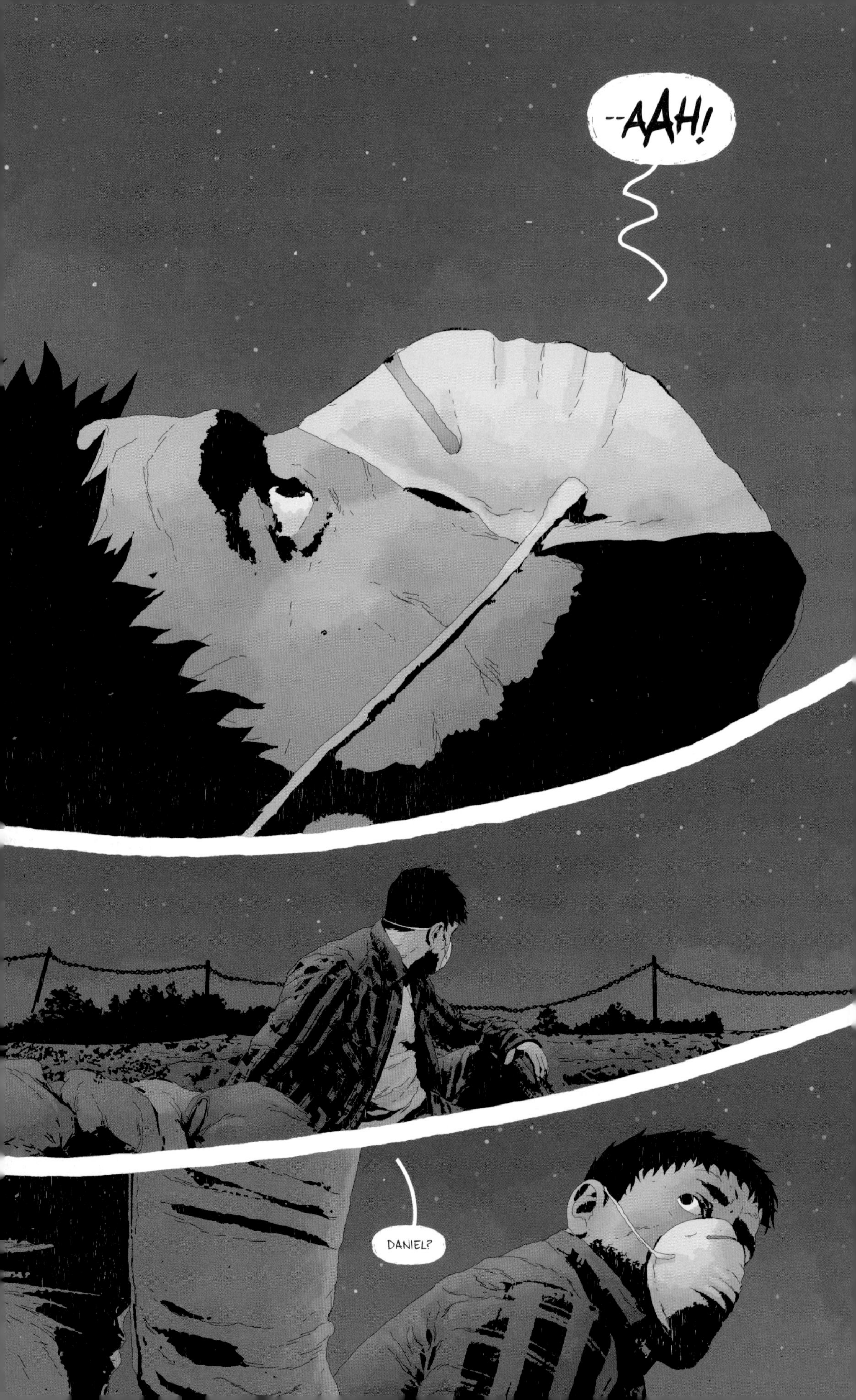
--AAH!
DANIEL?

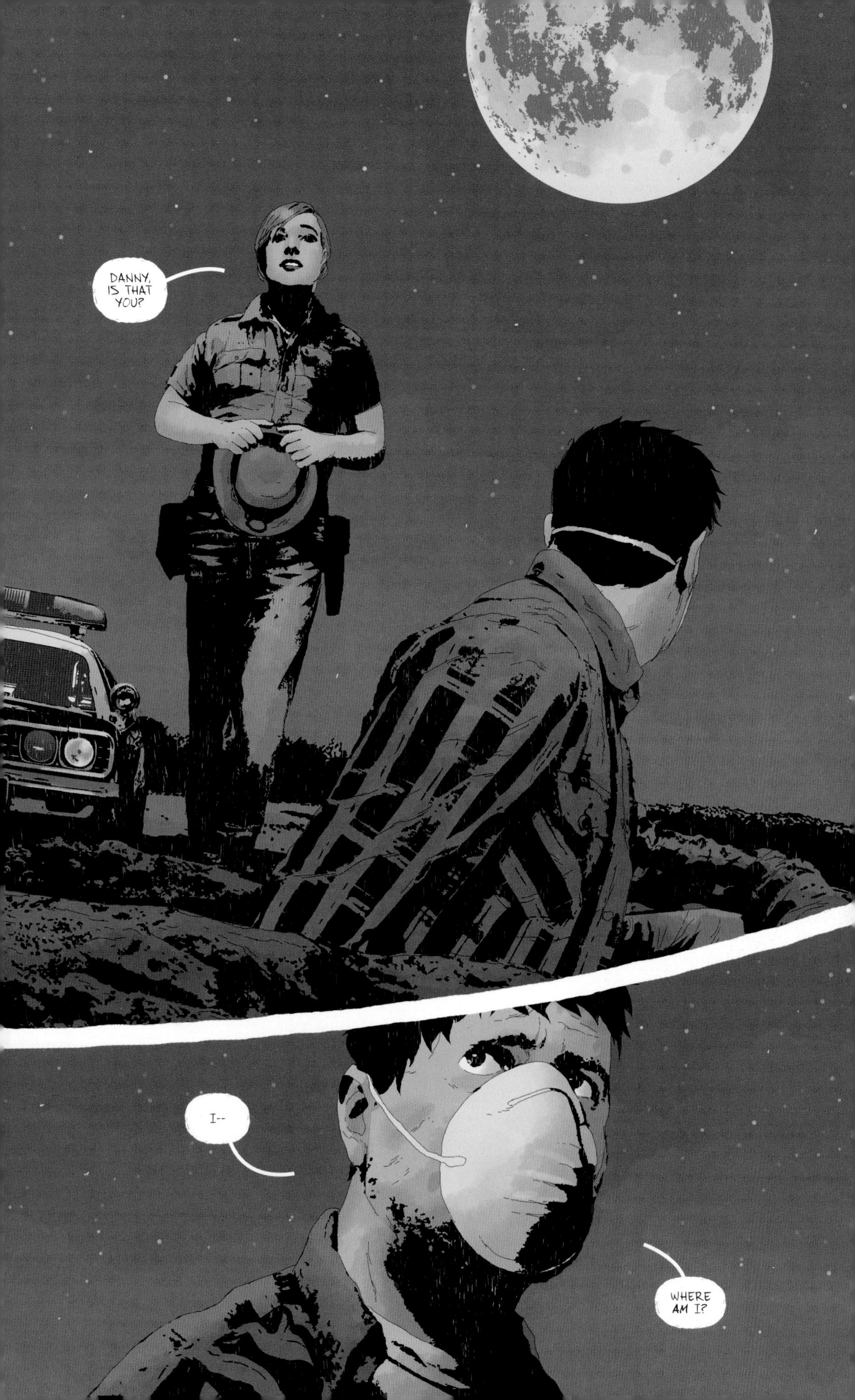
DANNY, IS THAT YOU?
I--
WHERE AM I?

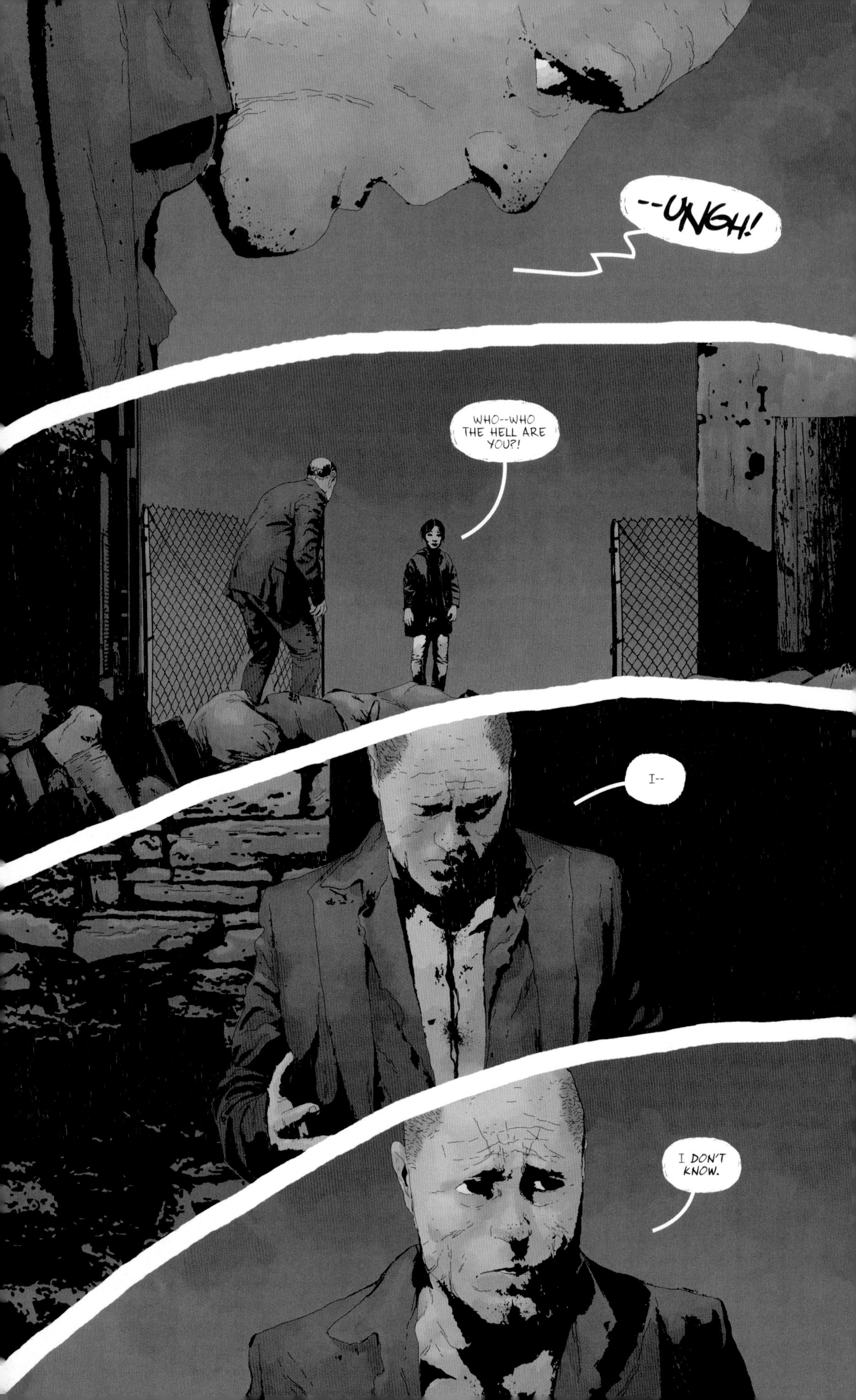
--UNGH!
WHO--WHO THE HELL ARE YOU?!
I--
I DON'T KNOW.

COVER GALLERY

#7B - TULA LOTAY

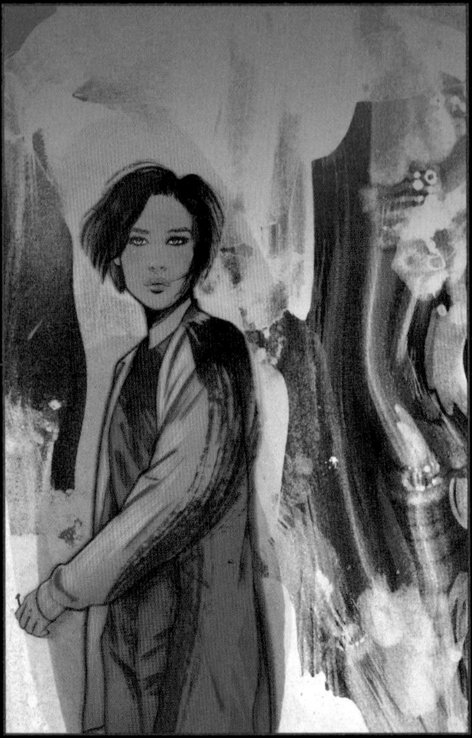

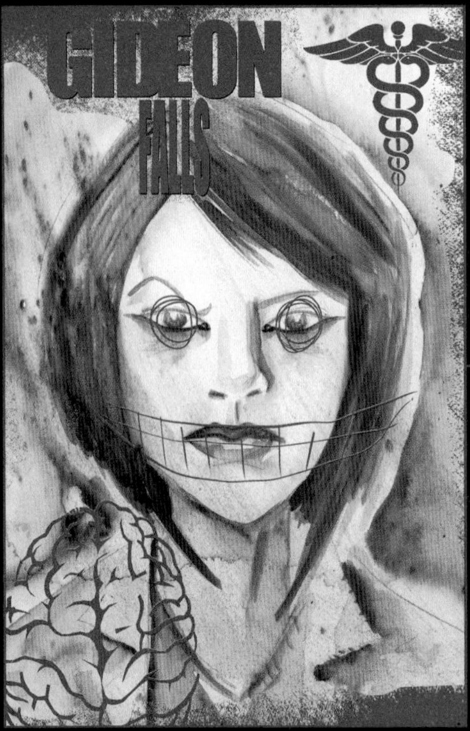
GIDEON
FALLS

#8B - JEFF LEMIRE

#9B - JAMES O'BARR

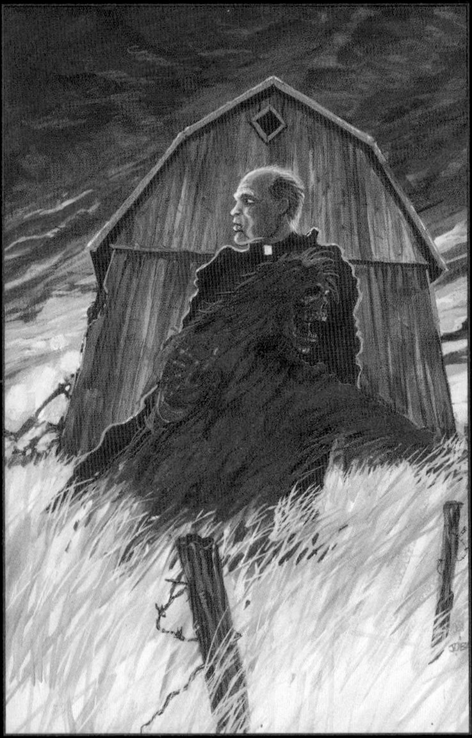

#9C - STEVE WANDS

#10B - CHRISTIAN WARD

#11B - MICO SUAYAN

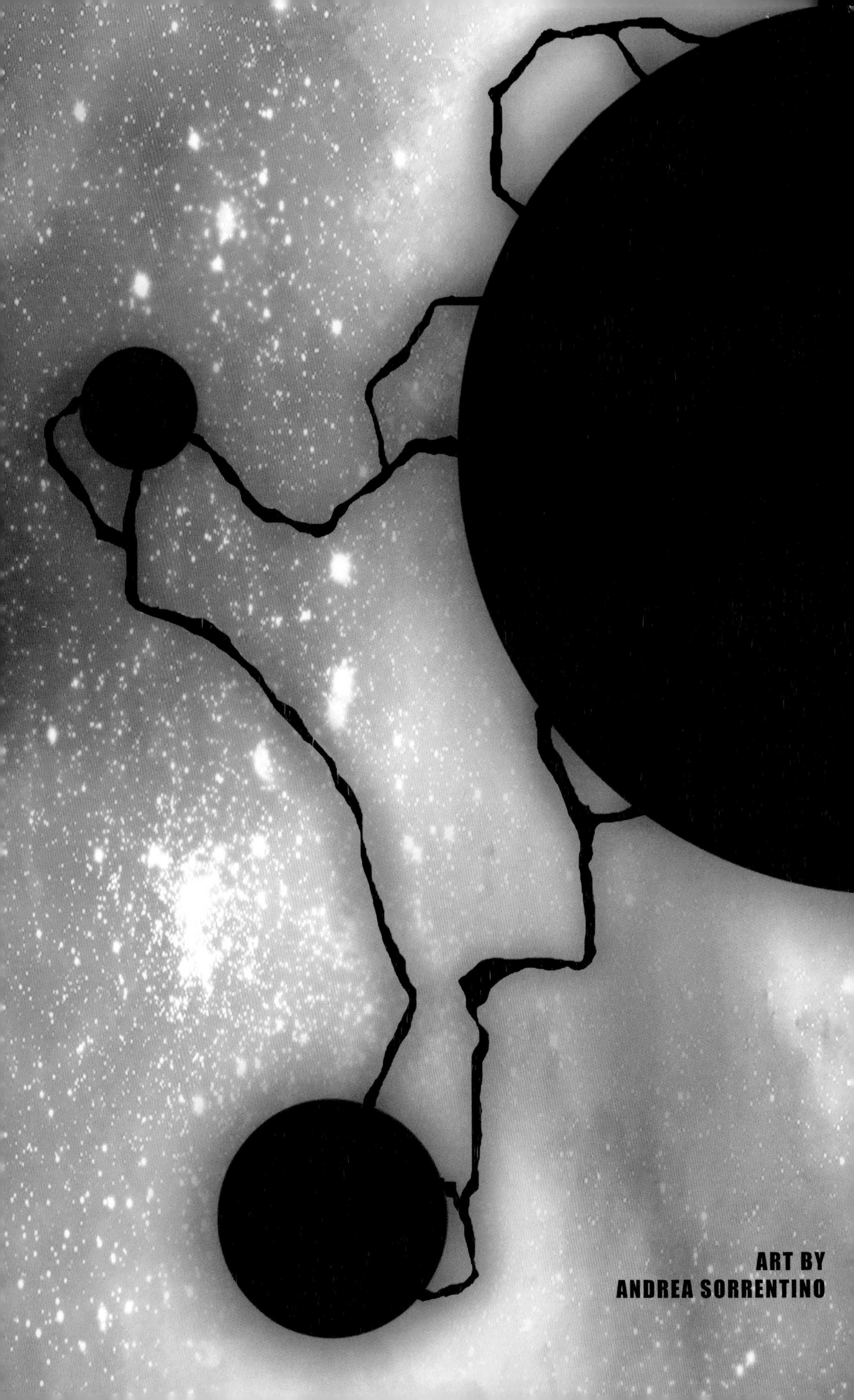
ART BY
ANDREA SORRENTINO

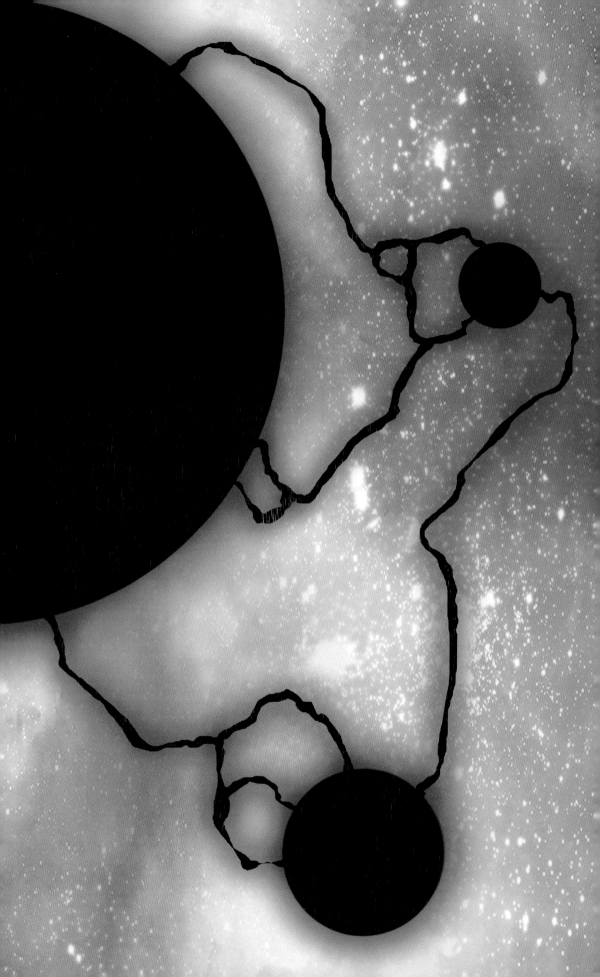

GIDEON
FALLS